UNTIL SUMMER ENDS

A novel

N.S. PERKINS

This book was a real bitch to write, so I guess it only makes sense I dedicate it to myself.

Author's note

Dear reader,

Before you start reading, I want to address the fact that while this book is a romance, it does bring up heavy topics. Our main character deals with endometriosis and primary infertility, which affect her life in many different ways. Other topics that are addressed include chronic illness, parental abuse, and death of a loved one. While I have tried to handle these themes with the utmost care, respect, and love, they might be triggering to some of you, and I want to make certain you all take care of yourself.

With all my love,
N.S. Perkins

Chapter 1

I used to say I would never step foot in Cape Weston again.

For eleven years, it was a promise that kept me going. I might have a bank account in the negative, and my sheets might smell like yeast from the microbrewery under my apartment, but at least I wasn't back there; I never would be again.

I guess I can now add *liar* to the list of things that are wrong with me.

The air inside my car is stifling, but I can't find the will to get out. I've been parked in front of my grandmother Ruth's house for the past ten minutes, knowing the second I step out, I won't be able to escape reality anymore. I'll truly be back, and she'll truly be gone.

I should've known if I ever returned to this cursed town, it'd be in service to her.

The weathered house looks more or less the same as it does in my memories, although the lack of smoke coming from the chimney and the wilted plants in the flower bed she used to care for like a child, are dead giveaways Ruth isn't here anymore. Even so, the screech of seagulls woven with the *whoosh* of the waves crashing against the reef behind the house reminds me precisely where I am.

Home.

I give myself one last minute of holding off the inevitable, then step out of the car and make my way up to the front porch, careful not to look at the neglected plants. If I start giving notice to all the tiny details reminding me of Ruth, I won't survive the day, let alone the next four weeks. The wood creaks under my feet as I lift the garden gnome that sits not so subtly next to the door and pick up the key underneath. I used to tell her how dangerous it was to leave her house key in such an obvious place. She'd laugh and tap my thigh before saying, "*Cassie, honey, no one bothers old bats like me.*" Then, she'd wink and lean back to sip her gin martini, and even if her words weren't reassuring, her posture was, and I'd drop it.

Today, I'm happy she was always stubborn and never listened to me. I didn't have a backup plan for where to stay if I didn't have access to the house. I don't think I'd be welcome at my sister's place, my childhood home is an obvious no, and with no income for the foreseeable future, I can't spend money on touristy motels in town, especially not during the high season.

The second I step inside, my breath catches at the memories that bombard me all at once. I can almost hear Stevie Nicks play-ing from the lime green vinyl player, Ruth's off-key voice in the background. Can almost smell Ruth's perfume wrapping around me on the evenings I found myself here, tucked against her on the corduroy couch. But now, it just smells like dust and damp because no one has been here in a month to open that ocean-facing window and let the salt-tinged breeze in.

My chest begins to burn as images of my last night here come back to me. A bruised face that led to a wad of cash being pressed in my hand, a kiss to my cheek, and an encouragement to get out of this place and never look back.

I realize I'm trembling when I feel my bags vibrating against my legs. Letting them fall to the ground, I cross the small house, passing the empty kitchen and dining room, and walk straight out the patio door and into a view of endless sea. The wind stings my face and ruffles the strands of hair that escaped my ponytail. My head is overcrowded, like a water balloon about to explode. I should have been braver and come back before. Why did I wait for her to be gone? Even if she's the one who suggested I go, I know deep inside, she expected it to be temporary. If not, why would she have named me as her estate executor? She would have known I'd never be able to say no to something like that.

Right now, I hate her for it almost as much as I miss her.

Get yourself together.

I repeat the mantra over and over, but I can't get the overwhelming wheel to stop spinning. I didn't get to say goodbye. Didn't even get a notice that she had passed until after her funeral was over. My nose stings as I try to get more air, but the deeper I try to inhale, the narrower my airways feel, like they're getting crushed from the inside, crumbling onto themselves.

Even with the sun hidden behind thick charcoal clouds, the air is warm, humid and thick with the sense of foreboding rain. Sweat drips between my breasts, down my back, and with my throat feeling dryer and tighter, I look out at the water and know there's one thing left to do. The only thing that could keep my teenage mind quiet when it burst into flames.

In an instant, my T-shirt and jeans are on the ground. Not caring that a neighbor could see, I run toward the shore in my matching set of black bra and panties. Ruth's house was built facing a rocky bank, giving the impression that it's floating over the body of water. For people who aren't used to it, it's terrifying to jump from the edge, but I know exactly where to aim so I don't hit anything.

So, I jump.

The shock of the water engulfing me—so cold, it burns—makes me gasp, and I have to swim up to cough out the water I inhaled. Hair plastered against my face, I choke and cough some more, swimming in place. I'm far enough from the shore that I can't lean against anything, the ground too deep for me to stand. My heart is galloping, this time for a different reason than it did a minute ago. I can't feel my body, almost as if it's gone numb, and I'm weightless. I wipe the salt from my eyes as I catch my breath, swallowing against my burning throat.

And for the first time today, I feel light.

Tilting my body back, I let myself float, getting rocked by the waves with my eyes closed. As much as I told myself I didn't miss this place, nothing compares to this feeling. My ears are covered by the water, drowning the outside noises, but mostly the inside ones. I don't have to think about the mistakes I made at work that forced my boss to put me on leave. Don't have to wonder about the faces I'll eventually come across in town. Don't have to think about Ruth lying to me for years, never telling me she was sick during our weekly calls.

I'm not sure how long I remain like this, simply breathing and floating, the temperature of the water becoming tolerable, then comfortable. When I open my eyes, the afternoon light has dimmed into early evening, and I realize I've drifted a little, so I swim back toward the edge. It's only about three feet in height, and when I was younger, I'd wait for the current to bring me closer to the bedrock, then grip the wall and hoist myself out of the water. I wait to do the same this time, except the current seems to have gotten stronger while I was relaxing, and now, when it brings me toward the bank, it's with a scary force. I don't reach the rock with a gentle boost but rather with a violent push that makes me bite my tongue as I hold onto the edge for dear life. The taste of blood fills my mouth, turning my face into a scowl as I try to pull myself out of the water.

And fail.

In my genius plan to jump into the water without a floating device, I forgot to consider that I hadn't done this in more than a decade and had probably lost a lot of upper muscle strength in that time frame.

I try to hoist myself up once more, but just as I reach for a higher level of rock, a wave crashes into my back, making me lose my grip and fall back into the water.

I lose sight of where I am for a moment, then heave in a breath when I reach fresh air. I try to grab another hold, but my rising panic and the worsening current makes it impossible. I can only grapple against the rocks before I'm pulled back down by the roaring water.

So, this is how I die. Too weak to do a chin-up. Embarrassing, honestly.

I don't have the time to inhale before another wave stretches over me, then rams me into the rocky wall. I'm dog-paddling now, trying to hold on to anything I can grasp, to no avail. When I meet air again, I gasp for breath, and that's when a loud voice calls out, "Here, hold on!"

Disoriented and terrified, I'm not sure where the voice is coming from, and as I continue trying to reach the wall, I feel something else: a hand. I hold onto it as tightly as I can, and before I can think of what is happening, I'm being pulled out of the water in one swift move, as if I truly am weightless.

When my feet hit the sandy ground, my legs crumble under me and I fall on all fours, wheezing and gulping air in.

"Jesus, are you okay? What were you doing out there?"

The panicked words remind me I'm not alone, and I have this person to thank for still being alive. Pushing my tangled hair out of my face, I stand on wobbly legs and straighten.

Then almost fall to the ground again.

I should've prepared myself to see him again. I don't know how I didn't.

And yet nothing could've prepared me for seeing Eli Grant again after all these years.

He's changed so much, and at the same time, he's exactly the same. His dark-brown hair might have grown longer, curling behind his ears and almost reaching his shoulders, but it's as messy as ever. His frame might be broader, but he has the same delicate fingers that used to build fires to keep me warm on windy summer nights and the same light-brown eyes that always reminded me of the leaves of late autumn, when they've just turned from red to amber.

"Cassie?" His voice is airy, smooth like velvet across my skin. His entire body is still, save for the hand he's slowly reaching out, as if he's just seen a ghost he needs to prove is real.

The last time I saw him, he was eighteen, face flushed and pupils wide, sitting almost exactly where we're standing now. It was dark out, only me and him and the ocean, and his lips had barely grazed mine before he'd said, "I'll understand, if you need to go." It was the end of the summer, and he'd just set me free.

"Hi," is the only thing I find to say. His khaki-colored sweater is wet, which reminds me of how he found me a few seconds ago. "Uh, thanks for helping me out there."

He ignores this, still watching me like I'm not real. "I never... What are you doing here?"

I point to the house behind me as if that's explanation enough.

"Oh. Right." His gaze softens. "I'm... I'm so sorry."

I nod. What else is there to say?

"So, you still live here?" I ask. It feels so stupid, to be talking about the basics like this, as if he didn't know every single crook and cranny of my mind a decade ago. As if he didn't use to be my everything.

He nods, too, and then we're staring at each other, both at a loss for words.

A gust of wind makes goosebumps rise on my wet skin, and as I lift an arm to cover my middle, we both seem to realize I'm in my underwear.

"Oh, God, here." He removes his sweater, then hands it to me, now looking away while I put it on. It holds his body's warmth and smells like fresh-cut grass and ocean air, the scent so familiar it almost brings tears to my eyes.

"Thank you." I should say more, figure out what he's been up to after all these years, but I'm still at a loss for words. I thought about seeing my mother and my sister, but I didn't even think of Eli, and now it seems ridiculous. How was he not at the forefront of my mind? Then again, when I left this place, I put everything related to Eli Grant in a box, tucked away in a corner of my brain, and every single day, I fought not to tug the lid off. It was the only way I found to keep going. Eventually, I had to let him go altogether.

He seems to be lost in the same trance, probably seeing two versions of me side-by-side, one seventeen and the other twenty-eight.

His throat works. "I can't believe—"

"Daddy!"

We both turn toward the sound, where a small girl is wobbling on chubby legs, her dark curls bouncing against her shoulders.

"Sorry," he tells me.

It takes me a second to realize what is happening. Eli gives me one last look before walking toward the girl. Her smile growing the closer he gets to her. Him squatting to welcome her in a hug, and her running faster.

I don't move, don't breathe, transfixed on the picture of her hand tightly clasping his T-shirt, on the sound of her giggle as he picks her up and on the faint trace of what I assume is chocolate on her cheek.

Of course he has a daughter. A wife. A family.

I take a step back, then another.

"Cassie, this is my daughter, Zoe."

I want to smile, to wave and go to her, to introduce myself and make her smile. A couple of months ago, I probably would have. Booped her nose, asked her about the chocolate on her cheek.

But today, it feels like being slapped with a future I missed out on, and I can't move. That is, until I remember even if I hadn't left, I still couldn't have had that with him.

I give her a weak, "Hi, Zoe," then start backing away toward the house.

"You okay?" Eli asks me, a deep furrow forming between his brows. The expression is too familiar, too reminiscent of the way he used to worry about me, when I still had a right to his worry.

I hum a response. "I—It was nice seeing you again." Then, before I can wait around and see just how badly I can break down, I run to the place I just escaped.

Chapter 2

I wake up the next morning with a jolt.

The mattress in the guest bedroom hasn't gotten more comfortable while I was away, and a familiar kink pulls at my neck as I straighten in bed. The golden ticking clock on the bedside table tells me it's almost 8:00 a.m., but I didn't fall asleep until 3:00 a.m. this morning, tossing and turning. It was all too much. Almost drowning, seeing Eli, and then coming back inside a house that felt drained of life... I didn't want to handle it anymore. Without bothering to eat dinner, I picked up the knitted quilt from the living room that smelled musty and felt like being wrapped up in childhood, then walked straight past the master bedroom. I'd feel like an intruder if I entered it, so I went into the room I used to occupy when I stayed over. Nothing had changed in it, not even the pink bedspread she got for me when I was twelve, as if she'd left it ready for me to use. Sleep evaded me, but I remained there, gaze lost on the cracks in the ceiling. It feels like only five minutes ago when I finally drifted off.

I stand from bed, then realize what woke me up when a high-pitched voice passes through the window. I pad to the bay window's bench where I used to sit for hours, knees tucked against my chest, staring out. It's oriented toward the Grants' house, which is how I noticed Eli for the first time. I had gotten to Ruth's place during the night and hadn't been able to go to sleep, so I'd sat here to watch the sun rise over the ocean, and at around five in the morning, my attention had turned toward the two people who'd come out of the house, carrying coolers and stacks of water bottles. Later, I learned Eli had been helping his father load his food truck, which sold burgers and lobster rolls by the beach during summer months and in mall parking lots during the off-season. From my vantage point, he looked short but gangly, at that strange period when boys have started growing but not symmetrically. I'd been ensnared by the way this boy, who looked to be around my age, interacted with his father. There was no animosity. No shouting or flinching at rough voices, and no things being thrown to the ground in tantrums. The older man was passing boxes and tin foil plates over to his son, who picked them up and stacked them in the truck, and the boy did so with a smile. I heard laughter coming from there, even at the early hour when darkness still colored the horizon. It looked like something out of a movie. I couldn't believe some families actually worked like that. Throughout the years, I continued watching the gangly boy who eventually turned into a man, and never lost that fascination.

Now, though, Eli isn't the one standing outside his house. A woman who could be in her late twenties or early thirties is knocking at his door in a frenzy. Her navy crewneck almost meets the hem of her jean shorts.

"Eli, open up!" Her voice is loud enough that I can hear it through the window. Her rounds of knocking continue, even when there's no sign of him coming to open the door after a minute. Whether it's because he's not there, or because he doesn't want to is probably what keeps me watching.

Another minute passes, and the woman looks more and more distressed. Even from here, I can tell she's crying by the way her shoulders are shaking and her back is spasming.

"Please, Eli," she shouts once more, but this time, it sounds less demanding and more desperate.

Finally, the front door cracks open, and out steps Eli, barefoot and dressed in pajama pants and a white T-shirt, muscles bunched from his crossed arms. He remains impassive in front of the woman who begins gesticulating and stepping closer. I can't look away, my breath fogging up the window, and when he finally moves, it's his head that tilts and turns.

Right in my direction.

I jump, backing up ten steps until I can't see anything happening outside, but it's too late. He clearly saw me watching, as if he could feel I was there.

My pulse is pounding from getting caught, but I feel a tiny bit better now that I can't see or hear them. It's not like it's the first time I've watched him from this exact spot, but this feels different. We don't know each other anymore.

There's no way I'll be able to fall back asleep with the way my body is pumped full of adrenaline, so I put on a sweater and walk out of the bedroom to the kitchen.

I didn't think to bring groceries with me yesterday, but I also didn't think about how there would probably be nothing in here. Someone—I'm not sure who—emptied the fridge, and the cupboards are mostly bare. My stomach grumbles, which makes me realize I haven't eaten since I left my apartment yesterday morning. I should grab my keys and go to the grocery store down the street, but the thought of all the people I might come across makes me freeze. I'm a grown adult, and yet being here feels like stepping back in time, into the body of a lonely teenager who would've done anything to be invisible.

I decide I'll be brave tomorrow, then reach for the box of likely-stale saltines that will have to do for now. Snack in hand, I walk to the kitchen table, still covered with Ruth's hand-stitched checkered tablecloth and take a seat while I pull my phone out of where I'd plugged it in the wall. I have seventeen notifications, including four from Emily, my favorite colleague who became my one good friend in the city.

Em: Hope you got there safe.

Em: Let me know if there's anything I can do for you.

Em: Can't wait to see you when you're back.

Em: Love you xx

I like her last message, then close the app, not interested in thinking any more about the job I was forced to walk away from. It might only be temporary, but it felt like a slap in the face nonetheless when Sariah—the chief nurse on the labor & delivery ward—met with me for the first time in six years to let me know I would need to take a leave of absence "for my own good". We both knew it wasn't *for* me, but rather because I'd fucked up, though she was nice enough to not say so.

My job has always been the one thing I pride myself on. Even when everything in my life was going to shit, I could at least tell myself I had the best job. I loved interacting with my patients when they got to the hospital in labor, being their advocate for the birth plan they'd drafted, accompanying them as they grew their family. And I was good at it. But as I listened to Sariah tell me about the terms of my leave and eventual return, I saw that silver lining crumbling like a sandcastle at high tide.

I snack on a few saltines, but I'm not that hungry anymore. I push the box away, and just as I stand to go get dressed and decide where I need to start with this whole executor thing, the sound of knocking stops me in place. At first, I think it's coming from Eli's place again, but when another set of three knocks resonates through the house, I realize it's here.

I didn't tell anyone I was back, but I guess secrets don't exist in this place.

Straightening my shoulders, I get to the door, but when I open it, I wish I'd have hidden inside and pretended I wasn't here. My sister stands there, her face a stony version of the one I used to know.

Keira and I have always looked alike. We used to joke that when she came of age, I could borrow her ID anytime. I left before that could happen. Now, though, we could not be more different. Her short, brown hair looks so kempt compared to my faded blond highlights and broken tips. She's clean-faced and dressed in athletic clothes, contrasting with my old pajamas I brought for the sake of comfort. What's most different, though, is the belly that seems ready to pop like a balloon under her shirt.

I feel the blood drain from my face as my gaze remains on that part of her body. Ruth told me she had a son three years ago, and I've even sent him birthday and Christmas gifts every year, but I wasn't aware of this one. I blink, the image of someone who looks so much like me with the one thing I'll never have stealing the breath from my lungs. I hate that it's the gut reaction I have, too. Jealousy instead of happiness.

"So, the rumor's true," Keira says in a sharp voice.

"Wh…" I babble something, but no real thought comes out.

"My own sister is back in town after a decade, and she doesn't even bother telling me." She lets out a low puff of air through her nose. "Figures."

"I just got here," I say, as if I was planning on contacting her in the next few minutes. In truth, I did consider it, then repeatedly pushed it to a later time. The guilt that now has a constant place in my chest swells.

She would never believe me, but I've missed my sister more than anyone else here. I wish I could step forward and wrap her in my arms, smell her neck and figure out if she still wears the tangerine perfume she used to spray in obnoxious quantities before going out when we were teenagers. I wish she could smile when seeing me instead of scowling.

When I first left, I made the mistake of going no-contact with everyone for almost nine months. I know now it was horrible of me, but when I got to the city, the only thing I wanted was to put everything that had happened behind me and to start fresh. In my head, that meant ignoring everything from my previous life, including my family. Was that smart? Absolutely not. But I was eighteen and afraid, my life had been turned upside down, and I convinced myself this was the only way forward. I eventually realized my mistake and reached out to Ruth first, who didn't hold it against me. She'd expected this when she told me to leave. Mom was just happy I'd finally called her. Keira, though, never got over it. In fact, she never answered my phone calls again after that. I spent the past decade trying to get in contact with her, to no avail. I emailed her on holidays and followed her life on social media, hoping she'd finally forgive me for being a stupid, heartbroken teen, but that never happened.

She hums, looking me up and down like she, too, wonders in just how many ways I've changed. "I didn't want to believe Eli, at first. My sister in Ruth's house? Impossible."

So, he's the snitch.

"I didn't know you two were friends," I say.

"Don't know a lot of stuff, I think," she snaps. Then, as if feeling bad, she explains in a smaller voice, "Xavier's friends with his daughter."

It makes sense. There's only one daycare around, and Zoe is probably around my nephew's age.

I swallow, then open the door wider. "Do you want to come in?"

"I don't need you to invite me into Grandma's house."

Even as kids, Keira had the gift of making me feel smaller than a fly. I always tried to remain on her good side, just so I wouldn't have to feel the knot that's currently twisting my stomach.

"Sorry." I'm not sure what I'm apologizing for exactly, but I know it's well overdue.

Her chin tilts up. "So, what brings you here?"

"Got a call from Ruth's lawyer." I pull my sleeves down, shivering against the morning breeze. "She made me the executor of her will."

Keira laughs then, the sound almost scary. "Of course she did." At my frown, she adds, "She named me, too."

I shouldn't be surprised. It makes sense that she'd name her two grandchildren, even though Keira was never as close to her as I was. Maybe that changed in the past decade, too. I sure wish the lawyer would've told me over the phone, though.

"So don't worry about it." She has her back straight, standing as far away from me as is physically possible. "You can go. I'll take care of it."

"I'm staying." The words come out more abruptly than I'd expected, and it's at this moment I see just how much frustration *I* have toward her. "I didn't get to attend her funeral. Wasn't notified until it was done." In fact, I didn't learn she had passed until almost ten days after it happened. When she didn't answer the phone for a few days, I started worrying, and only when I received the call from her lawyer did I get the dreaded news no one in my family had cared to share with me. That afternoon, I lay on my couch and stared at the ceiling for hours, too stunned for tears. Ruth was larger than life. She was the type of woman who asked her granddaughters to call her by her given name because she didn't want to feel like an old grandma. I couldn't imagine a world where she wasn't hosting barbecue parties for her girlfriends, gossiping with them like teenagers throughout the night.

"Didn't think you'd care."

My body steels itself, all the things I want to shout at her boiling inside. "Thanks for your visit, but I'm not going anywhere until this is done." If I wasn't sure I truly wanted to stay before, now I know I'm not going to move an inch.

Her dark-green eyes narrow, jaw tightening probably as a mirror to mine. "And how long do you plan on staying?"

"A month." Then, my forced sabbatical will be done, and I'll be able to return to my life. "I'll be out of your hair as soon as I can. Don't worry." In my wildest dreams, I could imagine Keira being happy I was here, but some part of me knew it would be like this, which is probably why I stalled in calling her yesterday.

"Fine." She lays a protective hand on her belly, which I follow with my gaze. "I guess I'll see you at the lawyer's office, then."

I exhale when she turns and climbs down the porch. However, my body freezes when she turns back to me. "Oh, and one more thing. Don't think about messing with Eli again. He's in a good place now and doesn't need your drama." Then, she makes her way to her truck and drives away, leaving me gaping. Somehow, this hurt more than all she's said before. She knew how I felt about Eli before. Knew how much I cared.

I didn't think I could fall lower than I already was, and yet every day proves me wrong.

Chapter 3

I was five years old when I learned there are different levels of love.

Before, I would hear the word thrown around as if it was a single unit that could not be differentiated. You either loved someone, or you didn't.□

That day, I was playing hopscotch outside while Mom mowed the lawn. My father hadn't come home the night before, and by the time his truck pulled up in our driveway, it must have been close to noon. Even through the windshield, I could see he looked sickly pale. Now, I know he was probably drunk out of his mind, but I didn't recognize the signs then. I was still playing in the middle of the pavement, and while I didn't have the reflex to get out of his way, he didn't slow down. The truck barely stopped in time, toppling over the bicycle I'd used earlier. Fear like I'd rarely known flooded my system in a millisecond, and when it came crashing down, I started bawling. My father got out of the truck, cursing, and didn't stop to see whether I was all right. He bypassed me and stumbled his way toward the house. However, he wasn't the one I cared about. I'd already turned toward my mother, the way I did when my grandmother Ruth would offer me a caramel square before dinner, and I had to make sure I was allowed to have it. Mom was the person I looked for when I skinned my knee. The one who made sure I wore my helmet before riding my bicycle and who was always on time for school pick-up.

I'm not sure what I expected of her. To walk over and curse him out? To tell him he had to be more careful next time? Maybe I just wanted to feel the comforting warmth of her arms around me.

But she did none of those things. Instead, she rushed over to him, leaving me behind.

And that's when I understood: Mom loved him more than she loved me. There were levels to her love, and I wasn't on top.

It was a lesson I still remember to this day. Even when my ex-fiancé left, I wasn't surprised. He might have loved me, but he loved the idea of being a father more, and the moment in the doctor's office we learned I could never get pregnant was the beginning of the end. You couldn't make someone stay when their love for something or someone else was bigger.

I haven't been in contact much with my mother over the years. A quarterly phone call is what I'm willing to give, especially since every time she picks up, the conversation is nothing but pretend. She tells me everything is great at home even though I know it can't be, and I act like my life is everything I ever wanted it to be, and that's that. Even when my father got sentenced to eight years in jail, we didn't talk about it. Ruth was the one who told me. Mom didn't think that was something I deserved to know—much like Ruth's passing. I'm still not sure why she didn't tell me about it. Keira's silence, I understand, as painful as it was, but I thought

Mom and I were fine. I can't wrap my head around the fact that she wouldn't tell me about something like that. It's probably why I haven't found it in me to visit her yet.□

□I tried yesterday, even got in my car and drove there, but the second I saw the house from afar, I turned around and went grocery shopping, thankfully not coming across any familiar faces.

This morning, I thought I'd try again but decided on starting my deep clean of Ruth's place instead. It's not like it's *only* an excuse. If I need to have this house sold by the end of the month, I can't waste time sitting around.

It's now been five hours of heavy cleaning, and I don't think I've felt this useful in weeks. Months, even. In other circumstances, I might've put music on, but today, I wanted emptiness. Even my thoughts silenced as I mopped and dusted. It felt good.

My shoulders ache as I bring yet another bucket of grimy water to the sink. I should probably take a break. My gaze drifts to my phone sitting on the countertop. Maybe I could start with a phone call to Mom. Might be easier.

After wiping my hands on my jeans, I grab the phone and walk outside toward the Adirondack chairs overlooking the cliffs. The sun is out today, casting a glare that would feel scorching if it weren't for the ocean breeze. Fine droplets of water mist along my shins as I settle into the chair. I flip the phone in my hands, then unlock it. Now or never, I guess.

But before I can dial Mom, high-pitched laughter from next door catches my attention.

Zoe pumps her legs with her light-up shoes on as she runs away from Eli, who's chasing after her. Some of her curls slip out of her pigtails and onto her paisley shirt as she gazes behind, giggling even harder when she sees how close Eli is. He's laughing, too, the sound deep and sharp, one that's so familiar, it almost takes me back to summer days spent in the water playing catch when *we* were kids. My childhood home isn't far from Ruth's, only a five-minute car ride, but as a child, we rarely visited, mostly because my father and Ruth were never on good terms. During the summer, though, I'd spend all my time here. Eli and I didn't attend the same school, so I soaked up every second of July and August. As I got older, I was able to sneak off more often to Ruth's during the school year, but it was never the same as summer, when I felt detached from the life I had in school.

I should probably look away, leave them in their moment of bonding, but I can't. The sight is too heartwarming to miss. My hand falls to my stomach as I continue watching the movie taking place in front of me. Eli's hair is disheveled, flopping around his face as he leans down to grab Zoe before she escapes him once more.

Since he doesn't seem to have noticed me, I take the opportunity to study him further. When he pulled me out of the water, I was so shocked—both from the near-death experience and from seeing him—that I didn't quite take in all the details that have made up Eli Grant over the years. But now, I can't unsee the way he carries himself with so much more confidence than before, or how he still smiles so easily. It used to take a lot to make me smile, but Eli never needed much. A joke, a bump of your shoulder, even just a weird sound, and he'd crack up.

From the way Zoe's laughter heightens with the roar Eli lets out, she seems to have inherited that beautiful trait. She continues running, her breathing so loud I can hear it even from here.

"I'll get you, Zoe Bear!"

She shrieks, looking once more over her shoulder, and just as she does, her whole body goes sprawling forth. Not a second later, a wail erupts from her. Eli is next to her in a moment, his expressive face turned into a scowl as he picks her up in his arms. I'm sitting on the edge of my chair, squinting so I can see what's happening, and when I notice blood on her leg, I don't think twice before getting up and jogging their way. I might look like a creep—again—but if someone doesn't come help quickly, there will soon be two patients instead of one.

"Hey, Zoe," I say as I reach the spot where she fell, dropping to my knees next to them. "I'm Cassie. Remember me? We met a few days ago."

She's still sobbing while holding onto her leg, not listening to a word I'm saying. Meanwhile, Eli has become stock-still, his face the color of ash.

"I'm a nurse. I take care of people with booboos all the time." Not true since I switched to L&D, but a white lie never hurt anyone. "Would you let me look at yours?"

That seems to reassure her, and with a wobbly lip, she nods.

"Good," I say. When Eli doesn't move, his gaze stuck on the small, bleeding cut on his daughter's knee, I touch his shoulder firmly and say, "Can you go get me some Band-Aids?" When he doesn't answer, I squeeze him again, this time more firmly. Finally, he looks up and almost jumps when he sees me, as if he hadn't noticed my presence before. "Band-Aids," I repeat, making sure he's looking at me.

He nods, then gets to his feet and walks away, looking only half ready to pass out. I'd call it a success.

"You took a mean fall," I tell Zoe as I push her tear-soaked hair away from her forehead. "You know what used to make me feel better when I hurt myself?"

She shakes her head, her sobbing having calmed to silent tears and her attention on me. She has the same wide-set brown eyes as her dad.

I lean forward as if I have a secret to tell her. "My mommy would give me a kiss where it hurt and then let me eat a popsicle afterward, and it was her magic trick. Think it could work with you?"

"My mommy isn't here," she whimpers.

"Then your daddy will do just fine."

Just then, Eli comes running back, breathless as he says, "I've got the Band-Aids." An entire box of them, apparently.

"Thanks," I say, extending a hand in his direction while keeping my gaze on Zoe. I seem to have calmed her, and I don't want the wailing to resume. However, when I don't feel a box, I look up, finding Eli's focus lost on the wound once more.

"Look away," I tell him as I stand to grab the bandages and baby wipes from his hands, then hurry to wash Zoe's cut and cover it. It's nothing big, but I still take extra care with it. "There. All done."

"I need the magic kiss," Zoe says in a small voice, her tears gone.

"Daddy, magic kiss," I tell Eli with a poke to his calf. "No B-L-O-O-D anymore."

He turns to me with an annoyed look. "I can handle the word."

My lips quirk up. "Just not the sight. Right."

He doesn't answer, instead leaning over to kiss the bandage over his daughter's knee.

I clap my thighs, then say, "Great. Now onto the second part. Zoe, want to get that popsicle?"

That gets her to stand and run to the house.

"You got to her quick, didn't you?" Eli says before running after her. I get up, too, but when I look at my lonely chair on the other side of the lawn, I decide to stay where I am, examining the house. It hasn't changed much since it belonged to Mr. Grant, except maybe for a fresh coat of paint and new shutters. It's simple, a bungalow with brown shingles darkened by the salty mist and large windows that I know offer beautiful views of the water. The curious part of me wishes I could examine the inside, too, see if it's just as I remember it, or if it feels as distant as the man who currently inhabits it.

A minute later, Eli comes back out with Zoe, who looks good as new with a pink freezie in hand. She runs toward her sandbox and when he's made sure she's fine, he walks to me.

"Thank you, for that."

"It's nothing," I answer, still watching his daughter who's begun filling buckets with sand and dead leaves while talking to herself.

"You remembered," Eli says after a moment.

"Huh?"

"About the blood."

I chuckle. "Hard to forget when you've passed out in front of me so many times."

"It happened, like, twice."

"Sure." The thought makes me glance at his forehead, where a scar is still present above his left brow from the time we were seventeen and playing with rackets in Ruth's yard. I've always been a terrible athlete, and when Eli hit the ball way too high for me to reach, I jumped to return his serve, but my grip was loose around the racket, and it slipped out of my grasp and right onto his forehead. He started bleeding, and the second he saw the red dripping to the ground, he lost consciousness. Then, when he came to, he saw the same dark spot of blood and promptly passed out again. He probably needed stitches, based on the size of the scar, but that day, I only covered it with three bandages and called it a day.

"I didn't know you're a nurse now."

It hits me then, that I maybe shouldn't have said it. I'd rather not talk about my job, or why I can leave work for so long. More than that, my position is technically waiting for me in four weeks, but who's to say I'll be able to keep it?

A patient has made a complaint about you.

I crack my knuckles, kicking my boss's gentle voice away from my head. "Yeah. A lot's happened in a decade."

"And yet you still haven't gotten rid of that nasty habit," he says with a dip of his head toward my hands.

I smirk. "You'll have to pry knuckle-cracking from my cold, dead hands." Nothing is better to relieve stress.

The small grin he wore leaves as he turns toward the water. "I still can't believe you're here, to be honest." He drags a hand through his thick, dark hair. "I'd assumed you'd never step foot here again." There's an edge to his voice; one I've never heard before.

"Me too," I say honestly.

His throat works. "You didn't tell me how long you were planning on staying."

"Four weeks." All the time I have to get my shit together.

He nods, then looks over my shoulder at Ruth's house, which is technically the real reason I'm here. Not to escape my life for the summer.

"I really am sorry for your loss. She was a great woman. Even at the end, she always had a smile for me when I'd bring her dinner or stop by."

My jaw slackens. I wasn't here for my own grandmother, didn't even know she was ill, while he was there, taking care of her in ways I should have. It almost seems like I should be the one offering condolences. I might have loved her more than words could express, but if his deep sigh tells me anything, it's that he probably was closer to her than I was, in the end.

"Thank you for doing that for her," is the only thing I find to say.

"Daddy, look!"

We both turn toward Zoe, who's holding what looks like a caterpillar between her small fingers like it's a prized possession.

"That's great, sweetie. Just release it in the grass now, okay?"

She does, giving it what looks like a kiss before leaving it on the ground. I both melt and shudder at the sight.

"She's adorable."

"She's something all right," he answers, grinning.

I haven't seen yesterday's woman back around here, and it's still not clear to me who she was, or if Eli has someone in his life. Earlier, Zoe said her mom wasn't around, but that could have meant she was at work.

"I'm surprised she took so well to you," Eli says. "She doesn't speak much to anyone but me and sometimes Keira."

"Maybe she thought I was her."

He looks at me then, from head to toe, then shakes his head. "You were never as similar as you thought."

My sister is gorgeous. Always has been, with her high cheekbones and heavy curves, and before, when we'd get compared, I always knew people meant I was the lesser, more ordinary-looking of the two. However, the way Eli says it, it doesn't sound like an insult. It never has.

He clears his throat when I've been staring at him for too long, making me snap out of it. It's just so strange, seeing this man who used to be a boy after all these years and realizing how much I've missed him. It's different than it is with my sister, who I still heard about through Mom. I don't know anything about the past years of Eli's life, and I crave to know everything I missed about the person I used to consider my best friend. I want to know how he met Zoe's mother, what happened between them, when he decided he wanted to become a father, what he's still doing in the house next door. But the distance is also what keeps me silent. We're not the teenagers we were, and I don't have the right to ask all this anymore.

"Daddy, come!" Zoe shouts, the sound breaking the trance of the moment.

"Duty calls," Eli says, taking a slow step back. "But it was, uh... It was good to see you again, Cassie."

Disappointment fills me as it sounds like a goodbye. *It was nice seeing you, let's do it again in another eleven years, yeah?*

"You too," I say, hoping my smile remains steady.

He looks at me for a second longer before nodding and turning toward his daughter in a jog. I remain in place, watching the way his body has become sculpted, trying to fill my head to the brim before I only have memories to keep me company.

Before I can stop myself, I take a step forward and say, "I'll see you around?"

A wave of nausea rolls over me as he turns, not answering right away. This feels like being in PE and waiting to see whether you'll be the last or second-to-last to be picked in the handball team in front of the entire class. After an interminable moment, he dips his head. "Yeah, I guess you will."

Not sure whether that sounded like a good thing to him, but I have a month to figure it out.

Chapter 4

I arrive at the lawyer's office first.

Yesterday, after I reached out to Keira to ask her where she wanted to meet, she only texted me the address. Nothing else.

A heat wave is starting, and the stuffy, coastal air feels suffocating, even at ten in the morning. I'm wearing jeans and a T-shirt, but I'm already regretting my choice of clothes. I couldn't figure out what I was supposed to wear to this kind of legal meeting, but with what I'd packed for the trip, my options were limited.

The office is located on the main street in town, which is bustling with families walking to the beach with chairs strapped to their backs and buggies with lunchboxes and towels behind them. To my left, a group of three children are squealing at a gull that's gotten close enough to steal a potato chip from their hands. One's barely old enough to stand on wobbly legs. I look away.

A minute later, Keira parks her truck right in front of me. She's wearing beige slacks and a pressed blouse that hugs the curve of her round belly. I didn't think to consider it the last time I saw her, but now, I'd say she looks to be around the beginning of her third trimester.

"Hey."

She passes me, not even stopping for a greeting. "Let's get this over with."

And hello to you, too.

I follow her inside, feeling like a grounded kid who makes sure to stay as silent as possible so as not to trigger their parent even more. The office is old-school, with massive, natural wood furniture and dark walls. It feels like stepping out of a beach town and into a high-end Connecticut office.

"We're here for Mr. Burton," Keira tells the young receptionist with an ice-cold tone. Apparently, she's decided she's being rude with everyone today.

"Sure thing," the receptionist says, tucking her long brown hair behind her ears. "Take a seat."

I sit in one of the chairs she pointed to, but Keira remains standing, her arms crossed, looking everywhere except in my direction. Low, instrumental music is the only thing occupying the space between us. The absence of words when we have so much to catch up on is so strange, it feels surreal. She's angry I wasn't there, but now that I am, she'd rather I disappear again.

I hang my hands between my knees, then say, "Is Xavier in daycare today?"

Finally, she meets my gaze, but only answers with a curt nod.

After another long moment of silence, she says, "Have you gone to see Mom?"

And we're off to a great start.

I scratch my jaw. "Not yet. I might go this afternoon."

"Right."

Actually, it'll probably be better if I just shut up while we wait. She seems to think the same, and after what feels like twenty lifetimes but was probably a minute, an older black man with gray hair and an expensive-looking suit comes out of the door behind the front desk, smiling.

"Mrs. McIntyre, Ms. Taylor?"

Crap.

Keira's head snaps in my direction so fast, I fear she might break something. "So, you're even too good for our last name now?" She snickers with a shake of her head. "You'll never cease to amaze me." Then, she walks forward to shake the lawyer's hand, not giving me the time to answer.

My knuckles crack as I tighten my fists. I want to run after her and shake her by the shoulders, ask her how *she* can bear to live with that name, but I know it's useless. It never bothered her like it did me.

I knew our family name was synonymous to an insult in town before I was old enough to understand why. When my father would cause mayhem and end up being arrested once more, it wasn't even the actions themselves I minded. I was used to them, used to the shame that inhabited our house like a fifth member of the family. What truly hurt was the way I was perceived because of them. Every time I'd think we'd gotten over the past crisis, and I was able to play with other kids without their parents telling them to stay away from "that McIntyre girl", when I could be just Cassie to them, he'd do another reckless thing, and we'd be back to square one. Eventually, there was no going back, and I remained Mac's daughter 365 days a year.

So yes, the moment I was able to, I changed my last name to my middle name, which was also Ruth's. Even if no one in New York knew who my father was, *I* did, and I wanted to be rid of that burden.

But this is not the time to have this conversation, especially with her simmering anger so palpable, so I ignore her comment and greet Ruth's lawyer as well, then follow him inside his office, where he invites us to sit and offers us each a glass of sparkling water.

"Thank you for meeting me today," the man says as he tucks his tie down and sits. "I'm Stephen Nelson, Ruth's lawyer."

"Nice to meet you," I say. We spoke on the phone twice, but always briefly, to settle things before today's meeting.

"First off, I want to offer my deepest condolences again. Ruth was a good friend of mine, and she was a great woman."

"Thank you," Keira says. I feel like if I say something about our grandmother, she'll bite my head off again, so I settle on a nod.

"Now, I'd like to know if she ever talked to either of you about what she wanted to have done after her passing?"

I shake my head but turn to Keira. While I didn't know Ruth suffered from heart failure, if she still saw Keira regularly, there's no way she hid it from her, so maybe they had the discussion at some point. I hate that Ruth decided to keep it all from me, even though I'm not surprised in the slightest. She was the proudest woman I knew. Never would have dared leave her house without a full face of makeup and a vintage, well-curated outfit.

"Not really, no," Keira says. At least there's that.

"All right, so let's start from the beginning." Mr. Nelson pulls two brown files out of his desk and hands one to each of us. Keira doesn't wait to open it, so I do the same. There must be around sixty pages in there, all written in legal jargon. I put the file down and glance back at Ruth's lawyer.

"Ruth was very specific in her post-mortem demands," he says, then scrolls on his computer before turning the screen in our direction so we can see the page he settled on. "First, she was adamant that her will be executed by both of you. If one hadn't shown up, she didn't want me to deal with only the other."

My brows furrow. What a strange demand.

"She also asked that a celebration be made in her honor, with all her close friends and family present."

"That's done already," Keira says.

"I wasn't there," I respond.

Keira ignores the comment, and Mr. Nelson doesn't seem to want to get involved.

Another wave of grief hits me, and I squeeze my thighs tight enough to leave nail welts in order to keep my cool. She wanted one last party, and I didn't even attend.

You're fine.

"Then, for the estate." He scrolls further. "I will read what she said, so there's no misinterpretation. 'To Keira, I leave my books, so she rediscovers the magic of this world. And to Cassie, I leave my scrapbooking material, so she can start seeing life from a new perspective.'"

Keira turns to me with a strange look, but I'm just as lost. I don't even know what the second part of that statement means. I've never scrapbooked a day in my life. At least Keira was always a big reader.

"'As for the house, I want it to be sold, as well as all the items in it, unless my granddaughters decide on objects they would like to keep. What isn't sold should be donated. Each girl shall receive ten thousand dollars from the sale. The rest shall be donated to the charity of their choice.'"

My sister's jaw drops. She didn't expect this any more than I did. And yet, once again, I should've anticipated it. Ruth was never one for material things. Everything in the house was bought in antique stores or garage sales. The kitchen chairs have always been mismatched, two contemporary and two in a Victorian style. The house had been passed down from generation to generation—otherwise she never would've been able to buy an oceanside property—but I'm not surprised she didn't want to give it to us. She knew she could change lives with that kind of money, and being generous, both with her time and money, is something that's so Ruth, I have to blink away the emotion clouding my eyes.

"'Moreover, all the steps must be done together, and all final decisions require agreement from both Cassie and Keira.'"

"When did she write this?" Keira asks, her voice poignant. "Twenty years ago?"

Mr. Nelson looks to be hating his life so much right now. "She had it edited a few months before her death."

"Ridiculous," she mumbles. "This will take an eternity."

"I have time," I say. "I can do most of it."

"Were you not listening? We need to both be there, all the time." She turns to the lawyer. "Is there any way we can do only parts of her requests? What happens if we don't?"

"Then the court will elect someone to do it."

"No way," I say. "Ruth wanted us to do this, so we'll do it."

"Oh, now you want to be sentimental?"

"Stop it," I grit out. "We're not doing this right now." I can't believe she wants to air out our dirty laundry like this. "And this is not about me. It's about her."

Her jaw ticks, then she turns to Mr. Nelson. "Fine. We'll do it, if we have no choice."

I exhale as Mr. Nelson says, "Thank you. And I'll be there to help you along the way, or if you have any questions."

"Is that all?" Before he's even answered, she's on her feet.

"Sure," he says, allowing her to leave without another word.

"Thank you," I tell Mr. Nelson before running after my sister.

"Hey, wait up!" I shout once I'm out the door, seeing her silhouette almost to her truck.

"There's nothing else to discuss." She pulls her keys out of her purse. "We'll deal with this shit, and that's that."

I feel like she's just slapped me, and after the whiplash this entire morning has been, I've had enough. "What's your problem?"

"My problem?" She takes a step toward me. "Are you seriously asking me that?"

"Yes, I am. You were acting like a child in there. I know—"

"You don't know *anything*." Her nostrils flare, cheeks burning. "I needed that money from the sale, Cassie, but of course, you wouldn't have known that."

"You're not being fair."

"And you were, when you left and let me deal with all our crap by myself?"

This is not the moment to let myself crack, even though everything in me wants to burst. She knew how it was for me here. How I was drowning in this town. For years, I would eat lunch in the janitor's closet at school, so I could eat without fearing someone would throw chewing gum in my hair. Keira could drown out the noise and make friends anyway, but I was never that strong.

"I'm here now," I say, forcing my voice to remain calm. "Let me help. Whatever you need."

She crosses her arms over her belly.

"And I'm sorry," I add, "about the money. Maybe there's a way we can—"

"It's fine. I'll deal with it." She licks her lips. "We'll do this, and then you'll be able to return to your great life far away from here."

Her words are a knife to my stomach, twisting and tearing. If only she knew.

She turns toward her car, but I say, "One more thing."

A long sigh leaves her lips, one I remember hearing when Mom would ask her to help clean up the kitchen. "What?"

"I want to organize something for Ruth." The idea wasn't fully formed in my head until the words leave my mouth.

"I told you, we already had her funeral."

"Not a funeral. Something like... a life celebration." She wanted us to do this, and if she asked for this request to be read when I was there, it means she wanted me to attend this event. "I'll host. You just have to show up. Please."

I wait for another sigh, but the only thing she says is, "Fine."

Then, she's gone.

Chapter 5

"So, what's new back there?" I ask, shielding my eyes and my phone screen against the glare of the setting sun.

Emily is slumped on the break room couch, one we've had countless heart-to-hearts on.

"Not much. Mitsy is complaining about her extra shifts, as always, even though she picked up the least of them out of all of us."

"I'm so sorry." I slow my speed-walk, looking at all the gorgeous new builds that have appeared in the neighborhood in the past years. Whereas the view was always beautiful, the houses on Beachside Avenue used to be shabby at best, decrepit at worst. Now, it seems like Ruth's and the Grants' are the only ones that remain in their original condition. Most have likely been bought by millionaires looking for a second house by the ocean instead of people living here year-long. The properties are massive, with pristine greige or white shingles, and large stone chimneys erupting from their sides. Old-school cerulean bikes with their cute baskets hanging out front rest against the porches, along with surfboards and beach chairs. In between each house, a magical painting appears, a sand dune that opens into bluer-than-blue water.

"Stop that," Emily tells me over the phone. "We've had staffing issues for the past, oh, I don't know, century?"

"Still." I hate the idea of letting down people who have given me a place to belong when I needed it most.

"Cassie. Shut up." She engulfs a handful of Cheetos. As paradoxical as it can sound, you'll never see a group eating as much trash as nurses, especially on evening or night shifts. It's as if we need the encouragement from a box of donuts or a mix of candy to get through the following hours. "Oh, actually? There is one new thing. There's this new anesthesiologist, and he's very much giving Mark Sloan vibes."

"Not a doctor, Em. Gotta resist those stereotypes at all costs."

"What can I say?" She shrugs. "You know what a good scrub cap does to me."

"What's the definition of a good scrub cap?"

"I retract my statement. Any scrub cap does it."

"Your standards are so very low," I say with a grin.

"Welcome to the current dating pool, my friend."

"Don't I know it."

"Speaking of which..." Emily's face turns a beet shade of red, shifting me on alarm right away. The last time I saw that half-guilty, half-pitying face, I was about to get temporarily fired.

"What's up?"

"Nothing, just... I saw Michael at the gym today."

I swallow. The reason for my loss of interest in the dating pool in the flesh. After he left, I couldn't imagine starting from scratch with someone else. I'd given everything, and now I was empty. If someone who'd wanted to marry me could leave, what stranger could want all of me?

"How was he?" A bird caws above me, giving me an excuse to look away. He never stopped using our common gym, even after our breakup. I was the one who had to leave, even though my best friend was still a member there.

"Good. I think..." She twists her lips. "I think he's met someone."

I nod. Nod some more. He met someone who can give him what I couldn't, probably. That thought hurts more than the idea of him with someone else.

"It's fine."

"Cassie..."

"It's okay, I swear." I smile, hoping it doesn't look as crazed as I feel. "It'll all be fine. I'll get through this month of family stuff, and then I'll be back like nothing happened."

In a softer voice, she says, "I don't think that's what Sariah had in mind when she asked you to take time off."

"That's because I didn't *need* time off."

I recognize her next expression all too well. It's one I've received countless times, by doctors, by nurses, and even by Michael. When he walked out of our apartment and out of my life, it wasn't with anger or with nostalgia. It was with pity.

"You haven't grieved, Cassie."

I don't know if it's the way she says it, or the word she uses—*grief*—that instantly makes my vision blurry. She's not talking about my grandmother, and we both know it.

"Being away won't change anything."

"Maybe it will." She's still looking at me like I'm two seconds away from breaking. "You weren't right, before you left. You looked like you hated every second of every shift."

She's right. I did. I hated seeing the expectant mothers coming in with their faces twisted in pain as contractions hit, one hand on their belly and the other holding their partner's. Hated hearing the wails of newborns piercing through the quiet halls during the night. Hated the happiness radiating out of their every pore when I went in the room to take vitals, or to help with breastfeeding techniques. Hated myself for hating it.

But what other choice did I have? Stay home to wallow?

"Maybe you should see this time as less of a punishment and more of a gift. Time to take a step back and see how you feel about everything."

I know how I feel about my infertility—hopeless. Lost. But she's made a point. I have a month to get back to a place where I can function in the presence of all these mothers, and if I want to keep the one thing that used to be great in my life, then I need to figure out a way to handle my shit.

"I will," I say, both to reassure her and to convince myself.

"Good."

I'm nearing the end of my walk, only a few yards away from Ruth's home, when motion attracts my gaze.

Eli is pacing in his driveway, wearing what looks to be a chef's white coat, only halfway buttoned. He's on his phone, and his free hand is running through his hair. He looks distraught.

I didn't think to ask him about his job in the past days even though he knows mine, but this wasn't what I expected. When we were young, he never had plans to follow in his father's footsteps. He was never decisive in what he wanted to do—an archeologist after he visited the Museum of Natural History during a trip to NYC, a math teacher while he was in the mathletes in middle school, a marine biologist during his ocean phase—but this option never came up.

"Hey, Em, I gotta go, but talk soon, okay?"

She eyes me warily before saying, "Sure. Take care of yourself, babe."

I force another smile I hope looks reassuring before I hang up and make my way to the man who I've rarely seen looking anxious before.

"Hey," I call out. "You all right?"

Eli looks up, then pulls his phone away from his ear and presses something on the screen.

"Minor crisis. I'll be fine."

"What happened?"

As he types something, he says, "One of my kitchen staff just called in sick, and we have an event to cater in an hour, so I have to step in."

So, he hasn't taken over his dad's food truck, then. A restaurant, maybe?

"Can I help with anything?" I don't know anything about professional cooking, but I'm sure I could learn quick if I'm given simple tasks.

"Unless you can get your sister or mine to answer their phones and agree to babysit tonight, then I don't think so, but thank you."

Right. He needs help with Zoe, not with his job.

I crack my thumb, watching as he makes another call. I hate feeling useless.

Except I don't have to be.

"I could do it," I say before I can second-guess myself. I can't work. I can't go see Keira, I'm not ready to go to Mom's yet, and being stuck in a space that reminds me of Ruth at every turn is stifling. But this, I can do. Plus, this could be some kind of exposure therapy. I've felt suffocated, being surrounded by mothers and babies recently, but Zoe isn't a baby. She's just one kid.

Eli's head snaps up, but after a second, he returns his attention to his phone, disconnecting his unanswered call. "I wouldn't ask that of you."

"You're not asking. I'm offering."

"Still. That's... It shouldn't be on you to do this."

His lips twitch, and while he's not being rude, it feels almost insulting, how much he's resisting my offer.

"We took our Red Cross babysitting class together, remember?"

That makes him chuckle once, and immediately, I get a glimpse of the old Eli. "Considering we were, like, nine and ten, and I remember exactly zero things from it, this is not the reassurance you think it is."

"But I always did have such a better memory than you."

He grins again but still presses another call button. I see the contact being Mrs. Peabody.

"All right, now this is seriously wounding. You'd rather have the old librarian who always smelled like weed than me?"

As if I've reminded him of who exactly he's been calling, he cancels the call. "Pretty sure that weed was medicinal."

"You are gullibility incarnated." I take a step in his direction. "Seriously, though. I've dealt with more shit than you could ever imagine at the hospital. I can take care of a kid for one evening, I promise."

His lips twist once more, and then he says, "Fine. Thank you. You'd be a lifesaver."

It's nothing big. He's allowing me to do him a favor. And yet, after the distaste I got from Keira this morning, and the reminder of my failure at work, this trust feels like a major win.

He tucks his phone in his pants and heads toward his front door. I assume it's an invitation to follow him.

"She's already eaten dinner and had her bath, so the only thing to do is maybe read her a story and get her to bed, and then you can do whatever you want." We walk inside, and while I want to take it all in and see what's changed over the years, he doesn't give me the time to. Eli is on a roll. As we walk, he grabs a package I recognize as his father's knife set, then closes a few cupboards that had been left open. "She's usually easy to get to sleep, but that's when she's used to who tucks her in..." He pauses, gaze darting at his daughter playing with Legos in the living room. He drags a hand through his hair. "You know, maybe I should call Keira again. She's usually home on Tuesdays."

It's a hit he's not even aware he's given. "Eli," I say, placing both hands on his shoulders. It's the first time I've touched really him in years, but now's not the time to notice how bulky his arms have gotten or how, from this close, I can smell the same Irish Springs body wash he used as a teen. "We'll be fine."

I don't pause to think about whose kid it is I'll be having under my care or what it is exactly I'm signing up for. He needs me. I can do that one thing for him. If I had time to consider this, I'd probably freak out at how I haven't taken care of a kid, not as a nurse but as a babysitter, maybe ever, but I don't have that luxury. Plus, Zoe looks to be the sweetest kid. How hard can a single night be?

His pupils are wide as he returns his attention to me. "Right. You're right." He turns and hollers, "Zoe? Can you come here, baby?"

She carefully positions her block tower before coming to us. Her pink pajamas are decorated with sparkly frogs, and her hair still looks damp.

"Cassie!" she says when she sees me. "Look, Daddy put a new Band-Aid on my booboo, and this one has little dogs on it." She still has a tiny lisp, probably from losing a tooth, which makes her even cuter, if that's possible.

"Oh, really? Let me see!"

She doesn't hesitate, lifting her pajama pants up to her knees while standing on one foot. I 'ooh' and 'aah', and the smile she sends me in return is as if I'd given her the moon.

Eli's posture relaxes. He kneels in front of her. "Zoe, I have to go to work tonight after all, but Cassie will stay with you. Is that okay?"

She doesn't give him an answer, instead turning to me. "Can I show you my fish? His name is Fish."

I grin. "I'd love that."

"All right." Eli remains on his haunches for a moment, discomfort transpiring from his every pore, but eventually, he does get up to go collect his keys. "I'll be back as soon as I can," he tells me. "Make yourself at home. There's leftover lasagna in the fridge, and—"

"Eli."

"Right." He rushes to his daughter, pressing a kiss to her forehead and saying something in a hushed voice that makes her smile. The sight should be framed, hung in this living room to be looked at every day. It makes my entire body melt. Louder, he says, "Be good!" Then, to me, he mouths a "Thank you so much," and then he's out.

It feels like a tornado has just passed through the house, the dust settling as silence returns. Zoe is still standing on one foot for unclear reasons, her round eyes on me.

"So. Where's that fish?"

Chapter 6

I'm halfway through my sixth episode of some baking show—who knew making cakes could be so stressful?—when Eli steps back through the front door. He looks like he's gone through an entire World War in the past ten hours. His hair is tousled, the dark-gray T-shirt under his unbuttoned white coat covered in a white substance I want to assume is flour, but in the state he's in, anything is possible.

"Hey," I say, leaning over the back of the couch to peer over at him. The Grants' house is mostly open-plan, and while it's bigger than Ruth's, it's still fairly small, enough that you can see the entire first floor at a glance. It's barely changed since I was here last, only a few different trinkets now sprinkled around. "Rough night?"

"You could say that, yeah." He throws his keys in a bowl, then removes his coat. I'm not sure whether it's the lighting or the stiffness in his body, but I barely recognize him. He looks...heavy. Like an invisible weight is pulling him down, and every second he remains upright is a struggle.

When we were kids, Eli would always be up before me, at least over summer break. I'd be dragging myself out of bed and he'd already be waiting for me in Ruth's kitchen, dressed and ready for a packed schedule. *"You'll sleep when you're dead,"* he told me one morning when I grumbled that I didn't want to go swim at eight in the morning in ice-cold water.

"Eli, I'd swear sometimes it's hard to believe you're not a ninety-year-old in a seventeen-year-old's body," I said, my pillow probably still stamped in my face. The only person I'd ever heard use this expression was Ruth.

"I'll try not to take it personally."

"You should. It was a very personal attack."

He grinned, grooves that would become smile wrinkles already etched into his skin.

That jumpy, almost hyper-excited kid is nowhere to be seen.

"Sorry I'm so late," he says now, padding over to the fridge. His shoes are off, and even though I've been in his house all evening, it feels strangely intimate, to be seeing him like this, knowing what kind of brand of socks he uses now. Like I haven't earned that privilege.

"It's fine. I had a great time." What I don't say is I played with Zoe for almost an hour before I finally enforced her bedtime. I couldn't get myself to burst her bubble. She wanted to show me every toy she owned, words spilling out of her faster than she could think them. In an hour, she went through her favorite animals—starting with the Froot Loops toucan—her dream vacation destination—the swamp from The Princess and the Frog—and what we wanted to do when we were grownups—I reminded her I *am* a grown-up, and she went with a magician.

I don't know where Eli got the idea that his little girl is shy.

By the time I got her to bed, she fell asleep before I could finish the first page of the book she'd chosen.

Eli stops by the couch to give me a doubtful look, then walks to the kitchen and grabs a bottle of beer from the fridge. "Want one?"

It's almost two in the morning. I shake my head.

He pops the cap before taking a seat on the opposite end of the couch. After taking a long sip, he says, "It shouldn't have fallen on you. I'm sorry."

"Stop it. I almost harassed you to do it." It's slightly more embarrassing when I say it out loud. "I wouldn't have been doing much else at Ruth's." In fact, tonight was a pleasant reprieve from it all.

He hums an unconvinced sound, then glances around the living room, and the heaviness only seems to grow. I notice him take it all in, as if seeing it from an outsider's perspective, from the toys swallowing the ground to the messy blankets I ended up covering myself with while watching TV. I feel like shaking him to figure out if I can get him out of this state.

Finally, his gaze lands on the pile of folded clothes on the coffee table, and he groans. "Please tell me you didn't fold my laundry."

"I didn't fold your laundry."

His eyes narrow. "My five-year-old suddenly learned how to?"

"You should never underestimate that kid."

"Cassie."

"It was on the couch. I couldn't just leave it there!" Plus, I've always found folding clothes to be calming. I love the repetitive pattern, the ability for my hands to busy themselves while my mind goes elsewhere.

He lifts the child-sized tie-dye tank top from the top of the pile, then quickly glances underneath. "Christ. I can't believe you've folded my boxers."

"I work in a hospital. You have no idea the shit I see on a daily basis. Your Fruit of the Looms won't ruffle me much."

"They're Calvin Kleins, thank you very much."

"Fancy."

He tries to crack a smile, but even that seems to take all his small change. "Really, though, I'm sorry for the mess. I hadn't realized how bad it'd gotten." He leans his head back, his scruff-covered jaw tightening. "I've been a little... overwhelmed, lately."

"Anything going on?"

He doesn't answer right away, and I have that same rollercoaster stomach-drop I had before, when he didn't want me to babysit. I keep forgetting we're not Eli-and-Cassie anymore. It's easy to remember when I'm away, but with him right here, close enough to touch, I can almost pretend we've taken a shuttle back in time. Jeannine, his mom, is outside tending to her flower beds while Ronald, his dad, is cooking something on the barbecue. His siblings are wrestling somewhere upstairs for the GameCube remote, and the two of us are here, fitting together.

But it's been a decade, and that fantasy is long gone.

"You don't have to," I rush to add. "I don't want to overstep."

"You didn't." He sighs, then takes another long sip. "I've had full custody of Zoe for a little more than a year now."

I feel my brows start to lift and force my face to remain neutral. I'm reminded of the woman shouting outside two mornings ago, and thankfully, Eli doesn't act like he knows I know. "And a month ago, her mother decided to come back from God knows where and ask to be let into my daughter's life again."

"Can she?"

"Legally? I have no idea. I'm just hoping she moves on, and we don't need to get to that."

So that explains the woman's desperate shouts the other morning, if that really was Zoe's mother.

"And if she doesn't? Move on, I mean."

"I don't know." He shakes his head as he traces lines through the condensation on his bottle. "It keeps me up at night, if I'm being honest. I'm fucking scared she'll be allowed in Zoe's life again."

"Why did she leave before?" I once again feel like I'm overstepping, but he's letting me, and I'm too nosy to let this opportunity pass.

His shoulders give a careless shrug. "Your guess is as good as mine. For leaving Zoe, at least."

"Were you...Were you together long?"

He looks up through his lashes, and I'm not sure if it's my hesitation at asking the question, or his realization of just who he's talking about this with, but a thickness settles between our words.

"Liz got pregnant when we'd just started hanging out. After that, we decided to try and make it work between us, but her heart was never in it."

But his was, I'm assuming. Eli Grant never half-assed anything. School project? He'd be on it the second he was out of class. Christmas presents? No one could find a more thoughtful, meaningful gift than him. He was probably the same when he learned he was going to be a father, looking up books on parenting. He wouldn't have gotten into a relationship unless he was ready to give it his all.

"We were never good together, but I wanted to give Zoe the best chance at a normal family, so we tried. And then, one day, she just got up, packed a bag, and told me she didn't want this life anymore. She left while Zoe was napping. She wasn't even two."

A burning sensation settles in my throat, at the simple thought of a parent doing this to their child.

"We've been okay, the two of us. It's a lot, but it's good." He wets his lips. "I don't want to put Zoe through that again. Having her mom, then losing her."

"Then don't stop fighting." I feel the words deep in my chest. That little girl deserves nothing but to feel loved fully and unconditionally.

Eli's honey gaze slips my way, and with only a look, I know he sees where that resolve comes from. I wouldn't want anyone to feel the way I did.

"Trust me, I won't." A long moment passes when we can't hear anything but our shared breaths, as if even the ocean and crickets have gone to sleep. His throat works. "But in the meantime, I'm a single dad who's worried 24/7 and trying to prove that I can do it by myself."

"Do you have any help?" He mentioned Keira earlier, and while she's been nothing but a thorn in my side this week, I'm glad she's there for him.

"Felix and Charlie help when they're around," he says. "But Charlie's in college an hour away and Felix is...not the most reliable. He's currently off backpacking in South Asia."

"Wow, I'd forgotten they're not kids anymore." His siblings are five and six years younger than me, and while they were often there when I was, they felt like background noise when Eli was my movie soundtrack.

He chuckles. "Yeah, definitely not."

"What about your parents?"

His face sours, and before he says the words, I know what they will be. I've seen grief too many times to mistake it. "Dad passed away six years ago. Another heart attack." His lips twitch. "Mom's spending her retirement traveling the world with her *much* younger boyfriend."

"Oh God, I'm so sorry. About your dad, I mean. I had no idea." Mr. Grant was one of the nicest people I met in my life. He never once shunned me for being a McIntyre, and he welcomed me to work with him and Eli in the truck during the summer without ever batting an eye. He knew finding a job in this town was a nightmare for me, and what money I earned from him allowed me to leave when the time came. I was never able to properly thank him for that, and I guess now, I never will. Once again, a sense of dread overwhelms me at the thought that I wasn't there to give Eli my condolences and support at that time. If I'd kept in contact, I could've been there for him the way he was for me so many times growing up.

"Would've been hard to know, since you never called."

My breath catches, and I know he hears it, because the steel in his face immediately melts; only because he's Eli, and he'd rather hide all his true feelings than hurt someone else. And the thing is, he *should* want me to hurt. He's right. I didn't call. When I left, I knew it meant I'd leave the best part of this place, too. I couldn't keep him tethered to me when I would never come back. It wouldn't be fair to give him a puddle of a relationship when he deserved the entire ocean. We'd ended before we'd had a chance to truly begin, and keeping him from better things by calling him every now and then and reminding him I existed seemed unfair. But I can see now that cutting ties completely could have seemed just as cruel.

I hurt him. The one person who only ever gave me joy. It feels like all I ever do is hurt the people I love.

Suddenly, I'm on my feet, grabbing my purse. I can't breathe right, and I need air.

"Cassie, wait." He's up, too. "I didn't mean—"

"It's fine. Really." The last thing I want him to do is feel bad for telling me the truth. "Thank you for letting me help out tonight."

I don't dare another glance before leaving.

Chapter 7

The boy doesn't remember a time when his life didn't begin and end with her.

Or rather, he does, but it feels like an entirely different life. Like he only realized what living meant the moment he met her. It might sound insane, but even at that age, something in his body recognized something in her. *Mine,* it said.

The girl doesn't remember the first time they met. She always tells the story of watching him through her grandmother's window before finally getting the nerve to ask him to play on his trampoline when she was ten and he was eleven, but that wasn't the first time they crossed paths.

It was an April afternoon, the kind of New England spring day where the hope of spring is crushed by a winter flashback. The boy was outside with his mother, helping her plant the bulbs for the bright yellow flowers she loved to see bloom over the summer, even though they would probably freeze overnight. He didn't mind the cold, though. Didn't mind the way he barely felt his fingers anymore. While the inside of their house was always chaotic, with his siblings play-wrestling in the living room and his father playing the radio too loud, the garden with his mother was a safe haven.

　　　　　　　　　　　　

He felt too old to say he missed spending time with his mother, but here, he could admit it to himself.

Dirt caked his hands and nails as he started digging another hole, but before he could plant the bulb, a rush of color brought his attention to the house next door. A girl was running toward the front porch, wearing tie-dye rain boots and a fuchsia coat. Her hair was wet, as if she'd caught rain along the way. She didn't stop running as she climbed the stairs and knocked on the door, but no one answered. The lady who lived in the house had left earlier in her car, so no one would. When the girl knocked again and still didn't get an answer, she didn't turn around. Didn't slump in defeat. She just stood there, reactionless.

The boy got to his feet.

"You can go inside if you're too cold," his mother said without looking up, but he wasn't listening to her. He could barely feel the cold anymore. To this day, he doesn't know what made him keep staring. Maybe it was the fact that the girl was wearing an entire rainbow, yet he'd never seen anyone looking so sad. Actually, sad wasn't the right term. Looking so *empty*. Like she didn't have any sadness to give anymore.

The boy walked over to the neighbor's lawn, and for a moment, he simply stood there, watching her. She looked to be around his age, maybe a bit younger. From up close, he could see that none of her clothes fit her. The purple jeans were too short, a line of skin exposed at the top of her boots, and the coat was two sizes too big, the sleeves hanging over her hands.

"She's gone," the boy said in a loud voice, maybe to inform her, and maybe simply because he wanted her to look at him.

Green.

It was all he could see when he finally got a good look at her face. Her eyes were the shade of burgeoning leaves in May, when their color is so bright, you cannot look anywhere else. They widened when she saw him, but she didn't look away.

Was it at this moment he fell in love with her? He likes to think maybe it was. It was game over for him from the start.

The boy wanted to walk up to her and ask why she had run in the rain. Give her a shovel and offer her to try planting a bulb in his safe haven. But she looked... fragile. Like one word from him, and she'd be blown away with the wind.

But he couldn't help himself. "Are you okay?"

She didn't say anything, only looked around like she didn't know where she was. As if someone else had brought her here. She blinked, then turned and leaned to grab a key from under a garden gnome. Without giving him another look, she unlocked the door and walked inside.

He'd never seen her here before, although he didn't hang outside much, especially over the winter. When he wasn't in school, he was usually inside, fighting with his siblings over who got to play the drums in Rock Band.

The boy walked to his mother in a daze and kneeled back in the dirt. His mother didn't ask what he'd been doing. She just clucked her tongue and said, "That poor McIntyre girl."

"What's wrong with her?" he asked, his mind still stuck on the haunted green eyes that had remained on his. As if she, too, had recognized something in him.

"Nothing's wrong with her. She just landed in the wrong family."

He didn't know what this meant, not really. He couldn't have known what was going on in the McIntyre household. Even years later, he never got the courage to ask the girl what had happened on that day she ran in the rain to her grandmother's house. Usually, he took what she gave him and didn't ask for more.

"Why was she alone?" the boy asked. Even at ten years old, his parents barely ever let him out of their sight. He couldn't imagine being able to run across town by himself.

"I don't know, honey." His mother looked at him and tilted her head. "I don't think anyone in that family has many friends around town."

He looked again at the neighbor's house, wondering what was going on inside. Did the girl know the owner? Or did she just take a lucky guess on where to find the key? Had she been able to warm up?

"The next time I see her, I'll invite her in," the boy said. If anyone needed a friend, it was this girl.

A beat passed before his mother answered, "All right, honey."

For months, he thought he'd never see her again.

And then, one August morning, the girl with the green eyes and ill-fitting clothes was there.

He never let her go after that.

Chapter 8

Walking up the front porch steps of my childhood home feels like stepping into an alternate universe. One I'd seen mostly in nightmares.

I didn't expect it'd happen this way. This morning, when I got up, I decided I'd pushed off seeing Mom long enough. I'd been here almost a week. However, I was still too much of a chicken to just go to her, so I kicked myself in the ass and called instead.

"I'm hosting a little something in Ruth's honor tomorrow," I said after she answered in an almost overly cheery voice. She was nice enough to pretend it wasn't strange that I hadn't visited her yet.

"Oh, honey, that's wonderful!" she exclaimed. "Would you like some help with the cooking?"

"I'm... I'm good, I think." My plan had actually been to get a mix of takeout and pre-made stuff, since I can't cook to save my life.

"Nonsense, I'll help you. Actually, why don't you come over? It'll be easier to do it here. I have everything I need."

"I—"

"Oh, we can make that cinnamon shortbread you love so much! Ruth loved it, too, when I brought her some."

I want to tell her I can't stand the taste of shortbread anymore. The last time I ate it was during the last annual Chowder Festival I attended. It's a kitschy yearly event with a few tents set up in the middle of town where merchants sell handmade products, and locals host an unofficial cooking competition, usually with—you guessed it—chowder, but Mom had decided to make her shortbread that year. Barely anyone had gone by her booth, so Eli and I had eaten most of it. And then, our day was cut short when my father got so drunk, he pissed himself in the middle of the lanes of tents, and Mom, Eli, and I had to carry him to our car. I'd thrown up all my shortbread once we got home. Eli had held my hair back and never brought it up again.

But Mom sounded so excited about it now, so I only said, "Sounds great."

I'm still staring at the house when the door opens, and for half a second, I don't recognize her. Age has morphed her face so much more than the eleven years I was gone. Her skin is sun-damaged and loose, her cheekbones too sharp. Her once-round shape now reminds me of Maine's white pines, spindly and slightly crooked.

And then, all the familiar parts of her hit me at once. The bird brooch she still wears pinned to her cardigan; a different bird for each day of the week. Today, it's the red cardinal. Her smile, always showing only half her teeth, like she wants to be happy but can't let herself show it too much. The upturned nose, the scuffed leather shoes, the brittle hair I inherited from her.

Some parts of me immediately turn on high alert, remembering what she allowed this house to become for our family. And yet...

How hadn't I realized just how much I missed her?

"Oh, Cassandra," Mom whispers, a hand over her mouth. Tears rim the bottom of her eyes as she takes two unsteady steps. She lifts her arms to me but stops them halfway, as if unsure whether I'll want the hug. I probably would have, but the pause has drenched me in cold water. We're both still, until my attention is pulled to the ground where an oatmeal-colored shape darts between Mom's legs.

"Dottie," I gasp, kneeling to welcome the dog we got for Keira's fifteenth birthday. Dad was gone at that time, but I don't remember where. He'd often leave for weeks or even months at a time, either to go on a bender with friends, or because he'd found the "next big thing" and was going to make us rich and successful. *Finally, they'll take us seriously in that goddamn town.* Those weeks were always my favorite. We'd watch whatever movie us three girls wanted in the living room, not needing to worry about the volume. That time, Mom had surprised us by finally getting a dog when my father had always refused, and I remember it as one of the happiest days of my life. She was the family's dog, but she always felt more like mine. Even when my father eventually returned, I'd prepared myself to run with Dottie if he didn't allow us to keep her. I'd found my confidante. My best friend during the school year when I was stuck at home because Mom didn't want to piss my father off by bringing us to Ruth's, and I was too young to go by myself. Dottie always knew when I needed comfort after some kid had stuck chewing gum in my hair. She'd come and nudge my thigh with her wet snout, and I could breathe again. Dogs always seem to read the room so much better than humans can.

"Hi, sweet girl," I say, voice raw. She's so much calmer now, her tail wagging softly as she approaches. She sniffs my hand once, then licks it. Mom and I aren't the only ones who've aged.

My throat tightens as I pet her yellowed fur. I've missed most of her life. She must be getting close to fourteen now. So much time I'll never get back.

"I was wondering when you'd come see her," Mom says, still standing. *When you'd come see me,* is what she means.

"I'm sorry," I say once I've straightened. Then, bitterness bubbles back up. "I had to get over the shock of learning about my grandmother first."

She inhales sharply. "Oh, honey, I'm so sorry. I..." Her nose scrunches. "I wasn't well after learning the news. I didn't feel like I could announce it to anyone else, and I honestly didn't know you two were still in contact."

It's possible Ruth didn't talk about me with Mom. It would've been just like her to hide how much closer I was to her than to my own mother. That doesn't erase the sting, though. "You still should've told me."

She flinches at my tone, and I instantly deflate. I don't want to be anything like the person who used to bring that kind of reaction out of her. Besides, I should probably cut her some slack. She did lose the woman she considered a second mother, and grief makes us do weird things.

"What's done is done," I say in a quieter voice. "Let's move on."

She nods with a grateful look, and then her face changes like a switch has been turned on, and she's erased the past minute in her mind.

"Ready to cook?" she asks. "Oh, I have so much to tell you!"

I follow her inside, immediately forgetting about the weird moment when I notice her walk. Whereas she used to run around the beach with us like nobody's business, her steps are now small and unsteady.

"Are you hurt?" I ask, hands braced behind her in case she trips and needs me to break her fall.

"What? No, I'm fine."

"Mom."

We reach the kitchen table that's covered in pots and baking ingredients, where she pulls a chair out and lets her body drop into it.

"I need to tell you about crochet club," she says, already pulling the bag of flour to her. "Oh, maybe you could attend! Wait until Eileen sees how beautiful you've gotten."

"Mom," I interrupt, still on my feet. "Can you tell me what's going on?"

"What do you mean? Take a seat, honey."

"You know what I mean." I take a quick look around the space, which looks exactly the way it did when I left, except there are empty coffee cups strewn on windowsills and dog hair on the carpet. While it's got nothing on Eli's place, Mom never would have let her house become this untidy before.

"I told you I had a bit of arthritis."

My brows jump. "A bit? That's not a bit." She'll probably need a walker soon.

"I'm fine," she says, then stares at me until I give up and sit. "Now, tell me all about how you've been doing."

Mom knows the big lines of my life. She knows about my job, about my three-year relationship with Michael, and our almost year-long engagement, but she doesn't know about all the footnotes and appendices. She doesn't know we'd been trying to get pregnant for years before we broke up. Doesn't know about the nights I spent eating takeout Indian food on the floor because he'd left with our couch, and I was too bone-deep tired to go shop for a new one. She has the summary during our quarterly calls, and that's all she has to know.

"I'm fine," I say, repeating her words from earlier. We both know we're liars, and neither can call the other out on it.

"Good. Good."

Eventually, I do sit, and she passes me a whisk and a bowl. Dottie settles over my feet, and once more, I'm hit with a wave of longing, for all this time I've lost with her. Mom tells me about her crochet club, then goes on to say what everyone in town has gotten up to. I don't particularly care whether Mrs. Waterford is pretending she's still naturally blonde at eighty, but small talk is always so much easier than talking about what actually bothers us.

Except by the time Mom starts rolling the dough, and I take a good look at her hands, I can't pretend anymore. Crooked joints allow fingers to climb over others, creating a jumbled knot of her hands. The sight alone is painful.

"You have rheumatoid arthritis?" I'd remember those hands from my medical textbooks any day, the swan neck deformities of the fingers unmistakable.

She shrugs.

"Mom, you acted like it was simple joint pain." Has everyone lied to me about their health issues?

"It is. It gets better at the end of the day."

I can't help looking at her poor fingers. She had trouble simply walking earlier.

"You can't stay here," I say, pointing at the house. It's a small bungalow, but there's no way she can do all the cleaning by herself. I doubt she could go down to the basement right now.

"Stop it. I'm fine."

"Mom. How can you take care of this entire place by yourself?" Maybe Keira comes over to help, but I know she works full time as a clerk in the town's dental clinic, and she'll soon have two kids. Unless my father did find a gold mine before going to jail, there's no way she can pay for a cleaning company.

"I manage." She lays her flour-covered hand on mine. "But thank you for worrying."

Worrying is not enough. She needs so much more from me.

"I can come over to help while I'm here, but—"

"Please, honey. Let me just enjoy having you here. We still have so much to catch up on!" She smiles again. It's too much.

"But..."

"No buts. I'm fine, I promise. The crochet girls help around when they come over, and when Dad eventually comes back—"

The world freezes. I don't hear the rest of her sentence, don't think I even breathe for a few moments.

"Dad?" I say, pulling my hand away. "You're waiting for *Dad*?"

She stammers, the only answer I need.

"You're still with him." My body feels numb as I stand.

I never expected Mom to leave him. He couldn't convince her to, no matter what he did. It didn't matter that all my classmates knew he was cheating with whoever he could find, that she'd always be looked at as less than in this town. But when I heard seven years after I left that my father had been arrested for assaulting a woman in the town's bar, I thought, *all right, this is it.* She couldn't stay with him after that. Couldn't stomach looking him in the eye, knowing he'd physically hurt another woman. I was convinced that would be her limit.

And yet, I never asked her. Never even brought up Dad's situation. Never told her I'd heard from Ruth he was in jail. She didn't mention it, either, but I'd thought it was our mutual agreement never to bring him up again. Now, I see a part of me probably always knew she would never leave. Nothing he could do would ever be bad enough. Not when it came to us, and not when it came to others.

"Cassie, it's—" She tries to stand, but immediately needs to hold on to the back of the chair. I go to her to help her regain her balance, but as soon as I know she's fine, I step away.

"I need to go." The air in this house has always felt so thick, so sparse.

"No, please. Don't go yet." I hear the strain in her voice.

I close my eyes. Breathe in, then out. *You don't want to be like him.*

Something wet touches my calf. Dottie's snout. I focus on it, on how her fur feels against my bare feet, coarse but also the softest thing I could conjure.

"We won't bring him up again," I say. "Ever."

She nods. "All right. All right, Cassie." She taps the table. "Now, please, sit."

It takes all the strength in me to do so.

Chapter 9

I was twenty-four the first time I hosted a dinner.

We never had anyone over when I was young. Eli was the only friend who'd come inside my house, and even that had been on rare occasions. Mom never had anyone over. Our dinners were always just the three or four of us, depending on where my father was at the time, until Keira got old enough to start going out.

I'd been working at Brooklyn Hospital Center for two years by then—I'd done a few rotations there as a student, too—and after being invited over by a few colleagues, it felt like it was my time to step up. I'd rarely been this nervous before. I'd had my clean slate, made good acquaintances, and yet I still spent my time feeling like an imposter. Who didn't know how to host a dinner party at twenty-four? I ended up spending way too much of my paycheck on those fancy cheeses and cold cuts, and I was so focused on not embarrassing myself, I forgot to actually enjoy it.

I'm feeling the same kind of jittery now as the doorbell rings. I wouldn't be caught dead saying how long it took me to set the table. The eyeliner I put on was supposed to make me look casually made-up but probably ended up making me look *made-up* made-up.

Keira doesn't wait for me to answer the door before she walks in, a smaller version of her holding her hand. While I'd seen him in pictures, this is the first time I get to see Xavier face to face. He's got Keira's sage-green eyes and her pointy chin, which means if I'd had a son, he could've looked like this, too.

I swallow, then kneel in front of him.

"Hi. You must be Xavier." I try to take in all the ways he resembles Rob, Keira's partner, instead of us. Small ears. Lanky limbs. Fluffy brows. *You can do this.* "I'm your auntie Cassie."

He doesn't react, not even with a hint of recognition. Keira probably never mentioned me. I picture my Christmas gifts, pushed down the trash before Xavier could notice them.

Eli and Zoe show up at that moment, and I'm grateful for the interruption. I thought it was important for Eli to be there tonight since he was such a big part of Ruth's life, especially at the end, so last night, I went by his place to invite him. His jaw was tight when he opened the door, like he was wondering whether I'd bring up the stinted way our night ended when I babysat Zoe. Lucky for him, I'm a professional at pretending. It runs in the family.

When he steps inside, his eyes remain on me just shy of too long. I really shouldn't have put on that eyeliner.

Keira brushes past me and disappears into the kitchen before I've had a chance to say anything to her, and Eli quickly rushes inside, too, when Zoe decides she wants to play hide-and-seek with Xavier—which is a horrible idea in a house filled with so many non-kid-friendly trinkets. Yesterday morning, while packing boxes, I found what looked like a sword from the Middle Ages in the guest bedroom's closet, and I would've bet a lot of money it wasn't fake.

I'm rubbing my sweaty palms across my dress when Mom shows up, completing our mismatched group. She's wearing her woodpecker brooch today.

"Come on, I'll help you settle in," I say as I grab her arm.

"I'm fine, Cassie," she says, but still holds onto me all the way to the table.

"Do you want us to serve something for the kids first?" I ask Keira and Eli, the latter fighting for his life with two kids running around like it's the last day of school.

"Xavier already ate," Keira says bluntly.

Eli has the decency to wince when he says, "I made Zoe eat before, too."

"Oh." I imagine the plate of sandwiches I made with animal-shaped cookie cutters I got at the store this morning, untouched in the refrigerator. "Yeah, of course."

Eli turns on a Pixar movie in the living room for the kids, who immediately melt into the couch and turn silent.

"So, let's get this started, hm?" Keira says. She goes to open the fridge, but I rush to stop her. No way am I letting her see those sandwiches. I don't need her to think of me as even more desperate than she already does.

"Sure, yeah." I'd also prepared a veggie tray with multiple dips and bread I got at the good bakery one town over, but now my skin is itchy, and I agree with Keira that this can't be over soon enough. Actually, this entire thing was probably a mistake.

Remember who you're doing this for. Ruth would've held the party of a century for me. I can do one dinner.

Eli helps me get the chicken cacciatore Mom and I prepared yesterday out of the oven, along with the green beans and potatoes. The entire table remains silent as I serve.

"This smells good," Eli says with a small smile in my direction.

"Thanks. Well, thanks to Mom."

Keira hums, then takes a bite.

I sit, then crack a knuckle under the table. "Thanks for being here. I, uh, I think I'd like to start by having each of us say one thing we'd like to remember about Ruth, or what we'd like to thank her for, or anything, really." I'd prepared a longer speech, about what this house meant to me, what *Ruth* meant to me, but I can only get those words out. I feel like a kettle about to squeal.

"Great idea," Mom says. She wipes her mouth. "I'm grateful to Ruth because I got my babies—and my grandbabies—" She gives a meaningful look toward the living room, then to Keira's belly. "—through her."

My bite of chicken feels like a golf ball in my esophagus.

Eli is next if we're going clockwise, which I guess we are because he clears his throat. "I'm grateful for all the times she took me in for dinner like it was no big deal." One side of his lips quirks up. "I'll never forget all the Kraft Dinner that lady made for me over the years." His eyes flit to mine, and I smile, too. At least once a week during the summer, Eli would come in and beg her to make some for us. Mr. Grant always treated the meal like it was an abomination on Earth, and even though I only found it okay, I couldn't get enough of how excited Eli got when we ate it. I probably begged Ruth to make it more than he did.

All eyes turn to me.

"I'm grateful for..." I put my fork down. How can I narrow it down to one thing? I'd thought of many potential answers, but somehow, none of them seem good enough now. So many small things that mean nothing in comparison to the woman she was in my eyes. I need to force my hands under my thighs to keep from cracking my fingers some more. "I'm grateful for the way she was always a guiding light when I needed it, and for the love she never ceased to give me."

Wrinkles have formed around Mom's lips. She cuts a piece of chicken, the knife squeaking against the plate.

I chuckle, the sound awkward. "And I'm grateful for her sweet tooth, and for the fact that she always shared her stash of candy with me." Every time I had a shit day, she'd pull out a bowl of whatever she'd decided to get from the gas station that week. *You know the great thing about adulthood, Cassie? No one's there to stop you from buying a good ol' bag of gummy worms for yourself.* I was eight the first time she told me that, and adulthood became a dream from then on. "Although my teeth probably don't feel the same."

"She didn't have a sweet tooth," Keira says around a mouthful of potato.

"Yes, she did."

"No, she didn't. She was a diabetic. Couldn't eat candy for years."

I open my mouth, then close it.

"But you didn't know that, did you?"

"Keira," Eli says, voice low.

She ignores him. "Actually, this entire evening is hypocritical, isn't it? You wanting to *honor her one last time*?" she says around finger quotes. "Where were you when she was actually here to honor? When she needed help?"

There's so much pressure behind my eyes, I feel like my head is about to explode.

"Keira, enough." Eli again. I barely hear him. Barely hear anything, save for the pulsing in my ears.

"She didn't tell me," I whisper. "No one told me."

"And why do you think that is?"

I blink fast. *You won't cry here.*

"Girls, please," Mom says.

"I don't know what you want from me." I *know* I wasn't there. I know I was the one who left. I've been hating myself ever since I got the call from Mr. Nelson telling me she'd passed. But Keira was there. She saw how bad it was for me. And that last night... I didn't have a choice but to leave. I guess Ruth never told her she was the one who encouraged me to go.

Keira shakes her head. "I want nothing from you." She stabs a piece of chicken and stuffs it into her mouth.

I look down at my own plate. It makes me want to vomit. I stagger to my feet, dizzy like I just drank a forty-ouncer of booze. "I need some air," I say, or maybe I just whisper it in my head. I'm not sure. I don't look at Mom, or Eli, or the kids in the living room who probably heard us.

The foggy, salty air is a welcome reprieve against my burning skin. My breaths are shaky, and when I drop into one of the Adirondack chairs closer to the cliffside, I feel like I weigh a thousand pounds.

I can't stay here. Can't do another three weeks of this. Of being guilt-tripped for doing the thing that saved me.

I look up. Most stars are hidden by the thick fog, but a few are still visible. I know looking at stars has nothing to do with the dead, but I still feel closer to her when I say, "I'm sorry, Ruth."

I'm not sure how much time passes before another body drops into the chair next to mine. I don't need to look to know who it is. A part of me will always recognize when he's around.

"I'm sorry about that," Eli says in his soft voice. "She's just hurt."

I don't bother telling him that being hurt doesn't give her a free pass to be a bitch.

"When did you two become such close friends anyway?" My words taste as bitter as they sound.

"She was there for me."

Somehow, the simplicity in that answer hurts even more than if he'd screamed.

"I know I've made mistakes." I glance at the few stars twinkling above and huff. "God, I've been drowning in that guilt for years. But I don't know what to do anymore. How to make it better."

The night I left, everything happened so fast. I went to Ruth's place in shock and jumped on a Greyhound with my mind blank. It was only when the bus stopped for gas somewhere in Connecticut that I realized what I'd done. I'd left my entire family behind without a single goodbye. And the worst part—the one I'll never say aloud—is that Keira was the last person I thought about when the guilt settled in. She'd left for college two years prior and hadn't even come home for Christmas that year. When I texted her, it sometimes took days before I heard back. It was like she'd cut me out of her life before I'd even left.

Even so, she never went MIA like I did, and while she might have moved out in a place of her own, she and I were still the only two people who knew what it was like to have grown up in that house, and I'd left her behind. I can see how painful that must have been. I was going through life on survival mode, but doing so alienated all the people I cared about most.

Waves crash somewhere in the darkness, sending tiny splashes of water onto us. I tuck my legs to my chest. "Coming back was a mistake."

"Don't say that."

"I've missed out on so much, but it's like it doesn't matter that I'm here now, because I'll never be able to catch up." I rest my head back. "My sister hates me. My mom's acting like some Raggedy Ann doll who doesn't blink or stop smiling while she's lying through her teeth. Even *you*'re being weird with me. And that's not a reproach. I'm just stating facts." Being with him used to feel so damn *easy*. Smiling, laughing... We didn't have to think about it. And now every one of his smiles feels like a pot of gold.

He lets out a deep exhale that holds eleven years' worth of feelings. "I'm sorry. You're right. I just... I guess I don't know how to act around you anymore."

"I'm still the same me."

"No, you're not."

That gets me to turn to him. The way he stares at me sends shivers down my legs.

"You left," he says, and my heart drops into my stomach.

"Eli—"

"Let me finish. You left, and you moved on to a bigger, better life, and I stayed right here. I'm still in my childhood house, for Christ's sake." He chuckles dryly, shakes his head. "I'll never fault you for leaving. A part of me always knew you would. But I also can't pretend like we're the same kids we were."

My chest feels too tight. "That means nothing. I didn't change by moving away."

"Then why didn't you ever call? Write?" he says, still calm, but the bite in his voice is back from that night in his living room. "I looked for you, you know. Even when you ignored my texts and calls. Even when you deleted your social media profiles. I searched your name online. Asked around. But you became invisible for years. I felt like our... like our friendship was nothing to you."

I let my eyes fall shut against the wave of pain that comes from opening that Eli box again. "That friendship was everything to me."

"Then why?"

"Because it would've only hurt us more, and in the end, it wouldn't have changed anything."

While I eventually got back in contact with most of my family and told them where I lived, Eli was the one clean break I needed if I wanted to survive. He would never leave Cape Weston—not with his dad's health that had started deteriorating in the past years—and I'd never go back, so even if I did call, I'd still never be part of his life the way I'd want to be. I'd always be looking at his life from a bird's eye view, never quite close enough to find the proximity we'd always had, and that would've been more painful than anything else. I'd have heard about him meeting new people, finding a girl, and I wasn't strong enough for that. But even worse than that, I didn't want him to keep hanging on to me when he could meet someone else, especially since he was never truly mine to begin with. I wouldn't have been able to live with myself if I'd kept my favorite person from living the life he deserved.

"I wish I'd had a say." He pauses. "I would've taken anything over nothing."

"I'm sorry. I really am." Goosebumps cover my skin at a cold gust of wind. "And even if it sounds messed up, I did what I thought was best at the time." Even my voice sounds exhausted. There's nothing I can do now but apologize and live with the shame. "And after a while, I thought you probably wouldn't want to hear about me anyway." I knew he'd miss me, just as I knew he'd move on. I might remain in the past forever, but Eli would find a way to thrive. Settle, find the right woman to marry, figure out exactly who he wanted to be. Even as a kid, there was a confidence in him, like no matter where he ended up, it'd be exactly where he always belonged.

"I don't think I could ever have wanted to stop hearing from you." He pauses, as if he's weighing how much to share, then looks behind me. "Sometimes I'd feel myself going crazy, not hearing from you, like maybe I'd imagined you. So, I'd ask Ruth about you."

She never told me.

We talked all the time, yet she never once brought Eli up. Maybe because she'd known it'd only hurt me to think about what I'd lost.

"I liked knowing you were out there doing your thing, even if I wasn't hearing it from you." For the first time, a hint of a smile touches his lips. "And then sometimes she'd let something slip, like how you'd choked on a piece of donut because you were eating too fast and needed some random guy in the street to help you, and I'd think, yeah, I didn't imagine her."

Despite the heaviness of his words, I find myself smiling, too. "I can't believe she told you that."

"No one was ever safe from Ruth throwing them under the bus."

I laugh. "She'd probably want that written on her tombstone."

"Knowing her, yeah, she would."

We smile at each other, my next breath coming easier.

Eli exhales, leaning back in his chair. "I'm sorry, too. About being weird. I can imagine being back isn't easy."

I swallow.

"And sorry for this dinner, too," he adds.

"Dinner? What's wrong with this dinner?"

I keep a straight face until I see the grin spread on Eli's lips, then start laughing with him.

Things between us will probably never be the same. But damn me if that laugh doesn't make me hopeful.

Chapter 10

I spend the following day burying myself in work. Ruth's house never ceases to be a box of surprises, with more items to triage appearing every time I look inside a cupboard, and a week has already passed since I got here. Our garage sale needs to happen within the next two weeks if I want to put the house on the market before I leave, which means I need to kick things into high gear. The distraction is good. The last thing I want is to think about the shitshow that was Friday night's dinner. By the time I'd gone back inside, Keira had already left, and it was just as well. I wouldn't have been ready for round two—or more like round four, at this point.

Just as I get out of my car, Eli's front door pushes open, and out rush Zoe and Xavier. I hold my breath.

"Cassie!" Zoe shouts before barreling toward me through the grass with her arms outstretched. Tension eases off my shoulders as I squat to welcome her hug. Behind her, Eli follows, a backward hat on his head and a comically small Hello Kitty backpack slung on his shoulder.

I didn't know this kind of combination would do it for me, but yes, it definitely does it for me.

Zoe steals the breath from my lungs as she slams into me. "Hi, honey," I say, squeezing her back. She smells like fruity shampoo and sunscreen. I don't think I'll ever get enough of her excitement when she sees me. It reminds me of how Dottie would always jump up and spin around when I'd get home. I could be gone for a few hours, and she'd welcome me like the long-lost love of her life. It made me feel like a thousand bucks, and I now have the confirmation it still does.

"Zoe, can you not jump our neighbors? Thanks," Eli says with a chuckle, then pulls the little monkey away from me.

"I vividly remember at least three times when you tackled me to the ground as kids," I tell him.

"Context, Cassie. We were wrestling." He wraps his large hands around Zoe's ears, which visibly annoys her and amuses him at the same time. "Don't expose my embarrassing stories to vulnerable ears." He smirks, then tips his head toward the packed car. "We're going to the beach. Wanna join?"

I look behind him, but no Keira has appeared. "Just you three?"

"Just us three."

I was going to do more work today, but I also wouldn't say no to a break. Plus, I told him I wanted our relationship to be easy again, and that won't happen if I lock myself inside and don't see him again until I leave.

"You don't have to," Eli quickly adds, then slicks his hair under his hat before setting it back on his head. I grit my teeth.

"Yeah, I'd love to, actually. Just give me a minute." I rush back inside and put on my one-piece black swimsuit and shorts. When

I cross a mirror and see just how bony I look in it, I cover my upper body with a thin sweatshirt, then go back out to meet them. Both kids are already settled in their car seats, so the moment I take my place on the passenger side, we're ready to take off.

"Where are we going?" I think to ask only once we exit the driveway. Probably would've been a good question to ask before agreeing to come.

"Just down at Moody Beach," Eli says, throwing a quick glance in the rear mirror, then at me. I will my cheeks not to redden. The last time we were at Moody Beach, I was seventeen, and Eli had just kissed me for the first time. We'd just spent the day in the water, and we were lying on our backs as the light dimmed around us. His hand was on my forearm, and when he'd turned toward me, I'd just known this was it. The moment I'd waited years for. He tasted like sea salt and sun, and I thought that was the beginning of forever for me. The next day, I was gone.

"Best beach around." I hope my voice doesn't betray the direction my thoughts went to.

"Cassie?" Zoe asks.

I turn around. "Yes?"

"How old are you?"

"Straight to the good questions, huh?"

"That's rude, Zoe," Eli says.

"Why is it rude? I'm just asking her age. I'm almost six," she says, raising five fingers up. I lean back to extend an extra one off the other hand.

"You're right, it's fine. I'm twenty-eight."

Xavier looks at me with wary eyes while Zoe's brows bunch. "That doesn't make sense."

"Why?"

"Because you're almost Daddy's age, but you're young and Daddy's old."

"Jesus Christ," Eli mutters under his breath while flashing for his next turn. Louder, he says, "Now *that's* rude."

I can't hold my laughter in. Even Xavier joins in. "Careful. You're practically geriatric," I say.

"You know what, kids? Cassie's too busy for a beach day."

I bump his shoulder, and he laughs.

Zoe whines, not understanding the sarcasm, so I turn and say, "Don't worry." Then, to Eli, I add, "I'm *definitely* staying."

Moody Beach actually *is* the best beach around. It's wide and usually less crowded, and it's a great spot for surfing. I don't do it myself—never saw the appeal, and I have terrible balance—but I love watching people floating on their boards, waiting for the perfect wave. I find it soothing.

After arriving at the beach, Zoe immediately bolts toward the water, and Eli follows, leaving Xavier with me. He stands next to the cooler and bodyboards, a foot tracing lines in the sand.

"Do you want to get the shovels out?" I ask. I don't need to look to know Eli brought some—along with a million other things—in his giant beach bags. He looks nothing but prepared.

Xavier doesn't answer for such a long time, I think maybe he's decided to ignore me. Then, in a low voice, he asks, "If you're mommy's sister, why haven't I seen you before?" He doesn't quite meet my eyes, which only heightens the blow. Like I'm a person his mother taught him not to trust. Has that question been sitting on his mind since Friday? Or has Keira talked to him about me since?

I crouch so we're at eye level. "Because I was away for a long time."

I don't know when this guilt will ever stop gnawing at my insides.

He doesn't answer. Doesn't ask more questions either, instead settling a little farther away. I get the shovels and buckets out and hand them to him, then return to my chair to watch him play. The last thing I want to do is scare him off.

When Eli and Zoe get out of the water, they join him and add more towers to the sandcastle he started building. I take the opportunity to slip away and dip my feet in the water. When I can't feel my toes anymore, I go back to my chair, and this time, it's not Xavier that I have to stop myself from staring at.

He's not yours to study anymore.

But that's easier said than done. The chest that used to be lean and tall is now bulky, muscled without being chiseled, like he doesn't waste time lifting weights but his life working in kitchens and taking care of his daughter has made him strong. Seeing Eli like this during the summer used to be my catnip, and I fear I may not have spent long enough away to get rid of that vice.

When he gets up and leaves the kids alone with their massive sandcastle, I force my gaze to remain on his face.

He unfolds a chair next to mine, then drops into it like his body is too heavy for him to carry.

"Drink?" I ask, holding out a juice pouch I grabbed from his cooler. He lifts a brow, to which I say, "Made myself at home."

"I put adult drinks in there, too," he says.

"Is there an age-limit on Caprisuns?" I take another sip that tastes like all of my best summer days.

"Guess not," he says with a chuckle, then sits and drains half of it. He makes a face, then shivers. "God, I'd forgotten how sweet that was."

"Nothing like a drink that's so sweet, it makes you more dehydrated than before."

His chair is close enough to mine that I can smell him, his usual sweet scent mixed with that of salt water and clean sweat. His skin is a gorgeous golden, the shade it always turned to during summer.

He leans back in his chair and closes his eyes, then releases the deepest, longest sigh I've ever heard.

"I feel like today's the only time I've seen you having a day off," I say. I've barely seen his car in the driveway over the week. Not that I looked or anything. One time, though, I saw a white truck with *GRANT CATERING* written across it, which answered my question about what he does for work.

"I shouldn't even have taken it," he answers, eyes still closed. "We're right in the high season, and my staff needs me. And there's a lot going on at home, and then there's choir practice tonight—"

"I always knew you'd look cute in a choir boy outfit."

He pops one eye open. "*Zoe's* choir practice."

"With Mrs. Hahn still? What is she, a hundred now?"

"And still as scary as ever. I never would've had Zoe go through that like I did, but she's the one who wanted to do it. Honestly, they're terrible, and I can't tell what they're singing half the time, but she loves it." He scratches his head. "They had practice an hour ago, actually."

"So why are you here?"

"Because I made the mistake of telling Liz about it, and this morning, I thought about how Zoe might see her there, and I choked." He rubs his brows. "But I also felt terrible about taking this from Zoe, so I took today off for a beach day." His gaze moves to his daughter, who's currently showing Xavier she can stand on one foot over a bucket. "I can't do it. It probably makes me a shitty dad, but I'm too fucking scared."

"It makes sense," I say. "And you're the opposite of a shitty dad."

He glances at me. "I'm pretty sure I'm the definition of over-bearing."

"No, you're not." I shrug. "You're... careful with her. With her heart."

Xavier shrieks as Zoe lays a splat of mud on his back.

"I should probably scold her for that," Eli says.

"She's laying down her territory. Leave her be."

He chuckles beside me.

Besides the kids, a family is set up with an actual tent and bar-beque, a baby sleeping in a cot on the ground. Pop music is playing from their portable speakers as two children eat the hotdogs the father just cooked.

"If I'd had to guess, I would've said you'd have had children first, out of the two of us."

A wave of nausea rolls over me. The sweet taste of my Caprisun turns bitter on my tongue, and I feel like spitting into the sand.

Unaware, Eli continues. "I never found you on social media, but when I'd meet your mom in town, I'd ask about you. She told me you were engaged. I was waiting for the day she'd tell me you were expecting."

He can't know what his words are doing to me. I can't fault him. We always did talk about how we wanted kids. I even dreamed for a long time I'd end up having them with him.

I don't remember a day when becoming a mother wasn't my dream. I knew I wanted it before I even understood what it truly meant. One day, fingerprint smudges would cover my fridge door. My floors would be covered in toys, strewn across all reachable surfaces, and I'd love the mess and chaos. My nights would be short, and my days would be filled with the kind of love I'd only ever seen in the Grants' house.

"I..." My mouth feels like I've swallowed sand. I've had to utter the words only once since I learned the news, and that was to

Emily. Sariah knew enough, but not the whole story. I could never bring myself to tell Mom.

"I feel like I just said something I shouldn't have."

I don't want to imagine what I look like. He's probably thinking that something happened with my fiancé, and it did, but that's the least of my concerns. It was simply the last handful of dirt thrown onto my grave.

"I can't have children."

For a moment, it feels as if the waves have stopped roaring, as if the specks of sand in the hourglass have paused their fall. People say time heals all wounds, and yet every time I so much as think those four words, it's as though my injury worsens, like the small blood clot has been picked away, only to restart the process anew. It will never get better. How could it?

"God, Cass..." The nickname, coupled with the heat of his gaze on me, almost makes me crumble. He doesn't offer an apology, no senseless encouragement, and that more than anything is what brings the tears to my eyes. He knows it wouldn't help. There is no silver lining in this. Not when I threaded my entire life around that dream. And only because he knows me so well, even a decade later, can he understand.

That profound recognition is what gets me to say, "I tried to get pregnant naturally for a year before I decided to consult, but even before then, I knew something was wrong. Could feel it in my gut. And after multiple rounds of investigations, I had my answer. Severe endometriosis."

My periods have always been painful. When I got them for the first time at twelve years old and cried for two days straight, sitting on the floor of the shower under the warm water until my father shouted that I clearly wasn't the one paying the utility bill, I thought I wouldn't survive it. I was told menstruating was painful for everyone, and I'd have to get used to it. Eventually, I did, or at least found ways to make them bearable. Hook myself on anti-inflammatories for the duration of it, go to school with heating pads hidden under my shirts, and pretend like twenty-five percent of my life wasn't composed of intolerable suffering. The endometriosis diagnosis never came up, even when I started having other symptoms, like IBS and painful sex. It should have been obvious to me by the time I realized I couldn't get pregnant, but I never put two and two together, probably still too fixated on the hope that we'd figure out a simple way to solve the problem. *You've been having sex wrong. Try this and you'll have a baby in no time!*

"Aren't there, I don't know, surgeries for that?"

"I had two already." It's still such a widely misunderstood disease, but surgery to remove pieces of misplaced endometrium in the belly is one known way to improve pain and infertility. I saw that surgery as a beacon of hope, but when nothing changed after the first one, I had to take off my rose-colored glasses. We tried another surgery nine months later, and while my periods did get a bit better after that one, I still couldn't get pregnant. In a sunlit office a year and two rounds of failed IVF later, my gynecologist clasped his hands and told me I should consider other options. "My body doesn't want me to become a mother."

"Cassie, I..." He looks the way I feel. Devastated, as opposed to the pitiful look I expected. His mouth opens and closes, but no word comes out. There are none to say. Instead, he places his hand on mine, warm and comforting like hot tea on a rainy day.

"I know."

He squeezes, and I offer him a small smile. He's still studying me, reminding me just what a good listener Eli Grant is. When you talk to him, he's not listening to have something to say in return, but like he wants to understand the whole story, leaving no stone unturned. Having him look at you like this makes you feel like the earth could be shaking under his feet and he wouldn't notice. I don't know how I ever forgot how good it feels to be seen by him.

"I'm sorry for asking," he says.

"Don't be. Friends should know these kinds of things about each other."

"Right," he says.

"And you would've been wrong anyway." My grin stretches, more natural. "Even if I'd gotten pregnant right away, Zoe would still have been born before, Teen Dad."

He rolls his eyes, color also having returned to his cheeks. "I was twenty-three."

"What I said."

He chuckles.

"I was still such a mess at twenty-three," I add.

"I was, too. Had to get my shit together." He glances at the kids, now playing with miniature dinosaurs in the sandcastle. "Still don't know whether I ever completely did, though."

"About that," I say. "I want to help out." The way he's running himself ragged cannot be sustainable. "It won't be much, but for as long as I'm here, I'll give you what time I have. I'm all up to date on my babysitting now."

Selfishly, I think it could be helpful to me, too. I have three weeks to get ready to return to the hospital, which means I have this amount of time to get comfortable around families and babies again. Even if being with Zoe never gave me the same feeling I had with newborns, I'm sure it could still work as exposure therapy.

"I can't ask that of you. You have an entire house to get in order."

"And the circles under your eyes could be mistaken for bruises."

"You've always had such a way with words."

"Flattery isn't going to help you."

"Thank God, because you'd be doing a shitty job of it."

I snicker, then say, "Please, Eli. I wasn't there before, but I can do something now."

He leans forward, thigh muscles bunching under his weight. "So, you're actually staying?"

"For July."

A moment passes before he says, "All right. I'll think about it."

I nod. Better than I could've hoped for.

"I want to go into the water again!"

We both turn toward Zoe who's jumping on her feet. Eli goes to stand, but I stop him with a hand on his arm. "I got it."

"You sure?"

"You said you'd think about it. This is you beginning to think."

He purses his lips but leans back in his chair. Winning with him always gives me such a high.

I get to my feet, and only then do I realize the mistake I just made. Going in the water means I need to remove my shorts and sweatshirt.

When I learned the news of my infertility, I stopped living for a little while. Couldn't eat, couldn't work out, could barely sleep or go to work. It got easier to simply stop looking in the mirror. I eventually regained some functionality, but the appetite never came back to normal.

I let out a breath. What does it matter, at this point? Turning my back to him, I remove my clothes, letting them fall on the chair. My swimsuit is nothing sexy, so at least it doesn't look like I'm trying.

"Hurry!" Zoe shouts before she starts running toward the water.

"You raised a real angel," I tease, throwing a glance back at Eli. I'm expecting an eye roll, but he doesn't even seem to have heard me, his gaze stuck on my naked back. There's so much heat in there, like the honey of his eyes has caught fire. Finally realizing I've turned, his eyes slowly climb my body, and there's no trace of humor in them. I recognize that look, too. And it makes me feel the same way I did when I was twelve and adapting to a new body, or when I was seventeen and wanted him all around me. It's as if he doesn't see all the ways I've changed, hasn't even noticed the loose skin and stretch marks.

I swallow, then turn and run with Zoe toward the frigid water, needing a good dousing of cold.

Chapter 11

Twelve Years Ago

The girl is in trouble.

She didn't need to tell the boy for him to know. The moment he picked up and heard her breathe out his name, he knew. He'd grabbed his jacket and car keys before she'd even said another word. By the time she told him she was at the police station, he was already in his dad's pick-up.

He'd never been to the police station before. Even had to look it up on his phone to remember where it was. And when he walks in, he feels out of place, like he, too, is about to be arrested just for stepping inside. He should probably get out of the house more.

What's the protocol in this kind of situation? *Hello, my best friend has been arrested for who knows what, and I'd really like to see her.* The small office doesn't look like how it does in the movies, and no one's out front to help him.

A door creaks at the back of the room, and as if he conjured her, the girl comes out with two police officers behind her, as if she's dangerous—which is insane, because she's this tiny thing, and he doesn't know a gentler person. She can be rough on the edges, but that's only because everyone has sharpened her. With him, she can allow herself to be soft.

The taller officer with the bushy brows lightly pushes her, and the boy suddenly knows how people may feel before they commit murder.

The girl shoots the man a glare before stepping away from him. Her hair is in a disarray, slipping out of her ponytail, and there's a red stain covering the sleeve of her sweatshirt, her right knuckles battered.

He inhales deeply. *Don't pass out. Please, for the love of God, don't pass out.*

For the first time in his life, he works through his fear of blood, because she's so much more important than a stupid phobia he should already be over by now.

"Is it yours?" he mouths as he points at the cuff.

She shakes her head, and he immediately feels better.

He should probably ask what she's at the police station for. Know what charges she's facing—because with the way these men are acting around her, she's the one who did something. However, looking at her, the only thing he wants to do is get her out of here.

"Can I take her home?" the boy asks the first police officer, trying his hardest not to show this asshole just how much he wants to punch him in the throat.

The officer looks him up and down, his obnoxious brows bunched, then says, "Sure, son." The tips of his boots brush against the boy's shoes. "But between you and I? Stay away from that family, will ya?"

Behind them, the other officer mutters, "Like father, like daughter."

The men are both speaking too loud for the girl not to hear every word they're saying. Her lips are pressed tight, a warm flush covering her cheeks. He's never been this heartbroken for her. And then, just like a switch flipping, the light dims in her eyes, as if she's resigned herself to her fate and stopped fighting. Somehow, that shatters him even more.

Without another word, the two of them exit the police station and walk to the parked truck. Even once they're both seated, the boy doesn't turn the engine on.

"Thanks for coming."

"Always." He doesn't question why she called him instead of her mother or sister. He likes being her emergency contact. A month ago, when his dad had a heart attack, she was there for him, too, waiting with him all through the night to see whether his dad would make it. The boy would never imagine not being there for her in the same way.

"Aren't you going to ask me what happened?"

"You'll tell me if you want to." He doesn't know everything about her, but he knows it's more than she's ever told anyone. All the stories he got from her had to be carefully extracted, and he treasures each part of herself she's gifted him, the beautiful and the horrid equally.

Still, he doesn't start the car.

"Last night was... rough," the girl starts after a long moment, which he understands as her father said or did some fucked-up shit. The girl cracks the knuckles of her left hand. "And I didn't feel like going back home after school today, so I hung around for the football match. Don't tell me it was a stupid idea. I know."

"I wasn't going to."

"I was just sitting there, and all of a sudden, Ashleigh Wright and Kyle Richardson where there, too, and they were saying some dumb shit about me. They wanted me to hear."

Of course they did.

"And then, Kyle decided to shout some crap about my mom being a..." She blinks repeatedly. "I don't know, Eli, it was like something tilted in me. I knew it was a cheap shot, and I knew he only wanted to get under my skin, but I just couldn't help it. It was too much."

The boy remains silent, not wanting to spook her into silence.

"So, I just walked over to him and punched him."

He jerks around in his seat. "You what?"

"In the face."

"Jesus, Cass." The boy looks down at her right hand's fingers, which he now realizes she's holding at an odd angle. He fights a wave of nausea. "Did no one take a look at those for you in there?"

She doesn't answer, instead giving him a smile. So goddamn soft.

"I'll bring you to the ER," he says, finally turning the engine on.

"I'm not spending hundreds of dollars on this. I'm fine."

"Cassie."

"Eli."

"I'll pay. I don't care." He can't stand the thought of her being in pain, and if the only hurt he can help is the physical one, then God help him, he will.

She places her good hand on his, relaxing his fingers off the wheel. "I'm okay."

The boy doesn't buy it for a second, but he can wait a bit.

"He's going to press charges," she adds.

"What?" The boy frowns. "But he's the one who started it."

"Technically, he just made some dumb insult. I'm the one who got violent."

Violent, his ass. How many times can a dog be kicked before it bites?

"So, what's going to happen?"

"The officers said because I'm still a minor, I'll probably only get community service hours, and there'll be a record to my name."

"That's fucking bullshit."

The girl shrugs. "I did it. I have to pay for it."

"But he deserved it."

"Yeah, he really did."

The car becomes silent, the girl still pulling at her cuticles. Most times the boy looks at her fingers, they look ravaged. Never as bad as today, though.

"He was wrong in there, you know. It doesn't matter what you do. You're not like your father."

"I know I'm not." She tucks a knee to her chest, her beat-up Converse resting against the seat. "But does it even matter when that's what everyone sees when they look at me?"

"I don't see that." He never has. Even when he grew up from that ten-year-old boy who first saw her outside her grandmother's house and started hearing the rumors about her family, he never looked at her any differently. To him, she'd always be the girl with the empty eyes whose face lit up every time she saw him. The girl who lived through hell every night and still showed up the next day and laughed with him. The girl who made every awkward part of him feel right somehow.

"I don't know how he can let this happen," the girl says, her gaze lost outside the window. "He has to see how he's ruining all our lives, and still, he keeps doing it." Her hands are trembling in her lap. The boy doesn't remember the last time she spoke this frankly about her father. "When I have kids, I'll do whatever I have to, to keep them away from this bullshit. And if it follows us, then I'll rip this entire town apart before I let them get hurt."

"And I'll be right there beside you, holding the match."

She turns to him, the green of her irises still taking his breath away after all these years.

She doesn't know he's in love with her. He's not being coy about it, but he's also never made a move. He's not ready to risk what they have. A friendship that's so much more than that. He's not ready to mess it up. Not yet.

So even if he wants to lean over and kiss her, take her in his arms and protect her from the mess that's all around them, he only takes her hurt hand in his and says, "But first, let me take care of this. Okay?"

She looks at him for a long time. Long enough that he wonders if maybe, just maybe, she feels the same.

"Okay."

Chapter 12

When Keira walks in for our planned triaging session three days later, she just says, "Hey," then settles in front of the boxes I assembled in Ruth's living room and gets to work, not saying another word.

I usually don't mind silence. Every day in the hospital, I'm forced to write notes while someone is shouting at the top of their lungs in the next room and ten different alarms are blaring next to my head, so when I get back home, I take whatever peace I can find. However, today, I'd take whatever noise I could get. Non-stop cuckoo clocks. A marching band. Anything to get the silence that weighs a thousand bricks between me and my sister out of the way. It's making my skin itch, and I've cracked my fingers so much in the past thirty minutes, my joints are hurting. I'd swear I can hear each of our pulses in the room. It's stifling. And yet, I won't speak first. She's hurt me, and I don't feel like being her punching bag any longer.

The only silver lining is the amount of things in here to focus on. Figuring out what is worth selling versus what can be thrown away is one hell of a task. Ruth wasn't a hoarder per se, but she did love to keep memorabilia from different periods of her life. There's no way she ever thought she'd use a ten-person porcelain tea set, but if I'd ever told her that, she'd have swatted me away and said, "*When you host your ten-person tea party, you'll be happy I was smart enough to keep this.*" The more days that pass, the less headway I feel I've made. The entire main floor is covered in piles I started making before getting sidetracked into another category of stuff. *To give. To throw away. Could benefit the local cat shelter? The costume shop might buy?*

I bring a full box outside, and when I come back, Keira averts her eyes. I'd say it feels like we're fifteen, but even when we were teens, our relationship was never this tense. We would fight all the time, but two minutes after she'd call me a bitch and I'd slam our bedroom door in her face, she'd come get me and ask if I wanted to go to the movies with her. Apart from Eli, she was my best friend.

I let out a long breath, then start on a new box. I write on it, *Tupperware-meeting ready.*

A huff of a laugh comes from my right. When I look up, Keira looks away like I've caught her stealing candy from a child.

I load my box of containers with and without their lids. Why didn't I think of turning music on before so it wouldn't be this goddamn quiet?

"I'm sorry."

I glance up warily like I hallucinated the noise.

"It wasn't fair of me to bring up Ruth," she says, and this time, I can see her lips moving.

I don't remember the last time I heard Keira apologize. The more our parents forced her to, the less she did it. My father could tell her to apologize for her tone, or she'd be grounded for a month, and she'd rather miss all the parties in the world than give in to him.

But here she is. Taking that first step.

"Thank you." I tuck a strand of hair behind my ear. She took that vulnerable leap. I can, too. "And I'm sorry I wasn't there to help with Ruth. Or with Mom," I add as an afterthought. "And that I wasn't there for you. The way I left... It wasn't right. I know it wasn't. It was never about you, but I'm sorry I made it that way."

Keira's face is still made of that impenetrable rock, every thought locked away so tight you could never dream of catching a glimpse at them. But still, she nods.

That's as close to an agreement as we've gotten since she came here that first morning.

We spend the next hour packing more boxes and emptying cupboards and closets, and while we're not chatty, she asks me to help her lift the heavy coat rack, and I make her a tuna sandwich while preparing my own lunch.

"So, did you have an idea for an organization you'd like to donate to?" I ask around a bite. Maybe she and Ruth did talk about it at some point.

She shrugs. "I still don't know why she chose to do that. I don't have any close to heart. Do you?"

I shake my head.

"I guess it would make sense to donate to a heart failure organization."

"That's a good idea." I don't have anything better to suggest that would be related to Ruth in some way, and I wouldn't want to give her money away to a cause she wouldn't have particularly valued, even if she gave us permission to.

"It feels like such a huge ask," Keira says. "That money could change lives."

She's right. Any place on Beachside Avenue could probably be sold for millions, just for that unobstructed ocean view. Ruth always told me how lucky she was that this house was in the family, and while I never wanted to live there, I never thought she'd want to sell it, either. I have a feeling it has something to do with the complicated relationship she had with her only son. It would've broken her heart to skip his generation and sign the deed to Keira and me, but she never would've been able to live with herself if she'd given him the house, only for him to sell it to pay for one of his bad habits.

"Will you be okay?" I ask. "Without the deal money, I mean. If you need—"

"I don't need your money."

I lift my hands in defense. "I wasn't offering."

I definitely was.

"Yes, you were."

I purse my lips the same way she does, and when we notice the mirror image, we both smile a little.

"We'll be fine. Rob and I just had to rework some stuff."

I want to ask if I can help with something else, but before I can, she stands and winces, one hand on her back to stretch, the other covering her big, round belly.

"How long do you have left?"

"Too fucking long."

I snicker. One of the most common answers.

"Back pain?" I ask, trying not to sound desperate for glimpses into her life as I bring our plates to the sink.

"Back pain. Heartburn. Lightning crotch. Nausea."

"Sounds like a blast." I'm only half sarcastic. I'd give anything to feel morning sickness and fatigue from sleepless nights spent tossing and turning, trying to find a comfortable position. "According to old wives' tales, the heartburn would mean it's a girl."

"According to different tales, I'm having both a boy and a girl at the same time. And apparently, the heartburn means they have a lot of hair." She returns to her box of mismatched cutlery. "It's a girl, though."

"Maternal hunch?"

"Ultrasound."

"Also does the trick." I imagine a baby girl with big green eyes and nails the size of a grain of rice. "Congratulations, by the way. I'm really happy for you." And I am. I could always appreciate the beauty of a growing family.

I never meant to bring my personal struggles to work. When I felt like crying at seeing the babies sleeping in the nursery, I would dig my nails into my palms and talk myself down until the urge dissipated. But one evening, I'd been having a rough time—Michael had come and picked up the last of his things that morning, and it meant the end of this story had truly arrived. I felt raw everywhere, like someone had peeled all the protective layers of myself and left me open for all irritants to burn. That evening, I witnessed the wrong thing at a time when I couldn't get control over myself. The mother who didn't want to wake up at night to feed her baby was probably overly exhausted, maybe even depressed. But when she asked my nurse colleague to do it for her for the third night in a row while her baby boy cried relentlessly in his cot, I snapped. It was so much more about me than it was about her, but it was still inappropriate. Sariah was right to tell me to take a break. In fact, she could've done far worse. I needed to get myself back the fuck in control. The pain will never go away. I'm not dumb enough to think a month away from work will close the wound. I just need to get my shit together, enough that I can pretend everything is fine in front of my patients, even when I feel like dying inside.

"Thanks," Keira says.

This feels good. Having a civil conversation with my sister. Maybe this is what will make this trip worth it. Finally getting back at least a semblance of a relationship with Keira.

"Are you still in the same apartment? What—"

Footsteps boom on the back porch before we hear a knock at the half-open patio door. "Hey, Cassie?" Eli's voice is unmistakable, and I wince. I quickly stand to go minimize the damage, but the glare Keira gives me says it's way too late. "I'm making spaghetti, and Zoe asked if— Oh, Keir, hi," he says as he spots her still seated at the kitchen table. "I didn't know you were here. I'll, uh, leave you to it." Looking back to me, he adds, "I'll bring you a bowl later." Then, he's gone, unaware of the chaos he just unfurled.

"Nothing is going on," I tell Keira before she can bite my head off. "I babysit for him sometimes. That's it." Now's not the time to mention the beach trip, or how we've spent a lot of time together in the past week before or after my time with Zoe while he was at work.

"You don't understand," she says. "This isn't some random guy. It's *Eli*."

"I know that."

"Do you? Do you know the way he was when he figured out you'd left? I'd never seen him like that, Cassie. Knocked on our door until Dad pushed him out, but he didn't care. He would've torn down the entire house. Would probably have killed Dad. I had to physically pull him away."

My chest feels like it's being sawed in two at each word. They take me back to the conversation the other night, when Eli told me he would've wanted to have a choice in the way I handled things. I made so many mistakes when I left, and I'm still feeling the ripple effects of them.

"I'm only helping him with Zoe," I tell Keira. "He's overworked. Nothing else."

"I *know* he's overworked."

When did she get so protective of Eli? When we were young, they barely spoke. She had plenty of people around her, but Eli was mine. I'd almost suspect something is going on between them if I didn't know how much Keira loves Rob.

The boxes and piles of items are forgotten at our feet. A muscle clenches in Keira's neck. "Did he tell you about his legal case?"

It looks like she wants to have trapped me. *You didn't know this, did you?*

I'm glad I can nod. It feels like being worthy of Eli's trust is something important, something valuable.

"Then you *know* you need to stay away."

"What is that supposed to mean?"

"He needs to keep a squeaky-clean image in town if he wants any chance at keeping full custody of Zoe."

It's a punch to the throat. A reminder that, in this town, I'll always be a McIntyre, no matter how many times I change my name. However, her point isn't fair. "*You* hang out with him." She might have had an easier time in town, but she remains his daughter, too.

"I don't have a record."

It takes me a second to understand what she means, which is crazy, because this event has been following me at every turn. Some stupid thing I did at seventeen has stayed with me for more than a decade. I was lucky it was a juvenile record which meant it didn't hinder my ability to get a nursing degree or a position at my hospital, but it did kill my chances of ever being able to adopt.

I'm shivering even through the god-forsaken heat of the house. It's as if every time I try to let go of my history in this town, it follows behind me like a shadow. It's everywhere I turn, just like it was before I left.

New York might have questionable odors and unbearable traffic, but at least there, I can be anonymous. It was what made me move there in the first place. I said goodbye to the idea of college for a while and took the overnight bus to the city, then used Ruth's money to pay for a month of rent and got a minimum-wage job for a year, until I could apply to college there. I wanted to be lost in a place where no one knew me, and I was.

I don't miss my apartment there. It's never felt like home—more like a place to sleep in between shifts, and since Michael left, it's felt even more impersonal. But right now, I'd give anything to be back there, if only to find that feeling of being insignificant.

Keira is still watching me like a lioness protecting her cubs.

"He needs help, so I'm babysitting," I repeat. "That's it." When she doesn't argue, it proves just how much she also believes Eli needs the respite.

"Please keep it at that. For his and Zoe's sake."

It's embarrassing and painful to think that simply being associated with me could hurt Eli, but it's probably the truth, and I would die before letting my presence in his life affect his ability to keep full custody of Zoe. It's not like I was planning on having more than friendship with him, but that fact seals the deal.

I guess we can be friends, so long as it's hidden.

"Don't worry. I will."

Chapter 13

Eli's yard has started to resemble a huge patch of beach grass. I'm sure a small dog like Dottie would get lost if it went running in there. The only thing that looks remotely okay in the yard is the small flowerbed I've seen him water a few times.

I've offered to mow his lawn. Twice, in fact. The first time, he was on his way out of the house with his chef's coat on and his hair pulled back in a low bun that had no business looking that good, and he barely had time to tell me, "Thanks, but I'm good," before jumping into his SUV and driving off. The second time was two days ago, and I was mowing Ruth's back lawn while Eli and Zoe chased butterflies—well, Zoe chased butterflies with aggressive moves of her net while Eli chased after her before she hurt herself. "It's no big deal," I said once he'd noticed the way I'd imperceptibly crossed over to his yard. The sun was setting behind him and Zoe, blurring their features to show only their silhouettes, one so tall compared to the other.

"I can mow my own lawn," he shouted from across the yard, but even from there, I could hear the humor in his voice.

"I know. But I can, too."

He took a few steps closer. "Are you trying to emasculate me?"

"Are you trying to tell me your masculinity lies in your ability to mow the lawn?"

"Dad," Zoe bellowed in a breathless voice, still running, "let Cassie do it so you can help me catch them."

I snickered. "Your daughter's a better feminist than you are."

"I'm not *not* a feminist. I'm an 'I can do it myself' guy."

"I know you are." My head cocked to the side. "I just don't care."

"No," he said, mouthing the word with extra intensity.

"No wonder your daughter's got such a hard head." The night before, she'd insisted we tuck each of her stuffed animals into bed, and when I told her we didn't have the time for that, she gave me a Yoko-and-John level of peaceful protest until I relented.

"We know what we stand for," he said with a grin, and since I honestly hate using the lawnmower, I didn't protest any more.

However, this has gone on long enough. I'm afraid I won't see his house from the street anymore if he doesn't do something about it.

I knock at his door, then stand back. The weather this morning is my favorite: a dry, warm day that promises heat in the afternoon, but that's still chilly enough to enjoy without needing any shade. It's the kind of morning where Eli would've woken me up at six-thirty to drive further down the coast to a less crowded beach with his surfboard thrown in the bed of his dad's pickup—when he got old enough to get his permit, that is. Before that, we'd just walk to the closest beach, and I would spend hours watching him on his board while jumping in and out of the water to keep cool. I'd snack on Sour Patch Kids and drink lemonade, soaking up Eli as much as I did the sun.

The door opens, showing a bare-chested Eli in loose shorts. My lips part, and my brain short-circuits for a second. I lose track of where to look when there's so much I want to take in. The deep groove between his pecs, the dusting of hair across his chest, the two birthmarks on his stomach I feel like tracing. Why the hell would I think about tracing his birthmarks?

"Hey," Eli says with a small but cocky smirk that makes me want to dig a hole and disappear into the ground forever. "What's up?"

I clear my throat. "I'm coming over to take care of Zoe so you can mow your damn lawn."

"I don't—"

"Yes, you do. Your lawn is turning into that of a frat house." His cheek twitches. "What are you, the lawn police?"

"Want me to call the lawn police?"

"*Is* there a lawn police?"

"Want to find out?"

He laughs, then opens the door for me. "Knock yourself out."

I'm almost taken aback he didn't fight me on this more. We're making progress, it seems.

"Thank you. I plan to." As I pass him, the subtle scent of his Irish Spring mixed with fresh ocean air fills my nose, and I'm taken back to all the times I just wanted to bury myself in his neck and smell him forever.

But that's in the past.

I move past him, then shout, "Zoe, want to show me your baby pictures album?" Lower, I tell him, "I've never seen a teen dad outside of television."

Three hours later, Zoe and I have ridden bikes, swam in the inflatable pool they've got out back—she swam, I kept her from hyperventilating by doing too many handstands in a row—and gone through all her baby photos. I had to force my face to remain neutral and not to ogle Eli too long, but Jesus, that man must have won awards for being the hottest baby dad on Earth. Mostly, though, he looked so freaking happy in all the pictures. Exactly the way I imagined he'd be with a baby in his arms, or a toddler on his shoulders. I patted myself on the back once we were done for going through that entire album without feeling sad. It seems I'm making progress, too. Eli checked on us a few times, always rapidly disappearing after I berated him that we were fine and he needed to get things done.

Later, while Zoe plays with Fish—don't ask me how they play)—I pull a laundry basket I'd spotted in the hallway to do some folding.

> The amount of Care Bear merch you have is concerning, to be honest.

I sent a picture of five-year-old undies. One bear is deformed from being overwashed.

Eli: You make me sound like someone the FBI should put on a watchlist.

Eli: FBI agent, I'm not a creep, I swear.

Eli: Also, STOP DOING MY LAUNDRY!!!!

And miss all this leverage opportunity? Never.

So, we've still got some work to do on him accepting help.

He should know he's the one who's doing me a favor by giving me something to do. I'd planned on going through Ruth's scrapbooking room this afternoon, so he gave me the privilege to bail. I haven't been able to make sense of that specific inheritance, and going through something she loved so much only amplifies how much I miss her. It's easy to forget whose stuff I'm giving away when it's rusted fondue pots or lamps, but the moment I opened the door to that room last night and saw all the pictures and containers of glitter I'd always find on her hands, my breath caught and I closed the door behind me. There would be no way to ignore these were her things, which would in turn remind me I'd never see those glitters stuck to her fingers again. I'm more than fine pushing that to another day.

"Cassie, I'm hungry," Zoe whines. "Like, so hungry I could eat a house."

I snicker. "All right, Gretel. Let's get you fed."

We climb down the stairs and enter a new living area. Gone are the scattered toys and overflowing recycling bin. The space smells like lemon sanitizer, the hardwood floors shining. From the back door, I can see the yard looks nice; the smell of fresh-cut grass entering the house from the open windows. In the kitchen, we find Eli scrubbing the floor on all fours, still shirtless, a light sheen of sweat covering his neck.

"Hey, Cinderella."

He looks up, then sits on his haunches. Zoe runs to him like she hasn't seen her father in days, and he welcomes her with open arms, pressing a kiss to her head as she laughs and tries to tell him all we've done today in a single breath. How lucky she is to be running to him knowing he'll catch her.

"Little miss is so hungry she's threatening to destroy your house, so I'll make dinner." I open his fridge, finding even that pristine. "If you're fine with grilled cheeses, that is." I've never been a great cook, and when it's just me, I'm good with dinners made up of crackers and cheese or a big bowl of cereal. With Michael, we'd order takeout most days after work, and I was fine with it.

"Please," Eli says, now on his feet. "I've been a victim of those grilled cheeses before."

"My grilled cheeses are fine."

"Sure." The little shit grins. "I'll make you dinner. It's the least I can do." He leads Zoe to the dinner table, where she immediately remakes the mess Eli just cleaned by pulling crayons and papers out. "But unless you want to eat chicken nuggets with a side of more chicken nuggets, I think we can have her eat first, and I'll fix us something later."

A dinner, just the two of us. It's dangerous. I know this even without having done it in years. Probably *because* we haven't done it in years. But Eli is a giver. He probably won't sleep for days if he can't pay me back in some way, and cooking a meal is a simple way to do so. We've eaten together hundreds of times before, from sloppy beachside hotdogs sitting on a curb beside his dad's food truck, to sandwiches he'd make for me when I came over during the day.

"Sure. Thanks."

"You got it." He then turns to the freezer and proceeds to cook just what he said for Zoe, all the while she snacks on goldfish crackers.

"They tell you to feed your kid veggies and healthy stuff," Eli says as he spurts ketchup on the plate. I look up from the emails I was answering; notices about coworkers' birthdays and new unit protocols, mostly. "But what they forget to say is your child will likely call you a monster if you add a single piece of broccoli to their plate."

I laugh just as Zoe pokes me. "Look, I drew us."

I almost choke on my saliva. She's somehow decided to draw us horizontally, with me on top of Eli—if "me" and "Eli" can even be used in this situation, considering the drawing that I assume is supposed to be me is one big blob of yellow and brown hair, and I'm dressed in a trash bag, and Eli is only in his yellow-body naked form. Meanwhile, Zoe is standing next to us, holding what looks like a torch.

"What are we supposed to be doing there, Zoe Bear?" Eli says over my shoulder. I hadn't realized he was there until his breath brushes down my back.

"I'm lighting a fire."

"Maybe she's the one the FBI should take a look at," I mumble. He makes a choked sound.

"And you're dancing," she says, like that's the most obvious answer.

In my ear, Eli whispers, "Not sure I'm familiar with that type of dancing."

I fold my lips between my teeth, and when Eli hands Zoe her plate and accompanies her through her dinner like nothing happened, I want to give him a medal. I haven't been able to remain as composed. Images I spent years trying not to dream about have snaked their way into my mind. Dancing, my ass.

Once Zoe is done, I go play with her a little more while Eli starts dinner—I'm guessing some kind of pasta sauce that smells heavenly—and then he's going back upstairs with her for bath time and bed. I finish scrolling through my emails, which I could've done without. For long moments this past week, the hospital slipped my mind, which is something that hadn't happened in so long, I'd forgotten how it felt not to be constantly burdened by something. This was a not-so-gentle reminder of what I'm going back to in two weeks. Then, I get to the texts I missed from Emily this afternoon.

Em: How are things?

> **Em: I miss you here. We had a code brown earlier. SOS.**

I chuckle. Code Brown is the word combination no nurse ever wants to hear.

> **Em: Any updates about hottie neighbor?**

I need to remember never to leave my phone unattended with Eli around.

> **Still hot. Cooking me a friendly meal tonight**

> **Em: "Friendly"**

We text for a few more minutes about the new anesthesiologist who's apparently sending *interested* vibes. When Eli comes back downstairs, I tell her I have to go and make sure my phone is hidden in my purse in case she decides to be sneaky again.

"Sorry about that," he says as he turns the heat up on the stove and stirs the sauce. "Two stories weren't enough tonight. She needed three."

"I told you, hard head."

"Yeah, yeah." He adds pasta to the pot of boiling water he'd asked me to start for him while I go set the table, rifling through a few drawers before finding the placemats, plates, and utensils.

"Can I help with anything?" I ask once I'm done.

"Yes. Open the bottle of wine in the fridge and pour yourself a glass while I finish up."

I'm not sure wine is the best idea in this context, but I also wouldn't mind a glass after the week I've had. I do as he says, pouring him one, too.

"I can't thank you enough for today," he tells me after taking a sip. "You've been a lifesaver."

I clink his glass. "Purely selfish reasons. That grass was killing me softly."

"Still. I needed it."

I give him another cheers. "Then I'm happy I was here."

His autumn eyes remain on me for a long time—so long, tingles start climbing my arms. Then, he turns toward his recipe and finishes preparing the meal.

The plate he brings me five minutes later smells like garlic and herbs, with large shrimps decorating the pasta, and the first bite I take almost makes my eyes roll.

"God, this is good," I say around a mouthful. The second bite is even better. "Seriously, I don't know when's the last time I ate a home cooked meal this good."

"That was Ruth's favorite recipe of mine," he says.

I take a gulp of wine to bring my bite down. "I never properly thanked you, for being there for her." Heat blooms across my chest, at the reminder that he witnessed the entire thing during our celebration for Ruth—which ended up being the opposite of a celebration—but he deserves to hear it, nonetheless.

"It was nothing."

"It wasn't. And I'm glad she got to eat food like this." Glad she had someone to talk to when she was probably spending most of her time inside her house. Glad for him in general.

"She helped me a lot when I first got custody of Zoe. It was the least I could do."

Of course, Ruth would have done that for him.

I put my fork down. "Was she... Was she okay, in the end?"

He knows what I mean. She was dying, obviously, but for Ruth, physical health would've been the least of her worries.

"Yeah. She was." He moves some of his pasta around. "She loved to talk about the past. About you, too. She was so proud, you know."

I do know. She told me every time we spoke. Still, it doesn't stop tears from filling my eyes. I nod at him, which I hope he catches as the thanks I want to give him.

We return to our plates, and I finish mine more rapidly than I'd care to admit. "Zoe doesn't know what she's missing."

"She'd agree to disagree." He looks down, a flush painting the tops of his cheeks pink.

"I never thought you'd follow in your father's footsteps, but now that I see it, it makes so much sense." Eli *would* be the person who'd want to spend his Saturday night locked inside a kitchen to make sure every guest had the best experience.

"I never thought so, either." He wipes his lips with his napkin. "After college, I was... confused."

My brows bunch. "But you loved studying business." By the time I left, he was up in the clouds with all the possibilities ahead of him.

"I did, for a while. And then it started to feel... meaningless." He quickly looks up, then returns his attention to his plate. "Dad had recently passed, and you were gone, and—" He stops himself abruptly like he's touched a beast we'd silently promised to leave alone. "I didn't know what I wanted anymore. I figured I'd start in a restaurant to make a bit of money, and I actually liked it. It didn't feel like being Dad's assistant anymore. I loved learning from the different chefs I worked under. Loved to see the customers happy and being able to make food my family and friends enjoyed. I never planned on doing catering or having my own restaurant. But when I'd been working at this place in Portland for a while, some acquaintances asked for catered meals for parties one summer, and after that, the contracts kept coming. Got some employees, and now here I am." He takes a long gulp of wine. "Having flown a little too close to the sun."

"You don't like it anymore?"

"I do. I just don't know how to refuse a contract, and I know everyone in my team wants a full schedule, so I agree to it all, and now there aren't enough hours in a day to mow my lawn and take care of my daughter without having my friend come over to babysit."

Friend. Such a weird feeling, to hear that word coming from his lips and referring to me. For all my teenage years, I spent each of my birthday wishes on having that word stop being attached to me. Now, hearing it feels like a gift.

"I have another task to get to in the next two weeks, then," I say.

He lifts a brow.

"Get you to learn how to say no."

He looks at me like I'm lucid dreaming, but I'll get to him if it's the last thing I do.

We finish our bowls, then I fill the sink with soapy water.

"I can do that." He tries taking the sponge away from my hands.

"Over my dead body, Grant."

"You've done enough."

"What did we just say about learning how to accept help?"

"That's not what we said. We said 'saying no.'" He pulls on the sponge. "And I'm saying no to you helping with the dishes."

I pull again, but this time, it surprises him, and the shock brings his body forward, enough that his chest brushes mine. I inhale sharply, that damn drawing creeping back into my thoughts.

The pulse in his neck is directly in my line of sight, beating so hard I can almost feel it.

When he steps back, he doesn't argue over the dishes anymore.

Once we're done, he follows me to the couch where I left my purse, and when I look up, he's handing over a wad of cash.

"What is that?"

"American dollar bills," the smartass says.

"What am I, your preteen neighbor? You're not giving me any-thing."

"You won't babysit for free. This is for the week."

I lean my back against the armrest. "I'm not babysitting, then. I'm hanging out with Zoe."

"I think we need to find you friends older than five."

"I like it that way."

He stares for a long moment, then moves forward to push it in my hand, but I shuffle away in time.

"Eli Poldrick Grant, you keep that cash to yourself."

He shifts again, and we're both on our toes, at war. "Pulling out the full name? Really?"

"It just has such a nice ring to it."

"I'm serious, Cass. You're taking the money." He lunges, but I move away faster.

"I think you've forgotten who you're dealing with."

"A pain in the ass?"

I grin. "A girl who once spent a week in silence to prove a point."

"And your sister still never let you use her iPod," he reminisces, laughing.

"You're not winning this. Better accept it." Before he can reply, I dodge under his arm, jump over the sofa, and make it to the door.

"What is this, parkour?"

"Call it what you want." I open the door. "I like Operation Get Eli To Be Selfish."

"Aren't people not supposed to be selfish?"

I lean my head against the frame. "I think it would do you some good to be."

Chapter 14

We're making good progress on the house.

Over the past two days, Keira and I have gone through most rooms in the house, which means I was able to schedule a meeting with a realtor Eli knew so we could finally put the house up. She came over to take pictures this morning. I'd planned on staying with her for it, but when she placed her tripod in the living room and said, "Oh, they're going to go crazy for this view," a lump formed in my throat, and I decided it was probably best if I left. This was happening. The last piece of Ruth we had would soon be gone. And with it, the last opportunity of finding a way to keep Keira, Eli, and their kids in my life.

I got in my car, then took the opportunity to bring some stuff over to Mom's; she's sentimental over stuff, too, and there were things like baby costumes or hand-knit clothes I knew she'd want to keep from Ruth's.

When I get to my childhood house, the driveway is full of cars I don't recognize. I grab the two boxes from my trunk, then knock on the front door, but no one answers. A loud jumble of voices comes from inside. I lean the boxes against the doorframe to get the door open, then walk into what looks like a golden age slumber party. Kitchen chairs are pulled up in the living room to complete a circle with the couch and recliner, and glasses of wine cover the coffee tables and even the floor.

"Oh, Cassie, hi!" Mom says. She tries to stand, so I put the boxes down and rush to put a hand on her shoulder.

"It's fine, sit. I was just bringing you some stuff. I'm sorry, I didn't know you were hosting a party."

"Not a party. I told you about crochet club!"

I didn't have the time to take a good look around, but once I do, multiple familiar faces smile back at me.

"Well, look at you," Eileen Horton says. She was one of Ruth's best friends, and I can't remember how many times I caught them drunk in Ruth's house when I turned up there unannounced.

"It's good to see you again," I say, struggling to keep my voice steady.

It feels like she knows exactly where my mind has wandered because her expression switches to mirror mine. "You, too."

"Join us!" someone shouts behind me. Susan, another of Ruth's girlfriends says, tilting a glass to her lips. The wine has made her eyes glassy and her pitch higher. Her firetruck-red hair is so bright, she probably had it dyed this morning.

"Oh, no, I can't. I was just dropping some stuff over."

"You have to! I want to hear all about what you've been up to," Eileen says, already squeezing herself away from Gertrude, the librarian who always let me borrow more books than I technically could. She was stiff with everyone, but because she was friends with

Ruth, she gave me that privilege that always made me feel special. Her austere air hasn't gone anywhere.

"I don't know how to crochet." Mom tried to teach me plenty of times when I was young, but I was never interested. I didn't go on to study science for no reason. I don't have an artistic bone in my body. I'm pretty sure Zoe's accidentally X-rated drawings are better than mine.

"Who cares!" Eileen says with a vigorous lift of her glass. "No one really does. Come here." She taps the now-liberated seat between her and Gertrude.

Only then do I realize they all have crochet hooks and balls of yarn around themselves, but no one actually has one in their hands. Eileen looks halfway drunk, Gertrude has taken off her cardigan—which all things considered is wild coming from her—and Susan is topping up everyone's wine. Her glasses are nowhere to be seen, even though I know from experience she can't see anything without them. Mom is just sitting in the recliner my father used to monopolize, a relaxed air to her.

"What kind of crochet club *is* this?" I ask on a chuckle.

Eileen grins. "The best kind."

"Now sit down," Susan says, and the small tap-tap she gives my butt makes me jump. "And join us."

I look around at these women who were mostly Ruth's friends, then at my mother who never had many people around her growing up. Actually, I don't remember her ever talking about a friend. She had no job and barely got out of the house. Her life was our father and us. She's smiling at me now, almost tentative.

"All right."

"Susan, I swear on all that is holy, if you speak about that cosmetic company one more time..." Gertrude looks ready to throw hands as she says this, her boyish haircut ruffled from how many times she's dragged her hands through it.

"I won't lie and not say what gave me that new porcelain skin."

"No one asked you that."

Susan smiles. "But you were thinking it." Her wild hair and boho clothes remind me of a fortune teller who sells crystals or bongs. I guess the face creams are tame, all things considered.

Eileen taps Susan's thigh. "I'd love to hear about it, darling."

"Well, good, because actually..." Susan leans down to grab her purse, then pulls multiple white tubes out of it. "I have these samples I can give you, and—"

"Oh, Jay-sus," Gertrude exclaims like she's performing an exorcism. "Another poor soul caught in the snares of a pyramid scheme."

"It's not a pyramid scheme!" Susan says, then proceeds to explain how the company is in fact a textbook example of a pyramid scheme. I keep my laughter quiet behind the wine glass that was practically forced into my hands.

"Stop it," Eileen chastises, her words slurred. "We'll make Cassie think we're crazy old bats if you go on."

"Damn right she should think that!" Gertrude says, making me laugh out loud. I don't think I've seen her exude that much intensity since I met her in first grade. I think I might like tipsy Gertrude, actually.

"I promise I don't," I say.

"Elizabeth should be there next time," Mom says. "She's young. You'll fit right in then."

Never would I have thought I'd say these words, but I actually wouldn't mind coming back to crochet club. This is probably the time I've felt most at ease in this house in... forever. It feels like a different place. I can breathe. There's also the fact that these ladies are wild, in the most respectful, loving sense of the word. Most of them ended up picking up their crochet projects, but no more than a few stitches were made before the yarn was put back down as another debate was started. No one argues or tells stories like them. The second I mentioned I was an L&D nurse, it was an invitation to share their childbirth stories in all their glorious details, which led to menopause horror stories, which then led to the women drinking more.

"Oh, I love this song!" Eileen shouts when Mom's old radio, still tuned to the same channel after all these years, begins playing Tom Jones' "It's Not Unusual." Then, she's on her feet, and Susan is right there with her, all dancing to the crackly song. Their moves are stinted, hindered by back pain or bad knees, but they don't seem to have a care in the world, dancing out there in the middle of Mom's living room like nobody's business. Gertrude watches them dance, and Mom remains seated but doesn't seem saddened by it. In fact, I don't think I've ever seen her as happy as she looked this afternoon.

I can imagine Ruth being there, too, standing to out-dance everyone here and singing at the top of her lungs.

Watching them feels like being back in some of my best childhood memories. Those nights with Ruth's friends, where they'd serve me cranberry juice in a wine glass and speak to me like I was equal to them in every way, will always remain etched in my mind. I don't know how these women made their way from Ruth to Mom, but I'm glad they did.

And being with them today, it *almost* feels like being reunited with Ruth. I bite a corner of my lips to fight the pressure building behind my eyes.

"Come on, honey," Susan says as she grabs my hand and makes me stand, effectively pulling me out of my feelings. "Show us what that young body got."

I don't like dancing. Never have. But now, with these women grooving to the music without moving much of their body, I can't help it, then laugh because this entire afternoon has been unreal, in every sense of the word.

I never thought I'd make happy memories here again. Everything about this town always felt wrong. But the past two weeks I've spent with Eli and Zoe, and now this afternoon with these ladies... It feels like hitting a wall headfirst.

And yet, I don't think I mind. Not one bit.

Chapter 15

"Just one more time."

"You've told me that eight times now," I say as Zoe reaches the end of the slide and is already running to the ladder to climb back up.

"One more," she says.

I'm a sucker. I really am.

The park is only a few blocks away from Eli's, but I should have left five minutes ago. Eli even texted me a half hour ago to remind me.

Eli: All good for tonight?

Yes, papa bear.

I approach the module where she is currently playing with a steering wheel connected to nothing. It's high enough that I can only peek my head through the bars for her to see me. "We'll miss choir practice if we don't get going soon, honey."

"I don't want to go."

I frown. "Why? You love singing." I've heard the choir's entire repertoire no less than twenty times since I've started babysitting her. It's... surprising, to say the least. I'm not sure what Mrs. Hahn is on while she picks the songs, but it sounds like good stuff.

Zoe avoids my eyes, which she's never done before. I've never seen that little girl embarrassed or awkward once.

"Zoe?"

She spins the wheel multiple times.

"Zoe, honey, is something going on at choir?"

"Amelia is mean."

"Who's Amelia?"

She doesn't answer, and a pit forms in my stomach.

"Is she part of the choir, too?"

She nods.

I don't know who Amelia is. She could be another adult teacher or a little girl. It doesn't matter. The only thought I have is *that little bitch*. A bright, funny girl like Zoe should never have any of that light dimmed.

"And what does she do?"

Zoe spins the wheel once more.

A cramp simmers in my lower belly, making me wince for another reason this time. The next week is going to be fun. I ignore it for now, focusing back on the five-year-old who's been acting weird since bringing up choir practice.

"Is there—"

"Zoe!"

A wave of cold douses me at the voice coming from behind me. It's foreign yet familiar, but most of all, it sounds overly excited. Before turning, I notice Zoe look up and watch as a million different emotions blur in her wide eyes. They're certainly not blank anymore, but I'm not sure I like this any more than the emptiness from before.

Sure enough, when I finally look over my shoulder, I recognize the strawberry-blond head that was shouting outside of Eli's door two weeks ago.

Fuck. Fuck, fuck, fuck.

I haven't discussed with Eli what I should do in this situation, and I intensely regret it. Zoe can't help me. Even if she wants to see her mother, I don't know that Eli would want that, especially without his supervision. I'm not close enough to the family to be able to make a decision like this, but I'm not sure I'll have a choice.

The woman—Liz, I think Eli called her—is walking toward the slide like I'm not even there, her arms extended as if she's going to ask Zoe to jump so she can catch her. Meanwhile, Zoe is still standing at the top of the slide, frozen. I don't know when the last time was she saw her mother, or what Eli has even told her about her mom. Another thing I should have asked before agreeing to watch her on a daily basis.

I hate my life.

"Hey," I say, placing myself between her and the part of the module she reached. She seems to notice me for the first time, and it's not a good look. Her nose scrunches like she's just smelled something pungent. "Hi."

"Who are you?" she asks.

"I'm..." My words drift away as something occurs to me. I know this person. I used to see her around although I'm not sure where.

School? Mr. Grant's food truck I worked at over a summer? It was never with Eli; *that* I'm sure of. "I'm the nanny," I say, only a half-lie. I'm not about to give her my name. That would be like handing over weapons to the enemy side. Even if I recognize her, she probably doesn't recognize me. "And we're just about to head back home." This way, Eli can decide what to do with this.

"I'll bring her back," she says, like I'm some dumbass who would just leave this child with someone I don't know.

"I don't think so." The bite in my words sneaks out accidentally—or maybe not so. I don't think I could ever play nice with someone who decided to abandon their baby to go live a different life. I understand why Eli is stern with her. In fact, I'm impressed he can keep cool at all. Behind me, Zoe is still quiet. I'm scared to see what kind of expression she's wearing now.

"I'm her *mother*," Liz spits as if she's the one who deserves to be angry.

I want to say that being a mother is so much more than just biology, but that would probably lead to a carnage I don't want to bring on Eli and definitely wouldn't want Zoe to witness. It's none of my business. I'm just a guest here. My personal issues with this person who had a gift and decided to let it go should not come into play.

"I have instructions to take her back home," I say instead, then turn to Zoe. "Come on, honey. Let's go."

"How dare you—"

I turn so fast, her eyes widen. "I'm going to take Zoe home, and you are going to let us go without a fuss," I whisper, making sure she doesn't break our eye contact. "Or else Eli will talk to his lawyers and tell them you're stalking the girl you lost custody of, and that won't help your case at all."

Her face is firetruck-red, breaths coming in pants like a bull. Meanwhile, I've steeled myself for whatever will come next. Eli has trusted me with the thing he cherishes most, and I won't let anything happen to her.

Her eyes narrow. "Do I know you?"

I fight with everything in me to keep my face passive.

"Aren't you—"

"I'm the nanny," I interrupt, my heart thrashing in my ribcage. "And now we're leaving."

My false confidence seems to do the trick because she only stares for a moment longer before she shakes her head with a stiff jaw and steps back.

"I'll see you later, Zozo! Mommy loves you!"

Even when she has turned and walked out of the park, Zoe doesn't move. I call for her, but her attention remains on the path her mother left through. I climb the children's ladder, then put a soft hand on her shoulder.

"Honey..."

She doesn't answer, but she does break out of her trance, going down the slide without a hint of her usual sunshine in sight.

She remains silent the rest of the way home.

I practically jump off the couch when I hear Eli's key turn into the lock.

"Hey, I stopped by Hannaford on the way over and thought I'd make—What's wrong?" Eli immediately lets go of the grocery bag and walks inside without bothering to take his shoes off.

"I went to the park just down the street with Zoe, and her mom showed up."

He throws his head back and releases a deep-felt but whispered, "Fuck."

Glad we're on the same page.

"I got Zoe home, but she hasn't spoken a word since, and I didn't know what to do. I didn't know if you'd want me to pretend I didn't know about her mother, or if you wanted me to call you at work, and I've been panicking because—"

"Cassie," he says, putting his warm hands on my shoulders, large enough that they cover the entirety of the skin left bare from my tank top. "Take a breath."

I imitate him as he does so. It's probably the first deep inhale I've taken since I heard Liz's voice.

"You kept her safe?" he asks.

"I tried."

"Then you did amazing. Thank you."

Eli's words have always had a drug-like effect on me. I could've biked to his place after being humiliated in class when people play-fought not to be paired with me for a chemistry project, and while I'd feel like crawling out of my skin, Eli would put his hands on my arms and tell me things would be better tomorrow, and I'd believe him. It's as if he was able to take some of the burden off my shoulders, and now I see that maybe it's because he took some of it on his own so it wouldn't be on mine.

"She does this every time she sees Liz," Eli says as he steps back and drags a hand through his hair. I miss the contact instantly. "She goes into some kind of quiet mode. I hate it. It takes time for her to get back to her normal self, and I never know what to do, either." He moves toward the kitchen where he leans across the counter, the muscles in his back stretching under his black T-shirt. Now that I'm calmer, it's as if he's given himself the permission to freak out.

"She's seen her often since she's... come back?"

"A few times. All ambushes. I wouldn't be surprised if she knew you were going to be there with her."

I wish I could give her the benefit of the doubt. I truly do. But a burning anger for the woman I've seen today has settled in my chest, and I don't know that any water will ever quench it.

"Are things looking good with your lawyers?"

He shrugs, then takes a seat at the counter. Deep circles line the underside of his eyes. "I don't know. They say I can probably win based on how she left in the first place, but I'm dreading going through that process and dragging Zoe along with me. It can't be good for her."

"I'm sorry." I take a seat next to him. Zoe is still upstairs, where she's remained since we got back home. When I offered her dinner earlier, she didn't want any, so I brought a PB&J sandwich to her room and left her in peace. That's what I wanted when I felt like everything around me was going to shit. Eli probably knows that's where she is because he hasn't asked about it.

"Not much else of an option."

I crack a knuckle, and the sound drags Eli's gaze to my hands, then up to me with a quirked brow.

"There's one more thing," I say. "I think she knows who I am. Liz, I mean."

"Who you are...?"

"A McIntyre."

"So?"

"So, she might use that against you." I feel nauseous. "I'm so sorry. I didn't think we'd come across anyone at the park, but I should've expected—"

"First off," he interrupts again, "you didn't do anything wrong. You were playing with my daughter. And second, who cares about your last name?"

I give him a look that says *you know damn well that everyone cares*. I didn't change it for nothing, but here, I'll never get rid of it.

"That's your father, Cass. Not you."

He's never understood that the two go hand in hand.

"But I do have a record to my name," I say in a small voice.

Eli squints, and only after a long pause does his expression change with recognition. "That wasn't your fault. He was bullying you."

I've always hated that word. Bullying. It feels like something you can round every ugly action in. Calling someone names, pushing them, giving them the silent treatment, making sure they never make friends... Those are all vastly different things. It's too easy to group them and summarize them with a single term. What my classmates or teachers did wasn't just bullying or intimidating me. They were ruining my life, day after day.

"It still happened, and it's never going anywhere." Even if juvenile records get erased after a few years, locals know about it, and people in Cape Weston don't forget. I swallow, then turn to him. "And the last thing I'd want is to cause you more problems, so I'd understand if you want me to step away."

"That's bullshit. I'm not letting you... I'm not giving any of them the winning point. Fuck that."

I'm not sure why Eli or the Grants never treated me and my family like everyone else in town. Mr. and Mrs. Grant were never fans of my father, but they were always civil with him and downright nice with my mother. And me? Walking into the Grants' house felt like entering a different world. I wasn't the same person there. Ever since I'd walked over to him at ten years old and asked him if I could use his trampoline, it was like I could just be Cassie with him. I waited for years for the other shoe to drop, for him to start looking at me with pity or disgust, but he never did. The only thing he ever showed was interest. He wasn't my favorite person for no reason.

"I just want you to know that the option is there," I say.

He leans forward, his elbow touching mine. "And I want you to know I don't want it."

"What if it causes issues with the trial?"

There's a pause before Eli answers, "I don't see how I could be faulted for hiring an old friend who's been nothing but kind to Zoe for babysitting purposes."

"Technically, you haven't hired me since I won't let you pay me."

He cracks a grin, some of the tension eased. "I haven't paid you *yet*."

"You can dream."

He snickers, and the light sound settles something inside me I hadn't even realized was brewing. I was scared, I think. Again, he's found the words I needed before I even knew I wanted them.

Despite all this time, I think Eli Grant is still my favorite person.

I clear my throat. "On another note, I think something's going on in choir practice. Something with a girl named Amelia?"

Eli sighs deeply. "Yeah. She's told me about her. She's..." He rubs a hand across the five o'clock shadow covering his jaw. "Fuck, I can't say that about a little girl."

"It's okay, I've already called her a bitch in my head."

He laughs out loud this time, bright and unfiltered. I realize now why I love hearing Zoe's laugh so much. When they're truly happy, it sounds the same.

"If you need me to kick some five-year-old's ass, just know I'm ready."

"All right, tiger." He nudges my knee with his. The contact is so easy, so familiar. I want more of it. "How about we keep you out of trouble for now?"

In a minute, he's turned this thing I've been ashamed of all my life into something we can joke about. He's magic, truly.

"I'll try."

I stand to grab my stuff, then turn to him. "So, you're *sure* you're okay with me coming again tomorrow?"

He gets to his feet, too, and comes to stand so close to me, I can feel his breath on my cheeks when I tilt my head up.

"Cass," he says, the nickname sounding like a rolling wave coming from his lips. "I can't think of a single day when I won't want you here."

Heat creeps up my chest. "So that's a yes?"

The backs of his fingers swish past mine. "Yes, that's a yes. So long as you keep the ass-whooping to your imagination."

"Yes, chef."

Chapter 16

Eleven Years Ago

The boy is drained.

After working all day with his father at the food truck, he hurried over to baseball practice, which ran much longer than expected. They're going to the state finals tomorrow, and while he's excited—this is probably going to be his last year playing the sport—he can't wait to get in bed and finally read the texts he missed from her.

However, he doesn't even need to wait, because when he looks out from his bedroom's window after getting out of the shower, he sees her, sitting on her grandmother's back porch. He doesn't need to see her face to know it's her. He can tell by the way she holds her shoulders just shy of hunched, and how she's not doing anything other than staring out into the ocean, the way no one remembers to do anymore. He used to find it strange, how she could just *watch* for hours on end without going on her phone or even reading a book. Now he knows it's her way of quieting everything out.

The boy throws on jeans and a hoodie and joins her outside. The summer day's warmth has dropped all of a sudden, wind blowing from the cliffs ahead. Still, the girl doesn't move, bracing the cold headfirst.

"What are you doing out here?" the boy asks as he settles in the Adirondack chair next to hers.

She turns to him, her gaze softening the same way it did when she was nine years old on her grandmother's front porch. Still, there's something tight in her expression today. "Dissociating. My stomach's been killing me."

He doesn't get embarrassed by this anymore. The first time the girl mentioned her periods to him, he freaked out, and she proceeded to give him a ten-minute lecture on how he shouldn't act like menstruating was anything other than a normal bodily function. Frankly, he would've reacted this way if she'd talked about any of her bodily functions at thirteen, but he felt scolded enough to shut up and take it in stride the next time.

"Give me a sec." The boy runs back to his house to grab the heating pad his mother keeps in the bathroom drawer, and a pack of sour worms he keeps in his room for the girl in case of emergency.

"You're an angel," she says when he returns. She places the pad on her belly and leans back with a groan, a worm already in her mouth. "I'm not sure I'll survive community service tomorrow."

After months of giving away her weekends, she's almost done. Soon, what happened with that shithead Kyle Richardson will be behind her.

"I don't know how many more hours I can tolerate getting catcalled or honked at while picking up trash."
"Who catcalls you?" The boy doesn't like the feeling of jealousy that claws at his chest, especially about something as dumb as cat-

calling, but he can't help it. This summer, it's gotten even harder to control.

"Whatever assholes happen to be on the beach." She breathes in through her nose and exhales through pursed lips. "I can't just sulk in peace. My simple existence pisses them off."

"I don't think that's it." The boy saw how some of the guys looked at her when he forced her to come to his high school's grad party last year. Sure, he noticed how some people acted like she had done something wrong by being there, but mostly, the guys looked at her like they would any hot girl. She just doesn't know the difference anymore.

"Keira told me to stop complaining about it when I called her earlier. I swear she's begging for another week-long silent treatment." The girl rolls her eyes. "She doesn't get it. She gets to be a McIntyre, and they leave her alone because she's gorgeous."

The girl's sister does have an easier time, but not because she's prettier. She simply doesn't give any credit to what people think about her. Eventually, people get tired of it and move on. His girl takes every hit to her armor until it shatters.

Besides, the two girls look like each other, and while it's true that the older one may have softer features, the younger is more interesting. Her strong jaw, the sharp slope of her nose... He could look at her for hours and never get bored.

"She has nothing on you."

She doesn't say anything back, but he doesn't miss the pink coloring in her cheeks.

Mist covers the boy's bare feet, turning them into icicles. How can she stay in this cold only wearing a light sweater? He pulls his hoodie off and hands it to her. She doesn't argue, which tells him just how cold she must have been.

"I could go for you tomorrow." He has his baseball tournament in the morning, but he'd work around it.

"You can't always be my hero, Eli Grant."

"I can try."

He wishes he could. Not just for the community service, but for everything. He can see how much she's struggling every single day, even if she'll try to mask it when they're together, and he has no idea where to start to help. She hasn't said it, but he can feel things at her place are getting worse. In the past weeks, when they went to the beach or hung out right here, he would sometimes speak and she wouldn't answer, as if she was truly dissociating from herself.

She's supposed to join his college next fall, but even if there's nothing the boy would want more, he's started to question whether it's the right plan. What if staying close to the man who's made her life a living hell is the worst thing that could happen to her?

Sometimes, he thinks of leaving it all behind and escaping with her. They could start again somewhere far away. But he's eighteen, she's still a minor, and this place is all they've ever known. It's where his father's food truck remains, where his siblings still go to high school, where he's started his business degree. And after his dad's heart attack last year, he can't imagine ever moving away from him, especially after coming close to losing him.

The boy knows the girl should go away for college. He *wants* her to go. She deserves a life away from this bullshit.

But selfishly, he can't imagine ever losing her. It's why he hasn't told her how he feels about her, after all.

"I'll be fine," the girl says as she stands, handing him the heating pad back. "I'm keeping the gummy worms, though."

"They're yours." Everything he owns, he thinks, is hers. His heart most of all.

Chapter 17

The pain rams into me like a freight train.

Endometriosis has given me the full scope of what a bad period could feel like. It can range from being nauseous and having a hard time going through my day-to-day life, to full-on crying and begging someone to take me to the ER because something must be truly wrong this time. Since my surgeries, it's been better, but today has got to be the worst one since. Every time I start to feel those mind-numbing cramps that turn me loopy, I forget how it could ever have been worse.

I woke up around 4:00 a.m. and the pain was so bad, I had to crawl to the bathroom to vomit. That was the first sign I was going to have what I call my 'disappearing days'. Days when I just want to stop existing, just for the pain to cease. I don't want to talk, to eat, to stand. Just disappear. The closest I can come to that is staying curled up in bed with a heating pad and try to fall back to sleep so I can spend the least amount of time awake. Fatigue drowns me, like my body is fighting a battle against itself. My bowels are in shambles, which is yet another unpretty part of this disease I discovered over time. The only silver lining with today is I didn't have to push myself to get to work.

It must be close to 5:00 p.m. now, but I couldn't say for sure. Thank God I wasn't supposed to babysit tonight. After drifting off all morning, I got myself to stand and get to the living room, where I turned on the television, mindlessly rewatching the first season of *Fleabag* while zoning in and out. I wanted to have a background noise so I could at least try to distract myself. The weather outside is just as gloomy, with thick rivulets of rain sliding down the windows. The ocean is barely visible through the thick fog. I'm covered in Ruth's dusty blankets, and I think I'd drink a hot tea if I had it on hand, but I don't trust myself to get up. I feel almost buzzed.

I'm just about to drift off again when my phone buzzes. I consider letting it go to voicemail for a moment but then remember it might be about Zoe. If Eli needed help with her, I'd find whatever strength I could muster to help.

"Hello?" My voice sounds as groggy as I feel.

"Hey. It's me," Keira says. "I'm at the hardware store, and I was wondering how many more cardboard boxes we need to buy."

"Hm." I pretend to take a moment to think because really, there's no way I can come up with a good answer today. "I'm not sure. What do you think?"

She pauses before asking, "Are you okay?"

"Mm-hmm."

"Okay," she says, not sounding convinced. "Think fifty boxes is enough?"

"Sure." I close one eye against the cramp that twists my insides. I may even release a little sound because Keira asks, "Are you sure you're okay?"

"I'm good." It's not the first time this has happened, and it certainly won't be the last. "I gotta go, though." This conversation has to end quickly if I want to make it out alive. "Talk to you later."

I hang up, then resume my vegetative state. I must fall asleep, because I jolt up from my slumber when someone knocks sharply at the front door.

I frown, then tuck the blanket higher so it rests over the bottom half of my face. I put the "For Sale" sign in front of the house yesterday morning, so it could just be a potential buyer, but I'm in no state to handle that today. However, I don't get the choice to ignore it when another trio of knocks resonates through the house, followed by a voice I'd recognize in my sleep calling, "Cassie, open up!"

This time, I do look at the time. Eli is usually not home until an hour past that. The curiosity is enough to get me to shout, "The key's under the gnome." Call it honoring the dead, I haven't been able to pull it out of there.

I could've remained silent and waited for Eli to leave, but knowing him, he'd probably have found a way to sneak inside by some vent conduit. Plus, it's not like he hasn't seen me in all types of embarrassing situations before. Surely, he can handle my bedhead and oversized Madonna T-shirt.

I hear rustling outside, then the squeal of the door opening. I should probably put some grease on there before the visits start. Just thinking about the mile-long to-do list I've made for myself makes me release another groan. I don't have time to waste being like this, but I can't avoid it.

"What's going on?" is the first thing Eli asks as he rushes inside. "Are you hurt?" He takes a seat next to me and brings a hand to my forehead, in full-on dad mode. I'd probably think it was cute if I wasn't in this state.

"I'm okay," I lie. "What are you doing here? Don't you have that big event tomorrow?"

"Keira called me. She was worried about you."

My pain medication must have buzzed me more than I'd thought. I stare at him, wondering if I might have hallucinated him. This entire thing feels like I'm dreaming.

"I get it," he says, and I'm fairly sure I feel his hand softly wrap around my ankle. "You're worrying me, too."

"I'm okay."

"Cass, you look like shit."

"Ever the uplifter, aren't you?"

His frown doesn't go anywhere, and he keeps watching me with a waiting look. I groan, then sit straighter. "I have really bad period cramps."

I wait for the narrowing of his eyes or the *that's it?* comment. Michael never understood why I made a big deal of my period. In his head, just like in mine before, something that half the world population experienced couldn't be so bad. Even when I received my diagnosis, he did show more empathy, but I always felt like a part of him remained wary. As if he didn't fully believe I wasn't exaggerating my pain. And I understand where he was coming from, I do. Something you can't see, can't feel, can only experience, is hard to grasp. But I also wanted him to know me better than that. No one in their right mind would pretend to feel like this and spend a week every month dying a slow death. Getting an IUD placed or taking the pill continuously never worked for me. Sometimes, I'd catch the barely audible sigh he'd let out when I said no to going out, and I felt like getting up to shake his shoulders and shout, "Do you think I want to be like this?"

I never did.

But nothing of the sort shows on Eli's face.

"It's the—"

"Endometriosis, I know," he says in the gentlest voice. "I did some research."

Now I know I drugged myself badly. Deep down, I know this is typical Eli, learning everything about a topic to be able to help someone properly, but it also feels ludicrous that someone would spend time on something like that. It's not like it's a condition that could kill me. In fact, it's so intangible that sometimes, I wonder if I've just convinced myself something was wrong with me.

My eyes flutter as another bout of cramps overtakes me. Still, I push through to say, "Where have you been all my twenties, Eli Grant?"

"I was right here."

Yes, he was. The place I never wanted to be in again.

A brush of his thumb on my calf. "What can I do for you that you haven't tried yet?"

The soft touch against my skin feels like a ray of light through a snowstorm. I'd missed the warmth of his skin, and I wish for a second he'd let his hand climb higher on my leg. "Just...stay here. Please." I sound like a child, and I'll probably want to throw myself off the cliff in front of the house tomorrow, but right now, I'm too exhausted to care. A part of me wonders who's taking care of Zoe, or when he's going to recuperate the time he missed at work, but that's also a problem for Tomorrow Me. I'm too selfish right now to let him go.

"I can do that," he says before standing in front of me and poking my head with his leg. I reflexively shift up, which gives him the opportunity to sit where my head was previously resting.

I glance up.

"Come on," he says, tapping his thigh once. When I still don't move, he softly pulls me down so my head rests in his lap. I let my eyes close. I had so little time with him like that. That last summer, we'd barely gotten closer before I had to leave. How many times afterward did I dream of being back in this exact same position? Twenty-nine-year-old Eli's thighs are stronger, tighter, but resting in his lap still feels like the coziest place on Earth. When his fingers land on my scalp and slowly start scratching, I almost purr. My nose is dangerously close to the seam of his jeans, but I can't get myself to care. I want to be facing toward him, tucked into his heat. I feel exposed, with his gaze free to roam over me, but it's not enough to get me to turn around.

"This is the first time someone has done this for me in years," I say after a while, my body more relaxed than it has been in the past twenty-four hours. Every breath feels like it's dragging me deeper.

"Done what?" he asks, the tip of a finger brushing my temple. Shivers dance down my back.

"Taken care of me."

I don't know how long he continues to play with my hair before I fall into a deep, uneventful sleep.

The sun has set by the time I wake up.

I'm not sure if it's the anti-inflammatories that finally kicked in or Eli's presence alone, but my pain seems to be in simmering mode instead of its previous raze-everything-to-the-ground, so I'll take it.

I turn my head and find my cheek is back to resting on Ruth's scratchy throw pillow. I only have a second to be disappointed Eli is gone before I smell something delicious wafting through the hallway. I stand, this time tucking my hair back into a tight bun. I'm careful not to look into any mirror as I make my way to the kitchen, since I'm pretty sure I don't want to know what I look like.

Eli doesn't notice my presence as I walk in, earbuds in his ears. He's muttering what I think are song lyrics as he whisks something—where he found the stuff to cook when everything is in boxes, I have no idea. My gaze snags on the corded muscles of his forearms while he uses the whisk so effortlessly, like an extension of his hands. There's something about capable men that's always done it for me, and since he's Eli, it *very much* does it for me now.

"Where have you hidden these moves all your life?" I say, leaning against the counter.

He doesn't jump, only looks up with a devilish smirk. "Enjoying the show, are we?"

He has no idea.

"What are you making?" I ask as I take a step closer, peering into the pan.

"Just an omelet. You don't have much in your fridge to work with."

"Aren't you a professional?"

He grins. "This felt like an episode of Chopped. What can I make with eggs, dried grass from the yard, a bag of stale marshmallows, and a Tupperware of questionable sauce?"

"That's my chili, you snob."

Amusement and shock flash through his eyes. "The situation is even worse than I'd imagined."

"It was good." Liquidy, maybe, but it did its job.

"I'm sure it was a valiant effort."
I poke him in the ribs. "Taste it."

"I'm a single father, Cass. I can't take those kinds of risks anymore."

He finishes making the meal as I go to the bathroom and change into cleaner clothes—aka a new pair of sweatpants and T-shirt. At this point, it's too late to pretend I look like something other than a troll today.

The food is ready by the time I return to the kitchen, Eli leaning back against the countertop with a rag draped over his shoulder. "You look better."

"I feel better." I sit down at the table, a plate steaming in front of me. "Thank you for this."

"For what?" He grabs a seat next to me with a plate of his own in his hands.

"Everything," I say with a hand motion toward the living room. I'm afraid of putting into words how intimate the moment we shared was and making him feel awkward about it, but I can't not thank him for it. "I truly appreciate it so much. It wasn't necessary."

He cocks his head, letting his fork down on the table, straight and perfectly lined with his glass of water. "You're difficult, you know that?"

"Thanks?" I say with raised brows.

"I mean, helping you feels like trying to move a brick wall."

"Wow, just keeps getting better."

He laughs. "As much as you give, it looks almost painful for you to receive."

"And look who's talking, Mr. I'll-do-it-all-alone-and-no-one-help-me."

"Are we... pathetic?"

"I think we might be," I say with a raise of my glass in cheers. He clinks it.

"How about we promise to accept each other's help, if only that."

"You've already accepted my help, if I remember correctly."

"Shut up and eat your eggs."

I snicker, then say, "I guess I can do that."

"Good," he says, his voice deep, and the simple word is enough to make me blush as I imagine what it might feel like to hear it in a different context. My hormones are truly out of whack.

"Speaking of eggs, these are fucking incredible," I say, shoveling more into my mouth. The appetite has come back out of nowhere, and now I could probably eat two more plates.

"You're too easy to please."

Damn you, brain, for yet again going there.

We finish eating, then I force Eli to stay seated while I do the dishes.

"What happened to accepting my help?"

"You've helped enough. That's my limit." The pain is slowly starting to build up again. I'll surely have a terrible night, but for the moment, I'll enjoy the reprieve I'm having.

He gets up, grabs a rag from the counter, then whispers close to my ear, "Screw your limit."

I have to focus on the veins in the wooden countertop not to meet his gaze. This is moving into dangerous territory. At least for me, it is.

"Your mom called earlier, by the way. I told her you were sleeping."

"Oh." For the first time, I'm glad to talk about Mom, if only for the change in subject.

"She seems happy you're back."

I shrug. "I met with her friends from crochet club on Monday. It was... nice."

"So, it hasn't been so bad? Being back, I mean."

I give him a smile. "Not all of it, no."

"Do you..." He wipes the inside of a glass that's already dry. "Do you hate it as much as you used to?"

It takes time for me to figure out the honest answer to this. "I guess it's different. Some parts are better, but it might just be because I know it's temporary. I don't have to worry about how I'll find a job around here with my name. Don't have to meet new people." I empty the water out of the sink and pick a drying rag. "My dad not being here anymore is probably the main part, though. I don't have to be afraid to come face to face with him for the time being."

"Hm." His glass is still turning, making squeaky noises. "Don't you think it's possible the town changed while you were away?"

I offer him a smile. He's always been a glass-half-full kind of person, and while I love that about him, it also makes him blind to certain things. "I don't think anyone's opinion about my family will ever change."

He hums again. We wash and dry in silence for a long moment, until he asks, "Didn't you ever miss it?"

"Huh?"

"This place. Didn't you miss it?"

"Yeah, I missed some things," I say, never taking my eyes off him.

His throat works, and suddenly, the air becomes heavy with everything that remains unsaid between us.

I hand him another plate and look down at the soapy water. "I mostly missed the little things. I remember when I finally got the money to buy a TV, and I landed on SNL while scrolling the channels. I almost returned it to the store. I didn't want to watch it on my own."

I don't like bringing up my leaving. It's almost like if I don't mention it, I can pretend I didn't hurt him. However, this time, it slips out before I can hold it in. I clear my throat. "It's funny, because thinking back, we definitely didn't get the jokes half the time."

"Yeah, we did." His voice is strained, but he still grins.

"Don't overestimate yourself, Grant." I hold out a bowl, which he grabs with a shake of his head.

We used to watch the show religiously on Saturday nights, and while we had to beg Mr. Grant to allow us to watch the "grown-up show" with him for the first time as kids, it eventually became Eli's and my tradition. Mostly, it was my excuse to spend more time with him.

I always felt embarrassed by how much I wanted him, and for how long. He might have returned my affection during my last days here, but I'd spent years pining over him before that happened. How many times did I blow out birthday candles while picturing what it would feel like to have him look at me the way I did him?

"I would always fall asleep before the end of the night," I say, putting a glass in the cupboard behind him.

"I was never great at flirting, huh?"

My breath catches as I pull back, so close to his face, I can see all the tiny freckles dotting his nose, his cheekbones, even around the scar on his forehead. It's the first time one of us has mentioned what happened between us before I left, a tiny crack in the ice that leaves me immobile, not wanting to fall through. However, he risked himself first, so I offer, "I didn't think you *were* flirting."

"I definitely was."

A long moment passes before I say, "I wish I'd known." I wouldn't have waited until the very last minute before getting with him. To know we could've had longer...

He inhales deeply, bringing our chests even closer. I should move away. I need to move away. But those amber eyes are on me, and I've never been able to look away first.

He wets his lips, and just as I follow the movement, hearing my pulse in my ears, his phone vibrates on the counter. We both jump, as if we were caught doing something wrong. He grabs it.

"It's Zoe," he says, typing something back.

"Who's with her?"

"Charlie." His sister's a medical student, which means she probably has other stuff to do besides babysitting right now. "Zoe asked her to tell me that she won't fall asleep until I show up and read her a story." He sighs, then laughs. "I might have overdone it by teaching her to always go after what she wants."

I lightly shove his shoulder. "Go."

I've never seen someone looking so torn. "But—"

"Go. I'll be fine." I give him my best smile. "The worst has passed," I say, probably lying, but there's no way he'll leave if I don't.

"We need to work on that deal of ours," he says, but he's also grabbing his things, so I guess I won.

"Another time." I accompany him out front. "Thank you again."

He nods, then pulls out something from his pocket. "Oh, I forgot to give you this."

A pack of sour gummy worms.

I take it, trying not to focus on the fact that he remembered. "Thanks."

He opens the door but doesn't walk away. "You will call me if you need something." Not a question, but an order.

"I will."

"Good," he says once more in that husky voice, and damn if I won't be touching myself to that word for years to come.

Chapter 18

After an awful night, the pain the next morning is back to a tolerable level. I might not be ready to run a marathon anytime soon, but at least I've been able to eat, shower, and feel like a regular human being again. A win is a win.

With all the time I lost yesterday, I immediately got to work when I realized I felt somewhat okay. The next big thing to go through is Ruth's art room, which I've been holding off on. Even after weeks of reflecting, I haven't been able to figure out why she wanted me to have this stuff. We never scrapbooked together, not even once. I did catch her doing it a few times, even watched her at one point, but that was it. While I had no interest in playing with different textures and papers, it was calming to watch her go through pictures and boxes of ornaments, kind of how it felt to watch Eli float on his surfboard.

After I ate a bowl of cereal—all the while dreaming of yesterday's omelet—I steeled myself to walk in, but nothing could've prepared me for what I'd find in here. If she liked to collect random items throughout the house, it was nothing compared to all the elements she hoarded for her hobby. There are more feathers in her drawers than in a zoo. Long, short, wide, thick, brown, white...

If there is ever a nationwide feather shortage, it's because Ruth collected them all.

I rarely saw all her scrapbooking things. Usually, she'd have them stored back in her art room by the time Keira or I came over. I did surprise her once when I walked in unannounced using the spare key. She screamed louder than I thought was humanly possible. *"It's as if you're trying to kill an old lady, Cassandra!"* She got so scared, she dropped an entire box of beads onto the ground. I spent the next two days on all fours, collecting the tiny beads back into their tray. They were apparently too expensive to vacuum.

I brush my hand over boxes and boxes of similar beads now, not knowing where to start. I don't *want* this stuff. However, I don't think I could ever get rid of something she wanted me to have, so I sit down and get started.

I spend the next few hours going through materials and old projects. It takes even longer than I'd planned, simply because I get distracted by everything I find. One of her countless books is open in front of me, the pages thickened with paper mâché, stamps, embroideries, and—you guessed it—feathers and beads. The album I picked appears to be dedicated to Ruth and her friends, following them over decades. Eileen, Susan, Gertrude... They're all there, sometimes dancing with huge 70s curls, sometimes sitting in a circle like they were during crochet club, this time with babies in their laps and glasses of wine in their hands. It's precious to get this kind of bird's eye view of their friendship.

I turn the page to find one where all the girls are now with their adult children, Mom and my father in the bottom corner of it. Mom is sitting in his lap, his thick fingers pressed into her thighs. This was probably a few years after I was born. I recognize the bangs Mom wore for a few years during my childhood. She's laughing, and he is watching her like she's all that's good in the world. I swallow and turn the page. It baffles me still how someone could look at her like that, then turn around and treat her like absolute trash. Things were already bad then, but you would never know based on this picture.

Even then, Ruth knew something was up with her son. I remember her inviting Keira and me over more and more often for sleepovers. She'd bring us to the zoo or the town fair. She'd step in as much as she could. My sister would often pass, but I never did, probably because I didn't have a group of friends to rely on. And through it all, Ruth never said one thing about her son. I can't tell how many times she listened to me talk about him, and while she nodded and sometimes cried, she never said what she truly thought of him. She stepped in to do damage control but was never able to truly let go of the boy she'd raised.

I turn the page to find a picture of Ruth with a sparkling cake in one hand and multiple Mardi Gras necklaces around her neck, wearing her usual wide-leg jeans and thick sweater. She's smiling her carefree smile, like the world has stopped for the night. A knot forms in my throat as I trace her face with my fingers.

I close the book, and just as I leave the room, a feminine voice from the foyer calls, "Hello? Cassie?" I barely jump. As comforting as hearing Eli's voice yesterday was, this one brings me right back to goodnight kisses and home cooked meals, no matter how long I've been away.

"Mom?" I ask as I make my way toward her voice. There, standing in front of the open front door, is my mother and Dottie at her feet, tail wagging. "What are you doing here?"

"I let myself in. I knocked but…"

"It's fine," I say. After all, she considered Ruth a mother as much as Ruth considered her a daughter. It's as much her right to be here as it is mine. "What's going on?"

She plays with Dottie's leash, her gaze darting around me. During crochet club, it felt easier, being the two of us. Like having all these loud, boisterous women as a buffer eased all the tension between us. Now, we're back to a gray zone of a relationship. "Keira called to say you weren't feeling well."

Warmth blooms in my chest. My sister can pretend she's indifferent with me, but her actions speak louder than her tough front.

"This might be silly," Mom says, and for a second, she reminds me of myself when I would ask if I could stay at Ruth's for the night, all hesitant and hopeful. "But when you were young, you used to love to curl up with Dottie when you weren't feeling well, so I thought I might bring her to you."

Silence envelops us, and while I wish I could speak, I don't trust my voice.

I'm not sure what makes me the most emotional. The fact that she thought about the best way to comfort me when we barely know each other anymore, or the fact that I so desperately wish she hadn't waited so long to do so. When I was a teen, yes, cuddling with Dottie was what I did when I couldn't leave home and felt so overwhelmed I thought I might burst, but the dog was not what I truly needed. It was a band-aid to the festering wound that would never heal until my mother decided to bring Keira and I somewhere else, where we'd feel comfortable to be home. Where I wouldn't have to wonder which version of my father I would get that night. I spent years waiting, all the while my father's addictions got worse and his behaviors became more senseless.

So many feelings battle each other. There's my inner child who sees her wire-frame glasses and brittle hair and wants to go hug her and drain all the reassurance I can get out of her, and there's the adult woman who thinks that, if I was able to have children, never would I let them feel afraid in their own home, even for one second. They would become my priority. I would never let my feelings come before theirs.

And yet the sight of her with my old dog at her feet makes the answer simple. She's not a bad woman. She's a woman who loved too much, and who couldn't put anything above that love. Not even us.

"Thank you," I say, leaning forward so I can pet my old dog on the head. "I appreciate it." Even though my cramps do feel better, I wouldn't mind spending more time with Dottie. She was the best heating pad, and after the next week and a half, I'll probably never see her again.

When I straighten, Mom is staring expectantly, her fingers knotted in front of her belly. I also won't see her for a long while after this is over.

"Would you like to come in? I was just about to make lunch."

It's as though a curtain has been torn open, allowing sunlight to seep through her face. It's such a rare sight. How could I let resentment take this feeling away from her? "I'd love that."

Chapter 19

"So? What do you think?"

Zoe chews one of the cookies I just pulled out of the oven, her gaze focused like a scientist wondering about a complicated theorem, and not like a five-year-old girl tasting what I thought was a pretty decent recipe. Her movement slows before she takes a deep swallow, closed eyes and all. "It's..."

I widen my eyes expectantly.

She takes another bite and does the whole process again before concluding, "It tastes like the food I give Fish."

Well, I have to give it to her, she's honest.

"When did you taste Fish's food, missy?"

"I thought it would be like Fun Dip." She makes a face, making me chuckle.

I'll take her comparing my cooking to powdered fish food over her silence any time. The jokes that usually had her laughing uncontrollably barely got a smile, and her toys were left basically untouched for a few days following the encounter with her mother. It was like she was a completely different kid. I vowed never to leave the house with her again if it meant preventing this from happening again.

Eli is actually working on this problem right now. He asked me to come over earlier while he went to some appointment with his lawyer, who, come to think of it, is probably Ruth's lawyer. I would've agreed to babysit no matter what, but the homemade meal he promised made it all the more appealing.

"You're harsh, I think," I say, which only makes Zoe giggle. She then steals two cookies from the pan and jumps down from her stool, running toward the living room.

"Not that disgusting if you're stealing more!"

I don't know how anyone could resist the laugh she lets out again. I could be in the foulest mood—which I was for a while after crossing paths with two girls who made my life in school a living hell and pretended they didn't recognize me today—and I still couldn't help but smile if I heard the sound.

As I'm following her toward the living room, a creaking noise comes from the front of the house, making me tense. Eli isn't supposed to be back for another hour.

I've never been brave. Not when facing bullies and certainly not when facing a possible home invasion. When I moved into my first studio in the city and had to live alone for the first time at the age of seventeen, I couldn't sleep for an entire month. Every noise would make me jump. I'd barricade my front door with two dressers before getting in bed each night.

I look back at the little girl snacking next to me. If protecting her means facing the break-in fears I've had since watching one nasty horror movie with Eli when I was a tween, so be it.

The knob of the front door turns, and I grab the first thing I can get my hands on—namely a wooden spoon—and rush toward the door just as it opens, weapon brandished.

I will deny I was the one who let out that shrieky yelp until the day I die.

Eli jumps back as he steps inside and sees me, wild-hyena style, and then, the prick has the nerve to smirk. "Nice," he says in that deep voice of his.

"You couldn't text?" I ask as I let the stupid spoon down.

"And miss that? Not a chance."

Asshole.

"Daddy!" Zoe shouts. It doesn't take a second before she's throwing herself into her father's arms, looking so tiny in them. He picks her up and settles her on his hip, then kisses her temple. I conclude right then and there that nothing is sexier than Eli in dad-mode.

"What happened to your braids?" he asks Zoe as he pets her head adorned with two tiny buns.

"Cassie made me these. She's *so* much better than you."

I chuckle. At least she's like this with everyone.

Eli throws me a look that only makes me laugh harder.

"She said she could make me a crown braid one day," Zoe tells her father like I'm some world-renowned hair stylist instead of a girl who watched YouTube tutorials to pass the time when I was thirteen. It's one thing I love about kids; how you could be the most ordinary person, and in their eyes, you hang the moon.

"Did she?"

"Yes." Zoe's eyes widen, then she turns to me. "You can make me one on my birthday." She says it like *birf*day because of her missing front tooth.

"We'll be at Nana's cottage on your birthday," Eli tells her.

"Cassie can come to Nana's!" To me, she says, "It's so much fun. There's fish in the lake, and sometimes they fight each other." I want to laugh as much as I want to cry, because based on Eli's face, I know I won't be here by the time Zoe's birthday turns up. If they're going to the cottage, it's probably sometime around August.

"Cassie will probably be very busy," Eli says, the humor also gone from his voice.

"Why?" Zoe asks.

I force a smile, then swerve the question. "I'll make you a braid crown tomorrow, if you want."

She still seems skeptical, but the promise does the trick. She swivels out of Eli's arms, and when he tells her it's bedtime, she says, "Can Cassie do story time?"

It's only then that I realize the mistake I made, spending this much time with her. Of course, she would get attached. *I* got so attached, I don't know how I'll leave. And yet the day is coming, and soon. My home is not here anymore. My job is waiting for me. And now I have this little girl who I have to leave, after she's been left so badly already.

"Your daddy will do it," I say, then pat her head in goodnight. Eli nods, and his eyes tell me some part of him knows what I'm doing. He doesn't say anything as he brings Zoe upstairs.

While I'm alone, I clean the kitchen we made a mess of while baking, then do the dishes and pick up some of the toys Zoe left lying around. Eli is back downstairs by the time I'm done.

"How did it go tonight?" I ask.

"Good, I think." He slumps on a stool. "We've got a court date in a few weeks. My lawyer said we have a solid case, even though judges usually rule in favor of the mother."

"That's good news."

"I'm still scared shitless."

"Understandable."

Eli leans forward to pick a cookie from the tray, but I slap his hand before he can.

"What?"

"You can't eat these." I should've thrown them away already, but I have a hard time getting rid of "good" food when there were a few times when I was young, I wasn't sure there *would* be food for dinner. Every time my father inevitably lost his job, Mom would do her grocery shopping at the dollar store and pretend like she wasn't hungry when her plate was smaller than ours. Then, my father would go out of town and find another job, we'd be better off for a few months, and the cycle would start again.

I figured I'd leave with the cookies and eat them no matter what they taste like.

"Why?"

"Your daughter compared them to literal fish food." And to a chef? I'm not dumb enough to risk it. I've seen his visual judgment of my chili already.

His lips quirk up. "I may have raised a monster."

I like to think I'm fast, but Eli is definitely faster. He steals one and bites in before I can stop him.

"You little—"

He interrupts me by standing to go spit his bite in the trash can.

"All right, Mr. Overreactor. They can't be that bad."

"Sweetheart, I think you've just tried to kill me."

I try to ignore the tingly way it felt to be called *sweetheart* and taste a cookie myself, then force myself to swallow it down. The only reason Zoe stole two must've been to pick at the chocolate chips inside of them.

"Okay, I swear they're not as bad when I make them at home," I mutter, still not throwing them away but moving the pan aside. "I wanted to give you these as a thanks, but I guess I'll need to find something else."

"Thanks for what?"

"For the other night. I really appreciated it."

"It was nothing."

Eli will never acknowledge that what he did *was* a big deal, so I don't bother arguing. Instead, I look around, trying to find something to give him. "I could teach you how to braid." That would mostly be a gift for Zoe, but two birds, one stone.

"I can braid." He looks like he actually believes it.

"Those braids were a crime against humanity."

"Who's the overreactor now?"

I grin, and he does, too. He knows I'm joking, that I admire the way he acts as two parents in one and does it so beautifully. I couldn't be more in awe of him, even if his braids do suck.

"Come on." I pull him by his wrist toward the living room, where I sit cross-legged on the floor. I pat the couch behind me. He obeys. "Now, watch how it's done."

I slowly braid my own hair as I give a step-by-step explanation of my motions. Then, I undo it and start again, and again. By the third braid, I go into the mechanics of French braiding.

"Got it?" I ask, undoing my last one.

"Sure."

"Great. Show me."

He didn't seem to expect having to practice, but he doesn't complain, either. Instead, he lifts my hair from my nape onto his thighs, so softly it sends shivers down my neck. I close my eyes. Having someone play with my hair has always been my catnip. Every Tuesday night for years, when Keira would be at soccer practice and my father would be at work, I would lie with my head in Mom's lap, and she would play for an hour while we watched the latest Desperate Housewives episode she'd recorded for us.

"Your hair is smoother than Zoe's," he says. He has a point that I barely have any texture in my hair while Zoe's curls make for the perfect canvas for hairstyling.

"Trying to find excuses?"

He tugs at the braid in warning, then starts again.

"Isn't it relaxing?" I ask. "I used to do this for my patients, when they were still in labor or had just delivered and had their hair in their face. I think I liked it as much as they did."

"Do you miss it?" Eli asks, not stopping his movements behind my head.

We haven't talked about the reason for my leave, but even if he hasn't said so, I know he's connected the dots and figured out the big lines. He's always been able to read me, and the tenderness with which he asks the question tells me he still does.

"Yes and no." I tug my knees to my chest and lean a little closer to him as he gets to the end of his braid. "I miss being with patients and feeling helpful, but I don't miss the way I felt before leaving. I hated the constant jealousy." I'm hopeful that when I return in a week, the break will have done me some good. So long as I'm functional again, I'll be fine.

Eli lays the braid on my shoulder, so carefully I barely feel it. I look at the swirl of blond highlights and brown, then swing it backward. "Start again," I whisper.

He undoes his work. Even without seeing him, I know he's focused on every word I'm saying, like he's inhaling it all to make sure he doesn't miss a part. I used to think he had a remarkable memory, before I realized he just has a talent for listening.

"You do know everything you were—*are*—feeling is legitimate, right?"

"Does it make a difference? It's not who I want to be."

A beat passes before he asks, "So, will you go back?"

"It's my job." I've been in the department almost as long as I've been a nurse. To me, it *is* nursing. "And I do love it." Or at least I used to, and I refuse to believe that my diagnosis will steal yet another thing from me.

"That's good. So long as you take care of yourself, too."

It's so strange to hear those words for the first time at my age. It makes my stomach buzz with the same exhilarating feeling I had when I laid in his lap last weekend. So many firsts at a time I thought I'd never experience any more.

Eli wraps the elastic band I'd handed him at the end of the braid, then shows it to me again. This time, I stand and go to the mirror. He appears behind me as I examine it.

"A little less criminal." I tuck a strand he forgot inside one of the holes. He didn't separate the three sections equally, so the braid is clunky in parts, but overall, it works. "We're at a misdemeanor level now."

"You're the worst, you know that?" he says, his expression saying the opposite.

"Yeah, I do."

"Good."

God, that word out of his mouth will be the death of me one day.

I keep the braid, liking that I'm wearing something he's made. When we were younger and would spend the night watching a movie, I'd sometimes get the scent of his soap on my shirt, and I'd smell it repeatedly throughout the day. It felt like I'd left with a part of him.

I go to the kitchen, then wrap the leftover cookies in the waxed paper and bring them to my purse. "I'm leaving with my disasters."

"Don't. I'll make you some."

"They're fine," I lie, then lean to grab my purse, where a wad of cash is pressed in one of the pockets.

I grab it. "Is this you trying to be subtle?"

He has the nerve to act clueless. I walk to him, then slap the money on the couch. "How many times do I have to say I like doing this?"

"How many times do I have to say you can't do this for free?"

"You pay me back with food."

"Stop being stubborn and take the money," he says, standing up.

I lift my chin. "Make me."

In hindsight, this was a mistake. His lips curl up before he pounces. I should've taken into consideration how much bigger he is. I swerve just in time to avoid his hand reaching for my front pocket, but by doing so, I trip backward, bringing Eli who's pulling at my shorts' belt loops down with me. I let out an *oomph* as we land on a heap on the couch, his weight crushing me in the best way.

We're both breathing fast, half laughing, half moaning in pain and shock, but the second our eyes meet, the humor dies out. His face is so close, I can count the freckles on his nose and cheekbones. Just below his right eye, a small cluster makes the shape of a cloud. How had I forgotten about it? How had I forgotten how his lower lip is slightly bigger than his upper one, and how, when he's exerted, only the top half of his face reddens? The details had slipped my mind, but now that I've seen them again, I know they've been permanently inked.

His knee is between my legs, thigh leaning dangerously close to my core, while his chest is flush against mine.

His eyes alternate between both of mine. We're too close. We both know we're too close. Yet, neither one of us moves. It's as if we know once we move, we won't be close like this ever again.

His tongue darts out, and I don't want to glance down, but I'm weak. I'm so fucking weak.

How could I ever have forgotten how much my body craves this man? He's always been my Achilles' heel. A strand of his hair tickles my cheek, a sensation I hadn't experienced before, his hair shorter the last time we were like this, and I want to feel more. Feel it everywhere.

"Daddy?"

We both jump at the sound, Eli on his feet in a second. Thankfully, from where Zoe is surely standing in the stairs, she can't see anything behind the back of the couch.

"What's wrong?" Eli says, his voice shaky, then clears his throat. I remain on the couch, hidden. We weren't doing anything wrong, but I don't want her to know I'm still here, and I don't think Eli does, either.

"Can you read me another story?"

"Sure," he says, and the fact that he doesn't tell her to go back to sleep like he usually does tells me he's as shaken as I am.

Tiny footsteps I somehow didn't hear before pad back up the stairs, followed by heavier ones. I sit up just in time to catch the glance Eli throws my way before disappearing upstairs.

And, like the coward I am, I leave before he has the time to come back and wonder what maybe, possibly would've happened if we hadn't been interrupted.

Chapter 20

The day is finally here.

After endless hours of triaging and back-and-forth trips to Goodwill, we're ready for the yard sale, with only a week to spare. That should leave me with enough time to make the final arrangements for the house to be fully ready to be sold by the time I leave.

It's barely past nine in the morning, and already, the sun feels like a torch on my skin. It's going to be one of the hottest days of summer, but it had to be done today, even if it means sweating buckets to get it done. Keira is already slumped on a chair behind me, and I feel bad she has to do this while heavily pregnant.

"Would you rather stay inside?" I ask as I adjust an empty picture frame so it's more visible. "I can take care of this and come get you if we get too busy." Ruth's house might not have AC, but the shade and open windows would be better than this. We're set up at the end of Beachside Avenue, so everyone passing on Main Street can notice us and easily stop by. It's less than a hundred yards away from the house.

"I'm good," she says, even though she looks far from it, repositioning herself in the beach chair that looks one move away from breaking under her weight. She winces as if she's having back cramps, which is probably the case.

A few cars slow down in front of our kiosk within the next ten minutes, and I pull out my best saleswoman smile, but no one stops.

"A lot of this is trash," Keira says, lifting a pullover I insisted on trying to sell for two bucks instead of giving away.

"That one's cute!" I steal it from her and fold it back up.

"If you're in the market for new cleaning rags."

"So, what if someone is?" I answer, refusing to give up on it. There might be a tiny stain I assume is mustard on the neckline, but it's not even that visible. Plus, for two bucks? A steal.

More cars pass us, this time with surfboards strapped to their roofs and floaties in their backseats. I'm instantly jealous of all these families who'll be able to jump in the glacial water to ward off the heat instead of burning on the side of the road.

"Garage sales are so weird," Keira says, still examining our layout. "I want to get rid of all this useless shit. You want it?"

"I have to say, we outdid ourselves with the randomness of this one."

"Want a coat rack straight out of the Titanic? How about a Utah travel guide that's older than the Internet?"

I grab the first item to my right. "Could I tempt you with a rotary cheese grater that may or may not still house an old rind of parmesan?"

"Or maybe a VCR player that doesn't rewind the tapes anymore?"

"Three individual golf balls?" Ruth didn't even play golf.

"A chair that will hold so long as you don't lean too far back?" She points to the struggling one she's sitting on.

"Don't forget the black cable that charges some unknown electronic item."

She holds up a stuffed animal that could be a rat or a squirrel, with beady eyes that are too wide for its face. "A kid's plushie that was likely haunted at some point?"

"It feels like it's staring straight into my soul." I fight a shudder. "I'm not sure whether it's supposed to be comforting to a kid or used as a threat."

"You know what?" She puts it in the bag under the table. "I'm keeping it to test it out."

"You're my hero."

She smirks, and before I can wonder whether her smile will disappear as she remembers who she's speaking with, our first client of the day arrives, rifling through all the shit like he might find hidden treasures in there (and unless his idea of treasure is a twenty-year-old mug that says "World's Best Grandma" then he won't find it here). A few others ensue. The cookies Eli baked and left in front of my door yesterday are certainly helping. On top of the box of the best chocolate chip cookies I've ever had was a note that said, *Gotta give those customers some incentive. x.* I'd like to pretend like I haven't been thinking of that 'x' since I read it, but that would be a lie.

Once our first wave of customers has come and gone, leaving with a few items, I take a seat next to Keira, who's remained on her chair most of the time. She's still rubbing a hand on the lower part of her belly, looking in pain. "Contractions?" I ask.

"Ligament pain," she answers. "I've been dreaming of a massage since week eight."

"Does Rob give you some?"

Something in her expression changes at that, but her straw hat hides some of it. "He hasn't been around much these past few weeks. Busy times at work." She leans back, then jerks forward when she remembers what she's sitting on. "I didn't expect the second pregnancy to feel this... lonely."
"I'm sorry."

Her eyes suddenly pinch in pain, making me jerk up. "What's wrong?"

"Little hellion decided to treat me like their very own soccer ball."

"They do like to be the center of attention at all times."

She looks up, and she must see something in my face because without talking, she takes my hand and places it on her belly. I never would've asked and definitely wouldn't have done it without permission, but it feels wonderful to be granted this gift.

It doesn't take long before a small bump of pressure appears against my palm, and my face breaks into a painful smile. Working in healthcare is strange. You can experience something day in and day out and be unphased by it, but the second it occurs to your loved one, it's as if you experience it for the first time. I'm not a nurse checking for fetal positioning or adjusting monitors. I'm a sister, touching her niece for the first time, and it's such a magical experience it brings tears to my eyes. Happy ones, this time.

"You've got a real Lionel Messi in there."

"If she could wait a few weeks before making her World Cup debut, I'd appreciate it."

I smile again, rubbing a thumb over her belly button when I feel another kick. Pregnancy is such a strange, wonderful, almost otherworldly thing.

"Do you still want them?" she asks.

I swallow, then shake my head once, and in one look, I know she knows. Mom must've told her at some point that I'd been trying for a baby, and even without the specifics, she seems to have understood that it's not in the cards for me. "Endometriosis," I say simply.

"You tried everything?"

I nod.

She doesn't say anything, only letting me keep my hand on her, smiling once more at the next kick, and then the next.

The sun continues to rise and becomes even more intolerable, forcing us to move to the shade between clients. We do get decent traffic flow, and sure enough, a couple more items sell. Who knew people actually wanted to buy used, rusty cheese graters?

There are a lot of new people in town, or at least people I don't recognize. It's mostly them that stop by our kiosk. That, and tourists on their way to the beach. We get the inevitable odd looks, too. While most move past us without stopping, Mr. Graham, our ex-mayor, and his wife pause by our table. They must be in their late sixties now, but I remember vividly when they were younger and acted like New England royalty. I'd bumped into Mrs. Graham in the grocery store by accident as a kid, and she'd reacted like I'd set fire to her house.

"Hello, there," Mr. Graham says with that fake, veneer smile of his.

"Cassandra," Mrs. Graham says, not even pretending with a smile. "Finally deigned to show yourself?"

I swallow, feeling like that little girl who was looking for her mommy in the grocery store again.

She looks me up and down, then glances at Ruth's house. "Your poor grandmother. With all your family put her through... May God bless her soul."

Not my father. *Our family*. Like Keira and I were just as responsible as him even though we were kids.

I want to say something, but no word comes out. I'm frozen.

Ruth loved us. I know she did. And yet Mrs. Graham's words make me wonder if, even just for a moment, Ruth was ever ashamed of us.

I brush that thought aside. It's not like it matters anymore.

"Thank you so much," Keira says with a sickeningly sweet voice from behind me. "And now, why don't you fuck off, hm?"

I want to turn and shoot Keira a glare. But the face Mrs. Graham makes before she shakes her head and turns around makes me crack up, even after her crappy comment. I don't think I've ever been this grateful for Keira's take-no-shit attitude.

The rest of the day goes by without any more hiccups. We get a few more clients, but mostly, we lay around in our chairs and chat. Later in the afternoon, a woman dressed like she's going to the country club—and whose house is probably already full of useless stuff—strolls through our kiosk.

"Excuse me, miss," she tells me. "Is the safe still available?"

Fuck me. "It is," I tell her.

I don't know why Ruth even *had* a safe, let alone one that's made of brass and is big enough to hold a small fortune in small cuts. I figured out her lock combination in one try—my father's birthday—and inside were a New York Giants hat and a stack of bracelets I know she bought at Claire's. Was it to trick potential thieves during a break-in? Something to show off to friends? I don't think I could ever understand that woman even if I had an eternity to do it.

"Fabulous. I'll take it."

I should've given it away. I knew I should've. Then, I could've used Eli's help to lift it in the car and drop it off. I don't know how Ruth even got that thing inside her house. It weighs more than a truck.

"Sure," I say. "Just back up your car, and I'll lift it in."

Beside me, Keira gets to her feet with one long groan.

"I'll go ask Eli for some help," I say.

"I can do it with you."

"You're pregnant."

"I very much know that. Now take your side."

"Keira."

She just gives me a look, and I know nothing will convince her. She might have a broken back and still push through the pain just to prove me wrong.

"Fine," I say, then wait for the lady's car to be right next to us before squatting in front of the safe. "Ready?"

She bends her knees like I do, then grips the bottom of the box.

"One, two, three," I say, then grunt as I lift that motherfucker of a safe.

"Fuckinghellhurryupl'mdying," Keira mutters, face red as we make tiny steps to the side until we push the damn thing to the lip of the trunk and let it fall backward. The loud boom it makes doesn't even cover up the animalistic sounds we release.

"Thank you so much," the lady tells me, then hands me twenty bucks and leaves. Talk about cheap labor.

"I just peed myself."

"What?"

Keira's staring at what is indeed a wet spot on her khaki shorts. "I just fucking peed myself."

"Are you sure you haven't broken your water?"

"Cassie, Jesus Christ, I can still tell when I've peed all over myself. Now help me before someone notices I smell like cat litter."

"All right, all right. I'll be back."

I run to the house, but as soon as I open the drawer where I stored my clothes, I know nothing of mine will fit her with this belly. I pull out various items before throwing them over my shoulders. Finally, I land on a beach coverup that can be tied multiple ways. That will have to do as a skirt. I rush back outside, breathless as I hand her the thin piece of fabric.

"Seriously?"

"It's not like I had a ton of options," I say, hands on my knees.

She huffs and puffs as she wraps the Hawaiian flower-patterned coverup around her belly and hips, then bends so she can pull off the wet shorts and throws them somewhere we can't see.

She looks down at herself once more. "This is what rock bottom feels like, huh?"

"See the bright side. You could've shit yourself."

And suddenly, we're both laughing, in a way I'm afraid I'm going to pee my pants and she's going to *re*-pee her pants if this goes on any longer. Keira walks back to her chair, then falls back in it a tad too abruptly. The coverup/skirt parts and she unexpectedly flashes me, which only makes us laugh harder. I drop to the ground because my stomach hurts too much, and I don't think I can stand a second longer. I don't remember the last time I laughed this hard, and most importantly, the last time I laughed with my sister. It's magical. Every time one of us sighs and thinks we're done, one giggles, and we're gone again. A car slows at some point, but once the driver sees us, they speed away.

When we finally catch our breath, I look up at Keira, whose cheeks are as wet as mine. She smiles, and it feels as close to a hug as anything I've ever gotten from her. I want to bask in this moment.

To our left, the kids previously playing in their pool now run around the front yard with water guns, their loud shrieks the embodiment of what summer feels like.

"For the record," Keira says, "you would've made a great mother."

"I know." And somehow, I'm not sad at all, because hearing those words coming out of her mouth heals a part of my heart I hadn't even realized was broken.

At 6:00 p.m., we called it a day, and Eli came over to help us pack into boxes whatever hadn't been bought to be brought to Goodwill tomorrow. He then invited the two of us to dinner with him, Zoe, and Xavier, who he'd babysat all day.

We haven't spent any time together since that moment on his couch, and I'm grateful for Keira and the kids being buffers tonight. I don't trust myself around him anymore. When he briefly touched my arm before he left to get dinner ready, I caught Keira watching the scene, and I waited for a berating that in the end never came.

"Well," I say as I finish my second counting of the money, "we made a grand total of 373 bucks."

"For all that work?" Keira says, and I have to agree with her. I almost feel like having written out a check for that sum of money would've been worth it just to not have to go through all that work. At the same time, today was a great day. Maybe that was the actual pay.

I hand her the bills. "I won't tell if you won't."

She eyes the money, then shakes her head. "Nah. We're doing this right, or we're not doing this at all."

I shrug, then put the money in my purse. I'll make a check for the heart failure foundation once I get home tonight.

I close the last of the boxes, then grab it and follow Keira back to Ruth's.

"I can't believe it's almost the end," I say, taking in the newly cleaned windows and the flowerbeds I brought back to life, at least partly. Soon, I'll never see that house again. My refuge for so long.

"Are you waiting for the sale before leaving?" Keira asks.

"Probably not." I have a shift in a week. It would be very surprising if the house was sold by then.

"Right," she says, her voice stiff, but thankfully, she doesn't add anything. After the good time we had today, the last thing I want to do is bring up my leaving, and the rift my absence has created between us.

We get inside, where I put the box down. The house is so empty, like a set of bones without the surrounding soul and body.

"Do you think she decided to sell it because of Dad?" Keira asks.

"That's my guess." My voice echoes in the bare room. I look around. "I do love the idea of this place being filled with more happy memories, though." I shrug. "And I know it wasn't what you expected, but I do think it feels very much like Ruth to want to offer whatever she owned to organizations that might change people's lives."

"It does."

Relief floods me that she sounds at peace with this now. I wouldn't have wanted her to remain angry at Ruth, and with time, she probably saw that it made sense for Ruth to make that decision.

She rests a hand over her belly. "And about that."

"Hm?"

"I was thinking earlier today, and we probably shouldn't put all the money into one organization."

"Okay...?"

Keira doesn't fully meet my eyes when she says, "I think Ruth would like to donate half the money for endometriosis research."

It's a gut punch, but one that doesn't feel all bad, kind of like when you jump into a cold pool and it steals your breath for a moment, but the freshness also makes your body feel alive.

Keira scratches her cheek. "She knew you always wanted kids. I don't know if she knew about your diagnosis, but if she did, I think that's what she would've wanted."

I don't have words. Don't know that I'd be able to say them out loud even if I wanted to. But to be seen like this by my sister? It's worth more than the millions of dollars this house will sell for.

Keira's not a hugger. Not with me, at least. But I hope with the tearful nod I give her, she feels like I've just wrapped her in the tightest embrace she could imagine.

Chapter 21

"Why are you looking weird?" Zoe watches me with narrowed eyes, and of course says this as loud as she possibly can.

I raise my brows, then turn to Eli. "Truly your daughter, huh?"

"I'd never have said that." His gaze dances across my body. "You look beautiful."

Three words that are so simple. Overused, really. Any man can utter them when you're asking for opinions on a new dress or when they want to get into your bed. But the way Eli says it, never pulling his eyes off me... I *feel* it. I'm wearing a white sundress and had a balayage done, so I don't have mile-long roots anymore, but I don't get the sense it's about that.

"You're not so bad yourself," I tell him, softly enough that Zoe, who's now skipping ahead of us on the sidewalk, can't hear. He's wearing a simple black T-shirt and beige linen pants, with his Ray-Bans sitting on his strong nose and his hair pushed back. Whatever product he's using on there is giving him this old money look I can't get enough of.

He smirks then, and the cockiness brings me right back to my last summer here, when we'd had a similar conversation, and I'd thought to myself, *Holy shit. Maybe this isn't unilateral after all.*

"However," he says, "you are *acting* weird."

"I'm not," I mutter, absolutely acting weird. We're walking through the quaint, scenic streets of Kennebunkport to a restaurant Eli all but begged me to come try with them. It's located on the deck of a renovated ancient sailboat that's now permanently anchored and apparently serves the best seafood in all of Southern Maine—a title every restaurant in the region bestows upon themselves, but who am I to say whether this one is the true best or not? I'm following closely behind Eli and Zoe, my gaze stuck to the ground.

Eli stops abruptly, so much so that I bump into his solid back. He turns, then puts a heavy hand on my arm. "It's going to be fine."

The truth is, I really didn't want to come. Eli only had work during the day to prep for an event tomorrow, so I thought I'd stay at his place for a few hours, then return home and finish posting the items we didn't sell during the yard sale online. That would leave Keira with less to do by the time I leave in four days. Most of the house is now empty, which makes it feel less like Ruth is occupying every room at all times. I'm not sure whether that makes it easier or harder. Sometimes, I'll pass by her empty bedroom and feel like my breath has been stolen from my lungs, because this is it. The true end. No more late nights under the stovetop light, talking until two in the morning about all the things I dreamed of one day doing. The more things I pack, the harder I think it's going to feel to drive away from this place. I was ready to tackle the last bit of work when Eli stopped me before I left and asked if I was in the mood for lobster tonight.

"Funny enough," I said, "I haven't even had lobster since I got here."

He looked like I'd announced I was signing up for an Iron Man tomorrow.

"You know what's way more criminal than my braids? That." Then he turned and called, "Zoe! Put your shoes on, we're going out." I have to say, the way he said it so confidently was very freaking hot, enough so that I didn't argue much. However, now that we're here, I wish I hadn't gotten mesmerized by the way the tendons in his neck strained and kept my head on.

"I don't want to cause you any more trouble than I already have," I say, looking away when a lady I don't recognize looks me up and down.

"You *haven't* caused any trouble. We want you around," he says, as casually as if telling me about the weather. "And whoever has a problem with me hanging out with you? They can say it right to my face." Then, he resumes his walk toward the restaurant, never letting go of my arm. He's not holding my hand or doing anything objectively romantic, but I still feel the heat of his skin on mine like a brand. Is this what it feels like to go crazy? Imagining every small touch as something more?

The street is full of sun-kissed families and casual-chic couples strolling around the port, small boutiques turning their signs to

Closed for the night. Zoe is still skipping ahead of us, truly back to her carefree self. I hope whatever happens with the custody trial won't affect her too much. I don't want to imagine her returning to that silent shell of herself. Actually, I don't want to imagine her in the future, period. I never thought I could get attached to someone like that in such a short amount of time, and the thought of never seeing her again in four days makes me queasy. I won't get to attend her final choir recital or hear the bizarre stories she makes up about her stuffed animals. Even if I come back to visit Mom, Keira, and Eli from time to time, it'll never be the same. She'll soon be in kindergarten, and then in school, and what we developed over the course of a few weeks will become some long-lost memory. In fact, it's probably best if I leave without saying goodbye and let her forget me without a fuss.

A pang of longing hits me at the thought. Can you miss someone you haven't left yet?

We reach the restaurant, and when the waitress settles us at the end of the terrace, with barely any neighbors, I feel myself relax. The boat is still adorned with large white sails that billow in the soft breeze, tied with thick ropes to the high mast. The town seems to disappear around us, giving us the feeling of drifting somewhere in the middle of the ocean. Lost. Peaceful. What I wouldn't give to have these two all to myself, somewhere not here nor there.

Don't go thinking like that when you're leaving.

"Fucks!" Zoe shouts as she jumps from her chair to lean over the railing. Below us, a quartet of ducks floats onto the calm water.

"Ducks, Zoe. *Ducks*," Eli says before dragging a hand across his bristled jaw. He looks at me. "If someone shouldn't go out, it's her."

"What?" I shrug. "They're pretty cute fucks."

"You know what? Never mind."

I chuckle as Eli leans back in his chair and closes his eyes against the sun bathing him in orange light. Behind him, the water is still, reflecting every cloud above. The sight is so beautiful, I wish I was a painter so I could frame the image forever.

Before he can notice, I slip my phone out of my pocket and snap a picture of him with Zoe in the background. It'll never reflect what it felt like to see it in person, kind of like trying to capture a sunset but never succeeding in showing its beauty on a two-dimensional frame, but it'll have to do.

Of course, though, when I click on the button, a loud camera shutter sound comes out.

Fuck me. Zoe must've unsilenced my phone earlier when she was playing with it.

Eli's eyes snap open, and while I expect a cocky comment with another of his smirks, he catches me off-guard by looking at my phone, then at me with what looks like longing all over his expression. Or is that in my head, too?

"Zoe was making a cute face behind you," I try to recover. He doesn't turn around, only staring at me. I feel naked.

"Here you go," our waiter interrupts by bringing crayons and paper for Zoe. I voluntarily take the distraction from my misstep and ask a million questions about the menu. We place our orders, and then we're alone once more.

Eli looks at the characters Zoe is starting to draw—assuming they *are* characters—but remains silent. It's as if his thoughts have suddenly dragged him a mile away.

I clear my throat. "Hopefully, she keeps it PG tonight."

That makes his lips quirk up.

I grab a crayon and hand one to Eli before joining Zoe on her sheet. Soon, our drawings intersect, and Zoe has a blast figuring out what the blends of our creations make.

"That's Daddy!" She points at a blot of brown and blue.

"Of course it is," Eli mutters.

Soon, our plates arrive, mine a sizzling lobster mac n' cheese that smells divine, and a lobster roll with homemade potato chips for Zoe and Eli.

"Jesus, this is good," I say. No matter how many restaurants in the city pretend they make the best lobster plates, they never hold a candle to the fresh lobster that's used to cook here. The taste takes me back in time to summer days, stopping by Eli's dad's truck for food before going down to the beach and spending the afternoon sunbathing while Eli read a comic book beside me. I take another bite and moan, loud enough that I look up, embarrassed, only to find Eli's gaze right on mine, his jaw tight. I give him an apologetic smile, then make sure to keep my amazement to myself.

"Cassie?" Zoe asks, mayo all around her lips.

"Yes, honey?"

"You don't look weird anymore."

I smile. It's easy not to feel weird when these two are around. "Thanks."

"Grant?"

We all look up to find Zach Steinberg, a guy who was a year older than me in class. We never spoke, but one time, Kyle Richardson crossed me in the hallway and shouted something crass, and the next thing I knew, Zach was shoulder-checking him and telling him to fuck off. It wasn't a big deal, but no one had ever done that for me, and I remember having a crush on him for the following six months, overthrowing my Eli-colored haze for that period. I keep my head tucked down as Eli stands.

"Steinberg. Hey, man." He gives Zach a classic bro-hug-back-clap thing. "It's been a while."

"We're still waiting for you to join again," Zach says, then looks around the table. When I feel his eyes on me for a long time, I have no choice but to look up, my cheeks on fire.

"Cassie, right?"

"Right." I appreciate that he leaves off my old last name.

Zach's smile widens. He was always good looking, in that blonde, skater-boy type of way, but now, he's turned handsome. "It's good to see you. I thought you'd left town."

"She did," Eli says but doesn't add anything, and a heaviness settles around the table for whatever reason. It makes my skin itch.

I clear my throat. "I didn't know you two knew each other." Eli and I did cross paths with Zach now and then around town, but I don't know that they ever spoke much.

"We were in the same adult baseball league for a while," Eli says. There's something strained about his voice. I frown at him, but he doesn't look over.

"Although that guy ditched us a few years ago and stopped hanging out."

"I've been busy." Eli's hand goes to Zoe's head almost out of reflex, petting her hair. Just like Eli had described her before, she's barely acknowledged the stranger, instead keeping her attention on her drawing while she eats pieces of lobster and bun separately. Something like pride blooms across my chest, that she never acted this way with me.

"I get it. But speaking of ball, we're looking for someone to fill a catcher's spot Saturday night. You up for it?"

Eli's smile returns briefly as he shakes his head. "I'm too old for that, I think."

"No, you're not," I say at the same time Zach harrumphs, "I'm as old as you are, dumbass." That gets Zoe to perk up, the bad word catcher, and Eli throws Zach a look. The poor guy raises his hands in defense.

"You should go to the game," I say, feeling Zach's eyes on me. I don't like having someone look at us and wonder what we are to each other, but I don't think Zach would be the type to make shit up around town.

"I'll pass for now," Eli says. "But thanks for the invite."

"It's there if you change your mind."

Eli nods.

"All right, then." The interaction is so weird, I can't be more excited that it's over. "See you around, Cassie?"

"Uh…" I'm not about to go into the specifics of my time here, so I just say, "Sure, yeah."

He smiles, then leaves to join a white middle-aged couple waiting for him at the terrace door.

Once we're alone, Eli digs back into his lobster roll, but I continue staring at him until he asks, "What?"

"What was up with that?"

"Nothing."

Zoe is completely focused on her drawings, so I lean over to him and whisper, "You looked like he'd just told you Santa wasn't real."

"No, I didn't."

I lift my brows, which makes him sigh. "That guy's just always had such a hard-on for you, it's insane."

I pull back. "What?" I'm fairly certain that guy didn't remember I existed until now.

He looks at me for a long time, then shakes his head. "You've always been blind."

"Or more like you've always seen things that weren't there."

He chuckles. "Sure, sweetheart."

There he goes with that name again.

And fuck me if it doesn't mess with my head even more than he already has.

On the drive back home, Zoe falls asleep the minute she's buckled into her car seat, so by the time we reach Ruth's house, Eli pulls up in the driveway and walks me to the door. Twilight has come and gone, only faint hues of red and dark blue coloring the sky. Otherwise, hundreds of stars blink down at us, the sky such a contrast to the one in the city only three hours away. It's sometimes hard to remember I'm not moving back to a different planet at the end of the week.

"Thank you for pushing me to come," I say, my back to the door. "I had a great time."

"Good." He puts his hands in his pockets but doesn't move. Even though Zoe was with us the entire time, it almost feels like we're coming back from a date, and I have no idea what to do with myself. There's a deep want for him that's lived inside my chest my entire life and that will likely never go away. It might have been lessened by our years apart, but now I feel it, whooshing inside me like a lighthouse that's been powered back on.

Eli's tongue darts to wet his bottom lip, and it takes all my willpower not to follow the movement with my eyes. God, this is bad. I'm not seventeen anymore. I know what happens once I leave. Keira's words come back to me, about how Eli was when he learned I was gone for good. Whether they're true or not, I would never want to be responsible for that kind of hurt again. This man deserves the world.

And yet, watching him watch me, I don't think I've ever wanted to throw caution to the wind as much as I do now. I *want* him to touch me. With Michael, and with my ex before him, there was an expectation to being touched. It would lead to a relationship, to the development of something serious between us, which was what I ultimately wanted. I wanted the after more than I wanted the now. It's the opposite here. I trace the hard line of his jaw with my gaze, imagine how he would press his lips to mine if he took that last step between us and finally allowed me to see if his lips still feel the way I remember.

He sees it, too. I don't know whether he wants it like I do, but the widening of his pupils as he takes me in once more is unmistakable. Still, he remains one step away.

I guess I should be grateful my craving is unilateral.

I cross my arms in front of my chest, then say, "Why didn't you say yes to Zach tonight?"

He's taken aback by my question. "What?"

"You should've. You used to love playing." He was part of a league in high school. He mostly practiced during the school year, but I did get to go see him play a few times. Even though I never knew where the ball was or what he was supposed to be doing, I loved cheering when everyone else was.

"That part of my life's over." As if by reflex, he looks over to where Zoe is still sound asleep in the backseat of his SUV. He even adds a small laugh, like the simple thought of him doing something for his own pleasure is ridiculous.

It's in this moment I realize, in the entire month I've been here, I haven't seen Eli do something for himself. Not once. Sure, I don't know what he does when I leave the house, but with the time he gets home from work and the hour he has to leave, I doubt it's much more than sleep. He spends all his waking hours taking care of his employees, of his clients, of Zoe, of *me*. When does he take care of himself?

"You're not a hundred, you know," I say.

"I feel like it, sometimes." He grins, but I don't return it.

It feels wrong. This good man, splitting himself in a thousand ways and being the best father I've ever seen, all the while forgetting he's only twenty-nine.

"Goodnight, Cass," he says, and with one last look, he's headed back to his car.

Meanwhile, all I can do is stare at his strong back and think, if I have one last goal before I leave, let it be this: get Eli Grant to have fun, for once.

Chapter 22

Eleven Years Ago

I t finally happened.

After years of dreaming about what her mouth would taste like and what sounds she would make when she gave up control, the boy kissed the girl.

It didn't happen the way he expected it to. In fact, he didn't know he was going to do it until his lips were pressed to hers. But when he turned to see her lying on her side next to him, the sun setting behind her silhouette, she looked like a goddess, like a supernova the second before it disappears, and it was no longer a want. He *had* to have her like this.

Thankfully, she seemed as eager for him as he was for her, whimpering the second he put his hands around her jaw as if she, too, couldn't wait a second longer.

It was a good day. The best day, really. He still can't believe it happened. *She wants him.*

Yet the harder he tries to be happy about it, the more heartbroken he becomes, because he doesn't see a world where this is forever. A person cannot be hopelessly in love with another and wish for them to remain near the people who make their life a living hell. It doesn't make sense.

And the girl knows it, too.

They've tried acting normal the rest of the day, basking in the glow of newly revealed feelings, but something doesn't feel right. He knows her well enough to figure it's not the kiss itself that upset her. She's trying to be happy, too, but something else is looming in the back of her mind.

Night fell an hour ago, and they're both lying on their backs in the boy's backyard, the waves dancing at the bottom of the cliff at their feet while Coldplay's "Sparks" plays from the boy's phone. The sky is illuminated by the Perseids; the yearly meteor shower that always made the boy believe magic might be real, if only for a couple of nights a year. It doesn't have the same effect tonight. He knows if magic was real, he wouldn't be in this situation right now, waiting for the love of his life to go.

They're supposed to be headed to the UMaine campus in two weeks. He'll be getting back to his roommates, and she's supposed to settle in her room at the dorms. Somehow, the closer they get to the date, the more he doubts that pipe dream will ever come to life.

It's strange, how when he was a kid, his dreams were extravagant. He wanted to build a boat from scratch and sail around the world with it. He was going to become a professional MLB player and be rich enough to get his dad to retire.

Now, his biggest dream is to live a simple life with her.

"It's getting bad," the girl said, the growing bubble of tension finally breaking. Her hand is already in his, but he tugs it closer to his chest. She keeps her eyes on the shooting stars. "His drinking has gotten worse."

She's only brushing the surface with this statement, he knows. The fact that she's even mentioned it is evidence enough of how bad it is.

He's never felt this helpless before.

"Come live here," he says, a hail Mary. "Or stay at Ruth's." The thought of anything bad happening to her in that house makes him want to puke.

"He won't let me."

The boy wants her to look at him. Whenever she puts distance between them, it's never a good sign.

He pulls her hand to his lips, kissing her knuckles. "I'm scared," he admits, which feels cowardly given everything she's going through, but it slips out of his mouth nonetheless.

Finally, she meets his eyes. "Me too."

It's the first time she acknowledges she, too, has doubts about the probability of their plans ever becoming true. Before, she would talk about the nights they'd spend discovering the college town and the parties they'd attend. Now, she's done pretending. They only need to last a few more weeks, but they can feel it slipping between their fingers. And even if they make it, they'll still be so close to home. Eli chose his college specifically for that reason. He wanted to be there in case his father had another health scare, and his family needed him. But for her? It might just be a prolongation of her penitentiary.

"I'll understand, you know," the boy starts before he can even wrap his head around what he's saying. "If you need to go." The words sound strangled, like they're being yanked out of his throat.

Her eyes fill, and then she kisses him. He doesn't know if it's because she wants him to stop talking, or because she's actually considering it.

It doesn't matter. He'll always take whatever she's willing to give him anyway.

Chapter 23

I'm leaving tomorrow.

The house is completely empty. The money from the furniture sale has been sent to the two organizations we settled on. I'm supposed to hear back from the realtor later this afternoon about a potential offer that's coming in for the house. I only have one thing left to do before I'm ready to go.

I don't bother knocking before I step inside the Grants' house, which is in its worst state of disarray since I walked in for the first time. Sleeping bags are strung over the couch. Bags of food litter the entryway, laundry is strewn everywhere, and half-filled suitcases are open on the floor. I'd forgotten Eli and Zoe are leaving for Mrs. Grant's cottage by the lake tomorrow until now.

"Cassie!" Zoe shouts from where she's "folding" clothes inside a suitcase, toppling over a pile of T-shirts as she runs into my arms. Eli looks up as I hug his daughter, brows furrowed.

"What are you doing here?" he asks, not necessarily cold, but not particularly happy, either. In the two days since the restaurant and the strange tension on Ruth's front porch, he's been more distant. When he returned from work, he didn't invite me to stay for a drink. It was as if I couldn't get out of his hair fast enough. I don't know what I expected for our last days together, but it wasn't that. I won't get into it with him, though. Not when I'm almost gone.

"I'm kidnapping you," I say, pulling him up from where he's packing in the kitchen. "Or rather the opposite of kidnapping. I'm forcing you away."

"Why?"

"Because I want you to go have fun." I push him toward his running shoes. He's already in a sportsy T-shirt and loose shorts. Perfect.

"I can't. I need to finish—"

"I'll take care of all of it." They're leaving for a week. I can figure out what they need for a few days away in a fully furnished cabin. "You will go to the baseball game, and you won't come back early. You'll stay out and have a drink or five with the guys."

"But—"

"I told you I'd get you to say no this summer." I take a step closer to him. "And that can also mean saying no to being responsible, for once."

He still appears hesitant, but when I hand him the glove I found in the basement—yes, I may have spent a lot of time looking for it while Zoe was napping yesterday—he finally cracks a grin.

"Thank you."

I feel like I've just won an Olympic medal.

He goes to give Zoe a kiss, grabs his stuff, and only gives me one last look before he's gone.

"So." I turn to Zoe. "What else do we need to pack?"

I get to explore the entire house to finish packing those bags.

During my time babysitting, Zoe and I have kept to the main living areas, the backyard, and her bedroom, so I haven't seen much of the rest of the house. Now, given the excuse to do so, I was happy to rediscover the rooms Eli and I made good memories in over the years. What I love most, though, is all the glimpses I get of Eli in unexpected places. The guest bedroom upstairs I stayed in once when Ruth was gone to Malaga with her girlfriends now houses Eli's work desk, complete with handwritten recipes and Post-its with random ideas like *portable fire pit for s'mores?* I wrote a yes on that one.

What gave the best insight, though, was obviously Mr. and Mrs. Grant's old bedroom, which has now become Eli's. I never would've walked in there voluntarily, only following Zoe in when she said it was where her dad stored the beach towels—it wasn't—but since I got a glimpse, I haven't been able to stop thinking about it. What else could I learn from Eli in there? The room was mostly neat compared to the rest of the house, with his khaki comforter pulled tight across the bed and pillows arranged neatly. Pajama pants were strung over the rocking chair while a pair of boxers sat on the floor. Images of what Eli might look like wearing only those may or may not have floated through my mind. A few picture frames sat on his nightstands, but I didn't have enough time to examine them, and I've spent the night obsessing over what else I missed in there.

After we were done packing way too many bags for a two-person, week-long trip, it was past Zoe's bedtime, but she was too excited to show any signs of fatigue. It took four stories, including an incredibly tedious one about a gnome who travels the world, before she finally fell asleep. Then, I came downstairs and watched TV for a bit, but my mind wasn't in it. It was stuck in that damn bedroom.

Finally, at midnight, I gave in and walked back in. Just for a little tease. I wouldn't sneak too much.

But here I am, thirty minutes later, full-on snooping. I wish I felt remorse, but I can't muster the feeling. I'm enjoying it too much. If I liked seeing Eli's calendar on the fridge or his packed lunches inside it for glimpses into his daily life, this is like winning the lottery. For example, on the shelves in his closet, he still has the baseball trophies he won in college. I didn't even know he'd played in college. I knew he was good, but I didn't think he was *that* good. Our time together was never about our separate lives. He did know most of what happened at home, and I knew he was going to graduate with honors, but we barely spoke about the time we spent in our respective schools. He knew I hated that part of my life and didn't want to relive it, and I guess he didn't want to sound braggy about the easy time he was having.

The picture frames on his nightstands end up featuring Zoe, his siblings, and Mr. Grant in what must be his forties. His head is out of his truck, and he's giving us what Eli and I used to call his president smile—all teeth, wide and bright.

Up to this point, I've kept myself away from the drawers, but God, they're appealing. The top one on the nightstand is open an inch, which is the most teasing image I've ever seen. The fact that I'm leaving tomorrow is probably making it worse. I want to absorb as much information as I can before I don't see him for who knows how long.

I glance at that drawer again. Cracked open is basically open, which makes it fair play.

Fuck it.

I tiptoe to it even though I'm alone with a sleeping Zoe in this house, then peek inside.

It's a typical bedside drawer; an amalgam of things someone would find in their pockets at the end of the day. Fluffy hair elastics, change, pens, receipts, random charging cables. I don't find any condoms, and a part of me is relieved, even though he could be keeping them somewhere else. I go to close the drawer when something catches my eye under the layer of items. I know I shouldn't touch anything, but I've seen something like this before. In Ruth's things.

I'm careful as I pull a piece of scrapbook paper out of the drawer. It's got Ruth written all over it, with feathers and fabric I've seen in her things, but also with collages I've seen her do before. And in the middle of the page, the main piece: a picture of two kids I recognize immediately.

It's him and me.

I'm fifteen, I think, making him sixteen. We're facing away from the camera, which explains why I never knew this photo existed.

Two years before he saw me as more than a friend. We're sitting cross-legged on the picnic table in Ruth's yard, looking at the water. Eli's head is thrown back, dark strands slipping back as he's laughing. I can hear it through the picture; this loud noise that could be considered boisterous, but that to me only ever represented happiness. I'm turned toward him, and while I'm not cackling like he is, the smile I'm wearing shows I'm simply glad to see him so happy. I know it, because watching him laugh was the best way to make me smile. I can't see my eyes clearly, but if I could zoom, I know they would have *lovesick* written all over them.

"Guess I shouldn't be surprised to find you here."

I jump back, so shocked I drop the scrapbook which falls in slow-motion over the bed.

Eli is leaning against the doorframe, his face unreadable. His eyes are glassy, which confirms he listened to me and had a couple drinks. His hair is wind-swept, a strand falling over his dark eyes. He looks delicious.

"You've always been nosy."

I can't say much to that. I *am* rifling through his things.

I can't find it in me to be quippy, either. Not after how rattled this picture has made me. Why would he keep it in his bedside drawer?

"When did she give this to you?" I ask, not bothering with apologies.

"The day you left."

It's difficult to swallow. That means after Ruth gave me money and a packed bag of stuff I might need, she went to see Eli in the morning to tell him I was gone. She gave him something to remember me by. She knew I wouldn't be back. Knew we'd never see each other again.

My eyes burn. I breathe through it.

"And you've kept it all these years."

"I have."

I blink. "Why?"

He takes a step forward, and while it's steady, something about him isn't. There's a part that was guarded all month that seems to have been unlocked.

"Why do you think?"

I close my eyes, the sweet scent of him now everywhere around me.

He steps even closer, his breath warm against my ear as he whispers, "Hasn't it haunted you, too? That we never got our chance?"

I'm trembling, heart like a hummingbird in my throat. If only he knew.

"You told me to go," I whisper on an exhale.

"I couldn't ask you to stay," Eli says now, looking as pained as he did that night eleven years ago.

I want to tell him that he should've, that if he'd given me a reason, I might have taken it, and yet I know he's right. I never would've been happy here, no matter how much I loved him.

"I still would've liked a goodbye," he says, his voice smaller. "I thought we had more time. Weeks, or days, at least. Why leave like that?"

My throat is tight, but I still say, "Because I knew if I saw you, I wouldn't be able to leave, and I *needed* to leave." The desperation in my words gets to him, because his eyes soften. I think a part of him must've known something had happened to get me to escape that way. And I realize now he needs more than that. "You remember the promise I made you when I was fifteen?"

His eyebrows string together.

"You told me if..." I inhale deeply, hating to relive that memory for even a second. "You told me if he ever lifted a hand at me, I had to leave. You made me promise."

Now his face doesn't just soften. It melts, every trace of anger disappearing from his traits, replaced not by pity, but by hurt for the girl I once was. The girl I fear I still am, sometimes.

"But I'm sorry I left that way," I tell him now. "If I could've stayed, I would have."

"I know you would," he says, and then he's right there, his nose to my temple, and he's inhaling deeply, almost like he wants to commit me to memory the way I did by going through his room.

His charcoal T-shirt looks soft. I reach forward, tracing a soft hand against the fabric over his stomach, and it indeed is soft, and hard, and warm. One of his hands lands on the small of my back, his touch as delicate as mine.

"Can I ask you something?" I say.

"Anything."

"Why haven't you kissed me?"

I feel his sharp inhale against my skin, but he doesn't move away.

I'm leaving tomorrow. I have nothing left to lose. "Tell me if I imagined it, but I thought there was... something here, still. Thought you might've wanted to."

"You think I haven't touched you for lack of wanting?" He leans down even closer, his lips brushing against my neck as he whispers, "Think I haven't dreamed of the way your mouth tastes?"

My inhales are shallow, head light. I arch to give him more space against me. His breath is warm on my skin. I want more.

Just as I'm about to beg for it, he pulls away and my body becomes frigid. "But I'm not kissing you goodbye. I can't do it."

I squeeze my thumbs under my fingers, crack them. Eli reaches forth, and I have a second of hope that maybe he's changed his mind, but he only pulls on my fingers so my hands loosen.

"So that's it, then?" I feel too raw, too exposed.

He drags a hand through his hair. "I don't know what you want from me."

I hate the despair in his voice. Hate that I'm the one who put it there, and that his words echo the ones I told my sister only weeks ago.

"I'm sorry. I'll go." I move past him. If he can't do the goodbye kiss, I can't do the goodbye, period. However, midway across the room, I turn. If we're leaving things like this, at least one more thing needs to be put to rest. "I hope you know it was never about you. You were always the best part of this place."

He wears his heart on his face—the hurt, the longing, the fear. It's all written on there.

He shakes his head as he rubs a hand over his mouth. I don't think I've ever seen him so perturbed. He's raw, too; all the emotions he's suppressed since I got here come back to the surface. I stand still as I watch him process it all. Then, his shoulders straighten as if he's come to a conclusion.

"Fuck it," he mutters, and in two steps, his hands are on me, his mouth presses to mine, and I take my first full breath in eleven years.

There's nothing tentative about it. He kisses me like a starved man, like he might have been dreaming about it since the moments our lips parted last. One of his hands grips the back of my head, his other arm wrapped around my lower back so I'm pressed as close to him as can be. I grip his shirt as he angles my head back to access more of me.

Just like the rest of him, his kiss is familiar yet entirely different. Whereas eighteen-year-old Eli was cautious and exploring, twenty-nine-year-old Eli is confident in what he's doing. The way his fingertips scratch my neck, how he's taken control of me... I don't think I'll ever recover. Seeing him, being close to him, was one thing, but this? There's no moving on from it.

The movement of his lips feels like an assault, nipping at my bottom lip when I grind against his hip, his tongue tangling with mine the moment I let him in. He's hard against me, and the feel of it makes heat pool between my legs. I don't think my body has ever felt this wired up.

His mouth tastes like mint and a hint of whiskey, but also like something that's entirely *him*. I stand on my tiptoes so I can wrap my arms around his head, wanting him closer, deeper.

And as fast as it all happened, his hands are gone. My swollen lips sting as I watch him step back. He breathes loudly, eyes not meeting mine. He rubs a hand over his mouth, again and again as he stares at the bedroom floor. As heavenly as I'm feeling, he looks like I've dragged him to hell. Finally, he says, "Guess you got your goodbye kiss after all."

"Eli..."

He walks out before I can say anything.

Chapter 24

Back when I moved into my first apartment in the city, I couldn't sleep for weeks. The amount of noise surrounding me felt otherworldly. I couldn't ignore the drunk people shouting in the street below at 3:00 a.m., or the honks and alarms going off at all times, or the neighbors having loud, intense sex all the time. It was like a zoo. My home might have sometimes been loud, but I'd never known anything except a quiet town, and here was constant stimulation at full intensity. It was unnerving, but also strangely exhilarating. I eventually got used to it and learned how to sleep through it all, even when my sixty-year-old roommate got diagnosed with sleep apnea and started using a machine that could rouse the dead throughout the night. It became the new normal. In fact, the first night I spent back in Cape Weston, I missed that noise. The utter stillness was destabilizing, kind of like the world had shut down around me. And now, I'm in a limbo where nowhere is comfortable. Not here, not there.

As the sun slowly rises above the ocean, I stand in the driveway, taking in Ruth's house one last time. Yesterday morning, the realtor left me a message to confirm they'd received a nice offer for a move–in date in September. A "lovely young family of four," she said. I should be happy nice people are going to get the house that was so good to me, but the only thing I feel right now is lost. I don't know what I want, don't know where I need to be, don't know what the hell I'm doing with my life. I gaze at the flower beds I've slowly brought back to life, turquoise hydrangeas starting to bloom. It's nothing close to how Ruth used to keep it, but I don't have a green thumb, and that was the best I could do. The gnome is still there, smiling at me, waiting for new people to keep the key I left under it. My gaze slowly drifts left, and the pressure in my chest turns into complete inability to draw in a breath.

Last night shouldn't have happened. When Eli left and didn't come out of the guest bedroom, I let myself out and cursed myself all the way to Ruth's house. This was not how the month was supposed to end. In fact, he was not supposed to come into play this summer. I was here to tie up some loose ends and collect myself before going back to my real life. I was not here to kiss the love of my teenage life and fall in love with his daughter. I was supposed to want to rush out of here once I was done.

So why can't I get into my car?

I should already be on my way to stop by Keira's and Mom's to say goodbye if I want to avoid as much traffic as possible. It's a perfect travel day, with clear skies and no chance of rain. The sunlight is warm on my skin even at the early hour, the sea breeze rustling softly through my hair. The car is all packed, filled to the brim with the stuff I kept from Ruth's, and all the scrapbooking material I haven't sifted through entirely yet. I'm *ready*.

My phone buzzes in succession in my purse.

Em: Can't wait to see you

Em: The whole unit is hyped that you're back

Em: Viet takeout tonight? xx

Em: Also, Betty has a thing on Wednesday night and asked me to ask you if you could cover her and do a double? LMK!

A knot settles in my stomach, one I haven't felt in weeks, and it only heightens my state of crisis. I thought I was doing better. These past weeks, I didn't feel dread when waking up in the morning. I thought I was, if not happy, then at least ready to function again.

I look back at the neighboring house, stock still in the morning light. Zoe will be waking up soon, padding downstairs so she can pour herself a bowl of cereal—or more like *try* to pour a bowl of cereal, drop most of the box next to the bowl, then ask for someone to come help her. That someone was me for a couple of days, when Eli was sleeping after having come back late from an event. He'll be getting up, too, his hair mussed from sleep, and also from my hands having tugged at it yesterday. Will he be thinking about that kiss the way I am, the way I did all night? Will he be regretting that he ever saw me again? Or regretting that we stopped after only a kiss?

My eyes alternate between my phone, my car, and Eli's house. Phone, car, house. Phone, car, house.

The last time I felt this lost was when Ruth told me to go all those years ago. It was the same dilemma, too. A place I never wanted to stay in, but the man in it who made me rethink it all. Except last time, I did want to see what was on the other side of that choice. The city represented hope. Now, I know what's waiting for me: shifts I will have to endure rather than enjoy, a lonely apartment, and an even lonelier heart.

Me: Free to talk?

Em: Always <3

When Eli gets out of the door while holding Zoe's hand, I'm waiting for him.

He climbs down the three porch steps before he notices me and stops. While Zoe's face lights up, his is blank. Or maybe blank isn't the right word. Guarded is more like it. Then, he takes me and my large backpack in, and confusion seeps through.

Looking at Zoe, I say, "I was wondering if you were still looking for that birthday crown braid?"

"Yes!" she shouts way too loudly for a Saturday morning at 7:00 a.m. She lets go of her father to hug me, then says, "I have to go say goodbye to my caterpillar friend. Give me a sec." She's off running toward the backyard before I can say a word.

Eli hasn't moved a single muscle, his expression wary. He's wearing a backward hat with a simple black T-shirt and jeans, and God, he looks good. He hasn't shaved this morning, and looking at that scruff only makes me remember how it felt on my palm, against my cheeks, my lips.

"I don't understand."

"I'm giving myself the rest of the summer." Giving *us* the rest of the summer. I'm not ready to go back, and I don't want to let go of this just yet. It'll be one last summer here, with him, for old time's sake. "If you'll still have me."

I went over my dilemma with Emily while she was on her way to the hospital, and she agreed I should stay. In fact, her exact words were, "If I see you at work tomorrow, I'll kick your ass." We do love a supportive friend.

His throat works. "Any particular reason why?"

I wrap my arms around my middle. "I heard there's a world-renowned choir recital at the end of August. Couldn't miss that."

Slowly, *finally*, his guard falls, and I swear, the small but genuine smile that overtakes his face could power an entire city.

"So?" I take a few steps in his direction, stopping far enough that it's safe. "Will you have me?"

"Yeah. We'll have you."

Chapter 25

The lake is an image of stillness.

We might only be an hour and a half away from Cape Weston, but I would believe you if you said we'd traveled to another country. Flatness and long strips of sand have been replaced by mountains and lush greenery, with large freshwater lakes interspersed throughout the land. The forest around the cottage is so dense, it's as if we're completely blocked from the rest of the world. I never want to leave.

I've been to this cottage once, when it still belonged to Eli's grandfather. I was fourteen, and I remember thinking I'd never seen a place so peaceful. Sitting in an Adirondack chair on the long dock that overlooks the water, nothing but the sound of birds chirping and wind rustling around me, I still agree. It feels light here. It also helps that an enormous weight has been taken off my shoulders by delaying my return to work. I feel like I can breathe again, knowing I have until summer ends to get myself ready.

The quiet is torn to shreds when Zoe comes running out of the cottage, dressed in a vintage princess costume—or is it a fairy? Behind her, Charlie, Eli's sister, follows, also dressed in a long, medieval dress. The two of us were never that close since she was five years younger than me, but I was genuinely happy to see her when we arrived yesterday.

"Lead me to your dragons, Princess Zoe," Charlie shouts theatrically, which makes Zoe giggle. The two of them run around the wide yard, Charlie going all-in with split jumps.

And then, the star of the show emerges from the cottage. I clap my hands while tapping my feet against the dock I'm sitting on.

"What a pretty princess you make!" I tell Eli, who obviously wouldn't have refused his daughter anything, even if it meant wearing a too-small velvet dress and one of those cone-like hats with hanging ribbons.

He curtsies when he reaches me.

"Where did you even find these?" I ask.

"The cedar closet downstairs."

I brush a thumb against the ribbon hanging by his face. He traces the movement with his gaze, which makes me realize just how close I've gotten. I let go, knotting my hands behind my back. He follows that movement, too.

We haven't mentioned what happened in his room since it happened, and I'm not sure whether that's a good or a bad thing. I don't know whether he regrets it and wants to forget it even happened. I know I'm torn about it too. I'm still leaving by the end of the summer. There's no future for me in Cape Weston. But then, I catch sight of him licking his thumb after opening a jar of tomato sauce and remember how that mouth felt against mine, and I'm not so sure I want to enforce my self-preservation instincts anymore.

"They're kind of scary," I say. The bottom of his dress has obviously been eaten by whatever animal or insect lives down here during the winter, and dark stains cover the burgundy material.

"Don't tell me. I had nightmares of these costumes for years." He fingers the velvet and shivers. "I don't even want to know where Mom got them."

"Some creepy guy on Craigslist, probably."

"My skin is suddenly very fucking itchy."

"Cassie!" Zoe shouts. "You need to be a princess, too!"

"Yeah, get your share of termites, too," Eli says.

"I think I'll stay like this, thanks."

The moment I say it, it's as if a magnet brings his gaze down my body, and he realizes I'm only wearing a bikini top and jean shorts. I've gained weight with all the meals Eli's cooked for me, and I now fill out both much better than I did at the beginning of the summer. This is the best I have felt about my body in months, and the way he's looking at me only makes me like it more.

"Eyes up here, Grant."

He has the decency to blush as he does look back up, but the lust in his gaze is unmistakable. Even wearing a nasty dress and stupid princess hat, he makes me weak in the knees.

"Give me that," I say, grabbing the hat from his head and putting it on mine.

"I think you make a prettier princess than I do." He has the audacity to tuck a strand of hair under the hat, the simple feel of his finger against my forehead enough to make me shiver.

I need to get my shit together. If the kiss was a one-time thing, I can't go around obsessing over his every touch for the rest of the summer.

A squeal pulls our attention to the lawn, where Charlie is currently on all fours, carrying Zoe on her back like a horse. That woman is a true medical student. She doesn't half-ass anything.

Another sound quickly makes me tense. Buzzing—too loud to be a mosquito. Automatically, I start slapping the air around me like a lunatic. Do I know it's the worst possible thing to do with bees? Yes, but I've never been good at remaining calm in this kind of situation.

"What the hell are you doing?" Eli says, the dock creaking under us.

The buzzing gets louder, the bee sounding like it's right in my ear. I run around the chair, not looking where I'm going so long as I escape it. In the end, I succeed.

By accidentally stepping off the dock and falling straight into the water.

It's not nearly as cold as the Atlantic Ocean, the lake warmed by long, scalding July days, but it still shocks me. I emerge a second later, gasping, the princess hat hanging crookedly against my temple, hair plastered to my face. Zoe is laughing from afar, and I'm pretty sure I hear her shout, "Mermaid princess!" At least the buzzing has disappeared.

To my left, a hand appears.

"We can't keep doing this," Eli says.

"It's just the second time."

"Just?"

"There was a bee," I say as I grab his extended arm.

"So?"

"I'm allergic."

"I'm aware you *think* you're allergic," he says, because of course he does. How many times has this exact scenario happened in my life? A hundred? Every time we'd have juice or soda on the beach, we'd get swarmed. I eventually learned to chug my drinks and toss them in the farthest trash can. He loved to tease me that I'd never actually had an anaphylactic reaction and that having had a rash after a bee sting as a kid did not automatically make me allergic to them, but I've always erred on the cautious side. "But was it stinging you?"

"Wasn't about to fuck around and find out. What with your amazing First-Aid skills and all."

"You'll never let me live that down, will you?" He's still holding on to my hand, his skin sun-warmed.

"You just give such great ammunition."

"You know what? Get your ass out of the water yourself," he teases, letting go of my hand and straightening up on the dock. Wet circles have darkened the knees of his jeans—jeans that are hugging every curve of his thick thighs and round ass, might I add.

"All right, all right." I hold my hand out again. "Please?"

The poor guy sees nothing coming. He leans forward because of course, he won't leave me to fend for myself, and the second I get a good grip on him again, I pull. He barely resists, toppling over the dock and splashing next to me.

Eli's dark hair sticks to his temples and neck when his head pops back up. He rakes it back. "You little shit." Humor is painted across his every feature, and God, how good it feels to see this man so unabashedly carefree and happy.

"That'll teach you to laugh about my allergy."

"It's a fake allergy!"

I grab his shoulders and start putting weight over them. "Want me to dunk you again?"

His hands land on my hips, thumbs pressing lightly against my waist. "I'd like to see you try."

We're too close. Our chests are nearly brushing, breaths mingling. Water droplets cover the freckle cloud under his eye and slip down his solid jaw. I want to follow them with my fingers, my nose, my tongue. I want to know if he tastes salty like I imagine, if the skin of his neck would smell like soap and salt air the way it did two nights ago. I feel him studying me, too, his grip never faltering. He's not moving away, either.

When his whiskey eyes meet mine, he licks a drop from his plush bottom lip as he gives my hips another squeeze, and I know somehow that if it was just the two of us, we wouldn't stop at that.

Yeah. Whatever happened between us? I don't think it's over just yet.

Chapter 26

People always talk about perfect summer days. You hear about sunlight so bright, you have to squint to see in front of you. There's a warm breeze and a gigantic pool or lake to cool yourself, and stacks of cold drinks and fresh-fruit popsicles that melt all over your hand before you have time to finish them. Close friends are around, or maybe it's just you, soaking up every single second of the peace and quiet to recharge your social battery.

Today is nothing like that. The sky is cloudy as Eli drives the boat toward the middle of the lake, a plush towel wrapped around my shoulders to counter the biting wind. The air is thick with humidity, tiny hairs slipping out of my bun and curling around my face. We're listening to Zoe's idea of a musical masterpiece—the newest Kid's Bops album. I just ate a cold sandwich made of almost-stale bread and the last slice of ham we had.

And to me, it *is* the perfect summer day.

I haven't been able to stop laughing since Charlie told us the story of the patient she saw at the hospital who had unfortunately "slipped" onto a lava lamp and gotten it stuck in an untoward place, followed by Zoe saying in a comically serious voice, "Daddy, that's not possible, is it?" Eli threw his sister a glare before changing the subject and asking Zoe if she wanted to go swim, which got her mind away from the lamp debacle. I passed on going in with them once the boat had come to a stop, and after they both jumped, I laid on my back, enjoying the luxurious leather seats on the back of the boat. Apparently, Richard, the man Charlie's and Eli's mother got remarried to, is not only a mechanic, but also the owner of fifty auto shops across New England. Now, the two of them spend most of their time at one of his properties in France, only coming back to the cottage every few months.

"Scoot over."

I open one eye to find Charlie hovering over me, her body shadowing the faint glow of the sun peeking through the clouds. She's holding out the plate of watermelon I cut before leaving, condensation having formed on the side. I give her enough space to lie next to me and lean on my elbows to take a bite out of the thick slice of fruit. Splashes come to our left, where Eli is throwing Zoe into the water over and over again, and she keeps asking for more, her mustard-yellow life jacket keeping her afloat.

"I wasn't happy when Mom remarried, but right now I'd marry old Dick myself if I could." Charlie finishes her own piece of watermelon, then lies down, her honey-colored hair tangling with mine. The boat *is* pretty great. I'm pretty sure you can call it a small yacht, actually.

"Sugar baby instead of doctor? I approve."

"I'm embarrassed to say how many times the thought has come to mind since I started school."

I've seen the way medical students and residents get overworked and underpaid—or not paid at all—so I can't blame her.

"Hospitals will do that to you," I say as I dig through the family-size bag of Sour Patch Kids Eli got for me on the car ride here.

"Right, Eli was telling me you're a nurse now."

I give her a half smile. I don't know her enough to spill my guts out to her, and yet there's a certain kinship healthcare workers develop between each other that can't be explained. You could find another person wearing scrubs crying in the hallway and join them in a bawling session, no questions asked. We see and experience so many hard things that only someone else in the field can understand. It's probably what pushes me to say, "I'm kind of in a 'rethinking my entire career path' phase at the moment, but yeah, I am."

She nods, and I can feel her understanding even without words.

"How long are you off for?" I ask.

"A week. Thank God."

Charlie's the kind of woman who seems to run a mile a minute with endless energy, but even through her giddy exterior, I can see the fatigue. Another hospital worker thing, probably.

"Zoe is really happy to have you here," I say.

Another delighted shriek comes from the water.

"I could say the same about you." Charlie turns her head to me, her gaze hidden behind her oversized heart-shaped sunglasses. "Speaking of, are you banging my brother?"

I'm glad I was done eating, because I would've choked right there. "Jesus, Charlie." My chest and neck flush so suddenly, I sit a little straighter for some wind.

"What? Too late to act prudish now."

"Why's that?"

"Because you've been eye fucking since I got here."

I wish I had more restraint, but I can't fight my gaze from drifting to him in the water. His daughter is using him as her own floating device even though he doesn't have a life jacket on, and despite his heavy breaths from swimming in place for so long, he lets her climb all over him, circling her small ankles with his hands while laughing.

"I'm not," I say, but even I can tell it's weak. Probably because while we technically haven't done anything more than kiss once, I've imagined doing more too many times to count. Last night, when we finished our three-way card game and Charlie suggested we go to bed, Eli followed me upstairs, and when our paths diverged—him toward the room he shares with Zoe, mine toward the one I share with Charlie—the back of his hand brushed mine, and our pinkies interlaced for barely a second. It was nothing, yet my body felt like a shaken bottle of soda, bubbles fizzing in my body and making me lightheaded. It felt like being young and spotting a cute guy on the beach, then daydreaming about your future together—except even in middle school, that guy was Eli for me.

Charlie hums. "Then you might not be banging physically, but you sure are banging mentally."

"I don't think I even want to wrap my head around the sentence you just created." I also don't want to think about the fact that she's not saying *I* am looking at him like that, but that we both are.

Charlie sits straighter, leaning her arms on the back of the boat and tilting her head toward another bout of subtle sunshine. "You can deny it all you want, but I know my brother."

"It's... complicated," I conclude. It's not like I could give her an answer even if I wanted to. The line between friendship and *more* has been crossed, both now and in the past, but beyond that, I'm clueless. Our situation isn't any less doomed than it was before.

Charlie doesn't try to dig for more. Instead, she looks back at him and her niece. "He deserves to have someone who brings him happiness."

The way she says it, her tone almost wistful, has my stomach twisting. "What does that mean?"

"He'd kill me if he knew I was telling you this, but he's had a hard time since Liz left."

"With Zoe, you mean?"

"With everything."

"I thought they were never serious." I try to keep my voice even, but jealousy still seeps through, which is stupid. We both had lives in my time away, and once I leave, he'll have one again. The thought feels like flames licking my insides, but it's the truth.

"They weren't, I think, but still. They were together when she left." She leans over me to pick a gummy from the bag I'd forgotten about, but she doesn't eat it, only twists it in her hand. "I think he felt guilty about it, too."

"Why would he feel guilty?"

She shakes her head. "In his weird Eli-way of thinking, Liz left because of him, which means he's the reason Zoe lost her mother. Pretty sure it's been keeping him up at night, although he'll never admit it to me."

I gape at her. This is crazy. No one would ever think Eli is responsible for any of that. Yet the more I repeat her words in my head, the more sense it makes. Eli *would* feel like it was his fault, even when he was the one who stayed. He would take responsibility for everything that could affect the well-being of his child.

When I was with Michael, we had this recurrent fight about cereal. It was stupid, but it drove me crazy. I have this particular brand of wheat cereal I like. It was what Mom and I sometimes ate for dinner when it was just the two of us. "A secret treat," she'd say with a wink, and I'd feel so special. Michael always said they tasted like ass. However, when he was done with his chunky, protein-filled cereal and needed a replacement, he would dig through mine. I rarely ate it, but when I had a craving for it, I wanted it there. And half the time, I'd grab the box to find it practically empty, only the crappy, crumbled pieces left at the bottom of the box. How many times did I confront him about it, only for him to say he'd get some for me the next time he went grocery shopping? He couldn't understand why it made me so mad. Couldn't take responsibility, even for something as small as eating my cereal, and here is this man, burying himself in guilt over the actions of someone else.

"I think part of him felt abandoned, too. After Dad died, it kind of felt like our main link was gone. We were... drifting. I had to leave for med school first, and then Mom met Richard, and they started traveling. Felix left a while after that for some tech job in Taiwan. Eli was the only one who stayed. And then she left him."

The small yacht rocks under us against the waves of another boat passing by. My eyes, like a pendulum following gravity, return to Eli. He's watching Zoe climb back onto the boat, but as if feeling me, he looks up. My favorite smile on Earth greets me, and my heart shatters anew.

"He's the best person I know." I don't mean to say it aloud, only realizing I did when I hear Charlie's hum of agreement. Eli hasn't looked away, and seeing my lips move without hearing what I've said has him quirking a brow up.

"Pretty sure he thinks the same thing of you," Charlie tells me with a tap on the thigh before she rises to help Zoe dry off. Meanwhile, all I can think of is, this man's heart needs to be protected with heavy padding and concrete, and whether I like it or not, I'm likely to be a sledgehammer to his glass walls.

Chapter 27

We return earlier than planned from our boat ride when a summer storm breaks across the lake. We try to hide under the barely-there cover of the boat, but we all end up drenched to our bones. Back at the cottage, we take turns in the shower to warm up while Eli gets dinner started; a hearty stew with bright carrots and potatoes bigger than my hands from the market we crossed on the way here, and a tangy sauce coating the tender pieces of beef. After dinner, Charlie does the dishes with Zoe who offers to help but only sends water splashing around and uses wine glasses as floating boats in the soapy water.

"I'll go make a fire," I say, heading toward the squeaky patio door overlooking the now calm water reflecting a barely-there sliver of moon. Even so, the dark water is shimmering, a silverish hue coloring the soft current.

"You don't have to," Eli says. He was picking up toys in the living room but is already next to the door, putting his shoes on. "I can do it."

"Sit your male-savior ass down and let her do it," Charlie says over her shoulder.

I stand on my tiptoes to whisper in his ear, "Wait until she learns you wouldn't let me mow your lawn."

"Is chivalry a bad thing now?" he says, to which Charlie and I answer with a loud, "Yes!"

He shakes his head, then says in a low voice, "For the record, I didn't want you doing it because watching you was too much of a distraction."

Goosebumps cover my arms—at his words or his closeness, I'm not sure. "Sounds like a you problem."

His throat works as his eyes alternate between mine. "Indeed, it is."

"Eli, let the poor woman get to her fire-making," Charlie shouts.

He steps back with his hands raised in defense, leaving me to go outside by myself. Frankly, I wouldn't have minded his help—I haven't built a fire since I moved to the city—but I wasn't about to admit it, and after a few tries, it finally catches. I call everyone out, and Eli brings out a jumbo bag of marshmallows. I'm pretty sure he got it knowing I can go through a regular bag by myself.

The fire is small and remains shaky throughout the evening, and no one dares say a word about it. We pass the bag of marshmallows around the circle, taking turns roasting them over sticks we found in the wood surrounding the cottage.

Charlie picks at her melted marshmallow with two fingers, trying to unstick it from her branch. "Isn't it weird how we're always so careful to thoroughly clean everything we eat with, but when it comes to marshmallows, we just grab random branches full of dirt and call it a day?"

"Risking salmonella is part of the thrill," I say, watching a flame latch to my treat, turning its edges brown, then black.

Eli leans over and blows a strong breath, extinguishing the flame. "You know you don't have to worry the local firefighters every time you toast a marshmallow, right?"

"I like mine to taste like pure soot. Sue me." I bite into the crispy, charcoal-colored sides of it and hum in pleasure. Pure, summery perfection. Some of the marshmallow drips onto my finger, which I lick before it can stick. When I turn to my right, I find Eli's gaze stuck on me, dark as the lake before us. Heat covers my body, and it has nothing to do with the shaky fire.

I grab one last marshmallow to grill and catch Charlie over the fire mouthing, "Eye fucking." I roll my eyes, but honestly, I can't really deny it. The way he was staring at me did make me feel like he was undressing me in his mind.

"All right, Zoe Bear, time for bed," Eli says, standing to pick up Zoe who's already half-asleep on one of the camping chairs.

"I'll take her," Charlie says, grabbing her niece from his arms. "I'm tired, too." She throws me a wink then walks inside. Eli doesn't resist for once, reclaiming his seat next to mine on the flat boulder that doubles as a bench, covered by an afghan that kept our bottoms warm.

This is the first time we've been truly alone since that night in his bedroom, and while nothing's changed, everything has. We can't brush this off as simple friendship. You don't kiss someone you feel nothing for like that. Like you'll die if you don't taste them.

But everything I told Charlie earlier was true; it *is* complicated. No matter how much we could want it to work, it can't last.

Light waves lap at the sandy shore of the lake, reflecting the flickering flames and the stars that speckle it like a million infinitesimal diamonds. My neck hurts from looking up, so I scoot off the rock and lie on the humid sand.

"Don't you want a blanket for that?" Eli asks even though he's already joining me.

"I probably ingested a few bugs and pieces of dirt from my stick just now. I think I can handle lying on the ground."

He chuckles, then exhales as he looks up, too, not in fatigue but in awe.

The Milky Way paints the sky like melted butter, while the Big Dipper and Little Dipper—the only two constellations I know how to recognize—are so bright, it feels like I could reach out and touch them.

"My father was the one who taught me how to spot the Dippers as big saucepans in the sky," I say. It's one of the first memories I have. Dad, with his hair not peppered with gray yet, pointing at the sky and telling me about them, like he was an astrologist, and he was sharing this secret with me. "For years, I thought there was actual kitchenware in the sky." I wrap my arms around my chest. "I wish I could go back to a time when I could be this naive," I say.

"Do you really?"

It sounds simple at first. Jumping back to a time when I didn't know how little control we have over our own futures? How holding on tightly to people won't make them stay, and how you can't erase where you came from, even if you change your name and move away? It'd be nice to have this bliss, even for a second. But then, it would also mean going back to a time when I had to endure what people said and did to me without being able to leave and build a life I could, if not love, then at least like.

"I don't know," is what I answer.

He hums, and we return to our stargazing, the fire crackling behind us, frogs croaking distantly. The scent of smoke blends with the citrus of Eli's shampoo and the musk and brine of the lake. The air has cooled since this afternoon, and the humid wind makes me shudder.

"You cold?" Eli asks.

I shrug.

"Come here." He lifts one arm to create a cozy nook for me to crawl into. It sounds like an excuse to touch me if I've ever heard one, and honestly, I would be stupid to say no to that. It feels like a silent boundary has been crossed, and we're both okay with it. I shift to my left, immediately comforted by the warmth of his body that's better than any weighted blanket I've ever tried. My temple leans on the side of his torso, his bicep under my neck and fingers carelessly draped across my shoulder, tickling me with each movement. It feels as if my entire nervous system has been rerouted to the spots where his body touches mine.

"This would be a good time to show off your astronomy skills and describe the sky to charm me."

"Sadly, I wasn't sure what you meant with your Dippers until you mentioned the saucepans."

"Right." I snicker. "You did admit when we were, like, ten, that you thought stars looked like the ones from Mario Kart from up close."

"Mario Kart is where I got most of my space knowledge."

"Surprised you became a chef and not an astronomer, honestly."

He laughs softly, and even though we both clearly know nothing about astronomy, we fall into silence as we gaze above. I might be clueless, but I do know that, just like watching the ocean, stargazing puts everything in perspective. How small we are in the grand scheme of things.

"Can I ask you a question?" Eli asks after a while.

I hum.

"What happened to that fiancé of yours?"

"How long have you been waiting to ask that?" A corner of my lips curves up, even though I don't particularly want to revisit this story.

His gaze drops to my lips, then climbs back up, too slowly. "Mostly since you've started to feel like mine again."

Mine.

Again.

I'm not a romantic at heart. I believe in steadiness and shared goals in a relationship. Never have I dreamed of being swept off my feet and carried into happily ever after. It wasn't something that could happen to me.

Eli Grant makes me want to dream.

I blink fast, trying to keep my feet firmly on Earth. He hasn't said this to convince me of something. That's one thing I love about Eli; with him, what you see is what you get. He's thought it, so he's said it.

The pads of his fingers continue brushing delicate patterns against my skin, not pressuring but relaxing.

"He left a little over six months ago."

Eli's jaw shifts to the side, but he remains silent. The flames flicker in his eyes, making their amber the color of spring honey.

"We'd been struggling to get pregnant for a long time by then, obviously, and I'd received my diagnosis more than a year before, but I'd only just been told by my gynecologist that it probably would never happen for me."

I've wanted to erase the moment he left since it occurred, but it's inked there, in bright colors. The wilting plant in the corner behind him, the leaves having turned from green to a murky gray, because I couldn't be bothered to water it. The Alicia Keys song I'd been listening to before he came in from work with avoidant eyes. The creases in his dusty blue shirt, like everything about his usually pristine self was rumpling. I was slowly bringing him down with me.

"*It's nothing against you, Cass,*" he said, not even taking the time to sit, a bag at his feet. He'd come out of the bedroom with it, his mind already made up before that moment. I was still by the sink where I'd been washing romaine lettuce for dinner, my hands freezing in the water. "*I just… I need this.*"

"He wanted kids more than he wanted me," I tell Eli, which sums up the theatrical breakup. Theatrical on his part, not mine. I did not move an inch, didn't even say a word. My fingers were bloodless, but I didn't move them away from the water. I was frozen. As he talked, apologizing and explaining his every thought, all I could think was, *I want them more than I want you, too.*

"That fucking asshole," Eli says.

I lift a shoulder. "I realized once he was gone that our relationship was more about a future family than anything else for me, too. We got engaged and didn't plan a wedding for two years afterward. Pretty telling."

"Still. He shouldn't have left because of that."

"I couldn't give him what he wanted."

"So?" His jaw shifts. "Cassie, he should've loved you for you, not for your potential motherhood. You don't ask someone to marry you then leave the second things don't go your way."

Except when he left, my potential motherhood felt like it *was* what I had been, and now it was gone. I didn't feel whole, so how could I fault him for it?

"You'd have stayed with Liz, if she hadn't left." It's more a statement than a question.

"Probably, yes."

"And would that have been a good thing?"

He doesn't answer. We both know the answer to that.

"We were done long before he left," I say. "I didn't even want him to touch me if I wasn't ovulating."

"Why?"

"It felt... I don't know, useless?" It should feel awkward to talk about sex with someone else with him, but somehow, it doesn't. I don't remember the last time Eli has made me feel uncomfortable. "Sex was always a reminder of what I couldn't give him. Like, my body was worthless, so what was the point?"

Eli shifts so abruptly, I barely have time to move away so my head doesn't bob to the ground. He sits upright, looking down at me. "There is nothing worthless about your body." He shakes his head, and even though his gaze doesn't move anywhere other than my face, it feels as if he's mapped my entire body in his mind. "Nothing."

A year ago, I would've laughed. How could a body that couldn't give me the one thing I truly wanted not be worthless? I would sometimes dream of unzipping my skin, of being able to walk out of it and find another. I didn't want anything else. Didn't need the long hair or the dimples at the small of my back. I would've walked into any other, so long as those masses of endometrial tissues weren't there. I would sometimes dream of it for so long, I'd start to feel numb, like I could truly detach from myself. But here, with the sincerity painting Eli's profile, I can see that maybe, just maybe, he has a point. When he lifts a thumb to my right brow, tracing it, then the other, I feel every single point of contact, feel like my body is thoroughly inhabited and not simply lived in.

His finger goes down my face, caressing the long line of my nose, the tight edge of my jaw, the plumpness of my bottom lip. I part for him, and when he slides his finger further up my mouth, I kiss it, top lip covering the tip of his thumb. A low groan emanates from his throat as he continues his teasing, pressing the finger an inch inside. I lick the pad.

It feels as if we're at a standstill, at the edge of a line we won't be able to come back from if we cross it.

I'm not sure who moves first; if it's his knee that climbs between my thighs, or if it's my hands grasping at his shirt and pulling him down to me. He tastes like marshmallows and the whiskey he'd been sipping, like sin and desire wrapped in a kiss. A moan slips out when he brushes his tongue with mine, and the kiss moves from sweet to possessive. Claiming. He breathes heavily as he brings his thigh higher, so it creates pressure against my core, making me gasp.

"Do you know how crazy you make me with those small noises you make?" He drags kisses down my throat, making me arch against him. His teeth tease the soft skin below my ear. "How often I've dreamed of seeing you like this after you moaned while eating?" A hand lands on the underside of my breast, and while I want him to move up, to push my bra away and finally touch me, he gives me the lightest of touches. "You're a fucking walking daydream."

I squirm so his finger finally touches me, and finally, through my shirt, he palms my breast, toying with the peaked nipple. It's been so long since I've felt a carnal craving like this, like I want to be touched just for the sake of the high. I feel like I just got a hit of some potent drug after being away for years.

"You feel so good in my hands," he says, his other one now under my shirt, palming me with a vigor I wouldn't have expected from him. He's finally letting all his restraint go. His lips are back on mine, kissing and sucking and licking. My mind is only filled with his name, repeated over and over like a mantra.

"Say it again," he groans against my lips, which makes me realize it wasn't only in my head.

"Eli," I gasp. I don't recognize the urgency in my voice, the unapologetic way I'm making a mess of his leg. And when he lets go of my breast and his fingers tease the button of my jean shorts, I feel like I'm about to burst.

"Can I?" he asks through heavy breaths.

"Is this considered public indecency?" I ask, even though every part of my body is screaming at me to stop joking and finally get him where I need him.

"I'll take my chances." His fingers continue tracing the line of my shorts, but he won't breach it unless I ask him to.

"Touch me," I whisper.

He wastes no time, slipping past my shorts, then my panties. I gasp at the first graze of his digit against my middle, but the moment his lips find mine again, I'm lost. I forget about why this might be a bad idea. No wrong decision could feel this good.

"Do you know what you do to me?" he says as his fingers move in tight circles, already lifting me toward an edge I haven't reached with someone else in a long time.

"I have an idea," I say, both because if what he feels is only a hundredth of what I do, it is still a tremendous amount, and because the hard length of him pressed against my hip isn't lying. He seems to move almost involuntarily, looking for friction at the rhythm he's offering it to me.

How long have *I* longed for this? My teenage years were spent dreaming of having him like this. I never had the chance to feel his hands on my body before I left, and the real thing is so much better than anything I could've imagined.

His mouth remains against my ear, whispering all the ways I'm driving him crazy as he listens to the sounds I make to find the perfect rhythm against my clit. I'm grasping at whatever part I can find—his back and then his ear, my legs shaking. It's too much but also exactly what I need.

I nip at his jaw, at his ear, but at one point, I can't move anymore, my body coiled too tight.

"I-I'm going to come."

"Good," he says, and that does it. I explode like an overblown balloon, spasming over his hand, my mouth parted against his neck as I hold on to him like I'll fly away if he doesn't keep me tethered.

My blood roars in my ears as I slowly come down from my high, feeling the loss the second Eli pulls his hand away from my panties. My hands are still buried in his hair, our eyes locked. I don't know how I could ever look anywhere when he's in front of me.

Slowly, he brings his thumb to his lips and licks it, and I'm immediately ready for more.

Softness blooms after the fire he's just shown as he leans to kiss my nose, then my lips. "Worth every fucking thing in the world."

Chapter 28

Something's wrong with my sister.

Ever since she showed up at the cottage this morning with Xavier for Zoe's birthday, I haven't known how to act around her. She's been distant; not only with me but with everyone.

I didn't even know she was supposed to be coming over until last night. After our moment outside, Eli and I spent more than an hour talking, one of my legs sandwiched between his, my temple on his chest and his soft breaths acting as the most potent anxiolytic.

"Are you okay if your sister comes over tomorrow?" he asked as he lazily played with my hair.

"You don't need my permission to invite a friend over." Especially since Zoe clearly wanted Xavier there for her special day. We'd been celebrating her birthday all week but tomorrow was when it really counted.

"I know, but I can still ask how you feel about something before doing it."

Funny how I'd never realized just how little I was considered in other people's decision-making until someone made sure I knew my opinion mattered.

"Then yeah, I'm good with it." I buried my nose even closer into his chest. "We're better now."

Except I'm not so sure we are.

I *thought* we were better after the yard sale. We went back to the lawyer's office together to sign the paperwork for the money donation, and brought the last of the boxes to goodwill in the same car. She even invited me for a sandwich at her place afterward. I felt like, if I'd left when I was supposed to, we would still have been okay.

But we've been walking in the woods for the past five minutes now, on a quest Eli sent us on to find wood for the fire tonight, and the only thing she's done is nod or shake her head when I ask a question.

"I don't think Zoe will ever take off the princess costume," I say as I bend to pick up a small stick. There are no ready-to-use logs in the trail around the cottage—obviously—so unless I improvise and pretend I'm a handy lumberjack, this will have to do. "She's had it on for five days. Eli is desperate."

"Hm," Keira says, not looking away from the path in front of her. Come to think of it, she hasn't grabbed a single branch either, only walked and stared ahead.

And then it's silence again.

She surprises me when she finally speaks to ask, "So, the two of you are a thing now?"

I almost trip over a rock.

"You're not as subtle as you think you are."

I honest-to-God thought we were. We barely spent any time together throughout the day. I didn't trust myself not to touch him reflexively. I guess I should've tried harder to not even glance in his direction.

"Is that what's up with you?" That would explain why she's barely looked at me.

"Nothing's up with me."

"Aren't we past the BS stage?"

"I don't want to talk about it."

"Well, I do." I stop in her path, so she has to stop walking. "Is it about Eli and me? Did I do something?"

There's a complete blankness in her gaze. "Believe it or not, not everything revolves around you."

"That's not fair." I thought we were past this snarkiness.

She shuts her eyes and exhales. "You're right. I'm sorry."

I give her time to find her words. The song of birds around us is so loud, it feels as if we've walked into a parallel world, one where it's just us two. Sunlight filters through the thick fir trees, illuminating the ground in a lacy pattern.

Finally, she says, "Rob's been cheating."

I blink. Blink again. "Are you sure?"

"If seeing pictures of her tits on my husband's phone isn't enough, I don't know what is."

"Keir, I'm so sorry." I want to step forward, to wrap her in my arms and absorb some of her hurt, share it so it's not so heavy, but she flinches when I move, so I keep my arms at my side, stiff and cold.

She brings a hand to her bulging belly, rubbing it mindlessly, like she's not only thinking about herself but about what it will mean for Xavier, and for this little one who isn't even here yet.

"I'm starting to think you had the right idea," she says, picking a leaf off a nearby maple tree and rubbing it between her fingers.

"What do you mean?"

"Leaving. Looking for a life better than this one."

"Is that what you think I did?"

She shrugs. "You left. You got *out*." Her eyes are shiny now. "I stayed, married the college boyfriend, did everything I was supposed to, and look at me now."

"I didn't leave because I wanted a better life. I left because I couldn't *breathe* here." I thought that was obvious. "If I could have stayed, I would have. You were stronger than me for that."

Her lips twist to the side.

"And I never thought I was better than you. I was *jealous* of you." My voice thickens. "I can't believe that's what you've been thinking this entire time."

"What was I supposed to think?"

"That I would've given everything to have your life. Probably still would." I let go of the bag of branches I've been carrying. "I'll never have kids. Never have a family like yours, messed up as it might be. And I'm not saying that to have your pity, or to make you feel like what you're going through isn't shitty, because it is. It really fucking is, and I'll kick Rob's ass the next time I see him. But I want you—I *need* you—to see that I never thought I was better than you." I swallow, then breathe through the knot in my throat. "I only ever wished I could be as strong as my big sister."

She kicks a rock. Cracks her knuckles. I'd never realized until now that she does it, too.

And then her arms are around me. "It's annoying when I'm pissed and you make sense."

"I'll keep that in mind," I say around a laugh, hugging her back.

She pulls back almost as fast as she came in, but I still feel elated from the simple touch.

"Egg his car when we go back?" she says.

"Count me in."

Later that day, after Keira and I have made our way back to the cottage, we go on another boat ride, and this time, Eli lets me drive for a while. Everyone is gathered at the front of the boat, looking at a pack of little *fucks* floating across the water—Zoe has now contaminated Xavier with her pronunciation—which allows Eli to step in behind me, so close I can feel the shape of his biceps around mine and smell the lemon popsicle he just ate on his breath. I shouldn't enjoy feeling like a seventh grader hiding behind the bleachers as much as I do, but that's the way Eli makes me feel. Like I'm carefree again.

Once we're done, Eli settles at the barbecue and makes enough burgers to feed an army. Zoe asks for maple syrup on her bun—even my sweet tooth could never—and since it's her birthday, no one says a word. We stuff ourselves with bright-yellow corn grilled to perfection and comically large, juicy heirloom tomatoes from the local market that burst with flavor on every bite. Eli serves the prettiest pink cake covered in edible flowers which excites Zoe to no end. She then opens her gifts, and I'm happy to say mine is her favorite (and clearly Eli's worst nightmare based on the glare he sends me when she opens the flute and starts blowing painful notes). By the time we've cleared the table, her crown braid is almost touching her plate, her entire body sagging with fatigue.

"All right, birthday girl, time to say goodnight," Eli says as he pulls her chair back.

Still half-asleep, Zoe says, "Can Cassie do bedtime?"

I don't think my heart will ever recover from demands like this.

Both Keira and Charlie give me looks with raised brows, but I pretend not to notice as I stand and grab Zoe's body out of Eli's arms. I won't make a habit out of it, but I can make an exception for her birthday. She clings to me like a koala bear, her hair smelling of sunscreen and maple. Eli's gaze remains on us for a long moment, expression feather-soft, and even without words, I know that whatever happened or will happen in the future, in this moment, he is the definition of happiness.

The stairs creak under our weight, muffling the conversation I can hear happening in the kitchen while plates clink and bottles of wine are thrown away. I skip the bathroom and bring her directly to her bed. Birthday celebrations include skipping teeth brushing. When I lay her down, her eyes flutter open. I go to undo the bobby pin holding her braid up, but her chubby hand stops me halfway.

"You'll be more comfortable if we take it out, honey."

"I want to keep it for tomorrow."

I brush a thumb over her messy, dark brow. "How about I promise to make you another tomorrow?"

Her eyes brighten like I'm a genie who's offered her three wishes. When I try to touch her hair again, she lets me. I undo the braid, then pick up the brush by her bed and untangle her hair. This used to be my favorite part of the night when I was a kid, when my mother would pick the wooden brush made of soft bristles and start from root to end, going over and over the same sections; sometimes while humming, sometimes while asking me about my day, and sometimes in perfect silence. I do the same with Zoe, taking my time, thinking she's fallen asleep from the heaviness of her breathing and the quiet that's so rare of her.

She makes me jolt when she says, "Cassie?"

"Yes?"

"Are you going to be my mommy now?"

My brush halts halfway through her tresses as a cave forms in my chest, so deep there's no visible bottom. Pure darkness.

I've had months to wrap my head around the fact that no one will ever call me mommy. No little boy will ever rush me not to be late for baseball practices. No daughter will ever ask me to do her makeup for prom. My fridge will never be covered in peanut butter-stained fingertips. I will never breastfeed, never attend gymnastics competitions, never sing crappy songs in the car during road trips to the beach. There's a new thing to grieve at every corner, and while I haven't accepted it yet, I've gotten used to the idea. But to hear those words coming from her mouth... It feels like someone dangling a carrot in front of me, and the worst part is, I know she wants me to grab it. There's so much hope in her question.

I don't even think this comes from her seeing me and Eli together and imagining we're a couple. This feels like it has everything to do with all the time I've spent with *her*.

I lean over her so she can't look away from me. "No, honey, I won't. You already have a mommy." I think back to the devastation I saw in Liz's expression when I saw her at the park. I'm certain I'm not lying when I say, "And she loves you very much, even if you don't see each other a lot."

Her lower lip turns down, and I wish I could've lied to her, if only not to see that instant disappointment.

"But you know what? It doesn't matter what you call me." I squeeze her neck where I know she's ticklish, and even if it's artificial, the giggle that escapes her loosens some of the tension in my shoulders. "I'll be your Cassie as long as you want me to."

"You promise?"

"I promise."

Even as I say it, I know some of me is lying. I'm leaving once summer ends, and as much as I want to be here for her, doing so from a distance will make it difficult, especially on her part. Still, I'll do what it takes. I'll visit. I'll call. If Eli allows me to stay in her life, I will be, in whatever form I can.

I take her hand in mine and dust a kiss to her palm, hoping against all odds that I'll be able to hold on to my promise no matter what.

Chapter 29

My first job interview was at one of the many local ice cream shops in town. I was fifteen and Lick It sounded like the only place I could possibly get a call-back from, even with my name. The place was falling apart, looking more like a dilapidated cabin than a shop, and it constantly smelled like mildew and curdled milk. I remember rarely having felt this nervous in my life. Changed my outfit three times, rehearsed answers for hours in front of the mirror, the whole deal. I needed the money to buy a car to feel like I wasn't entirely trapped in this town. I'd feel better knowing I had a way out. Of course, the person who interviewed me had to be Ashleigh Wright; one of the girls in my class who was particularly nasty to me. She didn't even pretend to ask me the interview questions, instead texting on her flip phone until I gave up and left the shop. I didn't get ice cream there all summer, even on the hottest days, and while Eli's dad was able to afford me a few hours every week at the food truck, I was never able to buy that car.

By the time I interviewed for my job at Brooklyn Hospital Center, I was slightly more confident. I'd had more practice over the years from small jobs I was able to land. I still vomited the morning of, but at least I was able to remain composed during the interview. When I left and was told by Sariah with a firm shake of her hand that she'd be in touch, I thought to myself, *this might be my last ever job interview.*

It might still be the case. I'm not planning on applying anywhere.

But...

It was curiosity that got me to type "nursing jobs near me" on my laptop. Curiosity that got me to click on the link of the small hospital two towns over I visited when I broke my arm at eleven by falling from a tree Eli and I had decided to climb (he'd fainted afterward and needed to be checked out, too.) Curiosity that made me look at their vacant positions.

When I hear the patio door of Ruth's house open behind me, I snap my computer shut so hard, the sound could be heard throughout town.

"What are you watching on there?" Eli asks as he comes up behind me and wraps his arms around my torso, his lips pressed against my neck. I feel his grin on my skin.

"None of your business," I say, not denying what he's clearly thinking. Better he believes I was watching porn than looking—curiously, *just for fun*—at available nursing jobs in Maine.

"I think I'd very much like to know," he says, his voice deep and low.

"Yeah?" I turn in his arms to find him dressed for work, with his hair tucked behind his ears. He had it cut when we got back from the cottage, the strands now curving at the base of his neck and falling across his forehead. It's somehow made him even sexier than before. I brush my fingers through it.

"Should I cut it more?"

I shake my head. "I like it like this."

"Good." He smiles, and even though I still have no idea what it is we're doing, I bask in this feeling of rightness. Like here, for a few weeks, we can pretend this is real.

He leans down to kiss me, but just before his lips land, he freezes, looking around the house. "What happened here?"

"What?" I turn around, realizing how strange the empty house must look to him. "Oh, yeah. I sold everything before the cottage trip." I was sitting on an Adirondack chair I pulled inside before he came in.

"So where have you been sleeping?" He's worked the past two evenings—and days—so I haven't seen much of him, except for when he came back from work and liberated me from my babysitting duties. Apart from a few make out sessions on the couch, we've been tame, mostly from lack of time. Every time I leave, I feel a rush of nerves because I know we only have so much time, and we're wasting some of it by not being together, but there's not much else we can do.

"Air mattress in the guest room."

"Is this a joke?"

"Don't worry, it's only half deflated. There's still some wiggle room."

"Cassie, Jesus. Why didn't you tell me?"

"Trust me, the beds at the hospital are worse." I have a love-hate relationship with night shifts. Sure, when the floor is quiet, you get to go lie down for a few hours, but the mattresses available to us are rock-hard and the blankets tissue-paper thin. I've learned to sleep on any and all surfaces, so long as I'm tired enough.

"You're not staying on an air mattress," he declares.

"Why not?"

"Because I have a perfectly available bed for you at my place."

"Does it happen to be the bed you also sleep in?"

His lips curve into a devilish smirk. "Would it be so bad if it was?"

I start smiling but shake my head. "We can't do this in front of Zoe. She'll be... confused." Especially after what she asked me at the cottage, the last thing I want is to add even more ambiguity to this whole situation.

Something sobers in his face, and I'm not sure if it's the mention of his daughter potentially getting tangled in this, or the reminder that whatever's happening between us is temporary.

"Right." He nods, then nods again. "We'll just pretend you're sleeping in the guest bedroom then."

"So there *is* another empty bedroom?"

"Yes, but you're not getting that one." His hands drift down my body, landing on my waist, long fingers curving around my back.

"Where's the honorable man who offered me a bed so I wouldn't have to sleep on the floor?"

He captures my mouth with his, a blink of a kiss, there one second and gone the next. "Who said I offered for honorable reasons?"

I wait fifteen minutes from the time Zoe's breathing turns deep and slow to finally join Eli in his room. I shouldn't be nervous, and yet I kind of feel like I'm going on a first date. I hesitated on what pajamas to wear, but since I never expected for someone else to see me at night when I packed, I didn't bring the best selection. I settled on a tank top and a pair of flannel shorts.

"Finally," Eli says when I close the door behind me. He crosses the space between us in three steps and pulls me closer to him. His hair is damp from his shower, and I once again wonder how it's possible for him to make Irish Spring soap smell this good. It becomes something else against his skin.

"Miss me?"

"You have no idea."

And then he's kissing me, and I forget to breathe. With his fingers tangled in my hair, we take slow steps backward until the backs of my knees hit the side of the bed. We both fall in a tangled heap on his soft comforter, his hardness pushing against my thigh. Still, there's no sense of urgency in his kisses. They're slow and deep, and the way his tongue tangles with mine in this unhurried way makes me boil from inside. I don't recognize my body with this man. Never have I felt this kind of want before. It's intoxicating.

"Do you know how grateful I am for goodwill right now?"

"I knew your chivalry was an excuse."

"Two birds, one stone." He cups my ass through my shorts, his pinkies toying against my skin at the hem. I want them off. I want *everything* off.

Bringing my lips back to his, I grab the bottom of his shirt to lift it just as his phone rings.

"Ignore it," he says, then takes his shirt off and lies back down, bringing me with him.

And then it rings again.

"Fuck," he says as he shifts away so he can stand in one swift move and answer, "What?"

I sit up, fighting a grin. I don't think I've ever seen him this rude before. He listens to what sounds like a male voice for a few moments, then leans his head back and groans. "Fine. I'll be right there." He hangs up.

"What's going on?

"Problem in the kitchen," he says, already putting his shirt back on. "Thirty extra people showed up to the event, and the organizers need us to accommodate them all of a sudden."

"So?"

"So I have to go help my team. There won't be enough food, not enough cutlery, not enough staff..."

"Isn't tonight your only night off this week?"

He drags a hand through his hair. Everything about his body screams tired. "I don't have a choice."

"How about saying no?"

"I can't. They're a good client. Booked us a year ago."

"And you did your job. You were ready. They made changes to their demands without telling you in advance." I undo the top button of my shirt. "That's not your problem."

"I know, but—"

"No but." I unbutton another, then a third one, exposing the top of my breasts.

"What are you doing?"

"*I* am getting ready for bed. It's late."

Eli's gaze is glued to my chest, not even bothering to hide where he's staring.

I lean back, uncross my legs.

"What is this? Blackmail?"

"I'm not torturing you, am I?"

"Honestly? Yeah, you fucking are."

"Let's call it incentive." I undo another button, now exposing my entire bra.

His feet bring him forward as I continue unbuttoning, as if dragged to me by an invisible magnet even he can't control.

He stands between my legs as I undo the last button, letting my shirt fall off my shoulders. "I did say I'd get you to be selfish."

His chest is rising and falling like he's just run five miles, maple syrup-colored eyes now obsidian. He lifts a hand to my breasts, but I lean further back at the last second. "You just gotta say no."

"You'll be the death of me," he whispers before crashing onto me. While the previous kisses were languid, these are wild and frantic, his hands everywhere. On my back, my neck, my breasts.

Through my bra, he teases a nipple between his pinched fingers, making me gasp in his mouth.

"You drive me insane, you know that?" He unclasps my bra, then pulls back and stares. I feel exposed, something I usually hate, but under his gaze, I don't mind so much. I couldn't feel insecure with the way he's looking at me. He brings a hand to my breasts, squeezing, then pinching. I arch my back, which rubs my core against the erection tenting his gray sweatpants. I shift so I can palm him through his pants.

"Shit." He pulls back, then lies on me. "You have to wait if you don't want this to be over in five minutes." With a nip at my jaw, he says, "Let me play with you first."

Just as his hand breaches my shorts and I'm shaking for him, he taps his phone and brings it to his ear. His finger traces soft circles on top of my drenched panties as he whispers, "Shh." Then, "Hey, Vince. About tonight? Tell them it's too late to change plans."

I can't believe he's talking on the phone while playing with my clit. I can't believe I like it.

The other guy—Vince—starts talking, but Eli doesn't seem to listen, only watching me as his fingers move my panties to the side and brush against my naked flesh. I inhale sharply, which he silences with a discrete kiss.

"Yeah. Uh-huh. But tell them we're not prepared for that kind of change, and they can call me tomorrow if they want to talk."

God, he's actually going to make me come like this.

Another bout of Vince talking, then, "Not tonight. I'm busy. Talk later." He hangs up.

"I'm so proud of you," I say on a sigh.

"Might regret it tomorrow, but nothing could've dragged me from here." With his now free hand, he pulls my shorts down to see the mess he's making of me. "Not with how long I've wanted to do this."

"Trust me," I pant, moving against his hand so I can get more pressure, more movement, more, more, more. "I win in that category."

He chuckles like I'm actually being funny. "No, you don't."

"I swear I do."

He circles faster against my middle, making my breath hitch. "Summer of grade 10? I was fifteen, you were fourteen, and I spent the entire time convincing myself I was only rubbing one out thinking of you because you were my friend."

Even through the fog of pleasure, I laugh. How could he even believe fourteen was the earliest I could've wanted him? I leave a kiss between his ear and his jaw that brings a curse out of his lips. "Christmas of grade 7. Wasn't thinking of sex, but still knew I wanted you." My parents had gone out on December 24th to dance at some bar in Portland, and Keira had gone to sleep over at her boyfriend's. I'd messaged Eli on MySpace and without me asking, he and Mr. Grant had showed up at my doorstep fifteen minutes later. I had dinner with their family, and after filling ourselves with stuffing and turkey, Eli and I went to his bedroom. We lay on the floor while listening to Coldplay's new album. I remember turning to him, the boy with bright-blue braces who'd made sure I wouldn't spend Christmas Eve alone, and thought my heart couldn't fit in my chest anymore. I'd had a crush before, but that was the moment I fell in love with him.

Eli's movements stop as he stares at me, the same way he did that Christmas night, with so much emotion in those brown eyes, and then he's kissing me again, even harder this time. I pull off his shirt a second time, the feel of his skin heavenly against mine. I feel my orgasm building from the way he's touching me, but as I chase it, I realize there's something I forgot to mention before coming in here and deciding to use my body as bait.

"I need to tell you something."

He pauses, a worried notch forming between his brows. "Everything okay?"

"Yes, I just..." This makes me feel so much more exposed than before. "I get pain, sometimes, with sex." Another sphere of my life endo has sunk its claws into.

"Okay."

"Okay?"

"Yes, okay." He goes to kiss me again.

I stop him with a hand on his chest. "You know that means penetration can be impossible sometimes?"

"Yes, I got that, Cass." He rubs a spot where he kissed me hard on my collarbone before, probably having left a hickey. "I'm not some dumb teenager who needs to fuck. There're so many more ways to have sex."

I don't think I've ever heard such sexy words.

He seems to notice the effect he has on me because he grins, then licks his lips. "You want an example?"

And then, he's lowering himself, farther and farther until his tongue gives my middle a long, hard stroke. I don't recognize the sound that comes out of me, and even less as he continues kissing and licking like he's starving, and I can't do anything but shake and moan.

"You taste just like I'd dreamed you would," he says, lips gleaming in the dim light before returning to my core. My thighs tighten around his face, pleasure cresting once more, but I don't want this to be over yet. I pull away, just long enough to flip him onto his back and straddle him facing away. Then, I pull his pants down just enough to expose his hard length. And just as I lean back down on him, I also wrap my lips against his length.

He quakes under me, his breaths sharp against my core.

"You okay up there?" I tease. "Pretty silent."

"I feel like you're actively trying to kill me tonight."

"Is it working?"

"Fuck, yeah, it is," he says before bringing his lips to me once more. I'm almost there already, shaking as I lick him from base to top. His musky taste and the way his grip on my ass tightens with every stroke of my tongue only makes everything more intense. He laps at me at the same rhythm I move against him, slow, then fast, adding one hand at his base.

"Shit, I'm close," he says, breathless.

"Me too." I'm barely able to continue my movements with the orgasm that's building. I become sloppy and he does, too—sharp, rough licks and sucks that end with me orgasming so hard, I gasp against his length.

Eli curses once more, his movements jerky in my mouth, and then he's pulling out and coming over our chests in long, hot spurts. Chest heaving, I let my body fall forward, not caring about the mess, too exhausted to hold myself up. He doesn't seem to care either, and we remain there for a long while as we catch our breath, his hand mindlessly rubbing my calf.

When I finally get myself to stand, it's only to cuddle closer to him. We'll clean off later.

He takes me in his arms and kisses the top of my head.

"I think this might have been a mistake," he says with humor.

"Why?" His hair is soft against my forehead.

"Because now that I know what your mouth feels like, I may never say yes to going in to work again."

"Mission accomplished."

I catch his laughter between my lips.

Chapter 30

"Can I do something?" I ask Mom for the tenth time. Dottie's sitting at my feet, looking up like she clearly wants food. I pick a piece of cheese and give it to her. Poor girl deserves it.

"I'm fine. Sit, please."

"I've been sitting all this time. I want to help."

I hesitated last night when Mom asked me if I wanted to join them at crochet club again, mostly because I still don't particularly enjoy being in this house. However, she sounded so hesitant over the phone, and I hate that I've become someone my own mother should walk on eggshells around. Granted, I haven't made it easy for her not to, but my anger reflexes are hard to tame. I felt like agreeing to this was a small step in that direction.

Without anything to do while waiting for people to arrive, I walk into the living room, where the same pictures from my childhood hang on the wall. One in particular has always annoyed me; the four of us are standing in front of a sunset at the Kennebunkport marina, smiling like we don't have a care in the world. Dad had called Mom some name a few seconds before, and Keira had comforted me after I'd started crying because he'd shouted. My eyes are still red-rimmed in the picture if you look closely. The picture is the definition of a lie. A moment that looks happy but was anything but.

Something clatters in the kitchen, and I'm there before Mom has even had the time to bend to pick up the spoon on the ground.

"I've got it."

She stops me with a hand on my arm, then leans to pick it up, except it takes her so long to get back up, for a moment I think she's stuck in a squat. Finally, her hand reaches for the spoon and her knees crack as she starts straightening and tries to find hold on the counter. To hell with her order. I grab her waist and pull her up, her entire weight suddenly resting on me.

When she's upright, she sighs deeply, then puts the spoon down. "I had it." She goes back to sprinkling paprika over the deviled eggs.

"Did you?"

She doesn't answer and finishes making her cheese platter like nothing happened, but it feels like a blinder has been pulled off my eyes. I take in everything in the house, details that had escaped me when I was here last. All the pots and utensils at arms' reach, the lower cabinets seemingly empty. The pillows piled on the back of the rocking chair. The furniture moved to rest against each wall, so the walking space is larger. The cane leaned against the wall, by the bathroom. She didn't use one when I was here before, but she clearly needed it.

"Why didn't you ever tell me it was this bad?" I ask, cracking the knuckles on my index finger. "I would've wanted to know."

Mom stops moving, her face turning soft. "My baby was out there living the life she deserved. What kind of mother would I have been to call her back here?"

"Mom..."

She takes a stiff step my way, then puts her hand on mine, so familiar in its warmth, and squeezes. She's never been the type to hold a grudge, but in this moment, I feel like I deserve it. It would probably make me feel better to feel her anger instead of her support.

"You were exactly where I wanted you to be."

"Well, I'm here now." At least, for the moment, I am.

"And I'm happy you are, but I don't want you to be my caregiver. I just need you to be my daughter."

I blink fast, but don't have time to answer before the doorbell rings.

I take a second to collect myself before I stand and open to Eileen, who gasps and jumps into my arms like we're long-lost lovers. "Oh, Cassie, sweetie, I'm so happy to see you again!"

After a moment, I hug her back.

"Oh, you have to come by the flower shop when you can! I'll make you a nice bouquet, on the house."

"If you're into weird arrangements, you found your woman," Gertrude says as she moves past us to walk in.

Eileen tuts. "You wouldn't know style if it hit you in the face."

"Same goes to you, sister," Gertrude says before tapping Eileen's butt.

"Cassandra!" Susan walks in then, also giving me a tight hug. I find myself smiling at all their affection. I didn't expect this kind of reaction from them, but I should've. They remind me so much of Ruth, even with all their quirks and differences. It makes me feel close to her to be here.

"I'm glad you're here." Susan says as she pulls away, and the moment she's taken off her shoes, she's pulling me by the arm toward a quiet corner of the living room. "I realized I hadn't had the chance to talk to you about something important the last time I saw you."

I hold my breath for whatever bomb she's about to drop.

"Susan, don't you dare!" Gertrude calls, but Susan trudges right on.

"Have you ever thought about becoming your own boss?" "Jay-sus, Mary, and Joseph, how long is this going to last?" Gertrude mumbles behind me, making me grin.

"What do you have against business owners?" Susan spits back. They're all so rude to each other, yet it's clear it's nothing but tough love. They've been friends for much longer than I've been alive. They would bicker all the time with Ruth, too, and while it made me uncomfortable as a kid, I can see the twinkle in their eyes as they give their quippy remarks now.

"I, uh..." Another set of knocks comes, and I jump to my feet. "I'll get it!"

"We'll talk about this later!" Susan shouts behind me. I hope we don't.

"Hi," I say as I open the door. "Oh, let me—"

My words die in my throat when I recognize the woman who used to be with the man that has lived in my mind for the past weeks. She looks just as shocked to see me, her extended fruit cake frozen midway to me.

"What are you doing here?" I ask. It doesn't compute, at first. The first thought that comes to mind is that she followed me.

"What are *you* doing here?"

"This is my mother's place," I say like it's obvious when it probably isn't. Keira and I both take after our father, and I've barely been here all summer.

She blinks. "I... Uh..."

"Elizabeth!" Susan shouts as she comes to hug her. "Cassie, this is my niece. I was just thinking how you two should meet! We need more young souls in this club."

"We met, actually," I say.

"Oh, wonderful! Come get a glass of wine." Susan disappears into the living room, where the ladies are pouring the wine like there's no tomorrow. Sounds like it's going to be another fruitful crochet session.

Liz's complexion is a nice shade of firetruck red. I would've expected anger from her, but she looks more uncomfortable than anything else. "I can go, if you want me to."

She holds the homemade cake closer to her, her hair parted in two French braids. *Zoe would love those,* I find myself thinking. Her nails are painted a bright shade of pink, some of it scratched off. Standing there, waiting expectantly, she reminds me of a younger version of myself. One who attended school cookouts and baking contests with an entire pan of cookies my mom would have baked the day before, only to have no one take one. I so wished someone would've let me in, made a space for me in their friend group, even just waved at me.

"No," I tell her. "It's fine. Come in."

"How many times will I have to tell you? I didn't know they had pot in them!" Eileen wails as she tries putting her shoes on. *Tries* being the important word here. The women are all so drunk, they can barely walk. Add to that the fact that Eileen brought pot brownies with her, and we've got a real dangerous gang. Thank God Susan's husband is here to pick them up and drive them back home.

"I will never believe you," Susan slurs before giggling. "Oh, some McDonald's would be good right now."

"Yes," Eileen says, holding the *s* a little too long.

"A universal feeling, isn't it," I mumble. Beside me, Liz snickers.

"Bye, ladies," I say louder with a wave. Mom's already in bed, thankfully pot-free. She didn't eat any of the brownies and went to bed a half-hour ago, claiming to be too tired to go on. She looked it, too. I wonder if that's another part of her illness she's hidden from me.

"Will we see you in two weeks?" Susan asks.

In two weeks, I'll be ready to leave, for real this time.

"Maybe," I say. I would technically have the time—I don't need to be back until September 1ˢᵗ, when I'm officially back to work—but I'd like to settle in before getting back to real life. Although I have a feeling I won't want to leave Eli until the very last second. Our days are filled with stolen touches and conversations exchanged through glances while Zoe tells us about her day at school over dinner. When she goes to sleep, we fall into bed together and discover everything we missed during our years apart. It's quickly become a new normal, which is lovely but mostly frightening. I don't know how I'll ever let it go.

"You better. You're a good spirit," Eileen says with a wink before turning and stumbling down the street while leaning against Susan. Gertrude is already waiting in the car, which only leaves Liz.

She was quiet during the evening, laughing softly when Susan made controversial statements with a surprising amount of confidence, and she contributed here and there, but mostly, she kept to herself. Nothing like the woman I saw shouting at Eli outside his house when I first got here.

"Do you need help with cleaning up?" she asks as I close the door behind me.

I go to say no, but when I spot the expectant look in her eyes, I falter. "Sure, thanks."

I fill the sink with warm, soapy water, then begin washing the decades-old wine glasses and the mismatched cheese plates. Liz picks up a rag and grabs a plate to dry.

"I'm sorry, if I intruded," she says after we're halfway done.

"If anyone was intruding, it was me." I learned throughout the afternoon that Liz has been part of the club ever since she returned to Cape Weston in May. She doesn't sound like she has many friends around town except for these ladies.

"I'm sorry about that day in the park, too."

I tip my head down, handing her another clean plate. Appropriate words are hard to find in this situation, but I end up saying, "I can't imagine anything about this is easy." She might have left, but she clearly loves her daughter.

"No, it's not." She stacks the dry plate on top of the others. "But I've had a lot of time to think since I got here. I realize Eli's doing what he thinks is right."

My skin crawls at the idea of talking about him when he's not around, especially with someone he's in a legal battle with. I don't want to say the wrong thing and risk messing things up. At least now I know she probably won't hold Eli and me being friends against him as she also hangs out with a member of my family.

"I've been looking for an opportunity to talk to you, actually," she says.

"Me?"

"I saw the way you were with her, that day in the park. She clearly loves you." Her throat works. "I'm glad Eli's girlfriend is good to Zoe."

"I'm not..." I don't finish my sentence, because I don't know how else I'd describe Eli's and my relationship. We're so much more than friends, but can I consider myself his girlfriend when it's only temporary?

"So, anyway, thank you, for taking care of my daughter." She clears her throat, rubbing at a spot on the wine glass that's already dry. "I've only ever wanted the best for her, you know? It's why I left. Thought I'd be a shit mom. *Was* a shit mom, probably." She wipes her nose with her forearm. "I was young and didn't know what I was doing, but there wasn't a single day where I didn't miss her like crazy."

"So, what made you come back now?"

She doesn't shrug, doesn't even hesitate when she says, "I'm better. Older. Ready. I think... I think I could be good for her now."

Sink empty of dishes, I pull the drain out, the sound of rushing water filling the room. "I need to be honest with you. Eli will put up a fight if you want shared custody." That's no surprise to her. They already have lawyers involved.

"I know," she says, still calm. "And that's normal. I'd do the same, if I were him. But it's not what I'm asking for. I don't want anything official. I just want to be allowed to see my daughter."

Her voice breaks on the last word, and my heart twists. I can't imagine being in her position. Having a daughter I could see from afar but not approach or hug or talk with. It feels like some of the nightmares I've been having, where someone hands me a little bundle of blankets that turns out to be empty when I open it. Except for her, it's not a dream.

"And if you don't get to do it?" I ask, not to provoke or discourage her, but because I genuinely want to know. She seems to understand that, too. "Will you leave?"

She shakes her head. "I'll be here and try again. I don't have anything else to lose, and I'm not giving up on her. Not again."

I don't answer anything, only give her a dip of my head that means everything.

Good answer.

Chapter 31

"I can't believe you actually asked him out on a date."

Emily huffs from her walking pad. "Why would I have waited for him to man up and ask me out when I could do it myself?"

"But during a C-section?"

She shrugs. "It worked, didn't it?"

"You're my idol, honestly."

"You know what? I'm mine, too."

I grin as I turn off the engine and get out of my car, the call disconnecting from Bluetooth and transferring back to my phone. "So, what will you do if it works out? Isn't it against the policy to date colleagues?"

"I guess I'll see after the date. Besides, I don't know that I'll stay in L&D forever."

"You're thinking of transferring?"

Her gaze flits away for a second, but it's enough to tell me she's actually thinking about this more than she lets on. A weight settles in my stomach. While I'm still not ecstatic to be going back to work soon, I figured I probably never will be again, and I'll just have to live with that. But losing the person that's been carrying me in the department for months? I don't know how I'll get over that.

She must see it on my face because she hurries to add, "Nothing set, really. Don't worry about it. Just some fleeting thoughts sometimes."

I make a humming noise. "It's okay, you know. If you want to change things up. I wouldn't want you to stay because of me."

"We'll see."

We say goodbye as I walk inside Eli's place, the smell of simmering garlic and tomatoes blending with the scent I've started to associate with comfort and home.

"Hi," he says, walking out of the kitchen to hug me. The cotton of his threadbare Coldplay T-shirt is soft under my cheek. "I missed you."

"I was only gone a few hours."

He kisses the top of my head. "Doesn't matter."

I close my eyes. It's a simple sentiment to say you miss someone, yet it feels so powerful to hear it. I don't remember the last time someone *actually* missed me. It's intoxicating, the way he makes me feel appreciated. I don't know how I'm going to walk away from it.

"I missed you, too," I say as we pull back, and he smiles before kissing me like he knew I did.

We head back into the kitchen, where Eli picks up a spoon to stir the reddish liquid on the stove.

"What are you making?"

"Testing a new recipe for the Chowder Festival." He scoops a spoonful of it and brings it to my lips before I can ask to taste.

"Oh my God," I say with a hand over my mouth. "This is insane." I don't even know what it's supposed to be, and I couldn't care less.

"I still need to tweak it."

"Don't. It's perfect."

He makes an unsure sound as he resumes his stirring. As easy as it is to make this man smile, it's difficult when talking about his work. He's so much harder on himself than he is about anything else.

I watch him work on starting his recipe again from scratch, 90s rock music playing from the speaker he keeps in the kitchen, and soon, I find my mind drifting back to my earlier conversation with Liz. A part of me wants to tell him everything. He deserves to know all the facts before making a decision. But then he brings his mixing bowl closer so he can continue cooking while wrapping an arm around my waist, and all my determination melts. This is nice. How many nice moments do we have left? I don't want to ruin it by bringing up the ex who hurt him.

"What's on your mind?" Eli asks, not even looking at me.

"Hm? Nothing."

"You know it's useless to lie, right?"

"And why would I be lying?" I ask, totally lying.

He grins, then picks up my hand to kiss the back of it. "Your fingers don't lie."

I hadn't realized I was cracking them until he says it. I lay my hands flat.

"So?"

I swallow. Now or never, I guess.

"I saw Liz today."

He stops moving, creamy liquid dripping from his whisk. "What? Ho—Did she do anything?" The whisk clangs against the metal bowl.

"She was at my mother's crochet club thing."

He stares, speechless. Even though I technically didn't do anything, he looks hurt.

"It was a coincidence she was there."

His nose twitches.

"I..." I push the bowl away from him and take his hands in mine so he's facing me. My thumb rubs over the dent between his thumb and forefinger. "Look, I'm not about to pretend like I know everything about her after one afternoon, but we talked, and she sounded like she's really changed."

He pulls away. "You're right. You don't know about her after one afternoon."

I purse my lips, but now that I've started, I can't back down. Not when I actually believe in what I'm saying.

"She made a mistake. Haven't you ever made one?"

He shakes his head, jaw tight. "Don't compare me getting shit-faced when I was seventeen to her abandoning her kid."

"I get where you're coming from," I say, voice low like I'm trying to tame a wild horse. "She did fuck up really bad. But if you—"

"And honestly, Cass? I'm sorry, but it's none of your business."

I jolt like he's just slapped me. It's probably what I needed, actually. A stark reminder that I'm not part of their family even if it has sometimes felt like it. But this is about Zoe, not me, so I say, "You're right, it's not."

His face falls like he realizes what he's just said. That no matter how much he might miss me, this thing isn't real.

I trudge on. "But I do know how it feels to be abandoned by a parent." It might not have been the same as what Liz did with Zoe, but every time my father fucked up and chose drinking or fighting over us, I felt a similar sense of abandonment, like my well-being wasn't worth prioritizing.

"And I know I would've given everything for my parents to have fought for me. To realize their mistakes and decide to change. I'd have forgiven my dad all his fuck-ups if he'd said he was sorry and tried to do better." I press my lips in a thin line, fighting to keep my emotions in check.

I don't fool Eli, though. Even annoyed, he reaches for my waist and caresses me through my shirt. I meet him halfway and place my hands against his soft, rugged, beautiful face. I take in the cloud of freckles, the scar above his brow, the caramel eyes. All so very familiar.

"Zoe's the luckiest girl in the world to have a dad who'd move mountains to protect her." I brush his cheekbones. "But if she can, why not give her the chance to receive even more love than she already has?"

Eli sighs deeply, his mint breath enveloping me, then leans his forehead against mine. The simple touch feels like getting booted up, like we've both laid down our weapons. I want us to fight on the same team, always.

"I'm so fucking scared."

My fingers tangle through his hair. "I know you are. And that's okay. What's important is you don't let that fear stop you from doing what's best for her."

"What if Zoe doesn't want to see her?"

"How about you let her decide for herself?"

A long moment passes before he finally dips his chin once, forehead still against mine. "When did you get so smart?"

"I was always smart. You were just too busy looking at my body to realize it."

He snickers, then pulls away so he can look at me. "All right. I'll think about it."

I hate that I've forced him to face a situation he's tried his hardest to avoid, but it's beautiful to see him doing it for her. I press closer to him, wrapping my arms around his neck. No one talks, only the sounds of our breaths between us. It feels like peace.

And that's when my phone decides to ring. We both reluctantly pull away. I frown when I see my sister's name on the screen. "Hello?"

"Cassie?" Keira says, her voice raw and high-pitched.

"What's going on?"

"She's coming," she says before groaning into the phone; a sound that I recognize from years of hearing it day in and day out. She's having contractions. Strong ones, from the way she's exhaling.

"Where are you?"

She breathes through the contraction, and once she's able to talk, says, "Hospital. I told Rob I didn't want him to be there. Thought I could do it by myself." Her voice cracks. My sister never cries.

"What can I do?" I ask. Eli stares with worried eyes and mouths, "What's she saying?"

"I can't do this alone," she sobs.

I understand then. She won't ask it out loud. She's too proud for that, but she called. That means everything.

"I'll be right there."

Chapter 32

The drive to the hospital takes twenty minutes. I make it in twelve.

I've never had to go to the maternity ward before, so I stumble in the hospital entrance, looking left and right like a headless chicken with my hair slipping out of my bun. Thank God I didn't eat any of those pot brownies tonight.

I run to the help desk, almost tripping over my unlaced sneakers. I didn't bother taking the time to tie them.

She called me.

She could've reached out to her friends, to our mom, but she didn't. She wanted me here. I'm not messing that up.

"Ma'am, are you okay?" A white man wearing a security outfit approaches me, his hand on what I assume is a weapon. A new low for me.

"Where's labor and delivery?" I ask, breathless.

He looks behind my shoulder to where my car is likely parked in a towing zone, then back at me. He seems to be wondering whether he should call backup, but I guess the place I'm looking for gives an explanation for the state I'm in because he says, "Third floor, to your left."

"Thank you."

I make a beeline for the elevator and rush to the nursing station of the ward once I'm up. It feels strange, to be on the other side of the counter. I ask for Keira's room, and a tall nurse with a kind smile brings me to her.

"I'm here," I exclaim as I step inside the room, dropping my bag to the floor and immediately going behind my sister to push on pressure points at her lower back. I don't think she even notices I'm here. She's sitting on an exercise ball, rocking her hips left and right while moaning through her exhales. I'd bet everything I have she's close to being fully dilated. It's a strange talent nurses develop in this department; the ability to tell how close a patient is to delivering just by hearing the sounds they make.

"I can't do it," Keira says, voice strained like she's been crying.

"Yes, you can. You did it before, and you'll do it again. Now, just breathe."

She doesn't listen and shakes her head. "I wasn't alone before. And—" Her sentence is interrupted by a contraction. Her body tightens, face twisting in pain.

"Breathe, Keira." My thumbs press harder against her lower back. I inhale loudly so she follows my pace. After a minute, her body relaxes, and I move so I'm facing her. With my hands on her shoulders, I say, "You're not alone, all right? So long as you want me here, you're not alone."

Her eyes well up, or maybe they were already teary.

We go through a half hour of the same pattern. I breathe with her, encourage her to drink and rest in between contractions, and soon, her nurse, Kelly, is checking on her, and she's fully dilated.

"I feel like I need to push," Keira groans.

"All righty, then," Kelly says, not taking my sister's tone personally. "Let's have a baby!"

She sets the bed up, and then Keira is pushing like a true champion. I'm holding her thigh up like a partner usually would and try my best not to overstep on Kelly. Today, I'm just a sister.

"Motherfuc—" she screams when the head is almost there.

"Hey, hey, look at me. Look at me."

She does, her face red and sweaty. I pass a cool, wet cloth over her forehead. "You got this. You're almost there. You're amazing."

She studies me for a long moment, then nods. It's the most trusting look I've ever seen on her, and one I never thought I'd see directed at me.

And then she's pushing and shouting, too—she's my hero for doing this without an epidural—and my eyes fill when I see the head crowning. I join the nurse and the doctor encouraging her to push. I let her squeeze my free hand so hard, I become numb.

And suddenly, like a sunray peeking through rain clouds, the softest, shrillest cry.

The baby is brought to Keira's chest, her arms shaking as she wraps them around it. The cries don't last long before the baby calms against Keira. And then, a beautiful, light silence settles in the room, the tension evaporated.

"Hello, you," Keira says, peering at her daughter's wrinkled face.

I've seen this hundreds of times before. I've cleaned babies and sucked mucus out of their nose and mouth while they were absorbing the heat of their mother's body. I helped mothers breastfeed and gave lessons on how to give baths for the first time. But this is like nothing I've experienced before. I'm in awe, gaping at this tiny creature like it's the eighth wonder of the world. I don't see the medical part of it. I just see them; a person I love so much and the new world she's just created. This small creature who will develop an entire life, who will grow to love and laugh and learn. It's as if I can see all that awaits her in a flash.

In this moment, I'm not thinking about me or the baby I'll never have. I'm not engulfed in grief and sadness. I don't drown in envy. The tears on my cheeks are from pure joy.

The baby slowly blinks as she reaches up, where Keira gives her her finger to wrap onto. My sister then looks up at me, and I don't think I've ever seen her this happy. At peace.

"Thank you," I say, not bothering to wipe my tears. "Thank you so much."

When I kiss her head, she lets me.

I spend the night with them.

Since I'm Keira's chosen partner, I don't get kicked out when visiting hours end, and I take the uncomfortable chair/couch/bed usually reserved for the other parent. I now understand why so many dads complain about it even though I'd never admit it out loud. The night is noisy, and poopy, and exhausting. It's wonderful. After a wild discussion on names—so many have to be crossed out because they belong to people we hated in high school—Keira looks down at her and says, "How about Billie?" It's random, not even close to her previous options, but somehow, it's right.

"Billie," I repeat, and that's that. She has strong McIntyre traits, just like us and her brother. I can't stop looking at her.

By the time Keira gets her leave from the hospital, I barely want to let them go. I drive them home with the car seat Mom brought this morning when she came to visit us. I didn't expect her to be emotional about the visit since I've never seen her cry, but she got teary when she rubbed a finger over Billie's pajama-clad foot. I thought I'd cried enough, but seeing all of us here, together, it did something to me. Like finally, being a part of the McIntyre family could be a good thing. A great thing, even. She left an hour ago, just before the pediatrician and the gynecologist came to do their final check-ups and gave Keira the okay to leave.

When I pull into her driveway, I hurry out of the car to help her out.

"I'm fine," she says while letting me take the car seat out.

"Let me take care of you for one last minute, okay?" I walk Billie to the front door, and only when I'm as far as I can go without entering the house do I put the seat down. "You call me if you need anything. And I mean *anything*."

"I will," Keira says.

"Promise me."

"God, you're annoying."

I don't give her the time to hesitate or protest before I hug her tightly. "You got this, all right?" A few hours after Billie was born, Keira called Rob to let him know. He broke down over the phone, while Keira kept her tears quiet. He's supposed to come over in an hour to meet Billie. "And if you need me to kick his ass, just say the word."

"If someone's kicking his ass, it's me."

"That's my sister." I pull back, squeeze her shoulders, then walk back to my car. I don't remember the last time I've felt this light. Like for once in my life, everything is just right.

When I finally make it to Eli's, I'm almost asleep on my feet. However, a bolt of energy spears me when I hear a female voice coming from outside the screen door.

I'm not a jealous person. Never have been. Michael had good female friends, and I never worried about him going out with them and their other friends. In fact, the thought never even crossed my mind to be anxious about it.

But now, my heart rate speeds up as I walk toward the back door. It's a horrible feeling. I definitely preferred indifference.

I slide the patio door with a little too much force. Only, I'm not met with a woman hanging out with Eli, but with Liz playing in the backyard with Zoe. They're sitting in the turtle-shaped sandbox, where Zoe appears to be showing her mother some kind of insect on her finger. Zoe is giggling, and Liz is radiant. To my right, about a hundred yards away from the sandbox, Eli is sitting on an Adirondack chair, pretending to read a book. He's doing a terrible job at it. His gaze is laser-focused on them, body ready to bound at any moment. He's wearing a taupe T-shirt that hugs his chest deliciously and makes the brown of his eyes look orange in the late afternoon light when he turns to look at me, as if feeling me staring.

I walk over to him, careful to keep some distance between us since I have no idea how he'll want us to act in front of Liz.

"You did it," I say.

"Someone I know is pretty convincing when she wants to be."

"Yeah?"

He nods, his gaze burning holes through my clothes. "Why are you so far away?"

"Where do you want me to be?"

He lets go of the book, not bothering to pretend he was reading it by marking his page, then taps his thigh.

"Are you su—"

He doesn't give me the time to finish before he's plopping me onto his lap and kissing me.

"But Zoe…"

"Is too busy playing to notice."

He's right. It's the first time Zoe hasn't spotted me walking in since that first day in July. It feels bittersweet, but I'm too happy for her to care.

"How did it go?"

"Good, I think." He keeps his gaze on them even with his hand tracing patterns on my thigh. His touch feels mindless, like it's a reflex now to have his hands on me in some way. Just like riding a bike. "We talked this morning about what she wanted to do. She was hesitant at first, but she's the one who ended up saying yes. She didn't want to talk when Liz showed up an hour ago, but she's loosened up now."

"I'm proud of you," I say.

"Still scared shitless."

"I know." I lean my head against his as we watch Zoe and her mother play. "That's why I'm proud."

He sighs just as Liz looks back and notices me. I feel like pulling away even though I don't technically need to, but the thought slips my mind when she grins and nods at me, then returns her attention to Zoe.

"I guess this makes everything easier," he says. "She doesn't want to share custody. For now, at least."

"And you're okay with having her around?"

"If that's what Zoe wants, then yes." His jaw shifts. "And honestly? It's a relief not to feel so angry at her. You'd think I've decided to forgive her for her, but really, I think forgiveness is more for myself."

"I'm really happy for you."

He squeezes my thigh. "How's Keira?"

"Great. Billie, too." I pull out my phone like the obsessed aunt I am and show him one of the dozen pictures I took.

"Beautiful," he says, specifically at the picture of me holding her. "I'm glad she called you."

"Me too."

He squeezes my hip. "And how are you feeling?"

I love that he asks the question. Love that he doesn't act like talking about it will make it worse. Love that he always faces everything head on, like he did by inviting Liz today even though he didn't want to. His bravery is subtle, but it's so impressive once you notice it.

And most of all, I love the way the honest answer feels.

"I'm good. Really good."

Chapter 33

The sky is a canvas of pinks and purples above the Atlantic a week later when Keira comes over for dinner. Inside, Eli is putting Zoe to bed while Xavier is already asleep on the couch. Keira and I are sitting on the back porch, a glass of wine in hand.

"God, I'm never getting pregnant and missing out on this again."

"Did you always want to stop at two?" I ask. By the cliffside, a flock of seagulls screech, the sounds lightly drowned out by the waves crashing.

She shrugs as she takes another sip. "Honestly, even if I didn't, the shitshow with Rob has just put a permanent end to everything."

"Has he been coming over?" While I've been around a lot to help this past week, I tried to stay away from the Rob subject in case she preferred not to talk about it, but since she brought it up...

"Twice. He wants more, but I can't stand seeing him." She starts pulling her short hair up in a bun. "And with the hormones? I never know if I'm about to start bawling my eyes out or kill him."

"I'm so sorry." There's nothing else I can say about the situation. It's plain shitty.

"He also told me he wants us to work on this."

"Will you?"

She shakes her head. "I don't believe in second chances."

I take a long drink.

"What about you?" she asks.

"Me?"

She gestures her chin in the direction of the house, now illumi-nated by the patio lights. "How are things with him?"

My face warms. Even though she knows we're... *something*, I'm not sure how much to tell her. I still feel like she might jump at me for making a move when she specifically warned me not to.

"Good." I swallow roughly. "It wasn't planned, you know."

She leans back in her Adirondack chair. "Doesn't matter. It was always going to happen. You two are like Velcro or something. Inevitable."

Even with the nerves of what she's going to say about us, some-thing unfurls in my chest.

"So why did you warn me to stay away?" I ask.

"I truly didn't want either of you to get hurt." Her lips quirk up. "I had to give it a try."

"Sorry we failed."

"He's happy. I can see it." She finishes her wine, looking at the patio door as if he's about to appear. "And you look happy, too. Just be careful with his heart."

I don't want to talk about the fact that if I leave, I don't know how either of our hearts will come out unscathed. I'm completely lost on that part. The more days I spend in Eli's bed, eating breakfast with him and Zoe, brushing our teeth together, falling asleep with our bodies tangled, I can't imagine walking away from it. I've thought about the hospital where Keira delivered again. Wondered if a change in scenery might be what I need. Things have changed around here. Maybe it's time I face it. But I'm too confused to dare bring it up with her, so instead, I say, "I'm really glad he had you these past years."

"I'm glad I had him, too." She stands. "I'll go see if Billie's awake." Just when she reaches the door, she turns and says, "You've got a gem on your hands. And he's lucky to have you, too."

I am melting.

Little Billie sleeping in her puppies onesie? Heart-shattering. But her sleeping while tucked in Eli's neck, his long fingers covering her entire back and head as he holds her close? Actually criminal. I haven't been able to look elsewhere. I thought photos of him with baby Zoe was enough, but they didn't do this glorious scene any justice. Every time he brushes his thumb against her little ear or looks down to make sure she's still sleeping, I want to throw my head back and groan.

"I feel like your turn is longer than mine," I say from my end of the couch. Maybe I can end this night unscathed if I stop watching him like this.

"Sucks to be you, then," he says with a wink. "I'm giving this baby back over my dead body."

"That's selfish."

"Could not care less."

I lean forward and whisper, "Are you sure about that?"

"Please don't use my kid as leverage, thank you," Keira says from where she's scrolling on her phone on the other side of the living room, Xavier still sleeping beside her.

That's when it hits me. The smell. I sniff once, then again, only to spot the growing stain on Eli's shirt.

"Oh my God," I say.

He frowns. "What?"

"She just shat on your shirt."

"No, she didn't."

"Karma's a bitch, baby."

It seems to be at that moment he smells it, because he looks down in horror to find his shirt covered in yellowy-orange poop. I start cackling.

"Oh no," Keira exclaims as she stands. "Oh, no, no, no."

"Can you help?" Eli tells me.

"I can't," I wheeze out, laughing too hard at his horrified expression to help. "This never happened to you with Zoe?"

"A first," he says, gagging when he looks again, only making me laugh more. Meanwhile, Billie is still sleeping soundly, her lips open like she's catching the best rest of her short life.

"Cassie, I'm dying here." He goes to lift her, only to show that the situation is even worse under her. "I can *feel* it."

Keira comes over with wipes, but she soon realizes the severity of the situation. "Okay, wait a minute. I need a towel."

He lets his head rest back. "I don't think I'll ever get this sensation out of my head."

I can barely breathe.

"All right, all right," Keira says as she jogs back with a white towel.

"White? You had to pick white?" I ask.

"First one I found." She goes to pick Billie up under her arms, then wraps her in the towel. "There you go. Not nice to poop on others, baby." She kisses the top of her head before taking her away to change her.

Eli and I stare at the mess on his shirt. "Will you help me get this off?" he asks.

I give his shoulder two taps, then kiss his cheek. "Not a chance."

After one long diaper and outfit change for Billie and a shower for Eli, everyone comes back to the living room, where Eli still asks to pick Billie up again, seemingly making her promise not to do this again. I then go through another half-hour of looking at the man I've spent more than half of my life pining over rubbing circles on her back—now clad in a dinosaur onesie—and leaning his cheek on top of her head. I love it and hate it at the same time. It's still the cutest thing I've ever seen, but eventually, a heaviness settles in my stomach. By the time Keira leaves, I'm emotionally drained.

I jump in the shower while Eli finishes cleaning up the kitchen, and when I come out of the en-suite, he's waiting for me on the bed, clad in only black boxer briefs.

"Did you have a good night?" he asks.

I nod with a smile, but he must notice something isn't quite right, because he stands with a divot between his brows. "What's wrong?"

"Nothing."

"Cassie."

"Really, I'm fine." I smile, but when he doesn't budge, I add, "Today was just a little harder. Watching you with Billie." Every time I saw his hand engulfing her tiny foot, I kept thinking of how, even if I was wild enough to imagine this for us, it would never happen. What I saw tonight will never be our reality, no matter what I decide to do with my life.

He doesn't say anything. Instead, he steps forward and wraps me in his arms.

"Are you sure you got all that poop out?"

"Shut up and hug me."

He doesn't need to ask twice. I understand why Billie slept so well against his chest, really. Nowhere is as comfortable as right here, with his sweet smell around me.

"You can say it, you know, when you're having a harder time. You don't ever have to pretend everything's fine. Not with me."

"But I wasn't *unhappy,* either. I had a great night. Sometimes it's just... all mixed together."

"Then you can say that, too."

"I don't want to ruin your happy moments," I say against his neck.

He pulls back so he can see me, his arms still around my lower back. "You won't ruin anything by being honest." He tucks a strand of hair behind my ear. "Don't you get it? I want you. All of you. Even the parts you think I don't want to see."

I swallow hard. "What if that changes?"

He laughs this time—a loud, clamorous Grant laughter. "Baby, I spent years forcing myself not to want anything. You're the first thing I allowed myself to have, not because it made sense, but because I wanted to." When he places his hand against my cheek, I rest on it. "Trust me. It won't change."

I don't give him time to catch his breath before catching his lips with mine. He immediately returns the kiss, his lips parting to allow my tongue in. My hands find their way to his hair, tugging lightly the way I know he likes. I don't know how I was ever supposed to stay away from this man. No one has ever made me feel as seen or understood. As safe. I feel like I know this man in his entirety, both the past and present versions, and there's nothing I don't like.

With his hands on my ass, he lifts me up and brings me to the bed. He never stops kissing me as he drags the straps of my tank top down my arms, as he frees my breasts from my bra, as he slides his hands under my skirt and makes me come.

Once I come down from my high, I feel his erection against my thigh, and even with this orgasm, I feel restless, like I want to climb into his skin. I lift my pelvis against his.

"Fuck," he exhales against my lips.

"I want you," I say.

He smirks, his fingers twitching under my skirt. "Am I not doing just that?"

I shift to grab his cock from outside his boxers. "All of you."

His lips part.

"I want to try," I add.

His gaze searches mine for a long moment before he nods, kissing me once more in a way that makes me forget everything except him. My hands are everywhere, in his hair, scratching his chest, palming his backside.

"All this talk about men being obsessed with asses," he teases, nipping at my lips.

"You have an insane ass. Sue me."

He chuckles, the deep sound reverberating to my middle. "Ditto."

I smile, too, but it disappears when he pulls his boxers off and exposes his hard length. He reaches back for me, pulling my skirt and panties off, leaving my shirt bunched in the middle of my stomach so I'm all at his mercy. His middle finger finds its way to my core, rubbing softly against my entrance, then dipping in. He groans.

"You're wet, but do you think we need lube, too?"

I nod. I haven't done this in months, and while this is Eli and I know he'll stop if I'm too uncomfortable, better put all the chances on our side.

He reaches behind me and pulls a condom and a bottle out of the bedside table—the one I didn't search during my snooping.

The edges of his jaw are razor-sharp as I roll the condom down his cock. I press a kiss to his lips before straightening. "I'd rather not think about why you have lube in your room."

"Trust me, I haven't used it in a long time." He pops the cap of the bottle.

"Is it past its expiration date?"

"Does lube have an expiration date?"

I study him for all of three seconds before deciding this lube could be from the ice age, and I'd still use it. I grab it from his hand, then rub a generous amount on him, then on me. He helps me, too, rubbing my core before entering one finger, then two, spreading the lube everywhere.

"Ready to face UTIs for you. If that's not..." My words die down when I realize just what I was going to say. Thankfully, he doesn't seem to catch on.

"I'm honored." The humor in his eyes simmers as he says, "What would make this better for you?"

I think for a moment, never having even considered that before. The penetrative part of sex has always felt more like a practicality to getting pregnant than anything else. It was never particularly good, but I never tried to make it better, either.

"Can we try with you on your back?"

He lies down on the bed without a word, and once I straddle him, he notches himself at my entrance "You'll tell me if it hurts," he says, not a question but a command.

"Yes, chef."

His face softens, his large hands landing on my hips, and the way he watches me makes me feel like I'm worth an entire galaxy.

Slowly, I sink onto him.

To say there's instant pleasure would be a lie. It stings, and I have to shift, so I can take him deeper. Still, the thought that we're connected, that a part of his body is inside me, makes me like it.

"Jesus fuck, Cassie," he hisses, head thrown back and exposing the delicious cords of his neck. I lean forward to kiss them, gasping at the feel of him. "That's it. Take me the way you need."

It's a freedom he's offering, to experiment so I can take what *I* want, first and foremost. Emotions swell inside me, but now's not the time to study them.

He kisses me, and I melt. I start moving again, and this time, the fit is better. I'm careful not to go too deep or too fast, protecting myself from cramps that could hit me at any time, and the thing is, Eli doesn't seem to care one bit. We're not having wild, back-breaking sex, but he still groans and whispers how good I feel, how gorgeous I look, how crazy I make him. And soon, the feeling of discomfort moves away, and with those small, careful moves, I find pleasure.

He seems to notice the change. My breathing quickens, perspiration slicking my back, and I hold onto him as I keep the same rhythm, a moan escaping me.

"Yeah?" he says against my lips. I close my eyes and nod, and when his finger finds my clit, it becomes almost too much.

"How does it always feel this fucking good with you?"

I don't know either. It's as if sex with him is an entire different thing from all I've experienced in the past.

I hold on tighter to him, my movements less controlled, the slickness from me and the lube rubbing on my thighs.

I see the restraint in his body, the way every one of his muscles is taut to make sure I remain fully in control. Pressure builds in my stomach, my inner walls clenching against him.

His thrusts get jerkier, and I'm barely riding him anymore, only rubbing myself against him so I can get all the friction I need, and before I can wonder if I'll actually come from this, the orgasm crashes over me, making me gasp against his exposed throat, my world tilting so I can only taste and smell and feel him. He follows close behind, careful in his movements as he groans and curses in my hair, his body twitching and his hands squeezing so hard it'll likely leave a bruise, just like he has every time we've been together. I can't get enough of it.

We remain like this for a long time, catching our breaths with my naked chest against his, fingers tangled in each other's hair.

"Eli?" I ask in a sleepy voice.

"Yeah?"

"I think I might like you."

He chuckles, then kisses the top of my head. "Yeah. I think I might like you, too."

Chapter 34

I'm in dopamine overload.

Most mornings this past week, I've gone to Keira's to fill up on baby cuddles. I pretend I come over to let her sleep longer, but I'm simply obsessed with my niece. Sometimes, Xavier wakes up early with us, so I also get my fill of playing with him. I am now an expert in all things cars. He's gotten used to me being around, and now, he doesn't bat an eye when I make his breakfast instead of Keira. We've come so far from the boy who would barely meet my eye when I arrived. At first, I was afraid he would ask me about his father, but he hasn't mentioned Rob, probably because he comes over every night to hang with the kids. During that time, Keira grabs dinner with Eli and me. Then, she returns home, and I get Eli in bed, all to myself.

It's been too good to be true, really. At first, it felt like I couldn't possibly feel this happy. It was too much. But then, I settled into it, so much so that I've started to slip up inside the house. Usually, on the mornings I stay home, I put my alarm clock at 6:00 a.m. and get up so I'm downstairs by the time Zoe wakes. However, when my alarm rang today, I was tired after Eli kept me up for hours, and I made the mistake of snoozing once. Then twice.

By the fifth time the ringing came, Eli grumbled, "If you snooze again, I swear to God..."

"You'll what?"

"Throw myself out the window, probably."

I lifted myself on my elbows, grinning after I turned the alarm off. "Didn't you say you liked having someone to wake up next to?"

"When it doesn't feel like I'm living on a construction site, yes." He covered his face with his pillow.

"I didn't know you could be so grumpy."

His voice was muffled as he said, "Humans crumble under torture, Cass. Everyone knows that."

"Fine, then." I went to climb out of the bed, but he stopped me with his arms around my waist and pulled me back down. His skin was burning hot against mine.

"Not so fast, you scoundrel."

"Did you actually just use the word *scoundrel* in a serious manner?"

"So, what if I did?" he said in a scratchy voice, his jaw coarse under my hands from his overnight beard.

I brushed my lips to his, and in a second, I was on top of him, everything in his body rock hard.

And then, his door squeaked open.

I jumped off him, then brought the cover up to my neck as if I could hide from Zoe's possibly traumatized eyes. Eli wasn't nearly as panicked as I was, only straightening in bed and making sure his groin was covered.

"Daddy, I want some cereal."

I don't know if it was because she still looked half-asleep, but she didn't blink at seeing me there. As if she'd seen her dad's friends in his bed countless times.

"Sure, baby," he said. Once she left, he got up and dressed into his pajama pants like he couldn't be bothered. I wondered if that was when the shock would hit him and he'd start freaking out that Zoe had caught us, but the only thing the smug bastard did was look back at me and wink.

It shouldn't have made me this giddy.

And now, four hours later, I'm almost skipping as I go to meet him at the Chowder Festival in town. It must be all that dopamine. I barely recognize myself, these days. Or rather, I barely recognize the person I'd become in the past year. Even the person before that, maybe. My shoulders are straight, and I don't avoid anyone's gaze as I find my way through the maze of kiosks, from middle-aged women selling handmade silver jewelry to farmers showcasing their bright, freshly picked vegetables. I ignore Mr. Garcias, my old Spanish teacher, when I notice him glaring at me like I'm still a student bringing trouble to his class. When I pass Ashleigh Wright and she smirks like she remembers how much fun she had ruining my life in high school, I look away.

Forget about them.

Eileen has a kiosk where she sells flower arrangements some-where out there, and if I pass her, I know she'll be happy to see me. Gertrude always participates in the chowder competition even though her eggplant soup never pleases anyone, and she'll be another friendly face in the crowd. *Eli* is here.

I can do this. I can stand proud in this place.

"Stealing my sleep and then skipping on me? Harsh."

I turn to find Eli leaning against his table, arms crossed over his apron, a curl of hair loosely hanging over his forehead. His smirk reminds me of the one he gave me last night after making me come more times than I ever had in a row, and that only makes him ten times hotter.

I did in fact skip his kiosk, entirely by mistake. Zoe is sitting behind him, a string of toys scattered in front of her tiny camping chair.

"You're facing a table of maple products," I tease. "You lost the competition before it even began."

"I'd expected I'd have to bribe you for your attention," he says before pulling a maple leaf-shaped lollipop from his apron's pocket like a magician. The same ones they sell in the kiosk opposite his.

He hands it to me, and as I open it, I fight the urge to kiss him, crowd be damned. I don't think I even knew what the word cherished meant until I got to experience Eli Grant as a partner. But this is a workplace for Eli, so I put the candy in my mouth to occupy it instead. It tastes like pure maple gold, and I let my head roll back because it's *that* heavenly.

"Are you actively trying to make me hard in public?" Eli whispers. When I open my eyes, there's nothing friendly about the way he's looking at me.

"I feel like getting turned on in public is just your thing."

Someone approaches the tent to our left, but Eli ignores them as he leans forward and whispers in my ear, "Nah. I think *you*'re just my thing."

I try to keep my grin in control, but it's too late. "You've got some customers to take care of."

"Don't go away yet."

"I won't."

"Good." He doesn't hide from anyone when he kisses my cheek, then returns to work.

I'm still smiling like a kid as I browse the maple products on the other side of the alley when Keira calls me.

"Billie miss me already?" I say as I tuck the can of maple syrup under my arm and smile at the vendor; a white-haired man in a plaid shirt and a particularly impressive mustache.

"Cassie." Her tone makes my stomach plummet.

"What happened?" My mind's already jumping through scenarios like an Olympic gymnast.

"Where are you right now?"

"The Chowder Fest. What's—"

"You need to leave."

"What's going on?" I ask, my mouth dry. Eli is watching me in my periphery, brows bunched, but I can't pause to explain what's going on. Even if she hasn't said anything, I can feel something big is happening.

Around me, people are starting to stare, although I don't think I'm making a scene. "Keira," I say.

An elbow knocks into my left ribs. The scent of cheap boy perfume overwhelms me. Somewhere farther, someone shouts. It feels like I'm in one of those horror movies where the rooms close in on the protagonist, and they can do nothing but wait to be squeezed out.

"I'll tell you when I see you. Just—"

She doesn't have the time to finish her sentence. Doesn't even need to tell me what's going on. I feel it in the air first, a shift in the molecules I've come to recognize. Commotion comes from down the kiosk alley, and the hairs on my arms rise. Every stare feels like a brand burning through my flesh, each sound too loud.

That's when I see him—long salt-and-pepper hair. A scruffy beard. Pale, stick-like arms. He's in a corner of the market, indifferent to the loud whispers and horrified looks thrown his way. One of his hands is in the pocket of faded jeans I recognize as well as my own while his other is holding something out to Crazy Al, a man we were always told to avoid.

The rules never applied to my father.

I can't think, can't breathe as I stare at him. I was never supposed to see him again. He should be in jail. Why the *fuck* isn't he in jail?

More people brush past me as they walk away, a lady even pulling her kid by the hand like it's dangerous to stay here, all the while looking at me with a mix of pity and disgust. I remain frozen in the middle of the way.

Crazy Al taps him on the back, and then he's turning my way. His eyes crinkle at first like he's not sure he recognizes me, and while I want to run and hide from his sight, I can't.

Whatever he was doing with Crazy Al is over, and I take too long to react and hide from him.

"Cassie-O!"

My mind becomes a field of white, and it's as if I leave my body and see the scene happening from above, like a floating ghost. My arms loose at my sides, knuckles getting cracked one after the other. My parted lips. My blank gaze.

"My girl," he shouts as he staggers my way, already out of his mind on whatever substance he could put his hand on. He's probably been out for less than a day, and he's already back to his shit.

There's motion to my left. Eli pulling Zoe behind him, even when she cries out to ask what's happening.

I have felt a universe of emotions when it comes to my father. I've gone through all the stages of grief with our relationship, time and time again. But the shame I feel now, seeing Eli protecting Zoe from him? From us? It tops it all.

The whispers get louder, blending into white noise as my father opens his arms to hug me. Even so, I hear a few clear words. *Shameful. Disgusting. Trash family.* And even with horror suffocating me, I still can't move.

"That's close enough," Eli says as he steps between us.

My father's nose crinkles. He doesn't even remember Eli. Ironic, considering he was always my whole world.

"This is embarrassing for everyone," Eli says in a low voice, close enough to my father that people around can't hear. "Get out of here."

My father doesn't answer. There's no fighting, not even cursing, but the tension is so palpable that everyone feels it, Zoe included. And the second I hear her cry for her daddy, I snap. The can of maple syrup I was still holding falls to the ground, sticky liquid exploding at my feet. Then, I do what I'm the best at.

I run.

The driveway to Mom's house is empty. The only silver lining in this situation. She still has time to leave before he gets to her.

I don't bother knocking, this time. I barge in, my pulse sky-high. "Mom?" I shout. *Please, let me be the first one to tell her.*

"Cassie?" she says in a voice much lower as she slowly peeks out of the kitchen. "What's going on?"

"Oh, thank God." I rush to her.

"What's wrong, honey?"

I don't want to imagine what I look like. Frazzled, breathless, teary. But coming here couldn't wait.

"It's…"

My gaze catches on a pack of Marlboro on the console beside the door. Mom doesn't smoke.

No.

I want to be wrong, but the moment I start looking, I notice it all. The dining table chair that hasn't been pushed back, in the way for Mom. The dirty pair of socks lying in front of the couch. The empty bottle of beer besides the bedazzled lamp Ruth had gotten Mom for her birthday one year.

Mom's shoulders slump.

"He *assaulted* a girl. Does that mean nothing to you?" I shake my head, then cry, "What will it take?"

"Cassie—"

"You know what? I don't want to hear it." I avoid her reaching hand and walk back outside. "I don't know why I expected anything else."

I'm halfway to my car when she calls out behind me, "Do you think I like this?"

I turn.

"Do you think when I was your age, this was the life I wanted for myself?" She's leaning on her cane, and despite it all, I feel bad for having made her walk so fast with her arthritis.

"Not everything is as simple as you think it is," she says, sounding defeated. "He owns this house. We have thirty-three years of marriage."

I know she has a point. I *know* it's not easy. But this has gone on too long. Now, it just feels like more excuses.

And I've heard enough.

"Whatever you say, Mom."

Chapter 35

Eleven Years Ago

T he lady isn't expecting anyone tonight.

Her friends left half an hour ago after their weekly crochet club that included a lot of snacking and very little crochet. She took the time to clean the kitchen before getting into her pajamas and washing her face, but before she can slip into bed, a knock comes at the door.

She's gotten used to visits from her granddaughters over the years, but they both have keys to the house. Her oldest granddaughter usually visits over the weekends, less so now that she's in college, but the youngest still comes over frequently. This summer especially, the lady has seen her most nights. Sometimes, she even hears the front door open when she's already in bed and in the morning, the room she keeps for her granddaughter is already empty.

It's not acceptable for a grandmother to have a favorite grandkid, just like a parent should not favor a child. However, in the privacy of her own mind, she can admit to herself that the girl has always had a special place in her heart. It must be because, even from a young age, she acted like the lady was important. Like she *needed* her. The lady's son became distant the moment he hit puberty, and as the years went by, he only got worse. She can admit this to herself, too. As for her oldest granddaughter, she always acted so sure of herself, like she knew her worth and her place in this world. But the youngest was a fragile one. She carried out like she had to apologize for existing. Even when the girl grew older and set some boundaries for herself, the lady never stopped worrying about what would happen to her precious soul.

And now, as she looks at the girl standing on her front porch, her hair plastered against her head from the rain, the lady thinks maybe the worst has finally happened.

She opens the door to her granddaughter, and the moment she notices the bruising on her cheekbone, she gasps, "Oh, my Cassie."

"I didn't know if you were asleep already. I-I'm sorry."

The lady opens the door wider for her and takes her into her arms. As soon as the girl lays her head on her chest, she starts trembling, silent cries jerking her body. The lady doesn't ask her a thing. She lets her feel whatever it is she's feeling, all the while soaking in her embrace. She has a feeling it'll be the last one she'll feel for a long while.

After a minute, the girl whispers, "I got back from Eli's too late. He was mad."

The lady wishes she would stop talking. She doesn't want to hear yet another horrible thing her son did. Doesn't want to wonder again where she went wrong. But she also needs to know. She won't be able to do what she has to if she's not convinced it's the right decision.

"Mom tried to get him to calm down, but he was out of it. He moved on her, and I tried to stop him, and..."

She doesn't need to hear more. She can put two and two together. She pulls her back and takes another good look at the bruise, seemingly expanding even still. It doesn't look like something that needs to be checked up, but it doesn't matter. It could've been a simple paper cut, and it still would've been a line crossed. Who's to say what will happen next? She's not going to wait to go visit her granddaughter in the hospital, or worse.

The lady breathes out through pursed lips and walks away.

She'd prepared for this. Every time she looked at the backpack in her coat closet and remembered that her granddaughter might one day need it because her son had finally done the unthinkable, the lady would start crying. She couldn't believe the little boy she'd watched chase butterflies in the backyard forty years ago could do something like this. Mostly, she couldn't help the guilt that ravaged her soul when she thought that, despite it all, he remained her son, and she loved him. How could she look her granddaughter in the face when she still wished for a miracle for her tormentor? Still, she planned. If the lady couldn't rid her grandchild of the man who made her life hell, then the least she could do was be prepared in case the worst happened.

She so wished she'd never have to use this backpack.

She hands it to the girl.

"What is this?"

The lady opens the bag the girl is still holding to find a wad of fifty-dollar bills tied together with a rubber band. She presses it into the girl's hand.

"We've reached the limit, my girl. Haven't we?"

The girl's eyes fill. She knows it, too.

The lady takes her in her arms again. "Go, my love. Go, and don't look back." She kisses her cheek, inhaling deeply the sweet scent of her shampoo, then pushes her out the door.

The lady doesn't look outside. She cannot bear it. She waits until the sound of wood creaking under light footsteps comes and goes before she lets her shoulders drop and sighs.

That night, she doesn't go to bed. Instead, she sits at her kitchen table with a full glass of gin and stares out at the dark water ahead. She doesn't cry. The tears will come later, she thinks, when the realization of what she's done settles in.

It must be ten in the morning when another set of knocks comes at her door, frantic this time.

She barely finds the strength to get herself up. She expects the girl's mother, maybe, or her other granddaughter. But she should've expected it'd be the neighbor boy who always looked at her girl with stars in his eyes.

"Have you seen her? Cassie?" he blurts the second she opens the door. He looks haggard, his dark hair sticking out in all directions. "She was supposed to meet me this morning, and she's not answering her phone, and I can't find her anywhere." He barely looks like he's breathing as he pulls at the roots of his hair. "Did I do something? Yesterday, we…"

He stops himself when he finally takes a good look at the lady. The loss must be written all over her. Still, he needs to hear it.

"I'm so sorry. She's gone."

She didn't think she'd ever see a heart break in real time.

It's not so obvious in the big picture, but it's all in the details. The flaring of his nostrils. The loss of focus in his eyes. The caving in his chest, like the place the girl used to inhabit was surgically cut out.

"She can't have left just like that. We didn't…" He blinks repeatedly. "We had more time."

She knows why the girl didn't go see the boy before leaving. It's the same reason the lady pushed her out the door last night. They both knew if they took a good look at the person they loved most in this world, they wouldn't be able to do it.

"Will she call me, at least?"

The lady's lips press into a straight line. If she knows her granddaughter, no, she won't. She'll want to protect him, which will mean letting him go. The boy seems to read this answer on her face. It feels like shooting a man already down, but she has no reassuring words to say. She's the person people come to for a positive outlook on a situation, but today, she doesn't have a positive bone in her body.

Instead, she goes to the scrapbook she was working on yesterday, when she didn't know her world was about to shatter. She finds a picture she took a few years ago, one she always loved because her granddaughter looks so at peace in it. She knows it's because of the boy she's looking at.

She returns to the boy, now even taller than he already was in the picture, and hands it to him. He looks down at it and immediately snaps his eyes shut.

"You were her world, Eli Grant." She squeezes his hand. "Thank you for loving my girl."

A tear slides down his cheek. "What am I supposed to do?"

"You move on." The boy is young. He'll be able to. Not like her.

"I can't." His head shakes sternly. "I'll never get over her."

She breathes through the thickness in her throat. If she starts crying with him, she'll never stop. "I don't think I will, either."

The lady doesn't know whether she'll see her granddaughter again in this lifetime. And if that means she gets to find happiness, then it'll have been worth it.

Chapter 36

I don't know how much time has passed since I left Mom's and got back to Eli's. I've blanked again. The only thing I know is by the time I hear the front door open and close, the sky outside the window is in this in-between state, with stars slowly blinking to life while fuchsia and orange still color the horizon.

"Oh, thank God," Eli says after climbing the stairs two at a time and finding me sitting on the bed in the guest bedroom. He's alone. "I searched—"

"Where's Zoe?" My voice sounds empty. *I'm* empty.

"At Keira's. I thought maybe it'd be better if she stayed there tonight."

I don't dare ask why. I don't think I can hear it right now. I won't be around for long anyway.

Eli steps closer, slowly, like he's afraid I'll jump and bolt. "How are you—What's this?"

I follow his gaze to the pile of clothes I've started gathering in my open suitcase. "I just started on some packing." Although by the time I'd gathered half my clothes around the house, I gave up. I'd rather leave it all here. It hurt too much to fold each piece of clothing that now had a memory attached to it. The shirt Eli kissed me in for the first time in his room. The sandals Zoe borrowed to parade for me, so big they slipped off her feet with each step. I won't want to see them again.

Eli looks like he's been punched in the stomach. His face has gone a pale shade of green. "W-Why?"

"I'm leaving in five days."

"But... Why?"

"That was always the plan."

"I thought..." He drags a hand through his hair. "I thought you might have changed your mind."

I close my eyes.

"Because you could, you know. Stay."

His sweet smell wraps around me as he approaches. I can't breathe.

"I'm keeping custody of Zoe. Liz won't fight me on it. There's no reason for us to hide anything anymore." It feels like a lifetime before his hand lands on the side of my neck. "We can be together. I *want* us to be together."

I squeeze my eyes tighter so the tears don't fall. It hurts too much to feel everything for this man and have to say no.

"This place isn't for me," I say when I trust my voice to remain steady. "It never was."

"I know today was rough, but—"

"Today was my nightmare." My hands are shaking as I get to my feet. "Didn't you see the way people looked at us? At me? It was just like being back in high school. I wanted to disappear." It was a feeling I'd thought I'd never experience again. I never wanted to feel this horrible in my skin again. I heard whispers all the way to my car, even in the parking lot where people had noticed the scene or had received a text about it. I'd never missed the invisibility of the city so much. I'd started to forget how it used to feel, but the stark reminder was just what I needed to wake up from my stupor. "This summer wasn't reality. This is."

"What does that even mean?" he asks, eyes pleading.

"I left in the first place because I couldn't stand being *that McIntyre girl* anymore. I changed my name. Tried to escape it. But today?" I point outside, the first tear slipping. "Today proved I'm always going to be that girl."

"You don't have to be."

My voice is barely more than a whisper. "They don't give me the option not to."

"And what about how *I* feel about you? How you made me fall—"

"Don't," I stop him with a hand up. Twin tears form tracks down my cheeks. "Please, don't make this any harder."

He wipes his nose with the back of his hand. "Is there anything I can say to make you change your mind?"

It physically hurts to see him like this, like tiny cuts all over my skin. He should never look this sad, and certainly not because of me. "If I stay, I'll suffocate again."

He was wearing protection before. A helmet, a shield, a bullet-proof vest. My words take them all off, and he deflates, as if I've finally hit him. As if he's realized the same thing I did a few hours ago: this is bigger than the two of us. There's no escape, no matter what we do.

His head hangs between his shoulders as he leans against the small desk next to me. "I thought I'd be enough to make you stay. Thought *we*'d be."

Breathe.

I make him turn so he's facing me, then take his face between my hands. His whiskey eyes are drowning.

I breathe deeply to control myself before I say, "If anyone could have, it would have been you two."

His forehead drops to mine, and the sigh he lets out feels like the weight of the world has landed upon his shoulders. Mine does, too. Even if I know I need to leave this place, I also know I'll be miserable without this. Without him. He's more than a friend. More than a crush. More than a lover. He's everything.

And so I bring my lips to his; not because I think it will change anything, but because if I only have a few days left, I want to absorb every second of them. I'll store all those memories, but this time, I won't lock them away. I'll keep them close, reexamining them under bright light whenever I miss him and remember all the little details that made me fall for this man.

I worry he'll move away, that he'll want to protect himself, but he doesn't. He kisses me back with a heightened fervor, like he, too, wants this storage of memories.

We fall backward onto the bed, but neither reaches for the other's clothes. Instead, we kiss for a long while, each stroke languid, each touch meaningful. We're taking our time, kissing not like we have all the time in the world, but like we don't and never want this moment to end. Our bodies are tangled, his hands at the base of my head, mine on his back, and I focus to commit it all to memory. Our kiss turns salty, a declaration of love and sadness at once.

When he pulls away, I almost cave at the defeat written across his face. "I can't leave." His throat works. "Zoe... Her whole world is here."

"I know." I hold his jaw between my hands, rubbing his cheeks with my thumbs. I'd never have asked him to follow me, either. *His* whole world is here, and it's time he thinks of himself for once.

His mouth twists to the side as he stares down at me. I blink fast, then drag his mouth back to mine. We kiss some more, and eventually fall asleep in the guest bed, still clothed, our limbs intertwined, not an inch of space between us. But no matter how tight we hold on, we both know we'll have to let go soon.

Chapter 37

The bell above the door of Eileen's Flower Delights rings as I enter the shop.

I've been wondering what to give Zoe before I leave, both as a reminder of me once I'm gone, and a thank you for the wonderful summer she gave me. It gave me hope that one day, maybe, I'll find something like it again. I'm also waiting for her choir recital before leaving, so I can't show up empty-handed.

As I take in the flower arrangements available for purchase, I can't help but smirk. Gertrude was right. These *are* weird. When Mom corroborated by telling me Eileen wasn't the best florist but everyone in town still buys from her because she's the only one around, I didn't quite believe her, but she wasn't lying. Bright orange Birds of Paradise mixed with delicate peonies and overpowering greeneries. Round, untrimmed shrubs planted in the middle of rose arrangements. Nothing makes sense. And yet, there are indeed customers around. I guess people around here are used to appreciating the thought rather than the bouquet itself. And isn't the intention more important than the final result?

"Cassie!" Eileen says as she walks in from the back of the store, holding a bouquet of flashy purple roses with plastic butterflies strewn across the stems with wool string. The flowers are bent at odd angles, one going as far as pointing downward. "What do you think of this? I've been toying with this idea for a while."

"The..." I'm not sure where to start since all of it looks experimental. "Butterflies?"

"No, of course not! I mean the flowers shaping a letter."

"Oh." I use all my strength to keep a straight face, not even trying to decipher which letter it is supposed to depict. "Beautiful."

"I think so, too!" she exclaims, and I understand now why people keep coming in. The pure joy she gets out of it is worth all the ugly gifts. She drops the heavy arrangement on the counter, then wipes her hands across her muddy apron. "What can I do for you, sweetheart?"

"I'm looking for a long-lasting plant to give to a friend."

She snaps her fingers, already walking away from the counter. "I have just the thing for you."

She leads me to a row of shelves decorated with different perennials and house plants, all of which are adorned with bright butterflies either hooked on the leaves or dug into the soil. It's actually perfect for a six-year-old.

Eileen picks up a plant with long, striped leaves. "The snake plant is a great choice if your friend doesn't have a lot of gardening skills."

Considering she forgets to brush her teeth half the time, I'd say that's a great assessment of Zoe. Plus, she'll love the name of the plant. For a moment, I think about what it would be like to watch her take care of it over the years, bringing it insects as if it was a true snake that needed feeding instead of watering it. I'm sure I'd always find all sorts of things in the soil; objects or creatures she'd have wanted to share with her pet plant. I crack my thumb knuckle.

"It's perfect."

"Oh, and I could dye some of the leaves, so it looks more ethereal!"

"I think we're good with the butterflies."

She purses her lips like I have no taste but still nods and leads me to the register.

"So, how are you doing?" she asks as she taps on her old-school cash register. I have a feeling her prices are determined as randomly as the flowers that go into each bouquet.

"Okay."

She looks up from her glasses, a brow lifted. "Really?"

This feels like a trick question. I don't answer.

She takes my credit card, then starts arranging the gift packaging around the plant. To say her creativity extends to her gift wrapping would be an understatement. She's meticulous with her work, too, so much so that I fear it will take an hour before I'm out of here. I'm not usually impatient, but Eli is waiting for me back home. Zoe is with Liz at Susan's place tonight, so we're going out. It feels strange, to have real dates only now that we know we barely have any time left. It's making us both hungry for more.

"You know," Eileen says as she cuts a piece of bedazzled sticky tape, "I didn't have the best family life either, growing up."

I stiffen. "Eileen…"

She glances up with so much steel, I stop myself. This is a *shut up and listen* look if I've ever seen one.

"As I was saying," she says with an overload of sass, "I didn't have the best childhood." Cut, fold, tape. "My father was... mean with my brothers and me. With my mother, too, although we rarely saw it."

"I really don't want to talk about this."

"But I think you need to."

I don't know when I started listening to Ruth's friend like she is my own mother, but her tone is so intimidating, I have no choice but to.

"My mother—God rest her soul—was a good woman, but she never did a single thing to protect us. She was always out late with friends, leaving us to fend for ourselves when my father got back home."

I swallow.

"I never wanted anything more than to have a mother who would be there for me. I would've done anything for her to see us. I don't think she even realized what was going on inside our home. I wanted a protector."

"I wanted a protector, too," I snap. Eileen isn't pretending to wrap the plant anymore. Her hands are resting on the counter, as if she's bracing herself.

"And you had one," she says. "You have no idea what your mother did to protect you."

"She stayed."

"And didn't you ever wonder why that is? That maybe her staying was her way to protect you?"

"I don't see how remaining with him could've helped us."

"But that's the thing. You don't know everything. In fact, I would bet you know less than the tip of the iceberg." She tilts her head. "Even Ruth was kept in the dark on most things."

I drag my tongue over my teeth, wanting to ask her how *she* would know, but she's been in my mother's life for a long time. She was mostly Ruth's friend first, but it seems she and Mom got close in the past years. If anyone knows about our home situation, it would be her.

Her voice softens as she says, "I'm not saying she was perfect. Your mother made mistakes. Of course she did. And I'm not saying staying was necessarily the best option, either." She pushes the plant in my direction. The gift-wrapping looks half-finished, but I guess that was the final result. "What I am saying is that she did what she thought was best for all of you, and you can think she didn't choose right, but her decisions were always made with you in mind."

Isn't the intention more important than the final result?

All the battle leaves my body at once. I lean against the counter, head low. "I don't think I can ever understand her choices."

"And maybe you don't need to." Her short curls bounce as she cocks her head. "Maybe you can just accept that she had her reasons, both for herself and for you girls, and decide to forgive her even if you don't understand them."

The retort that Mom stayed even after we were gone from the house is on the tip of my tongue, but what Eileen just said ripples across my mind. She had her reasons for herself, too. Maybe, just maybe, there were worse things than staying.

Although my anger disappears, a deep, all-consuming sadness overwhelms me at the thought of my mother still being in the heart of the cyclone, even all these years later. I was able to leave. It wasn't easy, and it created holes in all my relationships, and even now, it's tearing me apart, but I *could* do it. I can't imagine what it would've felt like to not be able to.

"Be gentle with her, all right?" Eileen says. "I promise you, as her friend, she deserves it. Deserves your love, too."

Toying with the inside of my bottom lip, I grab the plant and say, "Thank you, Eileen."

She smiles as if the intense last five minutes did not happen, and I'm just a regular customer. "Of course, sweetheart. I hope your friend likes your gift!"

I look down at the plant. As if knowing who I'm giving it to, Eileen added gummy worms on the dirt, not as a candy but as a decoration.

"I'm sure she will."

Chapter 38

Pure chaos has taken over Keira's house when I step in two days later. Shrill howls pierce the living room, where Keira is leaning over a wiggling Billie who looks very insulted that her mom is trying to dress her. Meanwhile, Xavier is dressed in a mix of different superhero costumes, with a Spider-Man bodysuit, a Batman mask, and some kind of gauntlet on his fist. He's jumping from couch to couch, every time coming close to falling and hurting the heck out of himself. I'm pretty sure that's crayon marks on the wall of the living room, too, but I'm not about to mention it.

"Oh, Cassie, thank God," she says, just now realizing I'm the one who walked in. I guess at this point, she doesn't even worry about thieves or kidnappers anymore. She does a double take as she rises with Billie, who immediately calms when she hugs her to her chest. Her expression transforms in question the second she takes me in. I don't know how she realizes something's up, but she does. Then, her shoulders drop.

"You're leaving again," she states, not even a question.

I don't answer, but my silence says it all.

"Xavier, go play in your room," she says without breaking eye contact with me.

"But—"

"In your room, now." Her tone leaves no place for arguing, and he doesn't. I send my nephew a sympathetic smile before he climbs upstairs. I hate that I'm causing even a hint of tension in their house.

I didn't want to do a goodbye tour. In fact, if I'd listened to my chaotic inner voice, I'd have left without saying a word. I don't know how I'll be able to handle all these separations, but skipping town in the dead of night would've been the cowardly thing to do, and I'm trying to do better eleven years later, even if it means torturing myself with a slow death.

"I can't believe I was this naive again," Keira says with a sharp shake of the head. "I was really starting to think this time was different."

"It is! It will be. You'll come visit." My heart is in my throat. Even though I believe in what I'm saying, I see the wall being erected between us, brick by brick with the warmth disappearing from Keira's eyes. Her entire body hardens.

"Like you invited me to visit the last time?"

"It's not going to be the same. I messed up last time. I don't want to lose you or the kids again."

"But you're still leaving us."

I can't go through this conversation again, so I summarize it with, "I can't stay."

"Don't say that. You *can* stay. You just won't."

My hand flies to my chest, rubbing. "Doesn't it kill you, every time you're associated with him?"

She adjusts Billie in her arms when she starts whining, as if feeling the brewing tension. "It'd kill me more to let him win and give away the life I've worked for."

"You've always been stronger than me."

"That's an excuse, and you know it," she spits. Billie lets out a small cry, and Keira breathes in deeply.

"I have a job back in the city," I say. "An apartment. A life."

"Another excuse."

I ball my shaking hands into fists. "You think I want to be like this?" I say, trying not to focus too much on how similar my words are to my mother's.

"You didn't even try to change."

"I did try." Little by little, I forced myself to go out there, even if I'd have rather stayed protected inside Ruth's place. I tried to be the person Eli wanted. Tried to be the sister Keira needed. But my father returning was the variable I didn't take into consideration. The one that made this dream unattainable.

"Not hard enough, then."

She's hurt. I can't fault her that, even if the hate in her glare destroys something I thought had been repaired within me.

"Well, we don't want your goodbyes," she says, sitting next to a pile of laundry and folding a shirt on top of it. "I'll find something to tell Xav, but that's the last time. You're either in my kids' lives, or you're not."

I look at Billie, so small still as her thin fingers twist into her mother's hair. I understand Keira. She's protecting her family from building expectations toward people who will end up flaking out on them. How many times did I wish Mom would do that for us? In a way, I'm proud of my sister for this, even if it kills me that I'm the person the kids might need protection from. I can't imagine not seeing Billie and Xavier again. Losing my sister. This summer, I found the person I used to consider a friend as much as a family member before, and the last thing I want is to give that up.

But you can't have everything you wish for. I know that better than anyone.

"All right," I say, swallowing so my voice doesn't crack. "I understand."

Keira hums.

"The offer remains open. Whenever you want to visit, I'll be there, with open arms."

Her lips twitch before she nods.

No goodbye, then.

With one last look at the hard lines of her brows and nose and at the small world inside her arms, I turn and leave.

Only once I'm outside and the door is closed behind me do I allow my face to crumple.

This entire situation is fucked. No matter what decision I make, I'm losing. There *is* no right decision. I'm trapped.

I take a good minute to get myself under control, then turn toward the driveway. I jump at the sight of the person leaning against her car not ten feet away from me, watching. Dottie is sitting at her feet, not even needing a leash.

"I figured it'd come to this," my mother says, her expression unreadable.

"What do you mean?"

"You decided to leave." She nods as if answering for me. I guess you truly can't hide anything from a mother. I'm not in the mood for another fight. I've already left every bit I had in there.

I reach her side and pull Dottie into my arms before leaning back against the car.

"I'm sorry, you know," Mom says. "I never wanted you to feel like you had to leave your home. I still don't." Her dark brown eyes fill, and she doesn't blink the tears away. "But I want you to know I understand."

I bite the inside of my cheek.

"I wasn't the mother you deserved, and you'll never know how much I hate myself for all of it."

My mind blinks back to the conversation with Eileen. *She did what she thought was best for all of you.*

I remember all the times Mom caught me eating sweets in my bedroom. Whether it was saltwater taffy from the candy shop in town, or cherry lollipops I'd gotten from my grandmother's stash, it was always the same scenario. She'd walk in while I was supposed to be sleeping and find me sitting under my covers, filling my mouth with sugar. It was always the best comfort I could find. Mom would pull the blanket from my head and tell me I wasn't supposed to eat those, especially after I'd brushed my teeth. Then, I'd try to bribe her with one, and after taking a good look at me, she'd say it was okay, just this once. I used to think my bribes worked, but now I see it was probably the sight of me being happy that stopped her from ever getting mad. I ended up getting three cavities repaired that year, but my mother never threw it back in my face. She's not like that. She'll do what she can to preserve the peace, to make a person feel good and grateful, even if she doesn't agree with their choices.

It's who she is. Who she's always been. And as angry as it's made me sometimes, it's a quality, too. Eileen's right about this. I might not agree with her choices, but it doesn't mean I have to keep holding them against her.

"It's a shitty fucking situation," I say, fingers buried in my childhood dog's fur.

"Language."

I roll my eyes, because I can't believe *this* is what she wants to focus on, but I rephrase, "It's a crappy situation. But we're stuck in it, and you're right that I can't know everything."

The road in front of Keira's house is calm; no sounds but the chirp of birds in the forest ahead. Thick fir trees hide us from the sun, the air almost chilly this morning. I turn to Mom, finding her gaze already on me. "I forgive you." I may never forget what happened to us as kids, but I can decide to move on. Let go.

They're only three words, eleven small letters, but saying them feels like unbuckling a belt that'd been choking me for a long time and finally taking in a deep breath. You don't forgive for others, Eli told me once. You forgive for yourself. And he was right. This is as much for me as it is for her. And more than that, I think I figured out that she and I aren't so different after all. We're both stuck in our messed-up coping mechanisms. Mine is to run. Hers is to stay and pretend like everything's okay. I can't wholeheartedly judge her for something I can't stop doing, either.

A hiccup comes out of Mom's throat. I exhale and lean over so the side of my head can rest against her shoulder. She smells the same way she has for as long as I've known her, like the strong floral perfume she gets at the local drug store. Dottie shifts in my arms so her snout rests on Mom's arm.

Will I ever understand her choices? Probably not. But that doesn't mean she deserves to bear all the blame for what someone else made us go through.

"And if you ever do decide to leave him and need a place to stay, you give me a call. Okay?"

She sniffs, then puts her sun-damaged hand on my arm. "Okay, honey."

Chapter 39

T he choir recital takes place in the community room behind
the library.

I thought there would be three, maybe four sets of parents out
here, but the room is packed. Apparently, choir is back in. I hold
tightly to Eli's hand and keep my face close to his shoulder as
we find our seats at the front of the room. If it were any other
situation, I'd hide in the back, but I want Zoe to be able to see us
out in the audience more than I want my anonymity. I'm leaving
tomorrow. This is the least I can do for her.

"I've been meaning to tell you," Eli says as we sit in the second
row. "This plant is horrible."

I look down at the gift I got for Zoe sitting in my lap. "I know."

"She'll love it."

I grin. "I know."

Soon, the lights dim, and the crowd shouts like this is a Beyoncé
concert. Two dozen kids come out and find their spots. Then, they
start singing.

"Stop laughing," Eli whispers in my ear as they enter a mash-up
of "Sorry Ms. Jackson" and "No Scrubs"; two songs these kids have
obviously never heard in their lifetime.

"You were right," I say, trying really freaking hard to keep my face neutral. "They're so bad."

"Yeah, horrible." Then, he whoops like this is the kind of show you throw random whoops for.

"You're overdoing it."

He snickers against my cheek, then presses a kiss to my jaw. He does it so effortlessly that for a second, I can imagine it; our life together. Drives to choir practices while listening to those terrible Kid's Bops covers, teasing each other in the kitchen while trying out new cookie recipes, attending school events together like we both belong here.

My throat tightens, and it becomes even worse when the music slows to "Amazing Grace" and Zoe steps forward for her solo. I'd be lying if I said she's a great singer. But I know the courage it's taken her to step out like this and stand tall in front of this group of kids who haven't been nice to her. It doesn't matter that she's off key or that her voice cracks on the highest note. It brings tears to my eyes all the same.

I feel Eli's gaze on me when I sniffle. Between the seats, he finds my hand and holds it. I squeeze tighter.

She looks so beautiful up there. Fearless. This little girl will grow up to live a grand, wonderful, happy life. And even if I'm not here to see it, I'll always cheer her on from the sidelines.

When the song comes to an end, I don't care about anyone else in that room. I jump to my feet and clap so hard my hands hurt. Eli joins me on his feet, too, whooping once more. A few others stand up awkwardly, and when "Unwritten" starts to play and Zoe returns in line with the others, we sit back down.

The concert doesn't last long after that, and the second it's over, the kids walk off stage and to their parents, not pretending to hide behind the curtains again. We stand to get to Zoe, but we're stopped by Mrs. Graham, the pleasant ex-First Lady of this town. Why is she even here? It's not like she has a kid in this group. Thankfully, this time she ignores me, only focusing on Eli as she tells him just how wonderful the food was at her son's birthday party last weekend. I ignore her, too, and look for Zoe in case she thinks we left before coming to congratulate her, but what I see is so much worse.

A little girl close to her age with bright-red hair and diamond studs gives her a hug, only to subtly pull at her ponytail.

Oh, now I'm kicking some six-year-old ass.

I head in their direction, but the path is clogged with people. I apologize and try to make my way in between bodies, keeping my eye on that little bitch and on Zoe, who looks like she's been turned to stone by Medusa. My sweet girl. I'd face all my teenage bullies again if it meant she didn't have to experience any of it.

It's as if the universe hears me, because the next thing I see is the little girl—Amelia, I assume—reaching out to a woman who's none other than Ashleigh fucking Wright. One of the girls who made my life a living hell for years. My insides physically revolt at the sight of her. But when I see her and Amelia throw Zoe a fake, sickeningly sweet smile, I know I can't keep quiet. Cold sweat gathers at my nape, but I still push through.

"Where are you going?" I hear Eli behind me, but I don't stop.

"Hey!" I call out once, then another time, until Ashleigh turns.

"Oh. Cassie, right?" she says with another one of her shit-eating smiles, as if she never bothered learning my name. I know it's fake. She would write it on the bathroom stalls all the time, always followed by some trashy take on me.

"Haven't changed one bit, have you?"

She continues smiling while her daughter sees another friend and leaves us.

"You know, being a mean girl in high school is one thing, I guess. Your prefrontal cortex is not yet fully developed and all that stuff. Still being one at twenty-eight, though, is pretty fucking embarrassing. But encouraging your child to be one to another kid? That's straight up pathetic."

Her smile has slowly slipped away, her powdered face now white under the bright neons of the community room.

"Grow up, Ashleigh."

I turn to find Zoe, but stop and throw over my shoulder, "Oh, and one more thing."

She's still standing there, looking like she wants to stomp her foot.

"If I hear your kid keeps bullying Zoe? I'll use that reputation you loved to throw in my face, and I *will* fuck you up."

Then, I leave, not even bothering to look back. Based on the weak sound Ashleigh just let out, I doubt Amelia will remain a problem. But if she does? I won't hesitate to come back and keep my promise.

"What was that?" Eli asks when I reach him and Zoe.

"Nothing," I say, smiling, then lean forward and hug Zoe as tight as I can, hoping it conveys how much love I hold for her. "You were wonderful out there."

The gummy worm snake plant is indeed a hit. Thankfully, it gets her smiling all the way home.

When I step out onto the patio, a heavy darkness surrounding the house, I can't find Eli, and for a moment, I have the fleeting thought that he left before we could say goodbye. Maybe he'd rather avoid it, so he got away while I was inside. But then I see the shape of him lying on his back on the lawn, arms behind his head, and I think, *of course he didn't leave*. He isn't me.

After we came back from the recital, Liz came over to see Zoe. She was at the recital, too, and when she gushed about her performance, Zoe *blushed*. It was the sweetest thing. While Eli still wasn't the chattiest with Liz, he did give her the time and space she needed with Zoe. And then, when it was Zoe's time for bed, she asked Liz to come up and do story time. I knew I couldn't handle an official goodbye with Zoe, so I walked over to her and gave her forehead a long kiss, then went into the shower while Liz and Zoe walked upstairs, and Eli snuck outside.

I walk over to where he's lying down and sit cross-legged. He doesn't move, eyes lost in the sky. The breeze is heavy tonight, whipping my hair across my face as water thrashes across the cliffs.

As much as I love the ocean during the day, there's nothing quite like it at night. Some people might see this infinite blackness as scary, but to me, looking out and feeling all alone in the world was always a comfort. With all the outside lights from the house turned off, it's so dark, I can barely see anything save for the faint glow of the Cape Neddick lighthouse miles away.

Silence stretches between Eli and me, the emptiness filled by the splashes and rumbles of the waves. It's as if neither one of us wants to speak first, like now that we're together again and with so few hours left, we don't know where to start. What can you say when the way you feel is beyond words?

But then, his little finger moves to the side of my thigh, and I exhale.

"What are you doing out here?" I finally ask.

"It's the beginning of the Perseids tonight."

The last time we watched them together, although I didn't know it yet, I was about to leave. I hate the irony. Still, when he wraps his arm around me, and I lay my head against his chest, I settle into the moment.

"Is now the time you finally tell me all about space?" I ask.

"Still only know the saucepans. Sorry."

"It's okay. You have other talents."

"Yeah? Like what?"

He's smirking now, and the lightness feels good compared to the distance he was exuding when I came outside.

I trail a finger down his stomach, the muscles tightening under me. "You give such...great..." I lean toward his ear, my hand stopping right above his belt. "Cooking advice."

His chest vibrates next to me. "That all?"

"I guess you now make passable braids, too."

"Wow. A real catch, aren't I?"

"Yeah. You really are." My next breath is heavy.

His gaze alternates between my eyes and my lips, but I interrupt the moment by gasping at a shooting star that crossed the sky in my periphery. It was so bright, there's no way he missed it. The sight always makes me so giddy, even if I know they're nothing but burning rock.

"Make a wish," Eli says, voice low.

"Have you already made yours?"

He nods, his gaze never leaving mine.

Since I started trying to get pregnant, all my wishes have gone to the same place. Birthday candles, eyelashes, four-leaf clovers, 11:11s... Gone to an aimless goal. This time, my wish is looking right at me, yet it feels just as out of reach.

Eli seems to realize this too, because he only tucks me closer to him.

I clear my throat. "Remember the first time we did this together, and you wished for a dog?" I was disappointed. While he'd wished for a pet like Dottie, I'd wished for him.

His irises are indistinguishable from his pupils, from the sky above and the ocean forward. "Baby, there's no moment with you I don't remember."

I don't know who moves first. Is it my fingers tangling in his hair, or his leg wrapping around my thighs? Do his lips reach for mine first, or is it my pelvis that starts rocking against his?

We kiss like two people inhaling all the air they can before diving underwater, like we know no matter how many wishes we get tonight, this is the end. Pressure builds behind my eyes, in my chest, and those emotions turn into frantic touches. It's the opposite of how we were in his guest bedroom. We take, and take, and take. Somehow, he's gotten on top of me, lips dragging from my chin to my neck, then to the top of my breasts. I stretch back, wanting him everywhere, but also needing him to stay close. He wastes no time tugging my loose, flowery skirt up and palming me through my lace underwear.

"You and that public indecency kink," I say on an exhale.

"Only for you."

Before I can protest, his head disappears under my skirt, making me see more stars than there are above me.

After, we lay once more on the ground, this time with half my body lying on top of his chest, our legs tangled. His fingers are tracing soft circles on my back, covering my skin with goosebumps. Hours could have passed, and I wouldn't know. I don't want to move. As if time could stop, and we could remain in this limbo forever if we remain still. His heartbeat is a slow metronome under my ear, as loud as the wild currents below. The eye of the storm, and yet no place will ever feel this peaceful.

His fingers on my back finally still. "I can't watch you leave tomorrow." The sound of his swallow is louder than anything else. "I can't."

I don't want to look at him. *I* can't. Not when I know it could reflect even just a fraction of the hurt that's ravaging my chest.

"It's okay." I force my voice to remain steady. "It's probably better this way."

He doesn't move to look at me, either. A precarious bubble has surrounded us; one made of words unsaid and feelings better left hidden. If he so much as looks at me, he'll see everything, and I think it might be the same if I did him. We can't do that to the other. Leaving is already hard as it is.

I close my eyes and inhale the sweet smell of his skin once more.

Keira was right. I played a careless game. No matter how much I've always tried, I was never good at not falling in love with Eli Grant.

Chapter 40

Dawn has barely won over night by the time I make it to my car, hues of purple coloring the areas of sky visible between the clouds. I'd already packed my things yesterday during the day, and it's a good thing I did, because there's no way I would've been able to when Eli and I went back inside well into the middle of the night. By that point, neither one of us could disentangle themselves from the other. When we made it to bed, we didn't talk. We didn't acknowledge what the morning held, or how this would be the last time we did this. We brushed our teeth side by side, his gaze catching mine in the mirror, and despite it all, he succeeded in making me smile once more. And then we wrapped each other under the blankets, his chin on my shoulder, his hand on my stomach, holding me just a little too tight.

When I slipped out this morning, I wasn't able to look at him. I wanted to—God, I wanted to—but I knew if I did, I'd never make it out the door. I'd have dragged it out, woken him up and asked for a solution, only to once again come to the conclusion that there *is* no solution. Not seeing him allowed me to pretend I'd see him later tonight, when he'd be back from work while I played with Zoe. He'd come in, give each of us a kiss on the cheek, then get started on dinner, not caring that he'd been cooking all day, because this time, it was for us, and that made all the difference in the world.

The outside air is cold, the wind even worse than last night, too sharp for an end-of-August day. I rush into my car, boxes of things from Ruth's hiding most of my rear view. I bring my hands to the steering wheel, then force myself to breathe.

My attention is dragged to a car pulling up in Ruth's driveway. Out comes a man who must be in his late thirties or early forties, carrying two cups of coffee inside. Not Ruth's house. *His.* The front door opens before he reaches it, and a woman in pajamas I assume is his wife welcomes him in with a kiss. The smile that reaches my lips is bittersweet. Ruth might not be here anymore, but another family will occupy her place, making more happy memories there. I hope they jump in the water, use the firepit and watch the movies while eating candy. Hope they love it as much as I did. Wherever Ruth is, I know she's smiling, too.

I look away when the door closes behind them, and without even thinking, my attention drifts to the house I'd forbidden myself from glancing at. I ink it to memory, too. The faded chalk in the driveway, the bright-white window shutters Eli repainted two weeks ago, the kid-sized shoes on the front porch—probably abandoned after Zoe decided she'd be more comfortable catching bugs barefoot.

I look away sharply, the tears catching me off guard. I need to leave now if I don't want to become a sobbing mess right here in this driveway. With straightened shoulders, I put the key in the ignition and start backing up.

"Wait! Cassie, wait!"

I pump the brakes, my head whipping up as a tall figure runs down the front porch stairs.

Eli is wearing nothing but sweatpants, his hair all over the place, a panicked look painted across his features. I roll my window down, and when he leans over it, red blotches covering his face, I don't think I've ever found him more beautiful.

"I couldn't let you leave like this," he says, breathless.

"We said no goodbyes."

"Fuck goodbyes." And then he's in my bubble, his lips on mine, hands in my hair, and I'm breathing again. I'm gripping his chest, soul-deep relief flooding me at this last taste of him. He's cramped through the window, our elbows and heads knocking against the edges. It doesn't stop us. He smells like Irish Spring and outside air, like what I imagine when I think of happiness.

Too soon, he's pulling away, his eyes glossy—with lust or with grief, I'm not sure.

His throat works, but as he tries to find words, nothing comes out.

"Will you call?" I ask.

The way his lips blanch is all the answer I need.

"I think you were right the last time. I don't... It'll only make things harder."

I nod, nod again, then turn back toward my steering wheel. "I understand."

This is it, then.

A strangled noise comes out of his throat. "I... If ever..." He doesn't finish his sentence. "I'll be here. All right?"

I dip my chin once more, but he doesn't give me the option to keep looking away when he brings my head closer to his lips so he can kiss my forehead. He remains close, his breath warm on my skin. "You'll always be the one that got away."

It looks as painful for him to back away as it is for me. When he's taken a step back, he pauses, as if to say something else, but then he taps the hood twice and keeps his attention on his feet.

I look in my rearview mirror for as long as I can, but he never glances back up.

I'm numb throughout the drive. I don't put on any music, audiobook or podcast. I don't think, either. I just listen to the voice of my GPS and eventually wind up home—if I can even call it that. Aren't you supposed to feel better at home than anywhere else?

Once I park in the underground garage, I turn off the ignition and lean back in my seat, staring at the concrete wall for a long moment. Long enough that I'm jolted to attention when Ms. Langley, my eighty-nine-year-old neighbor, knocks on my window with a worried look. When I turn, she presses a hand to her chest like she'd feared the worst, then slowly makes the trek to her car.

I get out and leave all my stuff in the car before I take the elevator up. I expect comfort to overwhelm me when I step inside my apartment, but the only thing I feel is nausea at the smell of overripe bananas I'd forgotten on the counter.

I go to the couch, sit, and wait. I'm not sure for what.

And then, finally, the tears hit.

I cry for Keira, for not being able to be there for her during this rough patch, and for having to leave when our relationship was just getting good again. I cry for Mom, who continues to live with a man who has never put her above his personal struggles. I cry for my niece and nephew, who I might not see again for years and who will grow up without me in their lives. I cry for Zoe, who became such an intricate part of my life in so little time. I cry for the job I have to return to, even though I don't feel nearly as excited for it as I should after being away for two months.

And most of all, I cry for Eli, and the loss of something that never had the time to fully bloom.

I'm curled over on my couch, the satin throw pillow under my cheek drenched in tears, my breaths cut through with hiccups. My vision is so blurry, I can barely see in front of me.

Despite having been alone in this place since Michael left months ago, it's never felt this lonely. I feel like crawling out of my skin, like the walls are closing in on me. Images I haven't seen in a long time flood my mind like a film reel I never wanted to watch again. Michael telling me he can't do this anymore, leaving with a gym bag full of clothes with a pitying look. My doctor tapping my hand like a simple touch could compensate for the world-ending news he just shared. Taking the overnight bus out of Cape Weston eleven years ago, crying in the last seat with a bruise growing around my eyebrow as I left the life I knew behind. Eli not looking up earlier when I drove away.

My hands are shaking as I pick up my phone and dial my best friend's number. She answers on the third ring.

"Cass, hey! What's up?"

"I'm back."

"Wait, what? Why didn't you tell me? I—"

"Can you come over?" My voice is shaky, the words barely audible.

She must hear all that transpired in the question because she says, "Oh, hon. I'll be right there."

Chapter 41

"Did yours deliver?" Emily asks as I sit at my charting spot.

I nod then laugh at the way she's sprawled on her chair, her eight hours of overtime transpiring through her every pore. She groans, melting even further into her chair. "It's so unfair."

"Don't be a sore loser." I pick up my department zip-up hoodie, the feel of its cotton as familiar as slipping into decades-old pajamas. "Mine was a fourth baby, so there was no competition anyway." I barely had time to call the doctor in before my patient Renata's baby girl was born.

"So, you're done now?"

I look at the digital clock behind her. "I guess." Not that I'm that excited to go back to my empty apartment.

That first night, when Emily arrived, she pulled me into her arms and let me cry on her shoulder for a long time. Then, she decided we were going to deep clean my place while she updated me on all I'd missed during summer. The cleaning was useless—I'd kept the apartment squeaky clean since Michael left—but keeping my hands busy while listening to all the department drama kept my mind blank, which was exactly what I needed. I'm pretty sure all the wild details she added about the anesthesiologist she went on one date with before determining he was a freak were fake, but I appreciated the effort all the same.

I was back at work the next day, and while I'd dreaded it, it was… fine. There was a new detachment in me, which made the job easier, if a little boring. My heart wasn't in it anymore. Maybe that was how it needed to be, though. When I cared, I couldn't tolerate it. Being a good nurse to my patients doesn't mean I need to be the person I was before, and while I don't feel nearly the same amount of fulfillment I used to, at least I don't get into shouting matches or come home crying, so I decided to take it as a win. I got my period in the middle of the week, and thankfully, this one was tolerable. I don't think I could've handled an episode like the one I had in July on top of everything. Even so, I pat myself on the back for surviving it by myself. I craved Eli there by my side again, his fingers tangled in my hair, cold compresses ready for me because he somehow always knew what I needed without me saying it. I felt comfortable living through my pain with him, bloated and moaning, and having that trust with someone, even for a single summer, is something I'll cherish forever.

"Hey, Cass?"

"Hm?" I sling my purse across my shoulder.

"You doing okay? Like, really?"

Sariah, my boss, asked me the same thing this morning, and when I answered I was great, she smiled and clasped my shoulder, the way she used to when I started working under her. "I'm proud of you," she said. "Glad your break did you some good." A part of me was proud that finally, I was able to properly lie to her. She didn't need to know I was still dying inside, although for different reasons than before my break.

However, with Emily, I can't hide it.

"I will be," is what I settle on.

She smiles sadly, then blows me a kiss. I return it before making my way out of the unit and to my car.

For the drive home, I put on an audiobook; some thriller I borrowed from my local library. Back inside, I'll turn it off only when Netflix will be on and will only close that tab when it'll be time to go to bed. My thoughts are too loud to be given any room.

When I park in the garage, something rattles behind my seat, and when I go check, my heart stutters. The scrapbooking boxes. I unloaded all my stuff from Maine with Emily when she came over, and we made sure to hide everything that could remind me, even for a single glimpse, of Cape Weston. I guess we forgot to do one last trip to grab the stuff on the floor of the backseat. The sight of the boxes is like being drenched in a cold wave of memories.

I consider leaving them there and acting like I never opened the door. Go back to my apartment, eat my single portion of watery lentil soup, and pretend I don't think about all of them 24/7 anyway.

Jaw tight, I pick up the boxes and bring them upstairs.

My plan is ruined.

I'm no longer only drenched. I'm flooded. Drowned. I haven't bothered turning on Netflix. At this point, it's not going to change anything. Silence fills the apartment as I continue rifling through photo albums. I knew Ruth liked to scrapbook around pictures, but I never realized just how important they were in her craft. She didn't create art around the photographs. She made the photographs come alive, with quotes painted in dark quill and themed papers that gave meaning to a two-dimensional picture. There's Ruth with her girlfriends and a child version of me, back when I would pretend I was a grown lady with them, and they would indulge me. There's Mom in her early thirties, holding a small Keira's hand, and a baby-sized me in her arms. Mom is there quite a lot, actually. If I hadn't known it before, it would've been obvious through the scrapbooks that Ruth loved Mom. Mom is in Ruth's art more than Dad is.

Keira and me. Eli and me. As kids, as teens, as would-be adults.

My throat is tight, but my eyes only get watery when I reach my college graduation picture, with my first stethoscope around my neck. I hadn't known how I'd ever pay for it, until a bubblegum-colored Littman stethoscope arrived at my doorstep the week before classes started. In the picture, my smile isn't close to the ones I wore in previous collages, despite having followed my dreams. I was supposed to be happy then. I swallow as I trace a finger across the face of that hopeful, naïve girl. By that point, I hadn't seen Ruth in four years, yet she still printed the photo I emailed her and put it in one of her most treasured places.

When I go to turn the page, the photo falls off, as if it hadn't been glued like the rest. Something on the back of it catches my eye, and when I understand what it is, tears spill over. I never thought I'd see Ruth's writing again.

My dear Cassie,

I stop reading there, my hands shaking so much I sit on them. I can't do it. She wanted me to find this. Wanted me to read this. But what if I read whatever she wanted to tell me and learn I've disappointed her somehow?

In the end, though, my curiosity will always win.

I hope you're not too mad at me. In fact, I hope by the time you read this, you're happy with the decisions I made.

Our lives are made of choices. We can't get around it, no matter how many times I wished I could live in one of those Barbie worlds you used to build in my living room, with shop girls going dancing at night and being told what to wear and who to become. Alas, I was only able to live those precious moments with you, and my life was filled with forks in the road I never wanted to encounter. But I did, and I had to live with the choices I made. And despite it all, I don't regret any of them because they have led me here, writing this letter to you.

I'm writing one to your sister, too, which she'll receive through your mother at some point, but I have to admit, it's a lot shorter and simpler. I had two hopes for her: to let you back in, and to recognize the love she truly deserves and go for it. I hope, through the books I left her, she will figure it out. But you, my dear, were a bigger challenge.

It all dawns on me then. The shared role of will executor. Naming me when I didn't live there. Giving us all those exhausting, time-consuming tasks.

I laugh through my tears. That damn woman played us, and she won, too.

I hope I'll have succeeded. As I said before, I have never regretted any of my choices, but letting you go was one of the hardest I ever had to make. I spent so many sleepless nights that first year wondering how you were doing, alone in a city so vast, it probably felt like an entire planet. I knew you had a better chance at happiness there, but I also knew your absence was a scab we had to be careful not to pull at in so many lives. Your parents. Your sister. Eli.

A sob catches in my throat.

Did you know he never forgot about you? Every time he visits me for dinner, he asks me how you are, and every time, I see a longing in his eyes I know only one thing could clear. I always tell him to contact you. He smiles, then says, "Maybe someday." Well, I hope that day happened, whether he liked it or not. That man is there for everyone. It was time someone was there for him. Plus, waiting for him to call you almost killed me before my heart did!

My beautiful Cassie, the girl who kept me young when so many made me feel my years and more. I'll never be able to put into words what you have meant in my life. I hope you see that all I did, I did with that in mind.

The best thing I ever did was tell you to go. I hope the second best was to get you to come home.

With all my deep, deep love,

Ruth

I can barely breathe as I bring the picture to my chest and hug it. Smell it, even, trying to find her lilac and vervain smell, but only finding rancid paper.

Wiping my tears with one hand, I turn the book's page with the other, landing on a picture of Eli, Keira, and me. I never saw that picture, but I remember that day like it was yesterday. It was a stormy summer day, with clouds so dark, it almost looked like night. I was twelve, maybe thirteen. Keira was sitting under the porch, reading a teen magazine that would inform her who her celebrity husband would be, and I was bugging her to let me read it. She kept calling me annoying and wouldn't budge no matter how much I whined. I was about to say I'd tell Mom she was being a bitch if she didn't pass it to me when Eli came up behind me.

"Wanna go swim?" he asked.

I remember frowning. "The storm's about to hit."

"So?"

It was crazy. It was supposed to thunder all evening. Eli wasn't even dressed in a bathing suit, his polo shirt and bermuda shorts freshly pressed, but the second he held his hand out to mine, I was a goner. I'm fully dressed in the picture, too, but I didn't care much. At this point, we only had a few minutes before we risked electrocution in the water, so I pulled at his arm and started running toward the cliff. In the picture, Keira's looking at us, the magazine resting against her crossed legs, her attitude giving off that of a fifteen-going-on-thirty-year-old. Meanwhile, Eli and I are jumping toward a blue-black sea. It should look nightmarish, but the happiness radiating out of the photograph is palpable. Or maybe it's just the memories I associate with the moment that are magical.

He wasn't going to go in the water. He probably walked over to come read a Garfield comic at Ruth's. Now that I think of it, he must've seen my sister and me fighting and thought of a solution to reach peace. He didn't want to get his clothes wet. That wasn't him. But he did it, for me, even when I didn't know I needed it.

He's always there for others.

Ruth couldn't have been more spot on. It didn't matter that I didn't ask for his help this summer. He was there regardless. So many people find excuses to bail or give you the bare minimum to keep you satisfied. Eli will do everything in his power to help, whether it's detrimental to him or not.

He's there for everyone, and yet people leave him all the time. His father, unwillingly. His siblings, when they left town to build a life somewhere else. His mother, traveling with her new husband. The mother of his child.

And me. Twice.

The man who would've given me the clothes off his back if I'd needed them only ever asked one thing of me; to stay. And still, I left.

It all hits me at once as I look around me; the aimless job, the empty apartment, the cold nook in my neck that's missing Billie's soft, round head. The selfies Zoe and I took on my phone I haven't been able to look at again. The sister who needs to find her own happily ever after. The untouched pillow on the left side of my bed.

I want it. I want it so bad, it physically hurts.

And I allowed people who don't even matter to push me away.

Last week, I told Ashleigh to grow up, but the truth is, maybe I needed to hear that, too. I'm still stuck in a limbo that's tainted by childhood nightmares, but I'm no longer that child. I won't be stuck in lockers for hours. No one will scare me in my own home anymore.

As if on cue, my phone vibrates beside my thigh, Eli's name popping on screen. I bite my wobbling lip.

Am I scared shitless of being stuck in another situation like the festival? Absolutely. I don't know that I ever will get over these feelings. But do I want to let these people who don't matter keep me away from my family and the love of my life? Because I'm afraid that's what he is. The one I'll never get over.

The man who only ever wanted someone to stay for him.

I spent my adult life craving a family. I looked for a man who could give me one. Chased stability and peace above all else. And when I received my diagnosis, my dream was destroyed; not just because I couldn't have children, but mostly because deep down, I knew it meant I'd never have the family I'd always yearned for.

Except I do have a family. One that's chaotic and rough, but one that's also filled with so much love.

I glance at my phone, the call now gone to voicemail, then to the scrapbook. There was happiness there. There always was.

I leave the picture books on the floor. I don't have time to pick them all up.

Within five minutes, I'm back in my car.

Chapter 42

I'm exhausted by the time I cross the sign welcoming me to Cape Weston. If the drive to New York was a blur of trees and overpass graffiti, this one was spent worrying over everything I got wrong, all through the night. My brain was fried halfway through Massachusetts.

I don't make a conscious decision on where to go first. It's as if my body takes over, and around the last stretch of dawn, I turn into my sister's driveway. As much as I want to get to Eli, I need to know things with Keira will be okay first. After I read Ruth's card, her words stuck with me, but mostly because they applied to Keira, too. So many people around her left, and she's stayed strong and present for everyone through it all. Her own sister shouldn't have done it, and while I can't change the past, I can make sure she knows I'm here now.

The smell of brine and petrichor that's omnipresent in town doesn't hit me as hard as it did at the beginning of summer, but it still feels like a warm embrace across my skin. It feels *right*. I've only been gone a week, but it feels longer when I come across the toys scattered across the lawn, and even more so when my sister's face appears in the doorway.

"Cassie?" Keira asks, not as abruptly as I'd expected, but more as if in shock.

"Auntie Cass!" a high-pitched voice calls before my legs are wrapped in a bear hug.

"Hey, Xav," I say, my chest squeezing at all the love poured into a single touch, especially from this one who was harder to reach. The time it takes for Keira to tell him to go back inside is another indicator of her stupor.

When we're alone, she keeps her gaze on the ground as she asks, "What is this? I thought I was clear I don't want any of this on-and-off thing."

I swallow. This was never going to be easy.

"I know. And I don't, either."

She glances up.

"I'm so sorry, Keir. For leaving again. For everything, actually. I... You're the last person I want to hurt."

"But you did." She crosses her arms. "Again."

"I know." I won't make excuses for it, either. She knows why I left, but that was never enough of a justification for her.

"So what? You've come back to tell me this?"

"I've come back to stay."

"Pardon me?"

"I'm done running, Keir."

If I wasn't sure before, the moment the words slip out of my lips, I know they're true. I *want* to be here, not because of the place, but because Keira and the kids and Eli are home.

Her nostrils flare. "For good?"

"For good."

She stares for a few seconds while blinking fast, her lips pinched tight, then glances behind me. "You can't be here."

"What?"

"You can't be here. You have to go to Eli's. Now." She steps onto the porch to rush me down the stairs.

"What?" I repeat. "What's going on?"

"You have to leave. Come back later."

"I don't understand."

"Just go!"

I almost trip with the force she uses to push me toward the driveway. She doesn't look angry, though. Still surprised. Anxious, maybe?

"All right, all right, I'm going." I give her one last questioning look before heading toward my car, nervous all of a sudden. Is something wrong with him?

"Cass?"

I turn around.

"You're really staying?"

"Yeah, I am."

She blinks, then dips her head, a small smile on her lips. That dip is the biggest beacon of hope I've ever seen.

"All right, go!"

I grin, then watch her walk back inside before I get in my car and turn on the ignition.

Again. And again.

The engine rattles but never turns on.

Fuck. Me.

I try two more times, but no luck. Keira's driveway is empty—she and Rob shared one car, so he probably has it now.

Well, here goes nothing. The rush with which Keira kicked me out had to mean something, and I can't wait around for the car gods to start working. With only one Uber and no taxi in town, I'd have a better chance at running.

So, that's what I do.

I run the three miles to Eli's house, so out of shape every breath hurts, and it's as free as I've ever felt. I receive a few weird looks, and while they crawl over my skin and give me the initial impulse to stop or hide, I don't. I force myself to look forward, to focus on who I'm running to, and ignore them. I'll probably need to learn to blow people off like Keira does so well, but that'll be for another day. I have to stop a few times to catch my breath and make sure I don't throw up, all the while promising myself I'll start exercising once I'm settled, no matter the outcome. If Eli has changed his mind or isn't certain he wants forever, I'll handle it and find a way to stay regardless. Ruth was right; I needed to leave, and I also needed to return once I was ready to face everything. Seeing my father for the first time after all these years made me act on impulse, but I don't want to be that person anymore. I can be stronger, if not for me, then for them. My people.

When I finally reach Beachside Avenue, the Grants' house looks like an oasis, gleaming under the warm glow of the early morning sun. It forces me to run faster even though my mouth tastes like iron, and my chest hurts so bad I fear I'm going to pass out.

And then, as if feeling my silent call, he's there.

He doesn't see me at first, but I would recognize that tall build from a mile away. He walks out of the house with bags strung over his shoulders, making long strides toward his SUV. I don't break rhythm, even as puts the bags in the car and walks back inside.

When I reach the driveway, I'm panting, folded in two with my hands on my knees so I can catch my breath. Thankfully, he's disappeared long enough for me to somewhat compose myself. When he returns outside with another bag hooked onto his shoulder and finally notices me, he stops dead in his tracks, at first squinting, then going slack-jawed. He looks so handsome, with his gray Coldplay faded T-shirt I know would smell like him and would feel so soft under my cheek. It hasn't been long, but my heart gallops as if I haven't seen him in years. His hair is wild, and his beard is already longer, probably not having been trimmed since I left.

He doesn't say my name, doesn't move, his bag hanging mid-air as he watches me like I'm a specter, just like he did that first day in July. I don't give him time to get over his shock and react one way or another.

"When I learned I couldn't have kids, I felt like someone had taken my only purpose away from me. Being a mother was what I was supposed to do with my life. Having that happy, loving family was all I wanted, and then that dream was gone."

Eli still looks shocked, but he takes a step in my direction nonetheless, as if even if his mind hasn't computed yet, his body knows where he needs to be.

My throat is dry, from the run and from saying things I've tried to keep pushed away for a long time. "Losing that changed everything. It made me hate the one thing I'd always loved. It felt like my condition had taken everything from me." Hands knotted in front of me, I crack a knuckle. "But being here this summer with you and Zoe..." My lips twitch at the burst of emotion in my chest. "It felt like she'd given me a new purpose. Like *you* had."

His face falls just as the bag does with a thunk, and then he's there, so close I could touch him. His eyes reflect everything I'm feeling—hurt and fear, but mostly hope.

"And it was scary. I couldn't imagine myself holding onto something as bad as I had with my other dream just to lose it again. And with the way this place has always made me feel... It felt inevitable."

I go to wipe at the tear that spilled, but Eli is already there, his warm thumb collecting it. His hand remains there for a moment, and I lean into it, feeling another surge of courage. He hasn't interrupted me yet.

"But I'm done being scared. I won't let my father, or these shitty people, take anything more away from me." I shake my head. "I won't. And I'll be honest, it's fucking scary to think about what's to come if I stay here, but you showed me to be brave even in front of the things that have the potential to tear me apart. So I'll face these fears." I swallow. "Because you're not a person to leave, Eli. You're a person to run home to."

The corners of his lips are blanched, his jaw tight.

I don't know what to expect from him. He could very well be done with the drama I've brought into his life. I take a deep breath as I wait for his answer, but the last thing I expect him to say is, "You know what I was doing before you got here?"

I pause, then shake my head.

He nudges his chin toward the car to our left. "I was preparing to leave."

My pulse stammers. "Leave to go where?"

"To you."

My brows furrow, the words spinning around in my head until his grip settles onto my waist, and I finally make sense of them. I almost sway into him, the relief as potent as a hard drug.

And Keira knew. That's why she sent me here.

"I tried to respect your choice, to see that maybe you don't love me as much as I love you, but deep down, I knew it wasn't true. We belong together, Cassie. We always have."

As much as I love you.

My eyes well up again, and his mouth tips up like he doesn't need me to say the words to know how I feel.

"I haven't had a teammate since my dad died. I looked for one. I tried with Liz, but I couldn't fight this feeling of loneliness." His fingers caress my hips. "Until you. You make me feel like you're on my team. And I was dumb enough to let you go before, but I'm not doing it again. Not a chance."

"So... What were you going to do?"

"Charlie was spending this weekend with Zoe, and then I would've figured it out. Tried long distance. Maybe given Liz a few nights so I could come see you every month. I don't know. I'd have found a way. I just knew I wouldn't lose the only woman I've ever loved for a second time."

I let my forehead rest on his hard chest, eyes squeezed shut. His chin dips to my shoulder so his breath is right against my ear. Even through the silence, I *feel* his love for me. It's palpable, as obvious as the dark color of his hair, or the sweet smell of his skin.

I want to get lost in his embrace and settle into this, but there's one last thing I need to clarify. I dig the tips of my fingers into his chest. "You... You know I can't give you a bigger family."

Eli pulls my head back so I'm looking at him, his wide eyes alternating between mine. "I need you to listen to me carefully when I say this. I *have* a perfect family. And you do, too. If you want it."

I sniffle, then stand on my tiptoes and finally, *finally*, kiss him. He tastes like sea salt and mint, like what I've been searching for all my life. The kiss is tender, filled with longing and with realization. It's a deal sealed, a promise made, a dotted line signed. Whatever's coming for us, we'll face it together.

"I love you," I whisper when we pull apart.

One of his true, light-up-the-sky smiles paints his face, and I know that no matter what happens in my life, this is the sight I always want to come home to.

"I know, baby." He slides his nose alongside mine, stopping with his lips hovering just above mine. "But now, why don't you show me?"

Chapter 43

"You have to stop snoozing."

Eli looks up from where he's kissing down my body, stopping at my belly button. His grin is devilish. "Look who's talking."

My back arches as he keeps his sweet torture going. His bed—our bed—is a sanctuary we have spent most of the past week in. After I was done with my big declaration, I realized I'd never taken into account where I would stay in Cape Weston. Ruth's house wasn't mine anymore. However, the second I mentioned this to Eli, he looked at me like I'd grown a second head and clamped his arms around me, scooping me up and carrying me to his bed. "You'll stay here, obviously." It sounded crazy to move in together when we'd technically only been truly together for the past five minutes, but this wasn't anyone. This was *Eli*.

"I don't want to invade yours and Zoe's space if you're not ready," I replied.

He lightly pinched my butt, making me squeal. "We've been ready for you for a long time."

And that was that.

Zoe spent last night at Keira's, which gave us a slow morning—although all mornings have been slow this week. We've probably indulged a little too much in make-up sex. I still need to go back and pack my apartment, but I don't have to do that just yet.

"Don't you have this big event tonight to prepare for?" I ask him now as he plays with the drawstring of my pajama pants while kissing around the band.

"I'll call in someone to replace me."

"You can't keep doing that." He's already taken four "sick" days in the past week.

His gaze is lust-filled when he flicks it my way. "Watch me."

I snicker, then pull his head up so I can kiss him. I feel his smile against my lips. "What happened to the man who wouldn't dare ask for anything two months ago?"

"He figured out there was something more important than pleasing others."

"Which is?"

Eli traces my jaw with his thumb. "Pleasing you."

I keep a straight face for a second before I burst out laughing, tugging his face to my neck. "Think you're being sly, Grant?"

He chuckles, his breaths sending goosebumps down my body. "I don't know, is it working?"

"Yeah, it is."

He kisses me once more, this time tangling his tongue with mine as he begins pulling my pants down.

I pull away. "*However*, we do need to get out of this bed. I need to get going on finding a job."

He groans. "I just want to have you all to myself for one more day."

I don't think I'll ever tire of hearing these kinds of words from his mouth.

"I can't live off you forever." I sit and tug one of Eli's T-shirts over my head.

"No?"

"No." I lean down to kiss his cheek, then walk to the bathroom to wash my face. Eli appears behind me a minute later, his naked chest still on full display in the mirror. I suddenly regret leaving the bed. He seems to realize where my gaze has landed because he smirks as he brings his arms around me.

It still feels surreal, that this is my life.

"Do you want me to come with you today?" he asks.

I shake my head. "I can't stay cooped up in here or with you forever."

Worry is etched across his features, and while I understand where it's coming from, I don't want him worried about me every time I leave the house.

I turn to take his jaw in my hands. "I'll be okay. I need to face these people at some point. Better get used to it." Do I want to see my father again? See my high school bullies? Not one bit, but it will happen whether I want it or not, and I'll have to slowly but surely become okay with it.

His throat works on a heavy swallow. "You'll call me if you need anything?"

"Yes, chef."

"You're not going anywhere?" he whispers, forehead dropping against mine.

It makes my heart ache to see and hear the doubts that I instilled in him, but I'll spend the rest of my life showing him I'm all in on this.

"I'm not going anywhere."

He kisses me, and in the end, we both end up being late.

My CV is clutched tight between my hands as I step into the York hospital for the second time in a month.

The day after I returned to Cape Weston, I had a long call with Sariah where I explained where I was at in my head. She was understanding and said she'd started expecting it. With Emily who's decided to follow my lead and apply for the open ER position, Sariah isn't in the best position with an already-understaffed team, but she didn't make me feel too bad about it. When that call ended, I felt like I'd broken away from a net that'd been cast over me. While my week back hadn't been so bad, it wasn't great, and I wanted to believe I could learn to love my job again. Maybe changing hospitals would be a step in the right direction.

I follow the same steps I took the day Keira called me in labor, although much calmer, this time. I'll need to bring my CV later to the HR department, but I want to first talk to the nurse manager who's on today and see whether they do have nursing positions to fill.

"Excuse me, miss!"

I do a double take, not sure whether the older lady sitting in the cafeteria chair is talking to me, but since there's no one else in another ten-foot radius, I guess she is.

"Can I help you?" I ask as I step closer. The pale, white-haired woman is facing two other elderly women, all three in powder-blue hospital gowns.

"Yes. You can prove my point by telling these two ignorants that whippets are true beauties."

"I'm sorry?" I say with a small laugh as the plump woman with her arm in a cast rolls her eyes.

"You know," the dark-skinned woman next to her says, "those long-legged, skeletal dogs that run fast and look like large rats?" Her voice is raspy, and she breaks into a coughing fit when she starts laughing. "Those are what Lois means," she chokes out.

"Oh, um…" The white lady looks at me expectantly, her lips pinched. Her arm is hooked to an IV drip beside her. I actually find these dogs so ugly they're cute, but I don't think I want to give my stance on this debate. "I'm not sure I know what those are. But are you ladies okay? Do you need help returning to your unit?" Most of the cafeteria is empty, and no one seems to be checking over them.

The feisty one—Lois—rolls her eyes even more intensely than the previous one did. "We're old, not dead yet. We can go get a coffee by ourselves if we damn well want to."

I know it's not her goal, but her remark makes me smile. I get the feeling if Ruth had still been around in ten years, this is exactly what she would've been like.

"Thank you for worrying, sweetie," the woman with the broken arm says. "We appreciate it, but we're just in this unit right there. Not far to walk back to."

I look to where she's pointing. The sign in front of the door reads **GERIATRICS AND PHYSICAL REHABILITATION.**

"Well, if you're not helping, you can go now," Lois says, brushing me off with a hand motion.

"Lois, stop being rude," the two other women say at the same time.

I can't stop smiling, even when Lois throws me a dirty look before resuming her argument for the cuteness of whippets. These three really do remind me of Ruth and her group of girlfriends.

I leave them and head for the glass doors of the geriatrics unit. The last experience I had on that kind of unit was in nursing school. I remember liking it, mostly because I enjoyed talking with the patients, but other than that, it's blurry.

Through the door, I see a dozen or so patients spread out through the hallways, some walking with a walker and a physical therapist by their side. Others are sitting in plush chairs, reading magazines or making puzzles. The nurses and doctors sit in the pod in the middle of the unit, chatting and looking to be having a good time.

I look back at the three ladies in the cafeteria, now smiling at each other like their previous quarrel is a thing of the past. Then, I glance down at my CV and back at the unit, still grinning. Somehow, it almost feels like Ruth played a role in bringing me to this exact place at this exact moment.

I take a deep breath, then open the door.

Chapter 44

Now

Sometimes, the man thinks back to the boy he once was. The one who accepted he would never be truly happy again. The one who liked to believe in shooting stars.

And then he looks around him at all the love he has, and he realizes maybe he was right to believe in their magic, after all.

Epilogue

One Year Later

The party is a success.

For her seventh birthday, Zoe wasn't sure whether she wanted a pirate or a princess theme. So, we did both. She also requested to pull out the insane costume from her nana's lakeside cottage, which means Eli is now laughing with Keira's new boyfriend—who she still only refers to as a friend, because God forbid she acknowledges she likes him—with a princess hat on his head.

He catches me staring from where I'm standing on the back porch, making sure the dessert table is perfect, and the second I grin at him, he says something to his interlocutor, then heads my way.

"I think you should consider replacing your baseball caps with this hat."

He places his hands at my lower back, just above where my jeans are resting. "You're just jealous I wear it better than you."

"That must be it." I finger the dusty material of the veil attached to the top of the pointy hat, finding a small hole in it. "The termites are really getting to it, I think."

Before I can stop him, he takes the hat off and places it on my head. "Ew," I say, pushing the veil away from my face.

"Sharing is caring, baby." He smirks before kissing me, and it's enough to make me forget about the bug trap he's put on me. I don't know when that feeling will start to fade. I've now had a year of daily kisses from him, and I still feel like I'm on the first drop of a rollercoaster every time he touches me. I hope it never goes away, and while I was doubtful at first, now, I'm seeing maybe it will be the case just because everything is different with him. Maybe the feeling stays when you find the right person.

"Think she's having a good time?" I ask him when he pulls back to kiss the top of my head and faces the crowd again. We didn't invite many people; just Mom, Keira and her family, Mrs. Grant with her husband, Charlie, Liz and her boyfriend, and two of Zoe's friends from singing class. After seeing how she was treated in choir last year, we changed her to classes given in the town over, and now, she has an even better time. The kids are nice to her, and we never have to hear about freaking Amelia or Ashleigh again.

Thankfully, we didn't have to worry about my father since he landed himself back in jail by breaking his parole only a few weeks after he got out. I don't know the planned length of his sentence, and honestly, I don't want to know. The less I think of him, the better I feel. Mom and I avoid the subject, and our relationship is back to a good spot. We both have our opinions on him, and I've accepted that.

"Yeah," Eli says just as Zoe starts running after her friend Leo with a foam sword brandished before her. "I think she does."

"A feminist icon."

He snickers, then looks behind us at the cupcakes he baked, and I helped decorate. "But I think it's time for gifts now."

My heart skips a beat. I've been able to push my nerves about our gift away for the party, but now, they're back in full force.

"What if it's a bad idea?"

Eli frowns.

"What if she feels like we're trying to replace her?"

"She won't. She's been asking for this for so long."

"But what if—"

"Look who's the parent hen now," he says with a wink.

Parent. For years, I grieved the loss of this word. It still feels surreal to me every time I'm referred to as one.

I don't have time to answer before he's calling Zoe over to open her presents, and then he disappears inside the house. Zoe completely disregards her friends the second she hears the word "presents" and runs over to me, her eyes wide.

"Take a seat, honey." I lead her to the chair at the end of the table, but she can't sit, too excited to settle down. She even throws me weird looks as she giggles. I don't think I've ever seen someone as excited to open birthday gifts.

We hear the bark before Eli and Zoe's present are even outside. It's sharp and high-pitched, the Golden Retriever puppy not even ten weeks old. And then Eli comes out with it, a red bow around its neck as it starts running toward me. Since I've cared for it for the past two days at Keira's while waiting to surprise Zoe, he's used to me the most.

Zoe gasps, immediately leaning in front of the dog to pet its ears. Her smile is as wide as the ocean, lighting her face with pure joy. I steal a look at Eli who's already staring at me with a grin. "You were right," I mouth. I shouldn't have worried. She could never feel like a puppy would steal the spotlight from her. Not with how much love we drown her in every single day.

"Hi, Sparks," Zoe says as she lies down so the dog can climb on her.

It takes me a second to compute that she already knows the dog's name—chosen by Eli based on our favorite Coldplay song. Did he slip up and forget to tell me?

I frown, finding him still grinning at me like all is right in the world.

"Cassie?" Zoe asks once the dog steps off her to run to Eli, then back to me.

"Y-yeah?"

"Did you take a good look at Sparks' collar?"

This is getting stranger by the second, especially when I catch Liz and Keira also watching me with a weird smirk. I throw Eli a "what the hell is going on" look, but he still doesn't act like anything's wrong, his hands casually stuffed in his pockets.

"Yeah, I picked it," I tell Zoe. I chose a violet one with fish on it just for her.

She snickers as she glances at her dad, then says, "Look again."

I don't know what is going on anymore, but I'm so distraught, I can only oblige. I lean in front of the dog to look at its collar.

And gasp.

The collar has been changed. Instead of the one I picked, Sparks is wearing a black collar, mostly hidden under his coat, where a simple diamond ring is dangling from the clasp. Tears immediately spring to my eyes while Zoe jumps up and down in my periphery. The world becomes a whirlwind as our loved ones clap and cheer while Eli undoes the collar, and then he's kneeling in front of me, the ring held up to me. Our surroundings disappear, and only he and I remain.

"I've always asked myself what was the exact moment I fell in love with you. There were so many possible options. I used to lie in bed wondering about it. And while I fell in love with you over and over again for most of my life, I think the moment it began was the first time I saw you."

I step forward to place a trembling hand on his cheek.

"However, I don't remember the moment I knew I wanted to marry you. I feel like I've spent my entire life wishing for it, even when I didn't know whether I'd ever see you again. You've always been the dream, Cassie."

I know I'm too early, but I can't spend another second without kissing him, so I do. I get on my knees with him and bring his face to mine.

"Yes," I whisper against his lips once I've pulled back.

"Let me ask the question first," he says with a grin.

"Fine," I say, then suddenly remember where we are, my eyes widening. "Oh God, did we just steal the thunder from Zoe's birthday party?"

Eli shakes his head. "That was the real birthday present she asked me for."

Can a heart explode? I turn around to find Zoe watching us with her hands clasped under her chin. I blow her a kiss.

"We both wanted you to officially be ours," Eli says, "because in our hearts, you already are."

And I do feel like I am. Eli, Zoe, and even Liz have made me feel like part of the Grant family since the moment I walked in their home. And with each passing day, they help lessen the loss of the children I will never bear by showing me I already have a perfect family. It might have taken a different form than I'd expected, but my wish did come true, in the end.

"So, Cassandra Taylor McIntyre, will you make me the happiest man in the world and become my wife?"

"Say yes! Say yes!" Zoe chants behind me as my vision blurs. I don't think I've ever felt this much joy in a single moment. During my first proposal, I felt like I was where I was supposed to be at that particular point in life. It was like checking a box. This is like finding out romance novels are real.

Eli leans forward and whispers in my ear, "Now's the time to answer, sweetheart."

Which makes me realize I've been keeping him on hold.

"I've wanted you for even longer, remember? Can't say no to an offer like that."

There's no surprise or relief on his face, because he already knew what I was going to say. Our love is honest and palpable. There is no doubt in it. And that love is the only thing I see in Eli's expression as he stands and picks me up to kiss me, my hair flying while he twirls me around. Cheers echo around us, mixed with the crash of the waves against the shore. Even if she's not here, I can feel Ruth clapping, too, from wherever she is. Her plan was a success, after all.

I'd told myself I could never like it here. Thought there was no happiness to be found in Cape Weston. But when I look at the people around me and at the way they make me feel, I see I was wrong. No place will ever hold as much love as this home, right here.

Acknowledgements

For a while, I didn't think we'd get here, mostly because I was a hairsbreadth away from giving up on this book so many times. However, I'm so glad I stuck with it because Cassie and Eli are so incredibly dear to me and sharing them with you is a true joy. For that, I need to give a million thanks to Melissa. You're an amazing content creator, a master of Canva, a helpful brainstormer, but most importantly, you're an incredible friend who gets me like no other and who is always there to either tell me my work doesn't suck or to help me make it suck less. I love you.

Next, I want to thank Clara, Lil, Sarah, Meaghan, and all the other readers who have posted about my books, shared them with friends, or mentioned them on their socials. You will never know what your words of encouragement and your excitement for my new releases mean to me. My motivation has yo-yoed so much over the (almost) two years I spent working on this novel, but every time I heard from one of you, it gave me the kick in the butt I needed to finish it.

Thank you to my beta readers for all your insightful advice and your laugh-out-loud comments.

To Karima, for bringing my vision to life and creating the cover of my dreams for Eli and Cassie. I'm infinitely grateful for your art.

To my friends and family, who have encouraged me in this career from the very beginning and who have picked up reading romance for me. Thank you, but also, you're welcome.

To my husband, who has listened to me complain about residency overworking me and stealing my writing time for the past two years. Thank you for doing everything you could so I could get more time to do what I love. I know how to write about love because of you.

And finally, to all the readers who have picked up my books and given me some of your time. I know how busy life can get, and I'll never take it for granted. Thank you for welcoming my characters with open arms, flaws and all, and for caring for them the way you do. I know with you, they'll always be safe.

About the author

N.S. Perkins lives the best of both worlds, being a family doctor by day and a romance author by night. When she's not writing, reading, or studying, you can probably find her trying new restaurants, dreaming about the next beach she'll be visiting, or creeping the cutest dogs in the parks near her house. She lives in Montreal with her husband.

Find her on:
Threads: @nsperkinsauthor
Instagram: @nsperkinsauthor
TikTok: @nsperkinsauthor
Website: www.nsperkins.com

Also by

A RISK ON FOREVER

THE INFINITY BETWEEN US

OUR FINAL LOVE SONG

WHERE TIME STANDS STILL

WHERE WE BELONG

WHERE HAPPINESS BEGINS